RAY GUNS AND LATE FEES

SPACESHIP MECHANIC
BOOK 3

JAMIE MCFARLANE

Formatted with Vellum

PREFACE

FREE DOWNLOAD

Sign up for my newsletter and receive a free Jamie McFarlane starter library.

To get started, please visit:

http://www.fickledragon.com

1

HIGH WIRE

Ghostmist Nebula, Garanod Enclave

"When will you be back, Kasit? We need to talk." Zenith Quel looked at the boy who'd seemingly turned into a man overnight. Thin, muscular and quick to smile, Kasit was every bit as attractive as his father had been, and Zenith worried that those attributes would put him on his father's path.

"I have a job to run for Mara Vell," Kasit said. "And before you object, it's a fluff run."

"Mara Vell is dangerous, Kasit," Zenith said. "Did you talk with Kha'rem? He has work over on Driftmarket for you. It's good money."

"I'll stop by Kha'rem's after my run."

"I don't like you getting in with Mara Vell."

"I'm not getting in with anyone." Kasit crossed his arms.

Zenith looked at her son with concern. She was only sixteen when he was born, and life since then had always been a struggle. She'd learned hard lessons while recovering from bad decisions, and she didn't want Kasit to have to relearn them.

"Easy money is a slippery slope, Kasit," Zenith warned. "Everything has a cost."

Kasit's expression softened and he stepped into his mother's space, wrapping long arms around her. "I'm not Dad, Mom. I have no interest in joining a pirate crew. Vell just needs me to move something out to Black Spire."

"You shouldn't be in Black Spire. Getta are all over Black Spire."

"It's a quick drop. They need me because I can get in from the backside. I won't even see anyone," Kasit said. Before she could object further, he continued, "Mom, I love you, but I need to live my life the way it makes sense to me. I promise, I'm not doing anything dangerous."

"It sounds dangerous."

"I'll bring back dinner from Driftmarket after I do whatever Kha'rem needs, okay?"

"Go, Kasit. Just be careful."

"You underestimate me, Mom. Nobody's faster on the fluxspan than I am." Kasit nudged Zenith's shoulder. "They won't even know I've been to Black Spire."

"It's a mother's prerogative to worry for her children. You're all I have, Kas."

"Same, Mom." Kasit kissed his mother's head before escaping through the front door to their bricked hovel, which sat within the large bowl that made up Havenfall District. Sliding a condenser filter into his nostrils, Kasit took off at a run.

Located within Ghostmist Nebula, Garanod Enclave consisted of five districts that occupied long, separated masses from a failed planetary formation. The districts—Black Spire, Driftmarket, Havenfall, Chainreach and Quiet Coil—had little in the way of codified laws, and each held subtly different customs that were unchallenged by anyone hoping to maintain the uneasy peace.

"You're late," Mara Vell's voice growled over comms. "You missed the ferry."

Kasit sprinted across Havenfall's bioluminescent landscape, which was dimly lit by failing ancient space station 'suns' that had been pushed into place long ago.

Travel between the districts was safest by ferries, which moved on their own schedules, sliding along spider webs of fluxspan rails that haphazardly stretched across the connecting passages of empty space. If one had enough money and enough guts, private cars could be hired to race along the rails, assuming the operator paid attention to the voluntary registry of rail usage. Collisions were common enough, as were detached cars careening out of control. Even so, ferries and private cars traveled considerably safer than rail sliders like Kasit, who used a simple sling and no shortage of acrobatic skills to navigate the morass.

Kasit grinned as he watched the ferry from Havenfall to Driftmarket began its slide across the glowing blue rail. Slicing through the crowd of queued passengers, who would be waiting another forty minutes for the ferry to return, he leapt from the platform and flung the end of his sling over the rail. A satisfying crackle of energy reverberated through his body as the magnetic latch caught and his weight settled. Adjusting his connection, Kasit took advantage of the bow in the rail to freefall toward the distant ferry. Once he was within a hundred meters, he slowed his approach with practiced ease, and at the last moment, he lifted his knees to land atop the vessel.

"I just caught it," Kasit replied to Vell.

"You take unnecessary risks," Vell glowered.

"Just keeping my skills sharp," Kasit said. "Isn't that why you hired me?"

"We will see." Vell closed communications, leaving Kasit to his thoughts as the light atmosphere of the nebula buffeted him.

"Someone took her grumpy pills this morning," Kasit quipped before scrambling to make sure he wasn't transmitting.

Approaching Driftmarket was always a view Kasit enjoyed. The smoothest of the planetary fragments that made up Garanod, Driftmarket had been hollowed out over the centuries and terraced into overlapping bazaars, which clung to the celestial mass like a sea of colorful barnacles. Navigation through Driftmarket was not for the fainthearted, as urban planning had played no part of its evolution. Stairs, spiral walkways, escalators and every method of conveyance joined otherwise unmanaged streets and alleyways. Having spent his entire life on Garanod, Kasit knew the area as well as, if not better than anyone, and his unique skills as a rail slider lent themselves to traversing the landscape.

Thirty minutes after leaving home, Kasit dropped lightly onto a cobblestone walkway. Straightening his shirt, he knocked softly on a salmon-colored door, though no light shown through the translucent glass, suggesting no one was home.

A sliver of light appeared, and a young woman peered out through the crack. Seeing that it was Kasit, she opened the door the rest of the way. "One of these days, you will not be so lucky. Mara requires precision in schedules. You were almost late, today," Pera, who essentially acted as an agent between Kasit and Mara Vell, scolded.

"And yet I wasn't," Kasit boasted, grinning. "Do you have it?"

"Were you followed?"

"There aren't five people in all Garanod who could have followed the path I took. And before you ask again, I did not see any of them on top of the Driftmarket ferry, nor running across the rooftops." Kasit rolled his eyes

"This is no game, Kasit," Pera warned.

"And yet I take great pleasure in it," Kasit said. "Do you have the package?"

Pera picked a leatherbound journal from a humble table that sat near the entryway. "Take this to the man in Black Spire. He will be wearing a red diffuser with this symbol on it." Pera spilled a measure of salt on the table and drew an arc, beneath which she smudged two dots. "He will be near the 132 rail, waiting for you."

"Red nasal diffuser with that symbol. This is supposed to be an easy job. What's with all the intrigue?" Kasit asked.

Pera brushed her hand across the salt. "It *is* an easy job. Finish it without attracting attention."

"When do I get paid?"

"Be patient. Payment is certain, but do not come back here."

2

FAILURE TO FOCUS

PATIENCE STATION

"I THOUGHT YOU WERE DEAD," Rix said, pulling Amari through the door to his mechanic shop at Bay 807 of Patience Station.

Amari had taken the form of a deckhand for the visiting freighter *Gordinox.* If not for her shifting her face back to 'Amari', Rix wouldn't have had any idea who had kissed him so abruptly. Such was the life of someone dating a Tejlari.

"Did you miss me?" Amari asked silkily as Rix pushed the door closed behind her.

"I thought you were dead. Even Kel thought you were dead," Rix said, holding her at arm's length, unable to return her flirtatiousness through the shock.

"But the crate with your grandmother's name...didn't that clue you in?" Amari asked. "I couldn't very well use my name. That'd kind of ruin the whole clandestine thing I had going on."

Rix clamped his jaw, but not because he was angry, at least not only. The flood of emotions he felt was unlike anything he'd experienced. Although he wasn't one to cry, his eyes burned as his face flushed.

"Oh, Rix," Amari said compassionately, pushing his arms aside and pulling him into a hug.

"You can't do that to me," Rix said.

Amari kissed the side of Rix's face. "It was the only way. I couldn't use any of my aliases. Work on freighters is about the only gig a person can get where IDs aren't well checked."

"How did you escape?"

"Oh, hon, you need to take something to heart. I was never in any real danger," she said. "My biggest objective was to stay under the radar, which I did. What do you think of the presents I shipped? I'd bet anything you can get more for them than the sixty-five hundred you spent. And thank you for putting up the money. For a minute, I wondered if you'd pay."

"If I hadn't, wouldn't *Gordinox* have come anyway?"

"Not for another two months," she said. "The human remains thing with an expedited fee put them over the top."

"Well, shoot," Rix said. "I'd have cleaned up better if I'd known you were coming."

"What's that about?" Amari asked, looking around the shop. "Normally, your shop is a whole lot cleaner."

"I just haven't felt all that energetic lately."

"Wait, because of me?"

"Well, kind of."

"That is *so* sweet," Amari said, her eyes tracking over to *Calypso*. "Dang. She got pounded. I didn't realize the damage was so bad."

"It looks worse than it is," Rix said. "We've taken out all the damaged systems and some that were in the way of getting to structural repairs. Unfortunately, we're short on funds, so repairs are going slowly."

"And I took your last sixty-five hundred credits." Amari looked at the floor. "I'm sorry."

"People are more important than things," Rix said. "I'd rather have you back than any amount of money."

"Please, you're laying it on kind of thick, don't you think?"

A smile tugged at Rix's cheeks. "Probably. But that's not the only thing chewing up funds." Amari raised an eyebrow. Rix continued, "I bought an apartment. We invested a bunch in the farms and brought in an investor. It's been busy around here."

"An investor? Who?"

"Skef," Rix said. "He has a one-fifth interest and is responsible for daily operations, including distribution in the station. Now that you're back, we'll need to negotiate how you want to participate."

"Do I still have an interest?"

"You're an equal partner with me. We both have forty percent ownership. Skef has the remaining twenty."

"Could you show me?" Amari asked.

"Sure." Rix switched to comms. "Kel, could you come down to the farm? We have a visitor asking questions about some of your merchandise."

"What merchandise? We're down to old ship parts and I thought you said you weren't interested in selling those," Kel said.

"I can handle the negotiations if you want," Rix said. "Bring Philo, too, would you?"

"Man, you're acting weird," Kel complained. "I'm on my way."

"Shall we go?" Rix asked, escorting Amari from the shop over to Bay 808, where four custom-designed hydroponic farms were located.

Only one of the farms was in full production mode, as the materials for the other three were still leaning against the bay's walls.

"You've been busy," Amari approved. "I was afraid that the power loss killed the seedlings."

"We lost two generations," Rix said. "You'd have to ask Skef about the seed supplies. He's getting ready for a harvest, which, if I heard him right, is just to collect seeds for future planting."

Amari moved around to the working farm's greenhouse door and let herself in. Instinctually, she slid out a tray filled with eight-centimeter-tall green sprouts. "These look amazing," she gushed. "They're almost ready to plant in the hydro-tubes."

"So I've been told," Rix agreed.

"What's with all the other material? And it looks like you've made changes to the design."

"Skef had ideas," Rix said. "We're looking to package all of this up and franchise it to other far-off stations in need of a stable food source that isn't reliant on constantly operational systems, like remote bases, big freighters, et cetera. It's not a huge market, but he's sure there's demand."

"I love that you guys are thinking big!" Amari said. "And these plants are doing well. I can't wait to see these hydro-tubes packed with produce!"

"What's the big rush, Rix?" Kel called from the doorway as she entered, the monkeyish but companionable Philo in tow. Shielded from view within the greenhouse, Amari's grin stretched ear to ear as she heard her half-sister's voice.

"Take a look in the crate that got shipped," Rix said, having hauled the large casket-sized crate over from the shop side over into the farm.

"That's kind of morbid." Kel shot him a strange look but went ahead and pushed the crate's lid off. "Wait, this isn't a casket at all."

"Hello, sister," Amari said, walking around the end of the greenhouse so she was in Kel's line of sight.

"I told you, Rix. No stinky pirates were going to capture Amari for any period," Kel said, running over to Amari. The two women hugged, Kel lifting Amari off the ground as she swung her around. "Welcome back, gorgeous!"

"Why, thank you," Amari said, separating from Kel and taking a theatrical bow. "Hello, Philo." Amari embraced the little alien, who was oozing with excitement over the reunion.

"What are we doing with the stuff in the crate, then?" Kel asked, jumping right to business.

"I used Rix's credits to buy spec items. I'm certain it's good stuff. Hopefully you can sell it."

Kel pushed the crate to the shelves where she kept items she hadn't yet sold and started unloading. "I don't know about sixty-five hundred credits, but there's value here. I'm tempted to rent a space in The Atrium."

"How much would that cost?" Rix asked.

"A small space is probably six hundred a month," Kel said. "That'd give us a thirty-square-meter windowed space."

"Is that big enough?"

"It is, for now," Kel said. "If we get enough traffic, we can always go bigger."

Rix checked his accounts. In the farm business account, there were fifteen hundred credits. In his personal, there were seven hundred fifty. Considering his partnership for the farm involved Skef and

Amari, Rix didn't feel right using that money to pay rent for his venture with Kel, so his decision was made.

"Will they do a partial month? Or maybe you could negotiate free until the end of the month and then six hundred," Rix thought aloud. "Who's leasing it?"

"Feriq. I'm not sure you know her. I wouldn't get excited about any freebies," Kel said. Amari nodded in agreement.

"Will you operate the shop if you're not out on a run?" Rix asked. "I don't have much free time."

"Sure, or I'll find someone to do it for me."

"Do you want a set of these shelves up there, or are you thinking something else?"

"The shop I'm looking at has nice display racks already," Kel said. "I'll want to add some decoration and branding to attract attention, but we can use profits for that. Give me a few. I'll see what Feriq is willing to do."

"Sure," Rix nodded. "Amari and I are going to grab something to eat. Want to join us after you're done?"

"Are you thinking Loose Bolt again? It seems like you never stick around. I bet it'll be quieter tonight. Did you like it, though? And did you tell Amari the big news?"

Rix gave Kel the exasperated look he often did when she asked him several questions in a row. "Big news is relative," Rix said, choosing the most interesting question. "Loose Bolt sounds good. How much liquor did you pack, Amari? I wonder if Greevo would be interested in it."

"You both talk like crazy people," Amari said. "What's this 'Loose Bolt' and what's Greevo got to do with anything?"

"Loose Bolt Lounge," Rix answered. "Fun new bar. Lots of spare parts turned into furniture."

"Oh, so you feel right at home."

"Truth."

"And your big news?"

"Couple of things," Rix said. "I already told you I bought an apartment."

"Yes ... there's more?" Amari asked.

"He's so dumb. He never toots his own horn," Kel said. "Yes, there's more. You're looking at Community Councilman Rix Banner now. There was this whole thing with Quixly and Greasle making back-room deals and skimming money from Patience Station, but I can tell you about that later."

"Okay, well, that is interesting," Amari said. "Congratulations are in order?"

"It's a paying gig!" Kel squealed before Rix had the opportunity to respond. Amari gave Kel a patient, amused smile and looked back to Rix for an answer.

"It's for the best. Quixly was misleading the council about station repairs. Garba had been doing something similar," Rix said. "I'm giving it six months to see if I come to hate the job. If I can hack it, I'll stay on."

"Is that how you're paying for the apartment? With your salary from the council? I didn't realize they got paid that much," Amari said.

"It's not a lot. Two thousand a month," Rix said. "And yes. Thudd Gaveshod is carrying a loan for the apartment since it was his property. He's also given me a sixty-five thousand credit allowance for a build-out."

"So you're not living there now, then," Amari clarified.

"We could, but there isn't furniture, walls, or anything useful at all."

"I'd like to see it at some point."

"For sure," Rix agreed. "Back to the other thing. How much liquor did you ship?"

"Oh, baby, I have some good stuff." Amari rubbed her hands together. "But if you're opening a shop, I don't think you want to wholesale to restaurants. I have four liquors and three spirit varieties. I have a total of twenty liters packed in two-liter bottles. We should transfer to smaller bottles for retail."

"Is that allowed?" Rix asked. "I know we did it when we relabeled Collie's Reserve, but that was with an agreement from Collie Berg."

"There aren't any applicable restrictions," Beverly said, choosing that moment to appear. As a four-hundred-nanometer-long symbiote who'd take up residence in Rix's skin, Beverly had no obvious physical representation. But she loved 1950s Earth culture, and her ability to project images onto Rix's HUD allowed her to show up near Rix, wearing any outfit, at will. In this case, she wore medium gray slacks, two-tone white and black saddle shoes and a gray pinstripe suit vest over a bright white shirt. The outfit gave her the appearance of a mid-level 1920s gangster.

"You love that mobster look, huh?" Rix said. "Share your image with everyone so they can enjoy it."

"I don't understand," Amari said. "What is a mobster?"

"There's a movie; *The Mob*. Broderick Crawford and Charles Bronson. We'll watch it later and you'll understand," Rix said. He had found upon leaving Earth that one of his favorite features of space technology was the ability to watch movies anywhere. He hoped his home planet would catch up someday.

When Amari raised her hands in further confusion, Rix continued,

"There was a time on Earth when alcohol was illegal—Prohibition. The mob took over distribution. It was a whole thing."

"I guess it was," Amari said. "I can't wait for movie night."

"Okay, Beverly. What's the spread on a fifth of alcohol?"

"Three hundred seventy-five milliliters of spirits will retail for twenty-five credits. Liquors, assuming high quality, for thirty credits. That would put the equivalent value of a two-liter carrier to one hundred thirty-three and one hundred sixty credits, respectively," Beverly said. "Previously, you've been selling wholesale for forty percent less. Also, given the lack of supply on Patience Station, you could certainly put a premium on the first bottles placed on the shelves in a retail environment. I'd recommend a scarcity approach, where you do not show the entire available stock."

"That's fifteen hundred credits for just the alcohol," Kel said, wide-eyed.

"Minus fifty credits for the smaller bottles," Rix corrected.

"Sure, right. I'm totally going to run the price up, though."

"I take it you like the retail approach, then."

"Yes," Kel said, fanning her way through Amari's crate, her eyes alight with excitement at her valuation of what had been brought back. "Add this to the stuff I have sitting around from my last run; I'd bet we have over ten thousand in inventory just looking to be sold."

"Sounds like you need to find your friend Ms. Feriq," Rix said.

"Go to Loose Bolt, I'll find you there, okay?" Kel said, barely able to contain her enthusiasm.

"We'll meet you there."

"She sure is eager," Amari said as soon as Kel was on her way.

"I have to wonder if she has the capacity to tend a store front," Rix said. "She's not exactly the type who likes to sit around."

"You're not wrong about that. At some point, though, you're going to have enough trade goods that you're going to need a way to get them sold. Maybe you could find someone else to tend the store," Amari said.

"Employees are expensive," Rix said, then changed gears. "Do you want to see my new apartment? No work has been done yet, but I'm getting close to finishing my floor plan."

"I'd love that. And it just occurred to me that with Greasle gone, Vigno and Jacknie locked up and Shixen dead, there's no reason I can't use my old apartment. My biggest problem is that they'll kick me out if we're not paying rent. Although, I'm not even sure who rent would go to, with Sable's management gone."

"Rent might not be a problem for a while. I happen to know that Community Council isn't looking to collect rent in old Sable territory for the next couple of months while we figure out the economic impact to residents," Rix said.

"At least that's a little breathing room. If you want to stay, we have a couch," Amari offered. "It might be homier than sleeping in that shop chair every night. That must be hard on your spine, unless humans are extra bendy."

"That's a mighty fine offer," Rix said. "It's getting late. Let's check out the apartment tomorrow and head straight over to Loose Bolt. I'd love a late dinner."

"Because of me?" Amari asked. Rix shrugged, not wanting to admit that he'd been in a funk after learning that she was likely dead.

The corner of Amari's lip turned up into a soft smile. "You're sweet," she said, grabbing his hand and pulling him toward the door.

It was after 2200 when they arrived at Loose Bolt Lounge and the bar was relatively quiet. The announcement of the pirate faction Sable's removal from Patience Station, along with the excitement of Community Council elections, had created a commotion earlier in the day, but the celebratory atmosphere had since dissipated. A few lingering partygoers had moved off to a couple of tables at the far end of the bar, which led Rix to usher Amari into a private booth opposite the bar.

"Are you hungry?" Rix asked.

"Yes. But you don't need to buy me anything."

"Nonsense. I've heard Greevo has a burger and potato wedges special that's hard to beat. Are you up for something like that?"

A green-skinned Grintok woman whose chin barely reached the top of the table approached. "Grill is closing in thirty minutes if you're looking for food," she announced. "What can I get you?"

"Are you still doing that burger special?"

"Yes. It's on the menu," she huffed.

"Three of those and two beers. Amari, what are you drinking?"

"Iced tea, please."

Rix sank back into the booth as the waitress hobbled off with their order. Sliding closer, Amari leaned against him. "It's been a long couple of weeks, hasn't it?" she sighed.

"I can't imagine what you've been through," Rix said. "It's been crazy around here, though, too."

"Would you believe I'd prefer not to talk about that, at least tonight?"

"Yes."

"What's in your way to fix *Calypso*?" Amari changed the subject.

"Money," Rix answered. "I was going to start looking at those salvaged frigates to see if I can recover any parts for *Calypso*. I have at least fifteen hundred credits in structural members that I wouldn't feel good about going cheap on. It's too much to ask that I find a working inertial system or navigational computers that could be reconfigured. If we have to manufacture all those systems, that six thousand five hundred credits I've been using for calculations will go to more like twenty thousand credits."

"Nobody talks about how expensive pirates are. I suppose a lot of freight companies have their ships insured," Amari said.

"Who can afford that?" Kel joked, sliding into the booth with them.

"Not us," Rix said, brightening slightly as the drinks arrived. "I heard something once that I initially had a hard time believing, but now I get it."

"What's that?" Kel asked.

"Small companies don't fail due to too few opportunities, but because there are too many and they can't figure out what to focus on. I feel like I'm doing that with all these businesses starting up and no plan on how to handle cash flow."

"Well, do I have good news for you, then," Kel said.

Rix grunted a laugh. "Do tell."

"I talked to Feriq about that boutique space. Not only will she give us the remainder of the month free, but she'll give us the next month free, too."

"What's the catch?"

"Three-year lease."

"What if we outgrow it?"

"I asked about that. She said she had other, larger spaces and she'd transfer the existing lease as long as the next one was bigger."

"Can we keep a boutique's shelves filled?" Rix asked. "If *Calypso* is running, you're looking at a minimum of twelve days, round trip."

"The question is, can we make six hundred extra credits a month with the difference between wholesale and retail pricing for our goods?" Kel replied.

"Do you think we can?" Rix scratched his head. "I haven't had a chance to look at the inventory of everything we have, and I have no idea if people around here are buying the stuff we have to offer. Six hundred a month isn't that big of a risk, but we're piling up leases. We'd talked about opening the boutique in the same space as the farm. I assume that's not working like we wanted."

"It's all about visibility," Kel said.

"Okay, things are volatile on Patience Station right now," Rix said. "What if you asked Feriq for a short-term lease, say forty-five days, so we could prove the concept? Would she go with that? We'd learn a lot in a short time."

Kel took a long drink of beer and set it down. "Dang, that's good. Greevo sure knows his beer," she said. "Did you know he brews this himself?"

"You're thinking about trying to distribute his beer, aren't you?" Amari asked.

"Well, maybe we could at least get the shipping contract," Kel said. "We were talking about running over to Xandarj system and checking out that Pocile Aerie junkyard for parts for *Calypso.* We could take *Gravitational Pull* and load up a single container with everything we have sitting around. They have this thing called The Trailer, which is a big old bazaar with no taxes. We could put out a table for a few days. You have those spaceship parts in Bay 808, and I have a crap ton of stuff I brought back from Majis."

"Hold on there," Rix shook his head. "First you were thinking a boutique, now you're thinking about a booth in Dralli Station over on Xandarj. I feel like we need to decide which way we're going here."

"I know," Kel said. "There are just so many fun ideas."

3

ALIGNING MOTIVATIONS

"THAT'S GOING to save us some cash, that's for sure," Rix said, crawling out from beneath the dilapidated freighter's sub-deck. Covered in a combination of soot and grease, he looked like he'd just slid down a fireplace chimney.

"You look ridiculous," Amari said over comms, wiping Rix's mask with her glove to help remove some of the grime. Her efforts were in vain, as a hand-sized smudge covered his visor.

"Don't, it'll make it worse," Rix said, pulling at the cabinet that he'd loosened from below deck. The cabinet resisted for a short time before it finally released and slowly tumbled over in the zero g conditions.

"What is that?" Amari asked.

"Industrial inertial system," Rix said. "Honestly, it's a piece of junk. No way am I putting it in *Calypso*."

"You sound depressed."

"It's not that. I've just tied up all my money into long-term investments and without a big payday, *Calypso* isn't going anywhere. It's a cyclical problem. We need money to make money."

"I thought you felt *Calypso* wasn't that bad."

"To repair that single structural member is over a thousand," Rix said. "I have three more structural members. I was working on the numbers. We're closer to forty thousand credits to get her going again."

"What are you going to do?"

"Start cutting this freighter up for recycle credits," Rix said. "It'll take me a few weeks, but if I work hard, I can make six, maybe seven hundred credits a day. I bet there's at least fourteen thousand in recycle credits in this one freighter alone. We have two more after that."

"Neither of which are in good shape," Amari reminded him.

"I figure I'll pile up the parts that have value and instead of keeping them, maybe we do just what Kel said and go over to *Xandarj* to sell them at their bazaar. I bet parts alone would fetch fifteen thousand, maybe twenty thousand credits. The work kind of sucks, but I don't have anything else going on."

"Except building out the rest of the farm with me and Skef," Amari said.

"How about this. You spend mornings with Atom and me salvaging this freighter, I'll spend afternoons with you building farms. Deal?" Rix asked.

"I'm up for that," Amari smiled.

"Where put this, Big Boss?" Atom asked, sauntering aft in the ruined spaceship. In his hands, he held the working components of a flight control system.

"Oh, no," Rix said, setting down the tools in his hands so he could look at the delicate part Atom had removed without his approval. "Atom ..."

"Atom do not good?" Atom worried in his halting speech.

Rix turned the part over in his hands several times, looking for obvious damage. With Beverly's help, highlights appeared atop critical components with notes about relative condition.

"Did you take that out, Atom?" Rix asked.

"How bad is it?" Amari asked.

"Atom take part. Greevo want part. Big Boss sell. Make money." Atom wrung his hands.

"Greevo told you that?"

"Yes. Greevo has list. Good credits this."

Rix turned to Amari. "It's not bad at all. Atom did a great job removing this part. I just can't believe he got it out in the time you and I were working on this industrial gravity generator. It's a delicate piece. Beverly, what's a component like this worth on the aftermarket?"

"There is damage at the C1 junction," Beverly said. "There are also three other bearings that have worn. If these are replaced, the value is twelve hundred fifty credits to an interested buyer."

"Cost of parts if manufactured on a non-priority basis?" Rix asked.

"We will need a pattern, but once that's done, ten credits in total."

"Atom have more, Big Boss. Come," Atom said, gesturing for Rix to follow.

A bit stunned, Rix and Amari followed Atom to the bridge, where they found that many of the systems had been removed and were chaotically laying on the deck, some partially connected, others caught up in a morass of wires and cables.

"Oh, buddy, this is a mess," Rix said. "I know we're looking at salvage, but we have to work clean as we go."

"Yes, Big Boss." Atom hung his head.

"Hold on, Atom did well here," Rix said. "This part alone has great value. I'm putting a repair plan into your work queue. We'll work together on how to do this in an organized way."

"Work queue?" Atom asked.

"Look at your HUD, see the blinking communication light?" Rix asked.

"Yes, Big Boss."

"Open it. There are pictures of what I need you to do," Rix said. "There are even a few videos showing you how to repair that flight controller." Beverly had built the communication and videos as they'd walked forward to the bridge.

"I see Big Boss," Atom said.

"Also, see how it shows where to put the parts that I need to look at versus the parts you're working on and the parts that are fully cleaned and repaired?" Rix asked.

"Much work to have many piles," Atom said. "Why work so hard? No fun."

"Not as much fun, right?" Rix asked. "Atom likes fixing things. We're just making small changes to the way that gets done, okay bud?"

"Okay, Big Boss."

"Run back into the shop and bring back a few crates," Rix said. "We'll get these pieces loaded and then we'll take them back and sort them, okay?"

"Sell Greevo?"

"After we repair them," Rix said.

Amari smiled and Rix caught her look.

"You can't help but add complexity and tasks to your day, can you?" she asked.

"I suppose not," Rix half-smiled. "There's a right way to do things and a wrong way. If we can fix a six hundred credit part and make it a twelve hundred credit part, that's the right thing to do."

"Even if you have to make manufactory patterns to finish the job?"

"Especially then," Rix said. "With good meta data, we list those pieces and show a video of us using them. Every time I do that, we get just a little more each day from the manufactory marketplace.

"I don't understand how your brain doesn't just blow up. You're tracking a million different things."

"Mostly, I let them track themselves," Rix said. "Right now, the farm and *Calypso* need a lot of attention. If I can get past that, I can think about advertising and bringing in some ship repair business. Here, help me move this gravitational unit back to the shop. It's not going to fit in the crates Atom is bringing."

"I love how you see value in Atom," Amari said. "Everyone else would have given up on him."

"Since I didn't grow up around here, I don't have any ideas about what people can and can't do. With some supervision, Atom does good work. He's a bit of a trainwreck if left to his own devices, but the good significantly outweighs the bad."

"Crates, Big Boss," Atom announced after Rix and Amari returned from their own trip carrying parts to the shop.

"Okay, bud, here's what I want you to do. Beverly is going to tell you which parts to put in which crates, okay? I'm going to hang signs where I want the different crates to go. Make sure you check with her when you bring them into the shop, got it?"

"Big Boss," Atom whined, not appreciating the oversight.

"I'll let you off work at 1600 this afternoon, and I'll pay for your dinner at Loose Bolt Lounge with two beers if you work hard," Rix said.

"Atom like Loose Bolt. Greevo and Kitka fun people. Atom like. Kitka no like Atom stay unless credits," Atom said.

"Well, you know what I'm offering. Work hard, I'd hate for you to miss out on Kitka."

"Atom work hard!"

It was 1400 when Amari and Rix got back to the farm after rearranging the shop to receive a stream of parts. In addition to creating places to put parts for pre and post repair, Rix cordoned off a large area for scrap to be reclaimed and dragged the unusable parts from *Calypso* to it.

"Do you ever get tired?" Amari finally asked at 1700.

"I got there at about 1400," Rix admitted. "You're the one who just keeps going."

"We have a lot of work left," Amari surveyed the bay.

"I estimate twenty hours left," Rix said. "I'm hoping we can find a good-sized battery in one of the other scrap frigates for the farm."

"Make it a reward for Atom," Amari said. "He'd love to play investigator and scour those ships."

"Do you think?"

"We need what, an atmo generator and a good battery? Tell him you'll give him five nights of dinner at Loose Bolt if he can find both of those things," she said.

"That's a great idea."

"Line up two parties' motivations and everybody is happy."

"I call that a win-win."

"Well, the win I'm looking for tonight is both of us getting showers and clean clothing, and I'll make dinner," she said. "After that, we can watch one of your movies."

"I'd like that. First, let's check Atom's work."

"Atom's been done for an hour," Amari said.

"Oh crap, I need to get money up to Greevo."

"Inspect the work first."

"Right."

Rix and Amari walked over to the shop, where they found Atom still hard at work, sweeping up the floor where detritus had fallen from the parts he'd moved around.

"What Big Boss think?"

"This is a good job, Atom," Rix said. "I'm adding a third beer, and you can come to work an hour later tomorrow morning. Set your alarm right now so you don't forget."

"Big Boss make Atom happy! Atom go Loose Bolt now and see Kitka!"

"Nope, Atom go take a shower and clean clothing, first. Trust me, Kitka will like a clean Atom."

"No fun."

"I hear you, buddy. Ask Amari what I have to do to get dinner tonight," Rix said.

"Am-girl, Big Boss need work?" Atom tilted his head to one side.

"No, Atom, Big Boss just needs to take a shower and clean his clothing. Once he does, I'm going to spoil him by making him dinner and snuggling with him while we watch a movie. Doesn't that sound nice?" Amari asked.

"No beers?" Atom asked.

"I take it Grintok aren't big snugglers," Rix said.

"I have questions," Amari agreed.

Just then, the station side door into the bay flew open and Kel burst in. "I have it! I know what we need to do! Buy me dinner and I'll tell you," she gasped.

"Whoa there," Rix said. "We were just getting done for tonight."

"Geez, it looks like a spaceship blew up in here. What's going on?"

"We're parting out one of the freighters," Rix said.

"That doesn't sound fun at all," Kel said. "Seriously, though, buy me dinner. I have a killer idea. You're both going to like it!"

Rix looked at Amari to get an idea of what she was thinking. She was smiling and shaking her head. "Sister, you have so many ideas banging around in that head of yours, I'm not sure how you walk down a hallway without falling over."

"That happens sometimes," Kel shot back. "Don't tell me you guys were going to try to go get mushy. And at a time like this, when the company needs us the most? Seriously, you've been with each other all day. You need to get out more."

"We were working all day," Rix said. "Work that I would suggest will turn into credits after a time."

"You and your slow-burn business opportunities. I have something that will make us real money right now, or at least when we can get a ship moving. Talk to me about *Gravitational Pull.* What if we put a jump drive and computer in her?"

"You want to go interstellar with *Gravitational Pull*? Are you crazy? That ship is like living in a can of sardines."

"I bet we can clear forty thousand credits if we do. Tell me you don't have jump drives on one of those freighters," Kel said. "Come on. It's just dinner. Hear me out."

"Only if you lay off the caffeine," Rix said. "You're talking a mile a minute."

"I have no idea what you're saying. Loose Bolt in an hour? That's enough time for a shower and a little wuggie-wuggie, right?" Kel was practically vibrating.

"I'm afraid to ask what wuggie-wuggie might be," Rix said. "What do you think, Amari? Do you want to grab a bite up at Loose Bolt? We were just there last night."

"The burgers aren't half bad," Amari said. "If I get a shower and some fresh clothes, I could go out."

"Booyah!" Kel celebrated. "I'll tell Greevo we're coming."

"I don't think reservations are required," Rix said.

"You're funny." Kel bolted from the room.

"You do know we're going to regret this, right?" Amari asked. "She's got some harebrained plan that's going to look good on paper and will fall apart at some point."

"Can I at least get a hot shower before we worry about it?"

"That's reasonable. You shower down here and I'll go back home. You have clothing you can change into, right?"

"Yes."

The two parted and Rix looked around the disarray in his shop. He despised the mess they'd made, but he knew that with an entire freighter of parts and scrap, it would get worse before it got better.

When he got back to Bay 808, he found Skef inside, working on the operational hydroponics farm. Knowing he had a minute, he joined the older man.

"How are your plantings?" Rix asked.

"You're just in time to see," Skef said. "I'm transplanting these tomato fruit plants today. They're looking exceptional. I'm glad the power cycling didn't ruin them. Give me another four weeks and we'll start harvesting."

"I can't wait. Anything more than tomatoes?"

"Several different varieties of smaller fruits and a few different leafy greens that generally sell well. With Sable gone, there have been more restaurant starts, and I've been getting inquiries about supply," Skef said. "We need more production capability now. I see you've been working on building the farm, but is there any possibility of hiring help?"

"How would we pay them? I was under the impression you would take responsibility for planting and harvesting."

"I can't run four farms without labor. I'm an old man," Skef said. "Are we out of the capital I invested?"

"Fifteen hundred remains from the panels I manufactured," Rix said. "We'll need another seven hundred of that to make hydroponic tubes and tubs. There won't be much left."

"Very well. I will pay Rook Hadden to help me for a time," Skef said. "Labor is not expensive, currently. We'll have to talk about how our company plans to pick this expense up once we start harvesting and selling our produce."

"Once we start selling, if we can't afford to pay for labor, we're not in the right business," Rix said. "Personally, I don't have enough income to pick up another salary, though."

"Who else are you paying?"

Rix gave a wry smile and shook his head. "That question sounds a lot like you wanting to get into my business," he said. "I don't mean to be rude, but when I say I'm tapped, I'm not exaggerating. You're changing our agreement, Skef."

"You've used ten thousand of my credits. I'm due some flexibility here. I own part of this business," Skef insisted.

"Hold on. A man is only as good as his word," Rix said. "If you're saying that you can change our agreement whenever you want, that's not going to work for me."

"You don't need to be dramatic," Skef said. "I'll hire Rook with my own funds."

Rix nodded tensely. "We'll have the other three farms put together in four days' time. If that's not going to work, let me know. I don't want Rook moving panels or installing anything without talking to me first."

"Are you questioning my understanding of how these systems are constructed? I've been building spaceborne farms since before you were walking," Skef spat.

"Skef, we have an agreement that you will honor about a separation of work duties," Rix said. "Until I'm comfortable with a new employee's capacity to do the work to my satisfaction, they're not to work on my farms. That was our agreement."

"There is no reason to be irritated," Skef said. "I will have Rook keep his focus to farming."

"If you want him to work with me assembling the other greenhouses, I'm open to that, but he needs to do the work in the way I direct, or I'm not interested in being part of it."

"What do you mean by that?"

"I don't have time to re-do work. If Rook makes errors because he's unfamiliar with what or how we're building the greenhouses, that will cause me extra work and potentially remanufacturing," I said. "I won't be part of a project like that. I'm too busy. We can part ways if that's unreasonable. I'll even give back the parts your money manufactured."

"I had hoped you'd be easier to work with."

"This doesn't need to be hard," Rix said through clenched teeth. "Let me know by tomorrow morning if we're working as partners or if you'd like to branch out on your own. I won't have hard feelings either way."

By the time Rix was in the shower, he was fuming. While picking fresh clothing after his shower, he was fully preparing himself for another confrontation. Fortunately, Skef was gone when he exited the shower room. Rix's stomps echoed through the room as he headed to Loose Bolt Lounge.

"Who peed on your shoes?" Kel asked, gliding a beer across the table to Rix as he joined her at a booth.

"Frustrating conversation with Skef. He's trying to change our working relationship. He's so darn irritating," Rix said.

"That's the general consensus," Kel said. "I was surprised you were getting into business with him, but then, you seem to be able to work with anyone. Not Skef, huh?"

"I gave him until tomorrow to make a decision on if he wanted to work together," Rix said. "I about popped him in the nose, though."

"I don't think a councilman should be brawling with another councilman," Kel said with dramatic concern. "People will talk."

Rix smiled. Kel's carefree attitude was helping him step back from the ledge.

"What did you figure out about your boutique?" Rix asked.

"Oh, I'm not going to do it," Kel said.

"You were all sorts of excited before," Rix said.

"Right, but jump drives for *Gravitational Pull*," Kel said. "Can you make that work?"

"I have no idea," Rix said. "Let's say yes. Well, hold on. We could take them out of *Calypso* for the moment. I don't think they were touched by the damage."

"But you'll see if you can salvage them first, right? There's no reason to make *Calypso* harder to repair?"

"Sure, let's hear what you have."

"Don't you want Amari in on this conversation?"

"I probably do."

"Okay, so I'll just give you a little teaser. Greevo has interest in taking a load to Garanod. They're paying forty thousand credits to move thirty-five thousand kilograms."

"Garanod?" Rix asked. "I thought we weren't telling anyone about that. How does Greevo know we have those crystals?"

"No idea, but he's on the way over. Ask him yourself."

4

FREEFALL

GHOSTMIST NEBULA, GARANOD ENCLAVE

STEPPING from the nondescript foyer into what was more alley than street, Kasit looked around. He hadn't spent much time down below in the Lager's End village of Driftmarket, mostly due to its reputation for shady dealings. Certainly, he'd raced across the rooftops, and many times had he slid across each of the twenty or so fluxspan rails that crisscrossed overhead. But "down below," as fluxspan sliders referred to the hard surfaces of the various districts, was not his normal gig.

"Kas, my frey, are you sliding today? Rig and I were thinking about picking up a game over on Drift. Are you up to play?" The voice in Kasit's ear belonged to his best friend, Wagg.

"Nah, frey, I been up since 0800 to Drift. Picked up a priority slide but got Kha'rem on my back shiny for lifting today," Kasit responded. As he spoke, he noticed a pair of gray-hooded individuals had started heading his way. He scanned for a quick way back to the topside while finishing his conversation. "Frey, I gotta bolt. Grab you back in laters."

"Be it then, frey," Wagg answered, severing their comms.

Kasit turned away from the approaching cloaked pair and as he did, they took off running. "You! Stop there!"

"Crazy grays, no stoppin' Kas!" Kasit shouted, starting forward only to find that another individual had been coming at him from behind and was nearly on him. "Crappin' nuggs!" he cursed, coiling his back muscles and springing off a half-height stone wall, his leap just barely clearing the sweeping arms of the figure who'd been behind him.

"Get down here!" one of the men demanded.

Without enough momentum to propel him to the awning above, Kasit took a horrible chance and kicked off a decorative pillar, sending him directly back toward the closest gray, who was more than surprised by his move. "Gaw, stupid slider trash!" the man yelled, flailing his arms.

As an elite slider, Kasit's primary skills were agility and audacity, and his next move required extra helpings of both. Planting his left foot on the still disoriented man's chest, he allowed his knee to bend until the man had recovered just enough to bring his hands back around. Straining, Kasit pushed off, kicking the man away as he propelled himself toward a soffit on the opposite side of the narrow alley. Blaster fire tore into the long-faded orange roof under Kasit's feet, peppering his leg with shards of canvas and poly lumber.

Kasit was already moving, though, having jig-jagged over the men below. "Snikes!" he exclaimed, landing on all fours atop the opposite roof. With hands grasping and legs churning, he clambered up the roof face and grabbed the peak, pinwheeling his legs over. Angry voices boiled up from Lager's End but, although out of sight, Kasit knew he had no business sticking around. Flipping onto his backside and using the slanted surface to his advantage, he dropped down into a roof valley and planted his feet when he reached the end. With a head of steam, he launched across the street below and raced away like demons had given chase.

"Wagg, snikes, gray cloaks just tossed bolts!" Kasit called, not daring to look back as he poured on speed. The telltale sound of straining engines caught his attention. While he believed, and was probably right, that no slider in all Garanod could catch him, he knew darn well that a good runabout pilot had acceleration he couldn't hope to match.

"Frey, what in the squishies? Why tossing bolts? Did you takes?"

"Negs. Real job," Kasit said. "Bringin' runabout!"

"How far from rails?" Wagg asked the only question on Kasit's mind. The fluxspan rails were Kasit's his only chance of escaping the runabout.

"Snikes, going to free down to Drift 1," Kasit replied.

"From Lager's? Don't do it, frey! Too far! You can't holds!"

Kasit leapt straight out from the edge of the high roofline. From the moment he'd kicked off from the gray's chest, he'd set the plan in motion, instinctively knowing the grays would follow him. In free fall, he caught the light breeze and spread his arms like a cliff diver, even as the runabout gained on him from behind.

Perfect aim was crucial. To miss the last rail on the lowest part of Driftmarket would mean certain death, as there would be nothing left to catch him. Kasit's heart thrilled as the steeply arced rail plunged away and to the side on its path to the distant Chainreach district. With small adjustments made by subtle body movements, he nudged himself into position.

"I'm flying now, frey," Kasit said. "Legend if I catch."

"Inky spot if you miss, Kas. Crazy frey. No miss!"

From the corner of his eye, Kasit caught a glint of light against steel and realized the runabout was not only still on his tail, but about to run over him. The only solution that he could come up with was to open his hand and allow the fluxspan sling to grab atmosphere and pull him out of line. He did just that, and he was rewarded with a thump against his chest as the runabout's cockpit glass punched into him, sending him sprawling and causing the sling to fly out of his hand.

"Oh, snikes!" he grunted.

"Frey?" Wagg asked nervously.

"No talks!" Kasit said, pulling his arms into a narrow diver's form, which caused him to speed up significantly as he chased the falling sling.

"Frey! Talks!"

"Nuggets!" Kasit exclaimed as he raced past the sling, grazing it with his hand. At the last second, an idea turned into action. He stabbed his leg out, snagging the sling with the end of his foot.

"Frey! Kas!"

Unable to process a conversation with Wagg and the task ahead, Kasit couldn't respond. Using his hands as small airfoils, he adjusted direction. He knew his speed was extreme, even if he managed to line up with the rail. Unwilling to accept any other option, Kasit flung the sling around just as he passed beneath the beaming blue rail. With wrists looped into the sling, Kasit's body weight heaved violently as the sling caught the rail, which had no give. The popping of cartilage felt deafening as Kasit's right arm pulled from its socket. He screamed in agony, even as the sling brought his body into alignment with the rail.

"No, frey! Kas, my brother!" Wagg cried out.

5

HIDEY HOLE

PATIENCE STATION

"This is nice piece," Greevo said, holding out the flight controls that Atom had reconditioned and sold to him earlier that day. "New parts. How?"

"It's just a matter of designing replacements for the pieces that are worn out and sending them to the manufactory," Rix said.

"Good work. Greevo know big buyers. Make many credits. Need zoomy ship go dark place," he said. As Greevo spoke, Amari settled into the booth next to Rix.

"You might not have heard, but all of our ships are in bad shape," Rix said. "No zoomy."

"Rix Banner good mechanic, Atom say."

"I like to think so," Rix said. "I'm working on building back my finances. We've had some recent setbacks."

"Sell Greevo meats and spirits from Majis."

"How do you know about that?"

Greevo shrugged. "Good price, sixteen hundred credits."

"No interest. We'll sell them for at least thirty-two hundred credits in our own store," Kel said. "We're done with wholesale pricing."

"No good. Pretty people not good make money. Greevo good. Be partner. Thirty bits. Greevo know many people. Kels go zoomy. Make big credits."

"What is he saying?" Rix asked.

"He wants to sell our goods for a thirty percent commission," Kel said. "His argument is that he'll make us that commission back because he knows the markets and has a bunch of contacts."

"Kel smart," Greevo said, nodding his head in agreement before looking back to Rix. "Kel go zoomy, make many credits. Go secret place."

"What makes you think we can get to the secret place?" Rix asked.

"Greevo know things. Make deal Rix Banner. Thirty bits, big price go secret zoomy," Greevo said and then walked off.

"See, I told you he had a deal cooking," Kel said.

"How does he have any idea that I grabbed those crystals?" Rix asked. "I didn't even think either of you two knew about them."

"What crystals, Rix?" Amari asked.

"Oh, I saw your little sleight of hand, alright," Kel grinned. She nodded in Amari's direction. "Tell her."

"I swiped *Bonehook's* Garanod jump crystals," Rix said.

"No," Amari gasped, scandalized.

"I didn't want Vigno and Jacknie jumping away before Dravari arrived," Rix said.

"Those crystals are hard to come by," Amari said. "Garanod is an interesting place. I have to wonder how Greevo figured out you grabbed them."

"He's smart," Kel said. "I bet word is out that those Garanod crystals went missing. He's on a fishing trip trying to figure out if we snagged them."

"How would he even get to that?" Rix wondered.

"Probably because he'd have done the same thing if he'd had the chance," Amari sighed.

"What do you think about partnering with Greevo to sell our loose cargo?" Kel asked. "He's a good connection, but I guarantee he'll skim off the top, no matter what deal we make."

"Why are we even talking about it, then?" Rix asked. "If we know he's going to cheat us, that's just a bad decision in the making."

"Not entirely," Kel said. "Greevo can probably make more for us than we can make if we have to pay for a boutique and an employee, even with him skimming something off the top. Negotiate a better share. He'll take it because of the skim. We can do a trial run with Amari's crate and the load I brought back from Gestalt. I'll run numbers with the best price I could reasonably expect. If he gets anywhere close, it's a good deal."

"How long will it take for you to run the numbers?" Rix still didn't feel confident.

"Give me a few minutes," Kel said. "I can get close."

Kitka arrived with beers, pushing them onto the table. "Burgers will be ready soon."

"Thank you, Kitka," Rix said.

"We could get as much as eighteen thousand if we combine what Amari sent and what I had in *Calypso's* hold," Kel said. "If Greevo takes a third, that'd leave us with twelve thousand, roughly."

"I thought you had buyers lined up."

"More like, I know who will buy the items. I need to talk to them first. I've made some contacts. I'm still working on it," Kel conceded.

"Okay. How about this? Send the list of items we have to be sold and ask Greevo what our cut would be if he brokered the items," Rix said.

"That's a lot of hypotheticals," Kel said. "He'll tell us a big number to get us interested."

"Okay. Do you mind if I negotiate this?" Rix asked.

"Do you think you can do better?" Rix shrugged and Kel gave him a half grin. "Okay, mister smarty earthman," she continued. "How about we make a bet?"

"Here we go." Amari smiled as she rolled her eyes.

"What are the stakes?" Rix asked.

"Five hundred credits."

"And the actual wager?"

"You can't negotiate a deal with Greevo in which you make more than twelve thousand five hundred for the entire lot I brought back, along with Amari's crate."

Rix extended his mug out to Kel. "It's a deal. I get five hundred credits off the top if we're over twelve thousand five hundred for those two bundles."

"What do you want to do about Greevo's Garanod deal?" Amari asked.

"I suppose it depends on the volume he wants to ship," Rix said. "I'm a whole lot more interested in fixing *Calypso* after we get cargo sold than I am in getting shot at by a bunch of anarchists."

"Why can't we do both?" Kel asked. "He's talking big numbers for a Garanod trip."

"Let's keep these deals separate, okay?" Rix pleaded.

"It's all you, baby. Greevo is on his way over." Kel rubbed her hands together. "Let's see the master negotiator at work."

"Your burgers," Greevo said, grinning widely as he placed food on the table. "Have you thought about my offers?"

"Sit and talk with us?" Rix asked. He didn't like that Greevo was standing, as it made him feel like they needed to rush through the conversation.

Greevo pulled up a chair. "I'm glad talk Greevo. Good business."

"Here's a manifest of the goods we need moved," Rix said. "For the first ten thousand, I'd go ten bits, next four thousand I'd go twenty bits, everything after that and you can have your thirty bits."

"Hmm, tricky deal. No good," Greevo said. "Twenty-eight bits all."

'I could go twenty bits," Rix said.

Greevo narrowed his eyes. "Not better deal. Twenty-six bits."

"I feel like we can make this work out," Rix encouraged. "How about you get twenty-five bits if you gross at least twenty thousand for the entire load. Otherwise, you get twenty-two bits."

"Eat burgers. Greevo come back."

"That sounded complex," Amari said.

"I can't believe you got him to negotiate." Kel slumped into the booth for a second before springing back up. "Oh, hold on, he's coming back."

Rix set down the burger, which he hadn't had a chance to eat. "What's up, Greevo?"

"Greevo have new offer."

"What's that?"

"Fourteen thousand credits now," he said. "No like thinking Rix bits."

"Make it fifteen thousand and I'm in," Rix said.

"Rix Banner make Greevo go hungry."

Rix stuck out his hand. "Fifteen thousand, and I promise we'll eat a lot of burgers."

"Greevo think Rix Banner is Grintok." Reluctantly, Greevo shook Rix's hand. "Greevo still want parts. Better deal Atom. No Rix Banner."

"We'll see what we come up with," Rix said. "When do you want to take delivery?"

"First in morning. Talk go hidey place, now? Good money. Better than crates."

"It's going to take at least a week for us to get *Calypso* up and running again. Can your deal wait?"

"One week okay."

"No harm in talking it out, then," Rix said. "What's this big, mysterious deal?"

"Take Greevo to hidey place with big containers. Greevo pay big," Greevo said.

"How do we get to this hidey place? How far is it?" Rix feigned innocence.

Greevo smiled, something that didn't take well to his gnarled green face. "Rix Banner have go-go rocks for hidey place. Greevo know this. Twenty-five thousand credits. Ride there. Ride back."

"Just Greevo?"

"Greevo, four more."

"Kel, are you up for a trip? Amari?" Rix asked.

Amari nodded, as did Kel, though she further added, "Twenty-five thousand upfront, Greevo pays fuel both directions and brings food for whoever he brings aboard. We have standards of care for the ship that'll need to be agreed to."

"Standards?"

"Penalties for cleaning and damages," Kel said.

"Never good deal," Greevo said shaking his head with a disappointed look on his face. "Greevo be poor if work with Rix Banner."

"I don't even know how we'd get to your hidey place," Rix said. "So maybe it's best if we let this deal pass. It doesn't sound like either of us will get what we need."

And with that, Rix picked up the burger that had been mostly ignored until that point and took a big bite. From his perspective, the burger was a far cry from the beef he'd become used to back home, but they were recognizable as food, especially when eaten hot, although that was a luxury he was not often afforded.

"I say twenty-five thousand. Rix no impressed. Why?" Greevo asked.

"Don't get the wrong idea," Rix said. "That sounds like a good deal. Add fuel to that, pay for your own food and we're golden."

"Rix Banner no have go-go rocks?"

"Doesn't seem like the sort of thing I'd talk about without money in my pocket."

"Give money back if no go?"

"Look, I don't know if I can go where you're asking," Rix said. "If we can't get there, I'll give the money back. That's as much as I'll say."

"Fix Kel ship. Find Greevo. Maybe make deal."

"I'll bring the items we've already promised first thing, unless you need them tonight," Rix said.

"Morning."

"Strange little man," Amari said as Greevo finally hobbled off.

"Shrewd negotiator," Rix said. "I hope not every deal we make with him is as hard as those were."

"Don't count on it. Grintok are known for their negotiating," Kel said. "You did a whole lot better than I'd have thought on those goods I brought back. Take your five hundred credits off the top."

"Sure. Because I won't just plow that money straight back into *Calypso*," Rix chuckled.

"At some point we're going to need to separate your money from mine," Kel said. "I get that I went broke a while back, but we'll dig out of all this eventually."

Rix's eyes were unfocused as he took a bite of burger, followed by a long drink of beer. "There we go," he finally said.

"There we go what?" Amari asked.

"I put in an order for the parts we need to get *Calypso* going," Rix said. "Our long-range scanning package didn't make the cutoff, and we'll need to do a few tasks manually while under flight for a while, but I got the bill down to twelve thousand. Tomorrow morning, we'll have structural members we can scarf in, and then we can start getting the hull closed in."

"Sounds good." Kel paused. "What was all that about the hidey place?" she continued. "Do you think he means somewhere other than Garanod?"

"I feel like he was reaching, and I wasn't about to show our hand until he had money on the line. There's no reason to be giving that kind of information away," Rix answered.

"That's smart. Greevo trades information just as much as he deals with black market items," Amari said. "That whole conversation could have just been a fishing trip."

"Nice use of an Earth idiom," Rix grinned.

"Beverly gave it to me," Amari said. "She wanted me to try it on for size. Did I use it right?"

"Perfectly. Since when did you and Beverly start chatting so much?"

"She has questions. I'm relatively well-informed. It's a relationship of convenience."

"You're too much," Rix shook his head, but moved on. "Want to go check out the apartment once we're done with these beers?"

"It's nice," Kel said. "It needs a woman's touch, though."

"It needs more than that," Rix said with less humor. "It's one big room. It needs walls, plumbing, paint, carpet, so many things."

"And you're letting Thudd pick all that out?" Kel asked.

"We never talked about it," Rix shrugged. "I don't like picking things like that out. I figured we'd just go with white walls and normal carpet. What's the big conversation?"

"Tell me you're just saying that to annoy her," Amari gaped.

Rix looked slightly confused. "Is there that much to pick?"

"Every surface, every fixture, every wall, every floor is a choice. There are hundreds of decisions to make!" Amari chided.

"I trust Thudd."

"Stop!" Kel said. She clasped her hands together. "If you trust Thudd, trust Amari and me to make these decisions. Do you at least know what you want for rooms? You have ninety-five square meters. You need at least two bedrooms, two baths, a kitchen, an eating area and some sort of family or entertainment room. You have a gorgeous view of the asteroid belt."

"Has Thudd set a deadline for design?" Amari asked.

"I haven't talked about it that much with him," Rix admitted.

"Amari, tell me you have this under control," Kel said, still looking exasperated.

"We'll get a drawing by tonight," Amari promised before turning doe eyes on Rix. "There are design services that can do much of the work for you if you're overwhelmed, Rix. Don't leave this to Thudd, though. Okay?"

"You'll help me?" Rix asked.

"Of course. Let's go look. I'm dying of curiosity now."

Rix took his last drink of beer and rose to join Amari and Kel, who were already standing. When their elevator reached Level 21, the trio stepped out.

"This is one of the nicer levels," Amari said, taking in the fresh paint and clean carpets. "You must have spent a fortune."

"No idea what a fortune is," Rix said. "The mortgage will eat all my councilman salary, though. I know that for sure."

"What a fantastic view," Amari breathed. After they entered the apartment, she'd walked straight to the bowed window and lingered there, gazing out. "We'll put your dining area right here."

"I was thinking bedroom."

"Don't waste this view on a bedroom. This is where we'll have morning coffee and romantic dinners." Amari winked at him. "Spend your money on finishes in this area. Living room in front of the other window. Keep things open between that living room, this eating area and the kitchen." Her eyes darted around the open space. "You can put the master bedroom on the opposite side, behind the living room, separate, with a private restroom and then another one for guests. The other bedroom behind the kitchen, closest to the hallway. It's not that complex of a design. Do you see what I'm saying?"

Before Rix could answer, Beverly projected low, opaque walls that were only a meter tall, but bordered each of the spaces Amari had listed off.

"That looks good, Amari." Kel nodded her approval. "You should install a top-shelf kitchen. Maybe get some real wooden surfaces."

"I don't cook that much," Rix said.

"But I do," Amari reminded him. "The value of your apartment is higher with a nicer kitchen. You don't have to have wooden surfaces, but that is a place you shouldn't skimp."

"Thudd gave me sixty thousand for the build-out."

"You might need more," Amari mused. "We can crunch this all together and get a budget worked out. Forget about all that, though. What do you think of the layout?"

"It'll work great," Rix said.

"If I'm staying in this second bedroom, I'd like to have a private bathroom," Kel said.

"Who said anything about that?" Rix asked.

"Uh, it was obvious," Kel said. "It's not like I'm here all that often, so there's no reason for me to have my own place. When I'm in town, though, I need a place to crash. This feels very practical to me."

Rix shook his head, a little relieved when Kel burst out laughing. "You should have seen your face just then," she giggled.

"You're not moving in with me?" Rix clarified.

"Not when I'm out sailing, no," she said, waiting a beat. "Seriously, you're so gullible. No, this is your place. I'll respect that."

"Sure," Amari said sarcastically, shaking her head.

"Look, I gotta get going," Kel ignored her. "Let me know what you work out with Greevo, okay?"

"Okay, Kel," Rix said.

"Do you still have time to watch a movie?" Amari asked. Rix smiled as the couple left the empty unit together.

Back in Amari's old apartment, they found Hutari stretched out on the couch watching fast-changing vids of aliens doing ridiculous things. She turned off the projection when Amari and Rix arrived.

"Hey, Mom," Hutari said. "And Rix! Are you two out of the closet now?"

"Mostly, people still think I'm Nefari, but I'll work on that over time," Amari replied.

"That works," Hutari said. "Sleeping over, already? You kids are going to be safe, right?"

"Hutari, be good," Amari warned.

"We were just thinking about watching a movie," Rix said. "You could join us. It's something from Earth, so it'll feel slow for you."

"That sounds fun," Hutari said.

Once Rix had slowed enough to sit still, though, the combination of being next to Amari and sinking into the soft couch put him to sleep within the first twenty minutes of the film. When morning finally came, he struggled to understand where he was, until he discovered Amari lying next to him.

"Good morning," Amari said, pulling his arm back over the top of her and holding his hand to her chest. "I'd ask if you slept well, but as far as I could tell, you slept like the dead."

"I missed the movie, didn't I?" Rix asked.

"All but the first few minutes."

"I'm sorry."

"Don't be. We watched it to the end. Hutari enjoyed it," Amari said. "There's coffee and a breakfast meal bar, if you'd like. I'm sorry we don't have much more than that."

"That's my morning ritual anyway," Rix said as the pair disentangled themselves so they could sit up.

"What's on the docket today?" Amari asked.

"Big stuff," Rix said. "We'll deliver Greevo's load, and by that time, the structural members will be ready for *Calypso*. It'll take most of the day to get those installed along with the missing hull pieces. I decided to have them manufacture those hull plates instead of making our own from the derelicts. It only cost another thousand, and exact fit will be a nice feature."

"That makes sense."

"I have a meeting with Skef today, too. I was a little hard on him last night, but man can he be irritating."

"He's a good man, Rix," Amari said. "Why don't you let me work with him. I bet I can get him headed in the right direction. It'd be a lot less stress for you."

"If you want to take a swing at it, I'm all in. We're partners in this deal, after all. He wants to bring Rook Hadden on as a worker. I just can't afford that since he was going to take care of all the planting, harvesting and sales," Rix said.

"Your primary issue with Rook is cost? Didn't Skef say he'd pay for him?"

"Yes."

"Problem solved?"

"Rook shouldn't start building those other greenhouses. He has no idea what we're doing," Rix tried to keep his tone even. "I need to make sure he knows what he's doing before he starts putting things together. Skef wanted Rook to do some of the building."

"You're okay with Rook doing work as long as it's only on Skef's side of things. You would need to work with Rook for a while to decide what else you're comfortable with him doing," Amari restated.

"That's about the size of things," Rix said.

"Let me take care of it."

"Skef might be looking to part ways. The conversation wasn't that friendly."

"Do you want to part ways?" Amari asked.

"Not if Skef will do his job and let me do mine," Rix said.

"I get it. You're both feeling time pressure. You have ships to repair and a shop that has parts strewn about everywhere," Amari said. "Skef is impatient because he is emotionally invested. Would you give me a shot at working things out with him?"

"Please do."

6

FRICTION AND GROWTH

It was 1000 when Rix returned to the shop after delivering parts to Greevo and picking up structural members for *Calypso* from the manufactory.

"Atom, what do I have you working on this morning?" Rix asked.

"Atom still moving parts," Atom said. "Big Boss need help?"

"Yeah, I'm going to need you to hold these pieces for me and make sure we don't get out of alignment while I tack them in place," Rix said. He'd spent thirty minutes rigging a harness to hold the largest structural member in place, but, given its mass, it was difficult to keep exactly in place.

"Okay, Big Boss," Atom agreed.

"Maybe when we're done with this, you could take a couple of loads down to the reclaimer. We're starting to stack up in here," Rix said. "Hold tight a moment."

"Reclaimer no fun," Atom said, steadying the big piece.

Rix zapped several short weld beads at strategic locations, tying the pieces together. "I know, but it's part of working in a shop. Now, would you mind if I asked a question?"

"Go ahead, Big Boss."

"Did you talk to Greevo about any of the things we brought back with *Calypso* from that last trip?"

"Talk to Greevo about supplies," Atom squeaked. "Big Boss mad?"

"I'm not mad. I'm trying to figure out how he knows I have crystals for a jump drive."

"Greevo much interested in cargos," Atom said. "I don't knows if says things."

Rix considered being angry with Atom, but he also understood that not knowing was hardly a confession by the small alien. Regardless, punishing Atom had little impact on his behavior, whereas positive affirmation seemed to yield significant results.

"I'd like it if we didn't tell things to Greevo that other people don't know," Rix said. "Greevo makes more money from me when he knows things I don't want him to know."

Atom quirked his head to Rix. "Rix Banner need secrets to make money."

"I do."

"Okay."

By 1300, Rix and Atom had fixed all the structural members in place and sent measurements for the replacement hull plating to the manufactory.

"Atom, I have a job for you that you might be interested in," Rix said.

"More cleaning parts?" Atom asked, looking at the deck.

"We have three derelicts, as I'm sure you know. I want you to see if you can find an atmo processor and a gravity generator that are in good shape. If you do, bring them back to the shop. But this is important, Atom. Don't break other components while you're removing those parts, and you need to clean up after yourself. Do a good job and I'll make sure you have extra beer and some more time off. Are you interested in that?"

"Atom like more beer." Atom bounced up and down.

"But first—at least two hundred kilograms to the reclaimer," Rix said.

"Okay, Big Boss."

With skeletal repairs complete and hull plating in the manufactory queue, Rix decided to take his medicine and move over to the farm. He wasn't looking forward to talking with Skef, but he knew he needed to do it. Arriving in the bay, he heard excited voices coming from the working greenhouse. Unable to see through the moisture collecting on the greenhouse panels, Rix had to hustle around to the door before he could figure out who all was present.

"Rix!" Amari exclaimed. "We have micro wheat berries popping! I can't believe Skef got these plants to maturity! Do you know what this means?"

Rix looked between Amari, Skef and a man he was unfamiliar with. Knowing it was impolite not to introduce himself, Rix stepped quickly to the new person and extended his hand. "Rix Banner, nice to meet you."

"Rook Hadden," the man said, tentatively accepting Rix's handshake.

"Rix, do you know what this means?" Amari repeated, unable to contain herself.

"We're making bread?" Rix asked, pulling both his hands and shoulders into a shrug–a universal *I have no idea* gesture.

"No, my boy," Skef said. "We have enough seed stock to plant entire beds of micro wheat. This is why I've been pushing so hard. Remember how greenhouse number four has all those sheet platforms with the lights and misters? This is what we'll plant there."

"I remember you saying something about that. You're looking at two hundred fifty kilos every three weeks, if I recall the conversation," Rix said.

"I'm impressed. I didn't think you'd be listening,"

"If my math is right, that's enough carbohydrates for seven hundred fifty people from one greenhouse," Rix said. "Or eight thousand credits annually, give or take."

"That alone sustains the quadraplex financially, along with a healthy rate of return for the investor," Skef nodded.

"You need number four up and running how soon?" Rix asked.

"The micro wheat berries will last a good while, so you have all the time you need to finish construction," Skef said. He sucked in a breath before continuing. "Yesterday, I allowed my excitement and expectations to potentially spoil an otherwise profitable working arrangement."

"We're doing apologies. I'm good with that," Rix said. "You caught me when I was feeling pulled in all directions. I agree, we're stronger as a team. Rook, would you like to help me finish up number four this afternoon? If we put an order in for the field sheets, they'll be done by the time we're ready to install."

Rook looked to Skef with poorly concealed confusion, and it became obvious that there'd been some conversation about construction duties. "Uh, sure, I'd love to see how this all goes together," Rook finally sputtered.

"And here you boys worked this all out by yourselves," Amari said, her eyes twinkling with mischief.

"We just needed a soft kick in the pants," Rix admitted. "Tell me, Rook, what's your experience with construction?" Rix asked as they exited the greenhouse.

"Most of the jobs I've had are labor," Rook said. "I help Thudd out from time to time with teardowns. Sometimes I help move panels for apartment buildouts. I'll be helping with your new place."

"You're familiar with panel glue ups?" Rix asked.

"Small pieces," Rook said. "Nothing this complex."

"All my designs have small videos of each step," Rix said. "If you register progress through your HUD, I have a program that catches errors and queues the next step. All the panels and mechanicals are stacked in order of installation. If you find a piece and don't know what it's for, you've missed something and you need to go back in the instructions and figure it out. Don't go forward until you do, it's just a whole lot more work."

"I wasn't expecting this much organization," Rook said. "It might take me a minute to get comfortable with this."

"How about we work on it together?" Rix suggested. "It'll go faster that way. Skef and Nerali are excited to get their micro wheat planted."

"That's all they could talk about," Rook said.

"Grab that end, would you? I'm on video 4A019," Rix said. "Take a minute to watch it. Once you get better at this, you'll be able to let the videos play while you're moving materials."

"This doesn't look too hard," Rook said.

"It's just a bunch of details. We make it easy by breaking the big tasks into small tasks until it feels easy," Rix said.

The two men worked in companionable silence, only speaking to coordinate movement of parts or when a piece needed bracing with an extra set of hands. Seemingly no time had passed when Amari reappeared at number four's entry, clearly not wanting to interrupt, but waiting for a moment to speak.

"What's up?" Rix asked, looking up.

"It's 1800, it'd be nice to let Rook go home for the day. Don't you think?" she asked.

"We're almost done," Rix said.

"I have the hang of this enough that I can finish up in the morning," Rook said, then put his hands up innocuously "Not trying to kick you off your own project. Just saying I've got it."

"Why not?" Rix shrugged. "The other farms are easier, too. If you let me get you started, I feel like I could turn you loose. You've a knack for construction, and I'll just be next door if you need help."

"I'll take that as a compliment," Rook smiled.

"I feel like I owe you a beer after the work we got done today," Rix said.

"I could grab one. Silca will be home soon."

"Silca is your wife?" Rix asked. Rook nodded, and Rix replied, "Ask her if she wants to join us for a burger. We've been hanging out after work at Loose Bolt Lounge lately. It's on me."

"You don't have to do that." Rook said.

"Ask Silca," Rix said. "We'll grab a beer, and if you need, you can take off after that."

"That's generous."

"Greevo is going to have questions about his load tomorrow, you know," Amari said as Rix started pulling off his dirty coveralls.

"I'll be interested to see what he comes up with."

"Do you want me to let Kel know we're grabbing dinner?"

"Only if you want to," Rix said. "Where's she been? Do you know? I haven't seen her or Philo all day."

"She's running loads for Thudd at the manufactory," Amari said. "Also, did you like any of those drawings enough to send to Thudd? He'll need that floorplan sooner than later."

"The first one, with the bedrooms on either side of the entry hallway, makes the most sense to me. You're right, having that bow window as an eating nook would be nice."

"I'm forwarding it to you. Maybe we could spend some time tonight picking finishes," Amari said. "You don't want Thudd picking that sort of thing for you. It'll be all black and chrome. He's such a guy."

"I'm a guy, too."

"But you like having people like me in your life, don't you?"

"If by 'like you' you mean 'dangerously gorgeous,' then yes."

"Ooh, that's the sort of talk you should run with."

Rook cleared his throat. "Maybe I'll just meet you up there?" He shifted from one foot to the other.

"Let's get going. I'll just stop by and see what Atom is up to," Rix said.

"We'll see you there," Amari said, hooking her arm into Rook's and leading him from the bay.

"Atom?" Rix called after entering his shop. Next to his workbench sat three freezer-sized subsystems that Beverly identified as two gravity generators and an atmospheric processor. The jagged metal hanging from rusted bolts and uneven dents in the cabinets told Rix that he'd overestimated the alien's patience and care for removing larger systems.

"Atom is unavailable," Beverly said, appearing in front of Rix in her Rosie the Riveter coveralls and polka-dot hair wrap. "Last I observed, he was upset and left the shop at 1700."

"Do you know what upset him?"

"There was considerable frustration in removing the subsystems. He was talking to himself in a most unflattering manner," Beverly said.

"Okay," Rix said. "Do we have a read on these units? Are they repairable?"

"All three units are heavily used, and without hefty maintenance, they could be categorized as being at their end-of-life. Being abandoned in a freighter left open to vacuum can be hard on equipment," Beverly said.

"Let's put that top of list for tomorrow morning. I'll have Atom work with me to take them apart and we can see what he was struggling with," Rix said. "I would've preferred he ask me for help instead of yanking them out like this."

"That was the source of his frustration. Atom is sensitive to an expectation of being yelled at for his transgressions," Beverly said. "Before you ask, you've been patient with him. He is frustrated with himself because he is afraid that he will disappoint you."

"Please send a message and let him know we'll work on the subsystems in the morning and get them fixed," Rix said. "There's no need to be upset about these things."

"Atom has the mental reasoning power of an adolescent," Beverly said. "It will take effort to work with his limited capacity."

"You're implying he might not be well-suited to working independently. I'll need to keep that in mind," Rix said. "Otherwise, I'm setting him up for failure."

"I agree with your assessment."

"Send him this message – *Atom, thanks for extracting those subsystems. It looks like we have some work to do to get them cleaned up. Let's work on them together in the morning.*"

"That sets a good tone, Rix," Beverly approved.

With nothing more to accomplish, Rix set off for Loose Bolt Lounge. When he arrived, he found Amari at a table with Rook and a woman Rix could only assume was his wife. "Hey all, sorry I'm behind. You must be Silca. You're even prettier than Rook said," Rix said, extending his hand.

"You're funny. And is this the hand wagging thing you were telling me about, Rook?" Silca asked.

"Have you eaten here yet, Silca?" Rix asked.

"I didn't even know this bar was here," she said. "I love all the parts he used to make the tables and chairs. It's such a spacer thing to never waste anything."

"That's a good motto," Rix said. "I've become partial to his proto burgers, but there are other things on the menu. My treat tonight."

Dinner was easygoing as Silca and Rook talked about life aboard Patience and how they'd met. The two couples separated an hour later, the food and drinks long finished and conversation topics whittled down to silence.

"Want to pretend to watch a movie tonight?" Amari teased.

Rix smiled. "Sure. Did you send the drawings to Thudd?"

"I did. Maybe while I have your attention, we could look at colors and the like. I have a few boards I put together that combine finishes and colors. I figured seeing it all together might be easier."

"You've put some thought into this."

"Do you like that?" Amari cocked her head to the side. "You act like it's an odd thing to do."

"All the houses I've lived in were already built by the time I moved in. About the most I've done is paint rooms and even then, I just used the same color as before."

"Then you have things to learn. I'll send these to your HUD. Pick as many of these as you like. That way, I'll get a sense of the style you like."

"I can do that." Projected on Rix's HUD was a rendering of the apartment, complete with walls, carpet, and kitchen appliances. With small hand movements, Rix navigated the space. "I like this one."

"The first?"

"Yes."

"Okay. Look at the next one," Amari said.

Rix knew better than to argue, so he swiped his hand to the left, bringing in the next set of design decisions. "I don't love red," he said, swiping left again without much exploration.

"Good. Don't be so fast to dismiss things. If you don't like one detail but like others, we can mix and match."

"Okay," Rix said. In all, Amari had compiled eight different partial interior designs, which Rix navigated, making small comments as he did so.

"You like warm tones," Amari noted. "You like the carpet from four, but décor six kind of hit your buttons, is that right?"

"It feels homey," Rix said. "What do you think?"

"I didn't give you any choices that I didn't already like," Amari said. "I wondered if six would be your thing. Is that a solid enough decision to send to Thudd?"

"Sure," Rix said. "I'm sending."

"We can worry about furniture later," Amari said. "Did Thudd give you a timeline for building out your apartment?"

"He said about two, three weeks," Rix said. "I thought we were working on this while watching a movie."

"Are you worried that we won't have anything to do during the movie?" Amari asked, a lilt in her voice.

"Oh … well … I guess no."

"You guess?"

"No. I can't wait for our movie," Rix said.

"You are certainly trainable, but it does take effort."

The two joined Hutari back at Amari's apartment. Victim to the couch once again, Rix awoke the next morning to the aroma of brewing coffee.

"That smells good," he said through a yawn, pushing blankets off and sitting up.

"I was trying not to wake you," Hutari said. "I have an early shift. Do you want coffee? I made extra."

"I'd love some," Rix said. "Do you mind a question?"

"Of course not, shoot."

"First, I need you to keep this quiet," Rix lowered his voice.

"That's fine."

"What do you know about Garanod?"

"You're not thinking about going there, are you?"

"I have a potential shipment that pays three times normal," Rix said. "Is it that bad?"

"I've never been, but I've heard stories. Garanod Enclave isn't like other places. It's complete anarchy. If you come across as weak, you'll attract the wrong kind of attention. I don't know if you belong there. You're a nice guy."

"And you read that as weak."

"Doesn't matter what I think," Hutari said. "It matters what energy you're giving off. Your energy is that of someone who might not hit back."

Rix nodded. "Violence isn't usually my first choice. You're saying I need to look meaner."

"Yeah," Hutari said, pouring a cup of coffee for Rix. "I gotta bounce. We can talk later if you want. Don't worry, I won't tell anyone."

"Thanks, Hutari."

"Also, thank you for taking it slow with Mom," she added.

Rix nodded and watched as Hutari exited. He walked back to Amari's room with his coffee and sat on the edge of her bed. "Hey, don't get up," he said quietly. "I'm going down to the shop. I have a load of parts to install."

"Do you need my help?" Amari murmured, curling her legs beneath the covers so she was closer to him, but keeping her eyes closed.

"Not this morning," Rix said. "Come down whenever you want, but I have Kel and Philo lined up for work later this morning."

"Are you sure?"

Rix leaned over and kissed Amari on the forehead. "Certain."

"I'll bring lunch."

7

SPECIAL DELIVERY

GHOSTMIST NEBULA, GARANOD ENCLAVE

"OH, SNIKES," Kasit hissed after a minute of racing along the rail toward Chainreach.

"Kas?" Wagg asked. "I thought I heard you splat?"

"So close. Arm dangly."

"Bad grays still chasin'?"

"No runabout chasin' a rail, Wagg, you know that," Kasit said.

"Checkin' rail sched."

"Thankin."

"Frey, fast slider comin' from Chainreach in thirty beats," Wagg informed.

Kasit stared down the rail, his eyes struggling to clear the tears caused by the extensive pain in his shoulder. At any other time, an oncoming slider would have been a welcome challenge. Without the solid use of his right shoulder, it would be considerably harder. Even so, as one of the best, he had tricks available. He started swinging, propelling forward as he lifted his legs out of the way, unclipped the sling, flew over the speeding private transport and reattached, all before his weight painfully settled onto the opposite side.

"Thankin' again, Wagg," he grunted.

"You be something mystical-like," Wagg said. "No slider good being all busted."

Kasit had a sharp mind and a keen memory. Chainreach hadn't been his actual destination, just the fastest rail away from Driftmarket. Envisioning the fluxspan rails leaving Chainreach, he reorganized his route with an eye toward easier transfers, as, with shock wearing off, his shoulder was becoming a real hindrance. Flipping to the five rail out of Chainreach, he bent and slipped an ankle into the handhold, replacing his hand and easing tension in his right shoulder.

"Two more transfers and I'll be headin' to Doc Amber. She always fixin' me up," Kasit said. Kha'rem will be spouting steam from his vents, though. I not be moving wares today."

"I'll take your shift at Kha'rem's today," Wagg offered.

"No workin' your mom's?"

"We runnin' slow. Rumor, mayhap big trader, lots of go-go parts comin' Patience Station. Three boxes be the word," Wagg said.

"Thankin' Wagg. You big frey," Kasit said. "Always rumor trade. Hopes for you."

Swinging wide, Kasit once again utilized his right leg to hold the sling as he switched rails, now headed toward Black Spire on a little-used rail that was known to have trouble maintaining power. For sliders, power outages were problematic, requiring leaps between dead spots, which Kasit would struggle with, given his shoulder. Being a gambler at heart, though, he preferred testing fate to slowing his approach, which would make him late, if only by minutes.

As if the gods of Gravenor were themselves looking after him, the power to Black Spire's 132 fluxspan rail held, and charcoal colored volcanic glass was soon racing beneath him. Approaching the distant, abandoned station, Kasit was unable to locate anyone awaiting his arrival. Hooking his left foot into the sling so that he hung upside down, he summersaulted from the rail, making sure to unlatch at the last moment.

Landing cleanly on the platform, Kasit found he was disappointed that none had been present to witness his athleticism, in spite of his grunt at the painful shock to his shoulder. He glanced at his watch and smirked. He'd arrived almost perfectly.

The sound of a slow clap snatched his attention as a shadowy figure emerged from behind a pillar supporting the level above. "I thought you would miss your window," a woman's voice announced. "Were you followed?"

"There is no one who can follow me." Kasit squared his shoulders, wincing.

"You are hurt." The woman wore a hooded robe that obscured most of her features. Kasit could only tell that she was not overly tall, and a tail of long black hair rested next to her neck. She reached out to grasp Kasit's right arm, but he pulled away. "You were chased. Did they stop you?"

"Someone knew about the pickup. They were waiting for me outside."

"Did you bring the package?"

"Turn your head," Kasit said, trying to get a look at the woman's nasal diffuser. She must have realized what he wanted, as she obliged, exposing the mark Kasit had been told to look for.

"Did you bring it?" the woman repeated.

Instead of answering, Kasit reached behind him with his left hand and fought to remove the worn book from his carrier pouch. With some adjusting, he managed to present it to the woman.

"You did well to evade those who followed. Forget this day."

"Hardly, it will take days recoverin'."

The woman's hand slithered out and deposited a credit chit in Kasit's hand as she retrieved the book. Without further conversation, she turned and disappeared into the gloom of Black Spire's nether. Kasit suppressed a shudder as he repressed the childhood lore of the monsters that lived beneath Black Spire.

With package delivered and chit in hand, Kasit needed no prompting to leave. Springing toward the fluxspan rail, he leapt from the platform and mounted with an elegant maneuver, avoiding impact to his damaged shoulder.

His return trip was uneventful, if painful. He landed on one of Havenfall's remote platforms, putting him kilometers from home, but close to the isolated Doc Amber. Walking along the path, Kasit smiled to himself as he watched the ground light up beneath his feet, stimulated by his passing. He inspected the chit as he pressed on, finding that it contained eight hundred credits, which was significantly more than he'd expected.

"What ails you child?" a familiar voice floated out from a grove of tall mushroom trees.

"Shoulder yanked, Doc," Kasit answered, turning into the trees. Multicolored glowing veins carrying power and nutrients linked the mushrooms in a complex network. He found Doc Amber kneeling between a pair of juvenile mushrooms, her long fingers buried in the vibrant soil and her blind eyes orienting on him.

"Sit," the woman said. "The young are too full of urgency. You must learn to slow yourself."

Kasit, knowing better than to argue with the old doctor, sat beneath a mature mushroom. As his bottom connected with the ground and his back with the trunk, the nutrient veins connecting his mushroom tree to the forest brightened and pulsed with renewed vigor. "Thank you, Doc."

"The forest thanks you for your gift of energy," she said, her peaceful voice floating through the air. "Was it worth the pain?"

Kasit could have played dumb and asked what she was talking about, but he thought better of it. Doc Amber's lack of sight was hardly indicative of her intuition. "I think so," he said, then hastily added, "I wouldn't have taken the job if I'd known there would be trouble, though."

"But you did know, didn't you?" she asked. Kasit bit off a quick denial and thought about the niggling warning he'd ignored. Doc Amber picked up on his internal struggle. "Good. Not all can even hear that voice. The truly remarkable learn to listen. Today was a good lesson. I hope that chit in your belt doesn't dull your brain for next time."

8

INSIDE JOB

PATIENCE STATION

WITH CLEAN CLOTHING and a cup of coffee in hand, Rix jumped on the nearby elevators and rode down to Level 8. He entered his shop to clanging coming from within *Calypso*.

"Kel, is that you in there?" he called. No response. Rix crossed the shop floor and stepped onto a ladder he'd set next to the opening in *Calypso's* midsection. Grunts from within gave him pause. "Hey, what's going on in here?" Rix tossed a leg over the edge of the unrepaired hull and stepped in. Further back, beyond the engines awaiting parts that would arrive within the next hours, a green figure stood at work. "Atom?"

"Wedged like broken soup bone," grumbled Greevo.

"Greevo? What are you doing on my ship?" Rix asked, a hand on the top of his head. "Knock it off already. You don't have permission to be in here."

Greevo turned to Rix, then looked back at the subsystem he'd been working on, and then back again to Rix. "*Calypso* not ready sail. Rix Banner work faster. Need sail."

"Bubba, I don't know what your deal is, but you need to step off the ship." Rix flexed his fingers. "I don't need to sail anywhere. We're just now getting this one fixed after the last trip. Now get to it. You've no business aboard *Calypso.*"

"Greevo help. Hold gravity generator running bads. Greevo has part sell Banner. Make better. Charge no much for work."

"You're not charging me anything."

This got Greevo's attention, and he stalked toward Rix with a glare on his face, still holding a long wrench. "We make deal. Banner take Greevo to hidey place. Greevo pay big. Greevo go quick quick. Must fix *Calypso* fast fast."

"My partner isn't here right now," Rix said. "So, we're not making any deals. I'm working on *Calypso* as fast as I can because we need her fixed for our own purposes. As for a trip to your hidey place, wherever that is, we'll need to talk about that with Kel."

"Rix Banner try for better price. Smart," Greevo nodded. "Much money for all. Greevo pay big big. Talk Kel Warp now."

"Okay, hold on a minute," Rix said. "Kel, are you there?"

"Do you have any idea what time it is?" Kel groaned.

"0700?" Rix asked.

"Right. It's nighttime."

"Well, Greevo is at the shop demanding to talk to us about his trip," Rix said. "I don't think he's going anywhere without you."

"Put on some coffee," she grumbled. "Have you seen Philo anywhere?"

"Not this morning. He's on the schedule to help with *Calypso*, isn't he?"

"Did he acknowledge that?"

"No idea. I thought you talked to him."

"Okay," Kel said. "Give me twenty minutes."

"Copy that," Rix said, turning to Greevo, who'd finally made it down the ladder.

"You can sit over there," Rix gestured to a pair of chairs next to the entry door. "Or you can leave and come back in twenty minutes."

Greevo didn't seem to hear him but instead had made his way over to the piles of parts Atom had been removing from the derelicts. "Where you get parts?" he asked.

"Salvage from those ships Quixly had tied up outside Patience."

"Hard work. Greevo already liberate good parts. Missed some," Greevo said, picking up a mechanical joint.

"We have a saying back home: *one man's trash is another man's treasure*," Rix said.

"Greevo take?" Greevo asked.

"No Greevo, you can't take my parts."

"Give good monies. Seventy-five credits."

"Rix, even in poor condition that mechanical joint is worth one hundred twenty-five credits," Beverly said, appearing in loose coveralls.

Rix pulled the part from Greevo's hands as Greevo looked at him with first confusion, then disappointment. "Greevo. When I decide to sell parts I've harvested, you will be one of my first stops," Rix promised. "For now, this is a distraction from my work on *Calypso*. How about a nice cup of coffee while we wait for Kel?"

"More interest," Greevo said, figuring out that the middle pile of parts wasn't as nice as the smaller pile next to it. He moved over, eyes full of greed, and Rix had to push on the smaller alien's shoulder to move him away.

"Take some rum in that coffee?" Rix tried, grasping at anything that might keep Greevo from ransacking his shop. The offer seemed to be just what Greevo needed to hear, as he turned to Rix with apparent intrigue.

"Yes. Coffee and rum is good good," Greevo said.

Rix made sure to take his time pouring out a measure of rum along with the coffee. Not unexpectedly, Greevo urged Rix to add to the cup until there were equal parts spirits and coffee. Rix couldn't have been more relieved when he heard Kel entering the shop.

"Is there a reason we need to be up at this ungodly hour?" Kel complained, accepting a cup of coffee from Rix. When her eye caught the flask Rix had brought out, she nodded to the rum, which Rix handed to her. "Better this way," she said, tipping the flask into her drink. "I'm already struggling."

"Time is now, Greevo. Where is this hidey place you keep alluding to, and why do you think we can get there? We don't even have coordinates," Rix said.

"Atom found Garanod crystals," Greevo said. "Tell Greevo."

"You want to go to Garanod," Kel said. "That's going to cost you. How long are you looking to stay? What kind of cargo are you hauling?"

"Not matter kind. Matter volume," Greevo said. "Two hundred meters three."

It wasn't the first time Rix had heard the term 'meters three,' as it was his translator's best interpretation of cubic meters, at least when talking to Grintok. "Forty-five meters is the max for *Calypso*," Rix said.

"Greevo know. Rix Banner has cargo ship. Make big smoke. Carry big load. Two big boxes," Greevo said.

"*Gravitational Pull* is hardly in any shape for interstellar travel. You've seen the smoke, apparently. There are so many things wrong with it. Besides, no jump drives on *Gravitational Pull*." Rix shook his head.

"Easy fix. *Calypso* bond. Two ships go as one. Small jump space is Garanod. Make easy big money," Greevo said.

"Sounds illegal," Rix said.

"Opposite of that," Kel said. "There's no law in Garanod. It's complete anarchy."

"So, pirates, then. Because we've done so well against pirates," Rix said.

"In fact, we have, dumbass," Kel said. "Sure, four-on-one in open space was dicey, but we came out alright. Before that, we dropped a couple of personal attack craft with limited damage."

"You're telling me Garanod isn't dangerous, that there aren't pirates and that we'd be just fine," Rix scoffed. "I'm not picking up what you're putting down, Kel."

"Look, *Calypso* is going to be in great shape, and she's got her needler turret," Kel said. "Ships with limited firepower sail into Garanod every day."

"Greevo not pay more ships," Greevo said.

"What about this 'doubling ships up to transit jump space' idea?" Rix asked. "Does that work?" His question was aimed at Beverly, but he wasn't surprised when he got two answers.

"I don't rightly know, Rix," Kel said. "We'd need to do some research."

"It's a matter of the combined mass of the vessels," Beverly said to Rix, who relayed to the rest of the group. "We'd need to check the jump space engines on *Calypso*."

"Greevo find new engines. Rent Rix Banner. Good price," Greevo said.

“What are we hauling and how long do you need to stay?” Rix asked.

“You’re thinking about this, Rix?” Kel asked, taken aback. “I’d have thought it was outside of your comfort zone.”

“It’s hard for us to make a decision without any details,” Rix said. “We should at least run the numbers. If you’re saying this is a bad idea, I’m all ears.”

“It’s not that. I just didn’t take you as someone who’d even think about going to Garanod,” Kel said. “But yes, let’s get details. Greevo?”

“I tell already. Two hundred meters three, mass sixty-two tons. We take four my people,” Greevo said.

“I don’t know how long of a trip it is reach Garanod,” Rix said. “Also, I need to know how long we’re staying after we get there.”

“Me not know trip. Rix Banner make trip plan, tell Greevo. Greevo stay four days,” Greevo said.

“Okay, and are we picking up return cargo?”

“Rix Banner nosy, ask questions. Greevo no like.”

“What about return cargo, Greevo? Stay with me, here,” Rix said.

“Greevo not know. Greevo think yes. Not big load. Forty meters three.”

“Give us the morning and we’ll get back to you, alright?” Rix said.

As they’d been talking, Atom stumbled into the shop, apparently having been out all night. He seemed unable to decide if he should stand by Rix or Greevo. The two Grintok exchanged a glance, followed by a couple of grunts that the translators couldn’t pick up. Atom gave Rix a questioning look but decided against asking anything.

“Atom bring parts to Greevo,” Greevo said, pointing at several pieces in Rix’s pile.

Without hesitation, Atom walked over to the pile and started gathering the parts. "Hold on there, Atom," Rix said. "What are you doing?"

"Greevo want parts. Greevo big boss."

"Greevo not big boss in my shop," Rix said. "Have you been taking Greevo other parts?"

Atom looked at Greevo, and there was another exchange of grunts. "Atom not have words."

"Greevo, are you asking my employee to steal from me?" Rix demanded, vexed.

"Atom Grintok before employee," Greevo said unapologetically. "Ships abandoned. Parts no cost."

"I see," Rix said. "Trust me when I tell you, those ships are not abandoned. I own them now, and they are sitting on a pier I've leased from Patience Station. Beyond that, Atom was removing those parts under my direction, and while I was paying him. You will return whatever Atom brought you, or you and I will *never* do business together. I won't even consider your journey to Garanod until this is resolved to my satisfaction. Do you understand what I'm talking about?"

"Rix Banner angry. Greevo make mistake," Greevo said. "Atom get parts. Bring back Rix Banner."

"Stop!" Rix snapped. "Atom works for *me*. You can't be ordering him around. Especially not in my shop."

"Atom know where parts," Greevo said, lifting his shoulders as if it only made sense. Even more irritating to Rix was the fact that Greevo wasn't wrong.

"Do we have an inventory of what's been moved?" Rix asked.

"Greevo no inventory," Greevo said.

"I've sent a list," Beverly said, to Rix's relief.

"When were you going to tell me about this?" Rix asked, fully realizing his question was aimed at both Greevo and Beverly.

"Not Rix Banner information. Free parts," Greevo said.

"I had it in mind to talk to you today about it," Beverly answered. "Fortunately, the value of the parts is under one thousand credits."

"Atom, do you know where these parts are?" Rix asked.

"Yes, Big Boss," he answered, carefully avoiding Greevo's eyes.

"Do as Greevo said. Go get the parts. Greevo, we'll talk later about this. I don't trust you right now, and I'm trying to figure out if I want to do business with you," Rix said.

"Rix Banner drink more. Too no bendy. Not good business."

"Out," Rix said, making shooing motions toward the door. "Go, Greevo."

"Talk Greevo later? Make good deal?"

"Just go."

Once both Atom and Greevo were gone, Kel turned to Rix and grinned. "Grintok are something, aren't they?"

"He admitted to stealing from me," Rix said, still shocked.

"Sounds like he'll send the parts back."

"He was also inside the ship, by himself, when I arrived this morning. I don't even know how he got in. He said the hold gravity generator was broken," Rix said. "As far as I knew, the hold gravity generator was in good shape."

"It might be worthwhile to inspect where he was working," Kel said. "It's probably innocent, but I don't know how he got in the shop. Do you have any cameras set up?"

"Beverly, do you have a take on this?"

"Atom gave him access at 0600 this morning," Beverly said.

"Show me." Rix steeled himself for the worst.

With streaming video as evidence, Rix and Kel watched as Greevo woke Atom with a comm, then instructed him to remove several parts from Rix's pile.

"He's a thief!" Rix said. "And he's co-opting my own employee!"

"Grintok have a much different perspective of ownership than other species," Kel said. "I wondered when that was going to cause issues. I suspect Atom sees Greevo as some sort of clan chief. His word probably supersedes yours in Atom's mind. You might need to tread lightly on that."

"I'm gonna lose my mind on this," Rix said. "I need to be able to trust Atom. If I can't, he can't work here."

"Sounds like you need to work that out with Atom."

"Sounds like I do."

Kel chuckled as she watched emotions play out on Rix's face.

"What?" he asked.

"You're normally so calm about everything. People can shoot blasters at you and you're not as perturbed as you are now. It's just funny. Different species come with their own baggage. You need to figure out how to deal with it and stop making assumptions based on your own experience."

"This sucks!" Rix complained.

"Dang, so close to actually cursing," Kel said. "But think of it this way: Atom is just responding to things the way he knows best. You need to let him know what your expectations are. If he can't do what you need him to, then maybe you let him go."

"Is Greevo going to feed him, give him a place to live and a place to work?" Rix asked. "It's not like he did that before I found him."

"So, decide how you want to handle it," Kel said. "I tried to warn you about hiring a Grintok."

"Gah. I don't want to talk about this right now," Rix said. "I've half a mind to tell Greevo to shove his dumb deal."

"And the other half of your mind? What does it want to do?"

Rix sighed. "Let's go check the mass capabilities of *Calypso's* jump engines."

"You don't know off the top of your head? And where are you going? *Calypso* is over here."

"Jump engine got taken out last week," Rix said, crouching in front of a jump drive that had been broken down into several large subsystems. "I'm just looking for a serial number plate to get specifications. Here we go."

"Boy, you sure just calm down when you start doing mechanical stuff, don't you?"

"No reason to bring emotion to machinery," Rix said. "It's all black and white."

"I might say that you could approach Greevo the same way after you figure out how Grintok operate," Kel said.

Rix was only partially listening as he reviewed the data coming back from the jump engine specifications. "Jump drives have wide bands of operation. This drive, if I'm reading things right, is good for four thousand tons. The next one in the line jumps to twenty thousand tons, and then ninety thousand."

"So, we can take both ships, then? What about *Gravitational Pull*? Would you feel good about taking it on a long trip? I mean, it smokes like it's on fire," Kel said.

"If you think the list of repairs necessary for *Calypso* is long, you're going to love what *Gravitational Pull* needs," Rix said. "I just spent another six grand on parts for *Calypso,* and I bet we have another three before we get ready to sail. If I want to go completely broke, I could plow six thousand more to *Gravitational Pull.* That's a good start, but it's only scratching the surface. Both ships need comprehensive overhauls on a bunch of different systems. We'll spend a hundred thousand credits before we're done, at least if I have everything my way."

"We don't have that kind of money, right?" Kel asked.

Rix snorted. "Not right now, we don't," he said. "Do you have interest in going to Garanod? We'd talked about settling down and taking less risky runs. This doesn't sound like that to me."

"I've always wanted to go to Garanod. It's everything Patience Station isn't."

"Like what?" Rix asked.

"First, it's huge. There are three hundred thousand people who call Garanod home. With no taxes and no government, it's a free-for-all. You can make fortunes in Garanod, if you know what you're looking for. You can also lose everything. Nobody cares."

"And if someone wants to shoot you and take your stuff, what then?"

"Well, that is a problem," Kel said. "We'll want to wear light armor so we're not easy marks. I've read that you want to make a deal with someone who has decent security when you dock so you don't attract the wrong kind of attention."

"Someone with decent security? Like a company?"

"It's a free market, so there are companies who offer docking and security as a package..."

"You just need to find someone trustworthy," Rix finished for her.

"That's the beauty of going out with Greevo," Kel said, nodding. "He'll know how to figure out who we can trust. Otherwise, he'll lose his entire load, and no Grintok is going to be okay with that."

"He needs to cover secure docking facility," Rix agreed. "Keep going. This is starting to make sense."

"Travel in groups. Stay armed. Pay attention to where you should and shouldn't be going," Kel said.

"Let's put together a contract and see what sticks. There needs to be a clause about paying for cleaning the crew areas after the trip is done. I'm not giving that away. We have fuel and docking space. They need to pack their own food. We'll pack our own. He said four passengers. Six is a lot for *Calypso*, but *Gravitational Pull* is hardly spacious." Rix rubbed his chin. "Beverly, what's one-way look like for time, considering *Gravitational Pull's* current condition?"

"With the information I have available, it looks like eight days, give or take twelve hours," Beverly responded. "There isn't a lot of available information, though, so I'd plan on doubling that for the trip out, just to be safe."

"Dang, sixteen days on *Gravitational Pull* would be brutal," Rix said. "And six people on *Calypso* would be just about as miserable."

"Four crew from our side?" Kel asked. "I'm assuming you'll ask Amari and leave Atom behind."

"That's what I was thinking."

"If we average worst case and what Beverly found, we're looking at a month of travel," Kel said. "For that, most crew would want six thousand plus room and board. Owners demand more than that, and that doesn't consider hazard pay."

Rix slid items around on the quickly forming logistics sheet that Beverly was helping him arrange. "Sixty-two thousand credits," Rix said. "Greevo isn't going for that."

"And he'll talk you down. You'll have to start with a bigger number," Kel said. "At what point are we not making money?"

"Fuel alone is eight thousand," Rix said. "Add atmo, food, sewage processing and we're at about twelve thousand, assuming we don't want to eat meal bars for the entire trip. Why?"

"Greevo will have done the math. He'll have a number in mind," Kel said. "We should figure out what he'll think is fair. I don't think sixty-two thousand is going to float with him. Generally, for a trip without extraordinary risks, you double the variable costs like fuel and such. That's a good rule of thumb."

"Thirty-six thousand," Rix said. "If we take that deal, our crew doesn't get paid a whole lot. Two older ships on that long of a trip will require maintenance when we get. Count on at least four thousand. My walk away point is at forty-five thousand credits. Where are you at?"

"Send me that sheet you're working on," Kel said. Rix flicked the datasheet to Kel, who looked it over. "There are good details on this. This is inflated, though. Forty thousand is the line."

"I'll start at sixty-five thousand, then," Rix said.

"When will you break the news?"

"It needs to be an in-person thing," Rix said. "I don't want him balking at a big number and us losing the opportunity. This kind of trip would be a feather in our cap."

"I don't know why you'd want a feather," Kel said, furrowing her brow for a moment. "But let's get to working on *Calypso* like we'd planned, and we can talk to Greevo up at dinner tonight. What's first on deck for work this morning?"

"A trip to the manufactory. We have a whole basket of parts to pick up," Rix said.

"Well, let's get going, then."

"I'm back, Big Boss," Atom called when he arrived, thirty minutes after Kel and Rix had returned with new parts for *Calypso*.

"Talk to me, Atom. Do you understand why I was frustrated that you took my parts and gave them to Greevo?" Rix asked.

"No. Free parts. Greevo want parts," Atom said.

"Not free. I bought those derelicts from Patience Station. I own them, along with their parts," Rix said. "I know you don't understand this, but you can't take parts and give them to Greevo without asking me first. I'm big boss here. Greevo is not big boss in my shop or on my ships. Does that make sense?"

"Not free parts?" Atom clarified.

"No free parts," Rix confirmed. "Just trust me, okay?"

"Okay, Big Boss."

9

FINE TOOTHED COMB

WITH SUPERSTRUCTURE REPAIRS completed the day before, Kel and Rix got to work laying out the unwieldy pieces of hull plating. If *Calypso* had been any kind of warship, the material would have been too heavy for the small shop. As it was, the pieces were just manageable for two people, and only if artificial gravity remained below one-tenth of the standard.

"Slow and steady, partner," Rix breathed, calmly guiding the two-hundred-kilogram sheet into place. When the sheet was within a meter of its place, he connected the magnetic end of a flexible clamp onto *Calypso*. The plating was still movable with the clamp in place, but its play was limited to only a few centimeters, allowing for fine adjustments. "She's locked down. Give me a couple of taps aft and starboard."

Kel pulled a hammer from her belt and adjusted the sheet as Rix indicated. Using the clamps for stability and existing hull plating for a template, they inched the sheet they'd pulled on neatly into place. Rix seized his opportunity and stitched several weld beads in place, inspecting the fit as he went. Between Beverly's attention and his own exacting precision, the sheet was soon secured, if not capable of holding vacuum.

"Who knew this was so much work?" Kel asked, locking in the next sheet and starting the process over again.

"If *Calypso* was any bigger, we'd need a shipyard to do this work. They have specialized robots that move these pieces like pancakes. They do all the welding too, and you can hardly even tell where their welds are, they're so well done," Rix said.

"You're so cute being all impressed by technology like that," Kel said, grunting as she urged the heavy panel toward Rix's outstretched hands. Repeating the same process a few times took until 1100 that morning, when Philo arrived.

"Heya, Buddy, you're just in time," Rix said. "Bring over that last little piece. We're just about to get her weathered in."

"Weathered in?" Kel asked. "There's no weather in space."

"Fine," Rix said. "Atom, how's work going?"

"Big stack, Big Boss," Atom answered.

"Can you bring back what you have, so far? I have a project for you," Rix said. "Finish up what you're doing first, though."

"Okay, Big Boss."

As Rix was talking, Philo jumped right in and was helping orient the final piece of hull plating as Kel tacked it in place. "I wondered if we'd ever get her closed in again," Kel said, panting.

"Not holdin' airs, Rixy," Philo pointed out.

"I was going to have Atom do the finish welding," Rix said. "His weld lines are the best I've ever seen."

"Atom make good welds, that's reals," Philo said. "What Philo do?"

"Want to get into that gravity generator? I have the new parts sitting on the workbench," Rix said. "Kel and I are going to be working on the steerage couplers."

"Okays, Rixy. Food soon?" Philo asked.

"You're right on time for food, Philo. We'll stop for lunch in forty minutes. How about you get started on that gravity generator?"

"Yup."

Rix grabbed the box of parts he'd set aside for the steerage coupling system. Some of the system's parts had been damaged, others ruined. He'd evaluated each piece's worthiness and had been lucky enough to find replacements for those deemed unsalvageable in the parts left behind by a previous tenant of Bay 808.

"Do you have this under control?" Rix asked as Kel wiggled into place between narrow girders beneath the disassembled engine.

"There's only room for one of us, so I better," Kel said. "Why, you got someplace better to be?"

"I thought I might go next door and see how Rook is getting along with the farms."

"Sure, whatever," Kel said. "Hand me the parts first, though, okay?"

"Okay."

Walking between the shops, Rix found only a single person working inside. With semi-opaque panels he had to navigate around, he'd expected to see Rook until, to his surprise, he found Amari. "I didn't think I'd find you here," he said. "Have you been working long?"

"Since around 0900," Amari answered, smiling. "Skef wanted to get these other trays planted."

"I thought he had Rook working on all this."

"He does, but there's more work than one person can do right now. Once all the farms are in production, Rook will be fine. Until then, he can use the help."

"I bet there's a robot for this kind of work," Rix said, watching as Amari patiently filled small indentions with seeds using a small device that doled them out perfectly as she passed it over top.

"It's not hard work, and I kind of like it," Amari said. "The dispenser takes care of all the hard work. I just have to get the seeds near the right spot."

"Sounds like a good job, then."

"Do you need help in the shop? It sounded like you were going to have a lot of help," Amari said. "This felt more peaceful."

"Nah, we're fine. I was just checking up on you," Rix said.

"Well, I like that," Amari said, leaning over so the two could share a small kiss. "You should come over more often."

"We were going to break for lunch in thirty. I'm making sandwiches with some of that new bread Petju made," Rix hinted.

"I'll get this sheet done, get cleaned up and come over."

Rix crossed over to the shelving he'd left in the space and lifted a medium-sized box of parts. So far, the trove of left-behind pieces hadn't amounted to significant savings, but he'd take any gain available, so he smiled as he extracted what he was looking for. On the way back to the shop, he noticed a delivery from the manufactory rolling down the hallway. At their current rate of work, they'd been receiving three or four deliveries each day, and he waited for the autonomous cart's arrival.

"More parts outside, Big Boss?" Atom asked as Rix dragged the delivery inside.

"One more," Rix said. "After lunch, would you be up for running weld beads for me on *Calypso*? I like how clean your beads are. It makes the ship's lines look nice."

"Big Boss like Atom work?"

"Of course I do, Atom is a good worker," Rix said.

"Yes! Atom do welds. Make Big Boss proud!"

"Hecks yeah," Philo said, joining them.

Lunch was a simple affair, and within forty minutes, Rix had everyone back to work, giving him time to inspect the jump drive engine that he'd found Greevo working on first thing that morning. "Beverly, can you figure out what he was doing back here?"

"It doesn't seem much of a mystery," Beverly said. "There are fresh scrapes against the crystal storage locker."

"How in the world does anyone trust him?" Rix asked, opening the locker and finding the ordinary backup crystals still in place. "Looks like he didn't get this opened."

"I assume he was looking for the Garanod jump space crystals," Beverly said. "He did not know you have been keeping them guarded."

"Something like that," Rix said, picturing the unlocked drawer in his toolbox where he'd set the towel wrapped crystals.

"Security through obscurity is generally frowned upon by experts," Beverly said. "It does seem to work for you, though"

"I'm just not expecting people to try to take things from me."

"That is common knowledge."

"Well, hold on. I didn't even know Greevo could get in here until recently." Rix said, looking at the cherry red lines of weld bead overhead where Atom was finishing hull repairs on the opposite side.

"Greevo will want to discuss business again this evening," Beverly informed, adding, "He is not a patient man."

"We have at least two days left on *Calypso*, and that's if we work nearly around the clock. *Gravitational Pull* is another matter. I still don't know what's causing all that smoking," Rix said. "It's something deep in that engine."

"A replacement of that engine is in order," Beverly said. "Otherwise, your fuel consumption will remain quite high."

"You think the engine's case is out of true, don't you?" Rix asked.

"That is a rudimentary description for what I believe to be wrong. I am no expert at the design of advanced spacecraft engines. I also do not have access to enough of the engine's internal surfaces to know if it is out of specification, or 'true,' as you call it."

"Only way to figure it out is to take it completely apart and start replacing things," Rix said. "There was this time I had an old Ford with a similar problem. I just kept replacing parts, each time thinking I'd finally found the problem. Do you know what it ended up being?"

"The case had been damaged so that it was out of true?" Beverly predicted.

"See, that's what I thought," Rix said. "I thought we had a warped block, but I got that thing milled down. Wasn't it at all."

"What was it?"

"I never did find out," Rix said. "I spent the better part of a month tearing that thing apart and putting it back together. The truck ran okay after that, maybe a little better than when I got started. I didn't have the heart to tear out that old engine and try again. Far as I know, that truck's still running, though."

"That's not a very good story," Beverly said. "Are you saying we should replace the engine without attempting to assess the actual problem?"

"No, but maybe we prioritize *Gravitational Pull's* problems like we would any ship and fix the most egregious issues. Once we get down the list far enough to start working on the smoking, maybe we'll already have a fix for it."

"That sounds quite optimistic," Beverly doubted.

It was 1900 when they'd all finished up for the day and found themselves back at Loose Bolt Lounge, not one of them energetic enough to consider making dinner for the night.

"Warp and Banner think about Greevo trip?" Greevo asked, bringing out the dinner they'd ordered. "Much dirt on face. Think work hard on spaceships."

"Do you want the entire proposal or the bottom line?" Rix asked, already irritated by the conversation. Amari rested a hand on his knee, trying to keep him calm.

"Number. Want number," Greevo said.

"Sixty-two thousand credits, with some discounts for fuel if we end up not using as much," Rix said. "Just like you, we haven't been out to your hidey hole. We don't know how long it'll take us to get there."

"Too much," Greevo said. "Make better number."

"I'm not negotiating against myself," Rix said.

"Greevo pay fifty-four thousand with five thousand penalty if take more than three more days leave Patience."

Rix sat back in his chair and took a good, long drink of the beer he'd become so fond of. Even with the penalty, Greevo was offering more than Kel had thought possible. He was certain Greevo knew something important that was being left out of the conversation.

"Fifty-eight thousand, no penalty, ten thousand up front to cover fuel and chandlery. Greevo's people bring their own food. We leave in four days."

"Fifty-six thousand, eight thousand fronted, we bring foods, leave eighty hours," Greevo said, extending hand as Rix had shown him before.

"That and you pay to clean the cabin once we're back," Rix said, grasping Greevo's hand.

"We go to hidey hole," Greevo cackled. "When load boxes? No wait eighty hours."

"I'll have them ready tomorrow morning by 0600," Rix said. "If you want them moved, I'll have them there by 0800, just tell me where to drop them."

"Greevo send address," Greevo said and stood in his chair. "Kitka bring more beers. Charge Banner. Celebrate."

Rix shook his head with disdain as the bar owner decided to celebrate with his money. He turned to Kel, who looked amused by the turn of events. "You're good with the price?" he asked.

"We're missing something," she whispered back. "There's a lesson in this somewhere. We'll know it when it shows up, I suppose."

"Aside from *don't let a Grintok think you owe them something*?"

"That's a universal lesson, Banner. So, we have three days to get two beat up old ships ready to sail? Feels like drinking should be the last thing on our minds," Kel said.

Rix brought up the interface he'd used for ordering parts from the manufactory and released the final three thousand in pieces he needed for *Calypso*, and six thousand more in parts he already knew they would need for *Gravitational Pull*.

"We need a schedule of who's working on what," Kel said. "Otherwise, we're going to be stepping all over each other."

"I'll work on that tonight," Rix said. "Amari, do you think you could run *Gravitational Pull's* cargo pods over to Greevo's pier tomorrow morning?"

"Sure thing."

"Beverly, I'm going to need your organizational help so we don't fall behind," Rix said. "I feel like most of the heavy lifting on *Calypso* is already behind us. I have maybe six hours of repairs, and then Philo and Kel can start reinstalling subsystems. I'm thinking fast, so I'm missing things."

"Talk me through what subsystems you're repairing tomorrow," Beverly answered. She'd shown up in the middle of the table wearing a conservative suit and sitting at a tiny wooden table, where she was writing feverishly in a green ledger.

"Mob boss again, huh?" Rix asked.

"It fits," she shrugged.

Rix nodded, then listed the systems he needed to focus on in *Calypso* before turning them over to Philo and Kel for reinstallation. As it was, he didn't love either of them working on *Calypso* without him being present, but there just wasn't time to do otherwise.

Choosing to sleep in Amari's apartment that evening, Rix was out of bed by 0500 the next morning, dragging the prior evening's delivery of parts from the hallway. After making coffee, he got right to work repairing the highest priority subsystems and delivering them to *Calypso*.

At 0700 Amari arrived. "I didn't feel you leave the bed last night. How long have you been up?" she asked.

"Only a couple of hours. I needed to get a jump on all this," he said, gesturing vaguely at the piles of machinery around him. "You're up earlier than I was expecting."

"I'm delivering the cargo pods to Greevo," she reminded him.

"Oh, dang, thank you," Rix said. "I'll help get them loaded onto *Gravitational Pull.* When you bring her back, I'll need you to retract the cargo rails and squeeze in behind *Calypso.* Do you think you can fit her?"

Amari gauged the distance behind *Calypso* with visual measurements on her HUD's sensors. "We'll fit."

With vac suits sealed and photonic barriers energized, Rix opened the large bay doors. For a moment, he stared out into space, taking in the asteroid field in the foreground and the distant stars behind.

"Are you doing okay, Rix? You seem stressed," Amari said.

"We're under the gun here," Rix said. "I wish Greevo wasn't pushing us so hard."

"You've run the numbers. We've got this. We'll keep working until we get it right, okay? You're not on your own here." She laid a hand on his shoulder.

Rix nodded. He had a good crew, although getting them to focus was often problematic. "Thank you, Amari," he said. "I'll work it out. I appreciate your help more than you know."

"You had my back when I needed you. Now it's time to learn that goes both ways."

"Is there a story about why you're so good at sailing old cargo haulers?" Rix asked, grabbing the long, heavy tools he'd need to lock the cargo boxes in place.

"There *is* a story," Amari said. "And, if you're good, I'll tell it to you. But not when your attention is split in a million different ways. I like to have your attention when I'm talking."

"I'm sorry I'm so distracted. I have a lot on my mind with all this. I'd have forgotten about delivering those pods if you hadn't shown up."

"Well, get your lever bar set in place. This is no time for distractions," she said, leaping off the pier, cutting the corner of the walkway as she sailed through space without the aid of anything but her inertia.

"Careful, Amari," Rix said, watching as she ran into the side of *Gravitational Pull* and grabbed a handhold, arresting her momentum.

"Get moving, Rix," she pushed back as she disappeared into the cargo hauler.

Rix started for the cargo pod but also kept his eye on the small vessel as lights illuminated within. A blue cone popped up at the back of one of the engines, and when the second engine started, a large cloud of black soot puffed out, momentarily engulfing Rix.

"Nice," he complained, stabbing the large lever bar into place.

"She has an attitude. It's like her signature," Amari laughed, expertly maneuvering around.

In all, it took less than fifteen minutes to lock the cargo pods in place, and Rix shook his head in admiration as Amari nimbly scooted *Gravitational Pull* away from the station. He was barely able to finish up his prior task before she returned, leaving the cargo ship tethered outside the bay. The pair were taking a coffee break when reinforcements arrived at 0800.

"What's the plan, Rix?" Kel asked, accepting a cup he poured upon her arrival.

Rix smiled. If he hadn't arrived early and gotten time to work on his own, the question would have been frustrating. Instead, he was ready. "I have you and Philo reinstalling three subsystems. That should take you to lunch time," Rix said. "I've put the first two in front of their enclosures, and we've sent video walkthroughs you should watch before doing the work. If you have any questions, interrupt me. I'd rather take a minute to explain now than hours to pull something out later."

"Look at Mr. Organization," Kel said. "It's almost like you've done this kind of work before."

"How about me, Big Boss?" Atom asked.

"Buddy, I looked at your welds. That's some great work you did there," Rix said. While he wasn't exaggerating, he also knew that Atom responded well to compliments. "I've marked three lines that need one more pass to fare them out. After that, take the paint gun and get a good primer down. Once that's dried, I have a paint program already loaded in your paint gun. One warning, though. Please be careful of over-spraying on the engine side, okay?"

"Copy, Big Boss," Atom said, taking the paint gun from Rix. "Atom make you proud."

"Are you ready for me to bring *Gravitational Pull* inside?" Amari asked.

"For sure," Rix said. "If you're up to it, could you remove that old exercise equipment from the ship, too? We can't get the deck repainted with it still in there."

"It can't be that hard, can it?" she wondered.

"Some of the parts might be heavy. If we need to reduce gravity in the bay for a while, we just need to let Atom know. It'll mess up his painting."

"Oh, good point." As the crew steadily worked, a stack of old, broken parts accumulated for future consideration, and the piles of replacement pieces dwindled. Hours turned into days, and sleep became elusive. On the second day, *Calypso* proudly pulled out into local space, destined for Greevo's dock, where cargo was onboarded. On the evening of the third day, supplies were loaded until both ships were full to the point of stacks of crates invading living spaces.

Finally, at 0400, four hours before the appointed departure time, Rix slipped a small wrench into the tool bag on *Gravitational Pull's* deck.

“Is that it?” Amari asked, stirring from the pilot chair where she’d fallen asleep several hours prior.

“Sorry, I didn’t mean to wake you,” he said. “I’ve been through these systems with a fine-toothed comb. We have issues, but we know what they are and can work with them.”

“You look like you could sleep for a week,” Amari said.

10

AUDITION

GHOSTMIST NEBULA, GARANOD ENCLAVE

An hour later, Kasit was finally on the path home. While he enjoyed spending short periods with Doc Amber, he could only take her mystical rambling for so long.

"You are too generous, Kasit," she'd told him as he'd peeled off a hundred credits from his chit after she'd twisted and pushed his arm, painfully resetting his dislocated shoulder into the socket. "And stay off that shoulder for at least a week. Do you hear me?"

"A week," he'd answered and bounded through the colorful overgrowth, the events of the day already fading from his consciousness. After twenty minutes, he finally came across a thin fluxspan line that would drop him within ten minutes of home. He leapt on, utilizing a figure-four leg cross to hold one side of the sling.

Covered by the ever-creeping floor of Havenfall, Kasit's home emerged from the landscape when he was just a dozen meters away. The colorful, energetic lines of biomass surged across the backside of his house, exposing that someone was inside and using power. For casual observers and strangers to Havenfall, the patterns of the biomass were mysterious, but it was Kasit's home, and he recognized what he was seeing.

"Mom? What are you doing home?" he asked, swinging open the entry and tossing his sling in the general direction of the shelving where he was supposed to store it. "I thought you were working today."

A man stood from a couch opposite the door where he'd entered. At first, he thought it might be Wagg, but when he realized a second figure still sat in a chair, he understood things were not as he'd expected.

"Sit, Kasit," the man in the chair directed. "We have things to discuss."

"Lights to seventy-five," Kasit called. "Who are you? Why are you here?" The man was no one Kasit recognized, that he wore expensive clothing was unnerving.

"Lights to sixty," the man directed. "Don't be rude, Kasit. Sit. This isn't a hard conversation. I just want to talk."

"I don't know who you are."

"Lirren Vos," the man said evenly.

"You're ... Lirren ... Vos?" Kasit stammered, immediately recognizing the name. As if to verify the man's identity, Kasit's eyes fell on Lirren's hands, which were covered with tattoos, his fingers sporting large rings. On Garanod, Lirren Vos was a name rumored to be high up in the Jeshifa organization, a violent group who used the hidden enclave as home base.

"You've heard of me. That'll make this conversation faster," Lirren said. "Tell me, Kasit of Havenfall. Where have you been? My associates lost track of you once you dove off the bottom of Driftmarket."

"I … I'm a slider. I was jus' slidin'. Nothing wrongs," Kasit said. "Hurt shoulder on Chainreach grab. Had to see a doc." To validate his story, Kasit pulled his shirt to the side, exposing a forming bruise along with a medi-patch that had been put in place to slow the damage.

"Protectin' source? Pera done you no solids," Lirren said, his perfect grammar slipping for a moment back to the gutter speech Kasit used.

"Not knowing Pera. Just slidin'," Kasit said unconvincingly.

Lirren pulled a package from a case resting against the chair where he sat. Opening it, he held up a journal just like the one Kasit had transported. "This was your package," he said. "I was your customer. It was a test."

"No understandin'," Kasit said.

"It's not that hard. I needed to see if I could trust you with important things," Lirren said. "We need a runner. Someone who can move small items without being caught. You that person. Diving off Drift-market with my informations, bad practice. Not make slide, Kasit gone … information gone."

Kasit considered what the man was saying, and he imagined that Lirren likely cared more for his book than some slider's life. "Trouble?" he asked simply.

"Never let it be said that Lirren Vos punishes anyone for a good gamble and a win. What if Kasit had dropped book? Or Kasit give book to gray hoods? Maybe trouble," Lirren said. "Tell me, Kasit. Did you look in my book?" Lirren asked. "Maybe you pick up a little information you sell later? Maybe I pay to know what you read, Kasit."

"No, I would never. Sliders just run. Have no interest in writin's."

Kasit's mind spun with questions. Why was Lirren sitting in his living room? "If your book, why do you need me to read it? I didn't read it" Kasit insisted, switching to formal speak. "I just slide for fun. I shouldn't have taken that job from Pera and Vell. I knew it was off."

"Your eyes give you away, Kasit," Lirren said. "You know this isn't the journal you ran. I'll come clean. I want the information in that journal. You're going to get it for me."

"How?" Kasit asked. "It was delivered."

"Good money in running for me, Kasit. I'd even get you a first-class upgrade for that cobbled sling you're sliding on. Work hard, I'd even spring for electronics. You could have oncoming maps in real time."

"What kind of work?"

Lirren's smile turned predatory. "It always gets down to this," he said. "Do you know why they use paper journals?"

"I don't. It seems inefficient."

"It is," Lirren agreed. "But it is also impossible to hack. No digital footprint means even my best electronics people can't see it, not beyond fuzzy images my gray cloaks caught today. You are fast, boy. Only reason I'm talking to you today is because you outran my best. Work for me."

"I appreciate you makin' offer," Kasit said. "I made promises. No organization. Can't go back on that. Here. Take the creds from the job." Kasit held out the chit that still held five hundred credits."

"Do you hear that, Busk? He'll buy me out with creds," Lirren jeered.

For the first time, the other figure spoke. "Kid thinks you askin'. Want me show him that no workin'?"

"What do you say, Kasit? Is Busk right? You think I'm askin'? Your slide this morning was brilliant. It was more than that, though. Do you know what it was?"

"A job?" Kasit asked, his voice small.

"Not bad," Lirren said. "It was a job. You sayin' right. It was somethin' else, too. It was an audition. Do you knowin' that word?"

"Busk hurt Kasit if no takin' job," Kasit said, eyes on the other, much larger man.

"Not a dumb kid after all. You come by this address tomorrow after 1700," Lirren said, flipping a piece of card stock at Kasit as he took a step toward the door. "Busk here will get you going with some new gear."

"If I don't show?" Kasit asked.

"You'll see Busk either way."

11

GARANOD HO!

"What are you working on?" Amari asked, finding Rix sitting cross-legged atop crates stacked behind her in the cramped galley space behind the pilot chairs. Sprawled across a makeshift table of three stacked of crates sat the complex inner workings of a system unknown to her.

For the first forty hours of their four-day trip to the Garanod jump point, Amari, Rix and Greevo had exchanged watch shifts and sleep schedules. Rix looked up from his work. "Side project," he answered. "I brought a pile of work from home. Figured I could put the down time to good use."

"We might need to get that vent working a little harder. Your solvent is smelly."

"Sorry about that," Rix said. "I'll get it covered."

"Is Greevo in the bunk?" Amari asked, glancing upward, even though a deck separated them from the bunkroom above.

With four Grintok passengers and both ships fully loaded with cargo and supplies, it hadn't been possible to keep the Grintok together.

Greevo often had strong feelings about various aspects of daily life, and Kel wasn't likely to take well to his input, so the decision was made to keep him off *Calypso*, leaving him on *Gravitational Pull* with Rix and Amari.

"Last I saw, he was playing some sort of game. Looked like gambling. I'm not sure how that works, given we're under sail," Rix answered.

"You've had quite a change, going from the frenetic pace of takeoff to all this enforced rest," Amari said. "How are you holding up?"

"Not moving around is driving me nuts," Rix said. "My muscles are feeling bad."

"You may regret bringing that up. I have an exercise routine we need to be doing," Amari said. "How many parts did you bring for repair?"

"More than I can fix," Rix said. "Something on your mind?"

"We should get a game going with Greevo, but you have to promise you won't let it get out of control," she said.

Rix gave a crooked grin. "What kind of out of control?"

"Grintok are crafty gamblers," she warned. "He'll own this ship before the end of the trip if you're not careful."

Rix held Amari's gaze. "You're not kidding around, are you?"

"No, I'm not," she said. "Figure out how much you're willing to lose and lock down the rest. He'll be persistent about getting you to bet more."

"Wow, you're worried about this. I'm good at cards. Ask Kel," Rix said.

"If you set a budget, and you take his money while staying within that budget, you'll be a legend," Amari said. "Make sure whatever you gamble is money you don't mind losing."

"That's not enough to get Greevo interested."

"What not interest Greevo?" Greevo's rasped from the ladder joining the bunk room to the main area.

"Cards," Rix said. "Amari was just telling me how good you are, and I was telling her just how much I don't like being separated from my money for no good reason."

"Now I've started something," Amari said. "You just remember what I told you, okay, Rix?"

"Game is sticks and stones," Greevo said, grabbing the assembly Rix had been working on. Rix was about to object, but Greevo was careful as he delicately placed it back into the open crate Rix had pulled it from. Rix rolled the remaining parts in the towel he'd laid out, set them into the crate alongside the assembly and then replaced the lid. While he was interested in fixing the assembly, the task was much more of a pastime than an actual job.

"We had a nursery rhyme called the same," Rix said.

"Drink important. No play no drink," Greevo said. "Be good worker. Get drink. Greevo get set up."

"Agree to stakes before you start," Amari said.

"Why talk? Greevo show game," Greevo said with irritation. "Girl play or girl talk?"

"Ten credits, no buy backs," Amari asserted. "He's never played."

"Ten credits," Greevo spat. "Not good. Why play?"

"Greevo, don't start already," Rix said as he was pouring a pair of drinks. "We don't need to always argue for everything. Don't you want to play?"

"No understand. Greevo always argue. Good for Greevo."

"Fine," Rix said. "Ten credits is the buy-in, or no drinks."

"Not fair."

Rix set down a glass containing half coffee, half rum. "Take even one sip and you agree," Rix said and settled back onto the crate where he'd been sitting before.

"Ah, good. Maybe Banner not so slow," Greevo said, taking a long sip of the spiked coffee.

And so, the journey continued. Each new day, Rix pulled out an additional ten credits, and by the end of the day or sooner, he'd lost the entirety of his stake. Finally, they reached the location where they believed the Garanod jump point to be, both ships coming to a stop.

"*Calypso,* come in, this is *Gravitational Pull,* over," Rix called over comms.

"This is *Calypso*," Kel answered. "Are you ready for us to initiate the bonding sequence?"

"That's affirmative," Rix answered. "I'll meet Philo out on the cargo pods, and we'll get lashed together as planned, over." Not knowing the sort of forces they might encounter, Beverly had suggested a physical connection between the ships, as jump space didn't have consistent physics related to electromagnetism.

"Good copy. Initiating joining sequence," Kel answered.

Donning his vac suit, Rix felt a thrill in his stomach as he depressurized *Gravitational Pull's* basement, which was directly below the main deck and gave access to the subsystems necessary for sailing. Small by any standards for space travel, *Gravitational Pull* was designed for shorter, intrastellar trips. Jumping such a small vessel between systems was uncommon, if only because of the cramped conditions endured by a necessarily small crew.

Opening the exterior hatch, Rix clipped his lifeline to a tether point and swung across to the first cargo pod on *Gravitational Pull's* cargo rails. Climbing to the top, he knelt, keeping close to the pod's surface, while Kel delicately tapped small thrusters, nudging *Calypso* into place atop the pods.

"Positive contact, Kel," Rix said, popping back up and hurrying to capture *Calypso's* mooring lines, which he attached to *Gravitational Pull's* cargo rails below. At the same time as Rix was executing this maneuver, Philo exited *Calypso* and did the same with mooring lines on the opposite end. The entire process took no more than twenty minutes, and the two returned to their own vessels after exchanging high-fives.

"I'm not sure why you're not more concerned about this," Kel called over comms. "I feel like we're overstressing those jump crystals. It feels wrong. We're not all that securely connected."

"Have you seen this go wrong?" Rix asked. "According to what I've read, we don't even need to be connected at all for this to work. The area of effect specified by our jump engines contains a whole lot larger area than these two ships. Are you calling a mission scrub?"

"No. I just want it recorded that I have a bad feeling," Kel said. "I'll enter jump space on your mark, Rix."

"Give it a ten second count down for gravitas," Rix said. "We're ready on this side."

"Here we go," Kel said. "Ten ... nine ... eight ..."

Rix's stomach flipped as they all entered jump space together. Kel had explained to him at length her own understanding of jump space, or the travel through a different dimension of reality which conveniently didn't follow the same rules of space and time as usual. Perhaps the most noticeable part of jump space was the odd smearing of light that occurred, or maybe the odd shift in the way energy related to things like acceleration, and walking felt like you were underwater, but without floating. The general rule of thumb, as Kel had explained, was it was just a great time to catch up on sleep, because no kind of productivity could be had while in jump space.

"Are we napping?" Rix asked, his voice sounding funny to his own ears. Without any resources to guide them, they had no idea how long they'd be in jump space. It could be a couple of hours or up to a couple of weeks, which was why they'd brought such a large volume of food along.

"Sticks and stones?" Greevo asked. "No need nap."

"Why don't you take a bridge shift?" Amari asked. "We'll take advantage of the down time and get caught up on some sleep."

"I'll make your coffee," Rix said, anticipating resistance.

"Fine."

After setting Greevo up with his heavily loaded coffee, Amari and Rix retired to the bunk room above.

"I don't know how he can make such a mess in such a short time," Amari said as they worked together to push Greevo's strewn personal items back into the case he'd brought along.

"At least we aren't sharing bedrolls," Rix said, picking up the sleeping rolls.

"Hold on a minute," Amari said, grabbing the buzzbroom and starting to sweep. By the time she was done with the nine-meter square space, she had a pile of crumbs and debris.

"Geez, we just did that three days ago," Rix complained.

"Partly, the problem is there isn't much private space. Greevo is eating most of his meals up here just so he can work by himself," she said. "Speaking of work, how are things going with your new job? Were they upset that you were taking a trip so soon after being elected?"

Rix focused on unfurling the bedrolls and straightening the blankets. "A lot of council business is done day-to-day with online communication. Actual votes are scheduled and the material is presented in advance. We've been working on the fiscal budget, which is a lot of discussion and even more research. They know I could be out of communications for a week to ten days, and they're fine with it. I raised a few eyebrows when I disclosed that we'd be outside of Galactic Empire space, though."

"I bet," Amari said, settling into her bed roll. "Do you mind if I ask a kind of touchy question?"

"Depends on how touchy," Rix said, though he smiled encouragingly.

"I know you like me, and we're good together," she said, nodding as if looking for a response.

"I agree with that."

"Why don't we sleep closer to each other?"

"Closer? We're practically touching," Rix said. "Are you asking why we're using two bedrolls instead of combining them?"

"I am."

"I've been wondering the same thing," Rix said. "I just figured that we've been running around like crazy people ever since we met, so it's been hard to feel connected."

"I've felt that too," she said. "The thing is, I want more and so do you."

"I do."

"Let's start small, then. We'll join our bedrolls, but no expectations or anything. If you want to cuddle me, I'd like that, but it's okay if we're just close ... sharing warmth."

Rix crawled forward and reconfigured the bedrolls to be connected. Turning his back, he stripped down to the thin leggings he wore beneath his suit and slipped into the bedroll, not looking in Amari's direction, though he could hear her changing into her night clothes as well.

"Lights to seven percent," Rix said. It was the illumination level they'd agreed upon before.

"Rix, you can look at me. It's okay," Amari said.

Rix turned, his heart racing. Amari wore a similarly thin, relatively modest gown, which didn't hide her allure. Gracefully, she slipped in next to him. "You're very attractive, Amari," he said, turning onto his side.

"I find you quite handsome, too," she said, turning away from him but also scooting toward him. "Hold me?"

Rix closed the distance and dropped his arm over her waist, relishing how the heat of her body felt against him. "We should have been doing this more," he whispered, his head only inches from hers. "Thank you for breaking the ice."

"I wondered if I'd ever trust anyone again," she said, wrapping her fingers around the hand he'd draped over her and pulling it to her chest.

"Can you sleep?" he asked a few minutes later. Tension drained from her shoulders, and she rolled into him slightly, her breath evening out. Rix smiled and fell asleep.

Six hours later, they'd moved only slightly, but in each iteration, Amari managed to keep her body pressed against Rix, even when he tried to give her more room.

"Rix, the end of this jump space leg is twelve minutes away," Beverly said, appearing in polka dot pajamas.

"*Pajama Game* hasn't even made it to the theatre," Rix said. "Did you see that on a poster somewhere?"

"It was in a magazine," Beverly said. "I'm surprised you know about it. That's a good catch."

"I like Doris Day," Rix said, shrugging.

"What's up, Rix?" Amari asked, stirring from her sleep.

"Greevo fell asleep. We've been down for six hours and are about twelve minutes from the jump space transition to normal space."

"Oh, I'm getting up," she said, and the two of them both attempted to crawl out of the bedroll at the same time, which was nearly impossible. Amari laughed. "You go first."

Rix grinned and backed out, grabbing his vac suit and pulling it on. Amari followed, and they worked together to tidy up. "Are you taking a shower?" Rix asked.

"Yes, but I'll wait until we transition," Amari said.

Dropping down the ladder, Rix scanned the main level and found Greevo fully reclined in a pilot's chair, snoring loudly. With only minutes left, Rix slid into the other pilot's chair, wincing as something crunched under his backside. Scooting forward, he turned to discover three partially eaten meal bars, still in their wrappers, now crushed beneath him.

"Greevo, wake up," Rix said. He knew better than to touch the alien, as he'd made the mistake before.

"No, Greevo tired. Do all Rix Banner work."

Rix shook his head but didn't respond. Greevo liked to complain and no amount of discussion seemed to change things, so Rix had taken to letting the grumpy alien have his say.

"Thirty seconds, Amari," Rix said.

"I'm secure," Amari answered.

Once again, Rix's stomach flopped and a feeling, like touching an electrical outlet, filtered through his system as the two ships dropped out of jump space.

At first, Rix thought they hadn't fully transitioned, as the space around them was colored with red, orange and blue hues, instead of the black void he was used to. He didn't have long to contemplate, as his comms chirped.

"*Gravitational Pull*, do you copy?" Kel asked.

"We're here," Rix responded.

"That's a first for me," Kel said.

"What's that?"

"Sailing into a nebula," she said. "If I'm not wrong, we're in the Ghostmist Nebula, which is way the heck out there."

"What's with all the colors? Oh, hold on, nebula are gas concentrations, right?"

"Got it in one. Would you believe there's actual pressure outside the hulls? It's not a huge amount, but it's something. There's even eighteen percent oxygen out there, and some other stuff, it's all inert. Might smell, though. Dang, we could breathe out there. It'd be cold, but you wouldn't die right away."

"Beverly, is that right?" Rix raised his eyebrows.

"The lower oxygen concentration would cause impairment over time, but for short periods of less strenuous activity, it would not be harmful."

"Philo, are you ready to help me get *Caly* unleashed?" Rix asked.

"Yup, yup," Philo answered.

"My scanners are picking up a lot of radio traffic about thirty hours out," Kel said. "Nothing in the way of ship traffic either, although transponders might not be a thing here. We might want to take a hint and shut ours down."

"Yeah, that's a solid idea," Rix said. "At least until we know what we're getting into."

Philo and Rix climbed onto the cargo rails of *Gravitational Pull* and disconnected the fat straps they'd tossed over the top of *Calypso*, as well as the magnetic clamps of the mooring lines.

"Rixy! We breathin'!" Philo said, dropping his helmet and waving his furry hands toward his face as if to pull atmosphere into his nose. "Smell old beer. Now thirsty."

Rix grinned and lowered the facemask on his vac suit. Philo wasn't wrong. The nebula carried a strong smell of hops. "I haven't had a good beer in a long time," Rix said. The idea of carbonation wasn't unfamiliar to the aliens he'd encountered, but the lack of barley and hops had made the taste of fermented yeast drinks less interesting.

"Philo have a good feelin' 'bout this," Philo said, rolling a wide strap onto a spool.

The pair worked efficiently, high fiving as always when they finished. They were hopeful that whatever version of civilization Kel had located only thirty hours away would potentially reduce what could be a much longer trip.

Rix entered *Gravitational Pull* to the sounds of arguing. By the sound of things, Amari was irritated by the mess Greevo had left behind, and Greevo was insisting that cleaning wasn't part of his responsibilities.

"Make coffee, Greevo come back," Greevo said, storming up the ladder to the bunk room.

"Tell me we get to leave him on Garanod," Amari fumed.

"I wouldn't be opposed," Rix said, grabbing the vacuum wand and connecting it to a port. "Any chance you'd be willing to make coffee?"

"For you, or the green monster that's polluting the upstairs with his stinky butt!" Amari asked, raising her voice for Greevo to hear.

"Girl stinky!" Greevo fired back, his head appearing in the opening between the floors. "Greevo no want stinky girl coffee."

"Greevo no get, then!"

Rix smiled and shook his head. He'd had plenty of irritating exchanges with Greevo, and he was amused that things had escalated with Amari before they did with him. Instead of participating, he gave the cockpit a thorough vacuuming, which it had needed before the trip. The amount of debris collected was appalling. When he was done, he moved on to the floor of the galley.

"I see you hiding behind that vacuum, you know," Amari said, pouring out a cup of coffee.

"Hey, check this out," Rix pretended to not hear her, though he put the vacuum away. On his HUD, Beverly was projecting a collection of large planetoid-sized masses, all near each other. "Beverly has a view on Garanod. Not what I was expecting at all."

"Is that a broken planet?" Amari asked.

"It is more likely that the planet cracked upon formation," Beverly answered. "It is equally interesting how dense the Ghostmist Nebula's gasses that suffuse the region are. The odds against this type of formation are extraordinary."

"Astronomical?" Rix asked with an ornery grin.

"I acknowledge your humor, Rix Banner," Beverly said. "Five masses separated by kilometers. I'm picking up significant radio transmissions from all masses. There can be no doubt that this is Garanod Enclave. Parsing the unencrypted traffic, I've discovered five districts: Black Spire, Driftmarket, Havenfall, Chainreach and The Quiet Coil. I'm gathering sufficient data to form a picture. Check your tactical display."

As promised, the broken planet, known as Garanod Enclave, appeared on their displays. As details filled in, Rix's attention was drawn to the small blue lines that formed a spiderweb between the masses. "Are those lines holding it together?" he asked.

"That seems unlikely, Rix," Beverly said. "I'll do my best to come up with better answers, though."

12

SIGNAL IN THE DARK

"KASIT, I am upset you have missed two days of work," Kha'rem said. "Had it not been for your friend, Wagg, covering your shift, and the belief that I would disappoint Zenith, you would no longer have a job. Clean work is hard to find in Driftmarket, as it is everywhere on Garanod, yet you act as if you do me a favor by simply presenting yourself."

Kasit carefully maintained his posture as the large, greenish blue Vesh spoke. Out-massing Kasit twice over, Kha'rem, like all Vesh, was more comfortable in the waters of the glowing inner lakes trapped within Driftmarket than he was walking on dry land. It was only the promise of trade that pulled him to the storefront where he bartered with eel, fish and various plants that had adapted to the subterranean waters where Vesh had evolved.

"I am apologetic," Kasit said, looking suitably abashed. He'd learned that while Kha'rem was a good businessman, the briny smelling man appreciated an apology, if delivered directly and without excuses.

"Your shoulder is damaged. Can you lift today? I have smaller tasks, if you need," Kha'rem said.

"It's good. I'm sorry, Kha'rem," Kasit said. "I missed a jump and pulled the bone from its socket. I nearly passed out."

"When will you stop this perilous sliding? Fluxspan rails are dangerous. Many have died in collisions with fast movers. I would not like to visit Kasit's release into the mists."

"I can't give it up yet," Kasit said. "It's the only time I feel free."

Kha'rem laid a wide webbed hand across Kasit's back. "For you, we will search for adventure. Now to the stores. You must pack frozen gillet with Wagg. I have orders for twenty cases."

"That's ... awesome," Kasit said, struggling to hide his disappointment. Gillet, a fish ranging in mass from just a few to over twenty kilograms, were a common source of protein in Garanod, as they were caught regularly by a crew who lived in the inner lakes. Gillet were delivered live in large water tanks. This required Kasit, and sometimes Wagg, to catch, disable and freeze the fish in fifty-kilogram cases packed with ice. Minor injuries caused by sharp teeth and pointy spines were common, though easily healed at the end of the shift with medical wrappings.

"Look who decided to finally show," Wagg said, arms folded in faux anger as Kasit pushed through into the pungent smelling storage room.

"Did you know we were doing gillet today?" Kasit asked, unfazed.

"Does it matter?" Wagg asked, relaxing his posture. "Better than the buzz eels. I'm so tired of getting shocked."

"All you have to do is wear gloves if we're doing buzz eels," Kasit said. "Bring some next time."

"No way, I only get three days out of a pair of gloves. I'm tired of paying for 'em."

"Truths," Kasit agreed, grabbing a polysteel case and unfolding it so it remained open. He pushed the box across the roller bar to his friend, who stopped it just beneath the ice dump, where he added five centimeters of crushed ice. They repeated the process five times, which was as many cases as they could manage in the space available.

Donning a special article of clothing that covered their throats and the tops of their chests and provided protective sleeves, Kasit dragged a large tank of water that sat atop a gravity plate over to Wagg.

"Clear!" Wagg said. Kasit lifted his arms as electricity coursed through the water, stunning the gillet. With gaffs, the two worked together to pull fish from the bath and stretch them out on the ice. With five in the box, the scale projected a bright blue light, indicating they'd reached full capacity. The pair rolled the case back to the ice chute, topped it off and closed it up. "Ready," Wagg said after lifting a gravity-suspended pallet next to the case. Kasit shoved the case onto the pallet, clearing their assembly line for the next go 'round.

"Kha'rem said we have to empty all the tanks. He thought twenty cases," Kasit said.

"Sure..." Wagg drew the word out sarcastically. "I'd put creds on twenty-seven cases, maybe thirty."

Kasit considered the tanks and did some quick math. "Ten creds says no more than twenty-four."

"Oh, we gots some action," Wagg said, carrying the next case over and filling the bottom with ice. "Did you hear the rumor? Crazy ship just showed, blarin' Galactic Empire transponder codes. Can you be believin'?"

"Yikes," Kasit said. "Where bein'?"

"Out some days in boot," Wagg said, referring to a boot-shaped section of the Ghostmist Nebula.

"Bein' rookie gonna hurts."

"I heard says transponders been doused. Think they bein' smart enough to jig-a-jag?"

"We'll be a hearin' for sure. Hope they can be escapin' the grays and Jeshifa," Kasit said. "And boys, I have somethin'. You never be guessin' who was in my hovel after my run the other day."

"When you busted your arm?"

"Yeah."

"I heard grays be chasin' a slider. You tolds me that it was you. Remembers?"

"No, this bein' different. Lirren Vos in my hovel, waitin' my homecomin'. Cool as could be. Wanted me to be spyin' for him."

"Bad yikes. Tell Zenith?"

"I can't tellin her that. She'd go lookin' for Vos. No goods for any."

"You bein' right. You spyin' for Jeshifa, now? Word get out. No credits for slidin'. Grays will be wantin' you out of game. Flusterin'! This is bad breaks," Wagg said.

"I had another thought," Kasit said, finishing off the next case. "It's bein' about your Galactic Empire friendins."

"Not my friendins. Just heard the rumor."

"What if we use that comm box you built? Tell 'em to do a big jig-jag or get troubles with Jeshifa or grays. Maybe they have credits for infos," Kasit said.

"If bein' trades, maybe dock Kha'rem. Kha'rem pay out finders. What thinkin'?" Wagg asked.

"Think they be receivin'?"

"No troubles for us if no."

"Maybe I stay at your hovel after works. We make radio signal."

"Buyin' dinner be Kas. Case twenty-three right here. Lots gillet to pack."

Kasit smiled. He had plenty of money on his chit, and the bet allowed him to buy his friend dinner without it looking like charity. "I need to be countin' better."

"Worry that Vos be looking for Kas?" Wagg asked.

"Been sleepin' in Morel Forest, not been goin' to hovel unless Zenith home. Nobody be messin' wit Zenith unless lookin' for troubles. She not be needin' Jeshifa troubles, though."

"Nobody needin' that kind of trouble."

13

SLOVEN

"*Gravitational Pull,* come in," Kel called over comms.

"What's up, Kel?" Rix answered.

"I'm establishing a tight beam communication. Are your systems in good enough shape for that?"

"I guess we'll find out. Go ahead. I'll work on capturing," Rix said, switching the stick control to the communication dish. With a mounted camera at the center of the dish, it wasn't hard to see what he was aiming at, especially as close as *Calypso* was. "Can you hear me?" he asked.

"You sound like you're inside a metal drum," Kel said.

"That's about what I'm getting, too. Hold on, I'm a little out of alignment."

"Are you doing that by hand? You know they make systems to handle that, right?"

"Maybe you forgot that I'm the one who installed the system you're using right now? *Gravitational Pull* has about a hundred small issues that need attention. Tight beam communication didn't even make the list. We're lucky we even have this much." Rix shook his head to himself before switching gears. "What's going on? Why the tight beam?"

"We just received a communication from Garanod. Apparently, they know we're coming," she said.

"That's not that unexpected. We're only a day out. Don't most places have good enough long-range scanners to pick up a couple of ships?"

"Not always," Kel said. "And not places as small or without government as Garanod."

"Okay. What's going on?" Rix asked as Amari scooted in next to him, her interest piqued by the snippets she'd heard.

"Communications were anonymous. They said our transponders were a mistake and that we needed to do a jig-jag if we don't want to get intercepted by the Jeshifa or the Grays," she said.

"Is that normal spacer talk? Jig-jag?"

"No, but it is descriptive," Kel said. "I focused *Calypso* sensors directly in line with Garanod Enclave. We have two groups of vessels headed our way under heavy acceleration," Kel said. "That's both the good and bad news."

"What's the good part of that?"

"Sensor blindness."

"I imagine you've planned a jig-jag in that case?"

"I have. In thirty seconds, we'll head off at forty degrees to port and ten degrees inclination," she said. "We'll keep that heading for two hours and then adapt based on what we're able to pick up. Assuming the ships coming our way aren't tracking us, we'll make new course adjustments later."

"Copy that," Rix said.

"Owe Greevo big if pirates take cargo. In contract," Greevo said.

"Not the time, Greevo," Rix cautioned.

"If they get too close, you can jettison the cargo pods," Amari said. "This old girl gets a whole lot faster and more maneuverable without sixty tons holding her back."

"No dump cargo. Owe Greevo big."

"It's good to look at all of our options," Rix said. "Don't take it personally, Greevo."

"Cargo personal. Much money."

"I have people I care about on these ships. Those lives are worth a whole lot more to me than your cargo. You're going to need to keep that in mind, or perhaps it'd be easier for you to sit up in the bunkroom, so you're not distracting me while I try to keep us from getting blown up, or worse."

"What's worse than getting blown up?" Amari asked.

"Captured and tortured," Rix said.

"If it's any consolation, most pirates don't take a lot of joy in that. They mostly just want your stuff. That is, unless you're mouthing off," she said, shooting Greevo a pointed look.

"Greevo not get hurt or cost Rix Banner big money."

Rix shook his head at the absurdity of the conversation. "We have a couple of hours. Are you needing some coffee?" he asked.

"Yes. Coffee important. Greevo feel jumpy."

"You're doing a good job of not letting him bother you," Amari said, joining Rix in the galley as he mixed coffee with rum.

"He gets grumpy if he doesn't get his rum," Rix said. "That he's not cognizant enough to serve himself makes me wonder who does this for him every other day. I guarantee it's someone, though."

"If we get into trouble, we'll need to put you in *Calypso*. She'll need someone running that needler turret," Amari said.

"Let's cross that bridge when we come to it," Rix said, handing the coffee to Greevo.

"How much coffee did you put in that?" Amari said, sniffing the air.

"Day like today, just a dash."

Greevo coughed as he took his first drink of almost pure rum. "Ooh, good coffee today, Rix Banner. Not save you from pay out if lose cargo, though."

Rix plopped into the pilot's chair next to Greevo and picked up his own coffee, which had no rum in it. He held the cup to Greevo in a cheers type of salute. Greevo reciprocated and took a long drink of the rum, which once again caused him to cough.

"Much fire in this coffee. Greevo like. Rix Banner make like this more," Greevo said.

"I'm always happy to make more coffee," Rix said brightly. "Bottoms up."

"What are you doing, Rix?" Amari whispered, even though it was likely Greevo could hear her. "He's half your mass."

"Greevo plenty big."

"And thirsty," Rix ribbed, clinking glasses one more time.

With this, Greevo finished his cup and set it down with a satisfied belch.

"Are you doing what I think you're doing?" Amari asked.

"Making our guests comfortable?" Rix asked. "If that's not a motto of our company, it should be."

Amari laughed as Greevo looked around, his eyes starting to swim and a dumb look coming over his face.

"Boy, I didn't get a lot of sleep last night. I sure am tired," Rix said with an exaggerated yawn.

"Oh, did I keep you up? I slept like a baby. I'm so sorry," Amari said. "You kept me nice and warm."

"Greevo stay up all night and keep ship going. Greevo big sleepy."

"Well, how about I help you up to the bunks. You can catch a couple of hours of sleep. We'll be just that much closer to where we're going."

"Greevo not need sleep. Greevo have works to do. What if pirates come?"

"Don't worry about that. We have a plan. We're a full-service shipper. That's why we brought *Calypso.* She's got quite a nice needler on top. What say I help you up to bed?"

"Maybe sleep short time," Greevo said, allowing Rix to steady him as he rose from the pilot's chair.

Standing beneath the entry to the bunks, , Rix pushed on Greevo's hairy backside as the small green alien scaled the ladder. "Not exactly the best view, back here," Rix complained, following Greevo up the ladder until he was able to push the Grintok into the bunk area.

"I don't know if you're a hero or a bad guy. You got him drunk so he'd leave us alone, didn't you?"

"He was getting nervous and escalating," Rix said. "I figured I'd take the wind out of his sails. He's going to have quite a headache when he wakes up, though."

"It was either him or us," Amari said. "I'm glad you chose the way you did. Also, you're wily when you want to be. I find that surprising."

"I like to keep things fresh."

The pair settled into a rhythm of cleaning *Gravitational Pull's* main cabin. With repeated scrubbing, decades of grime were finally fading, although they made no comment about the frequency of finding small pockets of debris both new from Greevo and old from prior occupants. At the appointed time, they returned to the cockpit, which newly smelled of citrus, and waited for Kel's contact as Rix focused the tight beam dish on *Calypso's* sending unit.

"I see you adjusting your dish," Kel's voice said over comms.

"What else are you seeing?" Rix asked, knowing that *Gravitational Pull's* limited sensor package wouldn't pick up anything smaller than a moon outside of a few kilometers.

"The two groups have split into three. One of them might have us. I'm not quite sure. We're going to make another turn," Kel said, attaching navigation instructions to her message.

"How soon before we cross paths, if that's going to happen?" Rix asked.

"Four hours," Kel said. "Do you want to raft up a minute and transfer over here? We could wait a couple of hours if you prefer."

"The closer they get, the more stress we're going to feel," Rix said. "Let's take care of the transfer now. Are you sending Philo over to *Gravitational Pull?* Greevo is kind of driving us nuts. I don't think he'll survive if he's left alone with Amari." Amari punched Rix in the shoulder. "Ow! What was that for?"

"I can handle one grumpy old Grintok," Amari said.

"For change of scenery, a couple crew would love to come over and ride along. Thranga has expressed interest. She misses Greevo." Rix couldn't help but wonder if Greevo missed his partner, too. He didn't dare to think that her transfer over to *Gravitational Pull* would brighten the alien's mood, though. "Also, Philo and Greevo get along well. Let's exchange the two of them for you," Kel finished.

"Amari, are you okay with that?" Rix asked.

"I'll hunker down in the pilot's seat," Amari said. "We're not that far from Garanod. I'll be fine."

"Cut your engines, Rix," Kel said. "I'll set down on the cargo pods and hold with magnetic clamps. Will you run an EVA safety line?"

"Can do," Rix said, killing *Gravitational Pull's* engines.

With practiced ease, Kel zeroed out the differences in acceleration between the vessels before using thrusters to nudge *Calypso* into place. Rix pushed himself out of his cockpit chair and started for the hatch that led to the basement. Amari joined him and for a moment an awkward silence passed between them.

"I'll see you soon," Rix finally filled in, wrapping his arms around Amari, who melted into him.

"Be careful, Rix. I'm starting to think I don't want to do this without you," Amari whispered.

After a short time, Rix pulled back and kissed her on the cheek. "I'm not going anywhere, Amari," he said as he started to climb down into the sealable lower deck. Amari grinned. "Ironic statement from a man leaving the ship."

"What can I say? I like a dramatic exit."

Amari's smile only widened as she threw a cleaning rag that was sitting in the galley. Rix dodged, dropping to the deck. As Amari closed the hatch, he waved, keeping eye contact the entire time.

Once in the basement, Rix grabbed a safety line and hooked it to a large interior ring before he donned his helmet and pressurized his vac suit. He opened the door, clipping the line to his suit, and pushed off, targeting *Calypso's* portside hatch. Having spent plenty of time in zero-g, Rix's aim was good, and he braked the spooling safety line to slow his speed. He grabbed a handhold on *Calypso* with an outstretched arm, untethered himself, clipped the end of the safety line in place and opened the already evacuated airlock.

"Welcome aboard, Rix," Kel said, greeting him. Behind Kel stood Philo and a Grintok, both patiently waiting.

"Rixy! Missin' my sticks and stones with you," Philo said.

"I've been playing with Greevo every day," Rix said. "He's yet to lose, so be careful."

"Greevo make good money at sticks and stones." Philo nodded with all too much familiarity. "Philo leave credits with Kels."

"That's a good plan," Rix said. "Thranga, if you make coffee for Greevo, there are two bottles of rum beneath the sink in the galley prep area. They have labels that say they're soap. They're not. I imagine you know what to do."

Thranga was an older, taller Grintok, much nicer looking than Rix thought a man like Greevo deserved. "Rum is good choice," Thranga said, tipping a mesh bag to Rix so that he caught sight of two more bottles. "Manage Greevo grumpies."

Rix clipped a strap to Thranga and then to the EVA line, which had been trapped by the closed exterior hatch. He repeated the same for Philo, even though he knew Philo could easily transit the line on his own. Stepping out of the way, he allowed the pair to enter the airlock and process through.

"What's that smell?" Rix asked as he removed his helmet. *Calypso* smelled of onion, garlic and spices he was unfamiliar with. While individually not particularly overwhelming, the combination was difficult.

"Can't say I'll miss Thranga's cooking," Kel said. "Everything is on the highest heat. We'll need new cabin air filters when we get home, and the bulkheads are going to need a solid scrubbing."

"I guess we knew what we were getting into," Rix said.

"Doesn't make it better. Come on up. I've been closing off the cockpit. It's not as bad."

Rix followed Kel forward, but his eyes wandered to the condition of *Calypso's* crew area. Dirty dishes lay haphazardly on just about every surface. Open food containers filled in every area, including the deck. Three Grintok barely acknowledged their presence as Kel and Rix passed, as they were engaged in their own game of sticks and stones.

"How are you faring with all this?" Rix asked.

"At first, I tried cleaning up after them," Kel said. "They just made more mess as I did. I gave up. I spend all my time in my bunk or in the cockpit. I'm not sure I'll agree to transport Grintok ever again, no matter how good the money is!"

"I'll back that," Rix said. "This is worse than anything I thought possible."

"How is living with Greevo?"

"Well, we outnumber him, and both Amari and I like to keep things tidy. It's a lot of work to clean up after him alone. I can't imagine four. I was hoping Greevo was just exceptionally bad. That doesn't seem to be the case."

"Amari's going to have words for you when you get back. Thranga is the worst offender."

"But she only has half a day or so to make a mess," Rix pointed out with half-hearted hope.

Kel closed the bridge door behind Rix, scoffing as she pulled out a bottle, which Rix discovered contained air freshener. "Yeah, we'll see how that works out."

"Are we still being followed?" Rix asked.

"Two ships gave up already and turned back. That leaves three still out here, and only one of those seems to have an idea of our course changes."

"How are you keeping track of them?"

"Once you get a read on a ship, they have to do something spectacular to get out of *Calypso's* sight picture. I was worried all our pursuers had the same tech. There's no good reason for them to split apart like they have, though. I'm guessing they are from competing gangs or whatever they call themselves."

"What kind of trouble are we in?"

"That depends on them," Kel said. "Mass appears to be about twice that of *Calypso*, but she's running heavy at her midline. Not exactly a warbird."

"Neither is *Calypso*."

"Right, but twice the mass means they better be ready to fight nimble," Kel said. "We give up a lot of cargo space for the ability to get out of sticky situations. With *Gravitational Pull* we can't rabbit, but with you running the needler and me dancing between the raindrops, I like our chances. Besides, intimidation is generally the goal. There's no value taking out a cargo vessel like *Gravitational Pull*. That's the prize. They'll look to talk a good game, then when that fails, they'll look to take out *Calypso*. We'll put *Gravitational Pull* fifty kilometers to aft so we can engage first."

"You've thought this out."

"How do you think I've stayed alive this long? It's not just because of my good looks."

"Not only," Rix chuckled.

"Good to have you back aboard," Kel said. "It's been a quiet trip. Although, I've seen more of Philo than usual."

"Grintok keeping him up?" Rix asked.

"They knock on his bunk to get him to play sticks and stones with them," she said. "He'll do it for a while, but it's not his favorite. He comes and hangs out with me just for some quiet."

"You love this, don't you?" Rix said, gesturing out into their view of the massive nebula.

"This view is unusual," she said. "I've never been inside a nebula before. If you pay attention, you can just start to see where Garanod Enclave is. I can't figure out if the settlers were crazy or genius. The atmosphere is generally safe, and it's a good temperature, but I don't think they can grow too much. Without massive imports, I can't figure how they survive."

"There has to be a food source," Rix said.

"It's warm, but not that warm," Kel said. "No plant life I'm familiar with would grow there."

"Fun to imagine what makes that all work, don't you think?"

"Now you're getting the allure of space travel. There's always a new mystery to be explored," she said. "And this ... this is huge. I've heard rumors of this place before, but I never thought I'd be sailing a ship here. I was half-convinced we'd be turning tail once we figured out the size of their welcoming committee."

"Four ships are plenty," Rix said. "Besides, I figure they can just wait for us to arrive."

"Or maybe they realize that if they attack everything that comes their way, they'll never get any decent imports," Kel said.

"I'm not sure the average pirate thinks that far ahead."

"Truth."

Time both sped by and crawled as they focused on the approaching point in space, where conflict as old as knights tilting down the line was destined.

"It's time," Kel finally said, breaking the spell the pair had found themselves silenced by.

"Give 'em hell, Kel Warp," Rix said earnestly.

"Make 'em bleed, Rix Banner."

"Don't wreck our ship. I'd love to have a new project for once."

Kel smiled. "No promises."

Rix exited the bridge, all thoughts of smelly galleys and unruly passengers dismissed. Opening the thin hatch that gave access to the needler turret, he grimaced as he discovered refuse strewn across the narrow ladder that led to chair above. Wiping with his hand, he cleared each rung as he climbed. Rix froze in stunned silence when he reached the chair. It was as if a wild animal had been trapped within. He feared serious damage and in fact, it looked like someone had started disassembling the controls.

"Kel, how much time?" Rix called, lifting a critical component that dangled, disconnected.

"Twelve minutes, get plugged in. There's no time to fool around."

"Our visitors were scrounging. I need twenty minutes."

"You don't have it," she said. "I can buy you an extra minute, maybe two."

"Do your best," he shouted, sweeping the mess from his seat as he searched for connectors that had been tossed aside. Fortunately, Rix had taken to carrying a small set of tools everywhere, enabling him to work quickly, after making a place where he could sit in and amongst the mess.

"Beverly, please give me the most efficient steps to get this restored," Rix said.

"On your HUD," Beverly answered, highlighting the location of several important connectors that were hidden in the dim lighting.

With fingers trained daily to grasp, twist, prod and poke, Rix started what at first looked and felt like an impossible task.

"*Galactic Empire-registered Vessel.* You will heave to. Clan Gray has laid claim to your cargos. Resist not," disembodied voice sounded over comms.

Rix wanted to respond but knew he needed to trust Kel as he fixed the problems step by step. "Beverly, put a first contact timer next to the repairs," Rix said.

"It'll be too distracting."

"It's all I can think about anyway," Rix said. "Do it."

"*Clan Gray Vessel,*" Kel answered. "We are a peaceful trading vessel, but do not be confused. If you continue your approach, we will engage. There will be no further warning. Disengage or discover why we fear not. Even now, our gunners are locking targets."

"You bluff," came the quick answer.

"Let's find out," Kel said, cutting comms. "Rix, you have forty seconds!"

Just then, a coupling slipped from Rix's fingers. It bounced off a rounded corner within the machinery and wiring and onto his leg before rolling off and disappearing into the seat's webbing. Seconds later, metal clanged as the coupling ricocheted off ladder rungs in its freefall to the deck.

"Crap, crap, shit," Rix muttered, thrusting his tools and the remaining parts onto a precariously positioned ledge.

"Rix? Those are not the words I need to be hearing from you," Kel called, tension thick in her voice.

Dropping his legs over, he slid down the ladder and to the deck. "Damn Grintok!" he cried out as his fingers sifted through the litter. "We're going to die to slobs!"

"This does not sound good. We need that turret, Rix. Talk to me!"

14

ATTRACTING ATTENTION

"HOLD STILL, RIX," Beverly said, hanging from a lower rung of the ladder, wearing an identical jumpsuit to what Rix wore. "Let me process."

It took everything Rix had to stop sifting through the layers of debris. "They're like rats," Rix complained as a strobe flashed, lighting small pieces of trash in a rapid search pattern.

"There!" Beverly said, highlighting the fallen piece. Just then, Rix was thrown into the portside bulkhead as *Calypso* tilted roughly.

"What was that!?" Rix asked, sensing the difference between a rapid directional change and an explosion. They'd been hit.

"Luckiest asshat ever!" Kel griped. "Is there any chance we're going to have an operational turret? I can't do this all by myself!"

"Did we lose it?" Rix asked, sighing a breath of relief as Beverly's strobe started flashing again.

"There, get it quickly before we get hit again," Beverly urged.

Rix closed his fingers around the part, along with a handful of cast-off wrappings. The stickiness on his fingers was an ancillary thought, although he worried that goo could impede the repair.

"Got it!" Rix said. "Hang on, Kel! Give me another minute."

"A minute? Are you kidding me? I have barely any cover out here and we've got a belly full of cargo. I'm like a pregnant quadle trying to outrun a jagger!"

Rix had to smile as he climbed the ladder. "You do know that I don't know quadles from jaggers, right?"

"Trust me. It's. Not. Good!" Kel emphasized each word with an abrupt change in heading. But, having been burned once, Rix knew better than to risk losing his coupling again. He latched an arm around the ladder as he gently opened his hand and retrieved the part from the small pile of garbage he still held.

"Keep it slow," Beverly encouraged in his ear. "I've patched into Kel's tactical display and am running a predictive routine to anticipate …" She was interrupted as Rix was tossed into the starboard side by an explosion against the portside hull. The familiar popping of his ears warned of atmospheric pressure loss.

Instead of dropping his coupling, though, Rix had clenched his fist, reopening it a moment later. "You were saying?" he asked.

"Why are you smiling?"

"You're trying to predict Kel and an attacking warship. It's an impossible task," Rix said, smirking.

"Not entirely," Beverly argued. "I should have tracked that turret. She turned right into the blast, though."

Focusing, Rix exhaled and deliberately pushed the little metal part into place. Careful not to cross-thread, he twisted it home. When the next course adjustment again sent him careening to the side, he fought to maintain downward pressure on the part. Thankfully, he recovered and released the magnetic handle of the wrench required to complete the job without losing his grip on coupling.

"Almost there, Kel," he said, sweeping his hand across the needler turret chair, driving more detritus into the ladder tube. Pulling the safety strap, Rix smiled with little humor at the propensity for straps to tangle in heated moments. Once again, he slowed his movements, methodically untwisting the harness to avert a tangle. Clicking the buckle together, he powered the unit and smiled with relief as indicator lights blinked across the console.

"I'm gonna need something, Rix!" Kel said.

"Turn into that ship!" Rix demanded as his own tactical display tracked the chasing vessel. The maneuver would give them only a moment of surprise, but it would also line up the needler turret.

"Ooh, that's gonna be dicey!" Kel laughed, finding it hard to suppress her emotions toward the reckless move.

As the predictive line of needler ammo stitched a yellow line, indicating the payload would miss, Rix adjusted and pulled on both triggers. The fastest stream of ammo was released at the highest velocity. The line turned from bright yellow to deep green as sparks erupted along the trail of deadly hole-punching ammo that likely pierced entirely through the enemy ship.

"Oh, good show!" Kel whooped with a throaty cackle. "Those first two shots had to be right in line with their cockpit."

"Maybe," Rix said, trying to adjust the turret's aim enough to reacquire his target.

"*Galactic Empire Vessel,* this is *Quibbler 12A,* we are requesting cessation of hostilities. We surrender!"

"*Quibbler 12A,* Power down that turret and adjust course on the attached heading," Kel said. "Failure of full compliance will be met with all possible violence."

Rix muted the comms. "All possible violence? Laying it on a bit thick, don't you think?"

"Are you kidding me? They were shooting at us with particle blasters. We got hulled," she said, fuming. "I'm ready to smoke the whole lot of 'em."

Quibbler 12A adjusted course so it pointed directly at Garanod Enclave, and its blaster turret settled into its cradle, powering down.

"We're new here," Rix said. "If we can avoid killing people, it's worthwhile."

"What in the hell happened back there?" Kel asked. "What was all the talk of rat nests and trash?"

"Someone got into the turret room."

"I hate passengers. I hate them with a passion. Tell me they got spaced," Kel said. "I might be willing to let bygones be bygones with *Quibbler*."

"You don't mean that," Rix laughed, unstrapping from the gunner's chair and gathering his tools.

"I might."

"You might," Rix agreed, descending the ladder. He tested the door leading into the main passenger compartment. While he was still in a pressurized space, it was possible he'd have to vent his atmo to move within the ship. "Feels like there's pressure in the main cabin. I feel like we lost atmo, though."

"Kitka apparently is skilled with hull foam," Kel said. "She's been giving me updates."

"Okay," Rix said, swinging the door open. "Are you tracking those other bogies?"

"Yes and no," Kel said. "They were too far out for us to need to worry about them outrunning us to Garanod."

"What guarantee do we have they won't fire on us there?" Rix asked.

"I guess I assume Greevo has a place for us to land. This is his show, after all."

"Okay," Rix said, uncertainty in his voice. "*Quibbler 12A*, you will heave to and prepare for boarding. Will you comply?"

"Do we have a choice?" returned a sulky voice.

"Have you started repairs? We're showing you're still venting atmo in twenty-four breaches."

"We don't have anything that will stop those leaks."

"Good copy. Comply with orders."

"What are you doing, Rix?" Kel asked over private comms.

"We're going to board," Rix said. "I want to disable that turret. Once I do, we can send them packing."

"Are you sure that's the good play, here?" Kel asked. "Maybe you should do something to their engines. Make them a little slower, or something."

"We'll look, okay?" Rix asked.

"Let's get Philo back aboard. We need someone at the helm on *Calypso*, and I'm not good with any of those Grintok being on my bridge."

"You're boarding with me?" Rix asked.

"Don't be dumb," Kel said. "I'll have *Gravitational Pull* raft up with us in ten minutes."

Rix nodded, even though Kel couldn't see him. "What kind of arms do you have aboard?"

"Come to the bridge," Kel said. "We'll look in the armory."

"On my way." Rix turned forward, kicking trash from his path as he did, which made him wince. Remembering their prior mistake, he turned back and locked the needler access hatch.

"Is it over?" Kitka asked, her scratchy voice taking Rix by surprise.

"I think so," he said. "We've disabled the ship that was attacking us."

"We need knowing when attacks," Kitka said, pointing up at Rix in earnest.

As irritated as he was with the prevalent trash, Rix understood her concern. "You're right. It happened fast, but you deserve better information," he said, which seemed to mollify the small green alien.

"I have this scatter gun that I keep around for just this sort of thing, Kel said as soon as Rix entered the bridge. "I'll use this." She turned to face him, swinging around with her what, at least to Rix, was clearly an old sawed-off shotgun. "It only has four loads," she said. "Makes one heck of a mess, but most of the time the pellets don't penetrate hull plating."

"I left my weapons back on *Gravitational Pull*," Rix said, glancing into the armory, which was just a locked cabinet inset into the bridge's aft bulkhead. "What in the heck is that?" His eyes were drawn to an aged pewter and woodgrain pistol with a copper trigger guard. The weapon looked like it was straight out of one of his science fiction magazines.

"The Starflare Ray?" Kel asked. "Might need to dial that one down a bit. It can be a little slow on its biggest charge, but put it at twenty percent, it's nimble enough. Strictly speaking, Starflares aren't legal in Galactic Empire, other than for show. You can't carry them."

"Doesn't sound like that'd be a problem on Garanod," Rix said, a big smile creasing his face.

"Why are you looking at me like that?" Kel asked.

"It's a ray gun, Kel," Rix said. "You have an honest-to-god ray gun."

Kel nodded patiently. "Well ... sure. I do. And?"

"I've always wanted a ray gun, ever since I was a kid."

Kel laughed. "Sure. Take it. Remember, though, anything over sixty percent power and you'll have a short lag before you fire. It also kind of makes a humming noise when it's charging for the bigger loads. There's an argument on if that's a good or bad thing."

"I suppose it depends on if you're looking to make a statement or a hole," Rix said.

Kel wrinkled her nose as she considered Rix's statement. "That's right. You have yourself a ray gun, mister Earth mans."

Rix couldn't help but grin like a kid who'd just discovered lost candy between the seat cushions of the couch. "We need to consider investing in body armor," Rix said.

"I thought we were going to get some for this trip."

"We spent too much money in repairs for *Calypso* and *Gravitational Pull*," Rix said. "And now I'm just hoping *Quibbler 12A* didn't damage anything important."

"This whole idea that there's not a government we can turn pirates over to is kind of messing with me. It's like it's our job to take *Quibbler*. Are you sure you want to let them go?"

"Have you looked at the ship?"

"Not in detail," Kel said. "Why?"

"That red color isn't paint, it's oxidation," Rix said. "Something in the atmosphere is eating the hull of that ship. My needles punched through way harder than they should have. I'm guessing that ship is a floating platform for that gun turret. If I'm wrong, we can make other decisions. I just don't need another crappy ship project."

"And you don't think we could sell it."

"I don't know," Rix said. "But if the inside is as bad as the out, it has almost no value."

"Except for the turret."

"Right. And I'm going to take something so important to that turret that it can't possibly operate without a replacement. I bet getting replacement parts out here isn't a whole lot of fun, either."

"Whoever owns that ship is going to want that part back."

"I imagine you're right," Rix said. "*Gravitational Pull* is here. Let's get going."

"Philo, you need to pull us right up next to *Quibbler 12A*," Kel said, meeting the little alien just outside the airlock. "Do you understand?"

"Kel and Rix boom boom the bad mans in ugly spaceship?" Philo asked.

"Something like that," Rix said, tapping the ray gun on his chest.

"Rixy be carefuls. Ray gun boom bigs." Rix held the Starflare out so Philo could see the setting on fifty percent power. Philo gave him a thumbs up. "Good Rixy."

With retractable lines attached to their belts, Rix and Kel pushed off, landing on *Quibbler 12A*. "Knock knock," Kel called, banging on the outer hatch with a small hammer.

"I don't think they can hear us," Rix said. Of course, it was at that moment that the hatch opened with a small puff of atmosphere escaping. "And they don't have an airlock."

"Small ship, maybe forty tons," Kel said. "No way they can afford the deck space for an airlock. Also, the pressure in this nebula is just about breathable, even out here."

Rix swung into view of the hatch with his ray gun pointed through the door. Two humanoid figures stood anxiously inside. Neither were wearing spacesuits, but both instead had small devices sticking into their noses. Seeing the weapons trained on them, the *Quibbler 12A* pair lifted their hands and stepped back. First through the door, Rix kept his ray gun trained on one or the other.

"Do you have this, Kel?" Rix asked.

"Let me clear the deck first," Kel said, pushing her shotgun barrel into the closest alien. "Back off, chubby."

The alien complied as Rix gestured with his ray gun where he wanted the pair to stand. They didn't so much as clear their throats as Kel continued her search. It wasn't a huge vessel, so minutes later, she returned.

"It's a mess, but they're by themselves. I didn't see vac suits. Apparently, these guys don't need 'em."

"Okay, hold down the fort," Rix said, slapping his ray gun onto the front of his vac suit, where it held tight. Instead of traversing within the ship, Rix instead climbed outside and up the heavily rusted port side. Once on top, he crawled over to the turret. Pulling a multitool from where he'd affixed it to his calf, he removed pins and nuts, at one point finding that he needed to use the small boltgun he'd brought along.

"Are you getting close, Rix?" Kel called.

"Just a couple more minutes," he answered, finally freeing the first of two three-meter-long barrels containing the concentrator electronics that formed the energized particles necessary to utilize the weapon. Moving to the second barrel, he repeated the process, only this time faster, as he was familiar with the process.

Rix wrapped the end of his safety cable around the pair of barrels after layering each of them with duct tape on both ends. Hand over hand, he started pulling himself back to *Calypso*. Once he was free, he used a remote trigger to cause the retractable cable to start reeling him in along with the gun barrels.

"Do you have a good exit, Kel?" Rix asked. "I'm done and have what I needed."

"That's the joy of these cables," Kel said. "If I connect to the back of my belt, I can just drift back and keep my sight picture."

"Beverly, can we dump the atmosphere in the hold? I'm hoping we have enough room for these barrels."

"I've instructed the atmospheric subsystem to recapture fifty percent of the pressurized gasses from the hold and bring artificial gravity to zero. Push the barrels into the ship at the top of the starboard side. You'll need to strap them to the starboard bulkhead, or you'll crush the crates below when gravity returns."

Rix decided that sliding the barrels in was best done by positioning himself in front of them. Movement of the payload could only be described as unwieldy and awkward, and had it not been for Kel showing up a few moments later, Rix might have been there all day.

"You took their barrels," Kel said, shaking her head and chuckling. "I was thinking you'd take their control sticks, or maybe a special circuit."

"I like to think of myself as an overachiever. I was looking at the price of the components of a particle blaster. Between the barrels and the energy particle formation chamber, we fully neutered *Quibbler.*"

"I wonder if there's a market for used particle blaster barrels," Kel said.

"Depends on the ownership chain for *Quibbler*."

"Would you sell it back to them?"

Rix shrugged. "Maybe. Depends on the price, I imagine."

"You're worse than I am," Kel ribbed.

"I doubt that."

The pair worked their way back out of the hold, then split up. Rix returned to *Gravitational Pull,* while Kel stayed on *Calypso*, greeting Philo as he returned aboard.

"Welcome back," Amari said, embracing Rix.

"Things okay here?" he asked, his hands lingering on hers as they pulled away.

"Greevo has slept off his rum and wants to talk," she said, shooting him a look that said *good luck*.

"I imagine he does. We'll follow *Calypso* back into Garanod ..." Rix noticed that Greevo was climbing down from the bunk room. "What's up, Greevo?"

"If any my cargo damaged, Rix Banner pay big," Greevo said.

"I'm done with that conversation," Rix said. "Do you have a contact on Garanod who can set us up with a secured dock?"

"No need secured dock. Garanod safe."

"That's not an answer," Rix said. "Beverly, see if you can find any sort of public station services."

"No good," Greevo grumbled.

"Do you have a different choice, Greevo?" Rix persisted.

"Yes. I contact. Make communications open," Greevo said.

This was the moment Rix had been dreading. Greevo was financially invested in moving his goods, but Rix didn't think for a moment that the Grintok was half as interested in the security of his and Kel's vessels.

"You have access to comms," Rix said. "Don't make promises about when we're arriving. You'll need to include me in that conversation."

"Bah," Greevo said, waving Rix off with a dismissive oversized hand.

"Rix, there is a public docking facility on the large planetoid mass called Driftmarket," Beverly said. "It will accept Galactic Credit chits or precious metals. The exchange for Galactic Empire chits is poor. There is a one hundred fifty-percent transaction fee that is added onto highly priced mooring services. There is, however, a promise of security."

"Give that to me in credits per day, would you?"

"Six hundred fifty credits each day for *Calypso,* twice that for *Gravitational Pull*, for as long as the storage containers are attached."

"Two thousand a day," Rix said. "Ugh. That's going to eat into our profits. We're contracted for five days in port."

"There might be other options," Beverly said.

"Book it for one day. We'll see if there's a better option once we arrive," Rix said. "We need somewhere to tie up."

"Greevo want go Chainreach," Greevo said. "Special hidey place."

"I'm done with secrets and hidey places," Rix said. "We can deliver your cargo wherever you want, but we're not docking anywhere I don't feel comfortable. Do you understand?"

"Rix Banner not good business," Greevo said. "Greevo make deal from Driftmarket. No happy."

"We're getting some attention, Rix," Kel called over comms. Looking at the linked sensor data, Rix saw that a fleet of smaller vessels was inbound. Unlike *Quibbler 12A* and the other larger ships, these were clearly made for short trips only.

"Beverly, what do they want?"

"I'm analyzing their communications," Beverly said. "It appears they're merchants, trying to sell us things like water, food, oxygen, even septic cleanout services."

"Secure our space at Driftmarket," Rix said. "Once we have a space, you can tell them we'll be discussing trades after we're settled in."

"Hold on there, Rix," Kel said. "I'm getting a comm from the same contact who gave us the jig-jag warning."

"Oh?"

"They're suggesting we reach out to Kha'rem," Kel said.

"Do we know anything about Kha'rem?"

"Local trader on Driftmarket," Beverly said. "I have a frequency for him."

"That sounds promising," Rix said. "See if you can reach him."

It took several minutes, but finally, a sonorous, low tenor voice answered Beverly's call. "To whom am I speaking? You have reached Kha'rem, trader of Driftmarket."

"Greetings Kha'rem," Rix said. "This is Rix Banner, and I have two vessels on approach to Garanod Enclave. We have trade goods aboard and are looking for a safe harbor in which to dock to make contact with trading partners."

"And how is it you have come by my frequency?"

"Maybe not the best conversation on an open frequency," Rix said. "I assure you that we are peaceful traders."

"The appearance of Galactic Empire vessels in our system is well discussed this day. Do you have a means of payment?"

"Full holds and a desire to establish trading partners," Rix said. "I'm sure we can come up with something. If you have dock space, your risk is significantly lower than your potential upside."

"Spoken like a true trader. Bring your vessels to my shores. You are welcomed for this day's passing."

"We will see you shortly," Rix said.

15

FLOTILLA

"KEL, can you get those ships off my starboard?" Amari called over comms.

As they'd closed distance with Garanod Enclave, the armada of small vessels swarming out from the pieces of the broken planetoid had grown. With atmospheric pressure at seventy percent, the vessels required no internal pressurization, and indeed many of them were open air skiffs that appeared to be little more than a large grav pallet and a couple of hot thrusters.

The mob of vessels, competing for attention, barraged *Gravitational Pull* and *Calypso* with communication requests. When those requests went unanswered, the boldest of them set themselves on collision courses, hoping to force a full stop of the pair of ship's approach.

"I have this," Kel said, arcing *Calypso* closely around *Gravitational Pull's* cargo pods. By adding a slow roll to *Calypso's* arc, the ship's stubby atmospheric wings became paddles that would flick away any craft caught between the two ships. "Do not change your pace. I'm transmitting our course on several frequencies. If they get in the way, they're making a choice."

"It won't look great if we go smashing up their citizens," Amari answered. "But I understand."

"Well, that was unexpected," Kel said before warning, "Rix, you have a border that just coupled to the front of the second pod. They're going to try to open her up.

"Good copy," Rix said, jumping to his feet and grabbing his new favorite weapon. He slid down the ladder rails into the basement and punched in an adjustment to equalize pressure with the nebula's gases. "If you'd told me a year ago that my job was repelling borders, in outer space, in the middle of a nebula, I'd have had you committed," he muttered under his breath. Clipping his safety line in place, Rix bounded out from the cab of *Gravitational Pull.*

"One rotation to starboard," Kel instructed. "If you can't get them, I can get a bead on their skiff with the turret. It's not like they're moving."

Rix clambered forward, keeping the corner of the cargo pod between him and the skiff. As he moved, Beverly projected a three-dimensional scene, combining *Calypso's* view with her knowledge of Rix's position. Projected onto the cargo pod ahead of him, outlined figures still hidden from direct view were carrying long-handled equipment from their skiff.

"Freeze!" Rix called, leaning over the edge of the pod.

Ordinarily, sound would not travel in outer space, but with the nebula's atmosphere, his amplified voice carried quite well. The figures evidently heard him, as one of the two swiveled and fired. Rix anticipated the shot, and with Beverly showing a predictive path of any oncoming projectiles, he was in no danger. Taking aim, he sent a crackling ray of energy with a *buzzap*. It was a close miss, which sent a clear message.

"Get off my ship or the next one will do the job," Rix reiterated through his vac suit's amplified external speakers.

"Eat dirt, Galactic scum," came the answer, along with a barrage of shots that exposed that the shooter wasn't exactly sure where Rix had gone as he'd ducked back around.

With wireframe outlines of the pair of thieves, Rix was able to line up his shot before exposing himself. When he popped up, he acquired a sight picture and held the trigger just a bit longer, the ray gun's capacitor humming as it charged. *BUZZAP!* The sizzling ray of photonic energy struck the aggressive thief and sent him reeling off into space.

"Drop the tools and get off!" Rix demanded, swiveling toward the second thief, who'd started hammering inelegantly at the locks on the cargo pad.

"Don't shoot! I'm going!" The second thief said with more irritation than fear.

Rix dialed down the weapon's energy, but the second thief was slow to get moving. *Buzzap*, the third shot rang out, lighting the air behind the recalcitrant border. The shot delivered Rix's message better than any words could have and set the thief sprawling before he sprang back onto his feet and raced for the parked skiff.

"Kel, I need cover. I'm going to see how much damage they did," Rix called, crawling over the corner of the cargo pod and tromping over to the locks.

"I'm right above you, but you sent a good message. The armada is backing off," Kel said just as Rix arrived at the cargo pod's manual door locks. "What's the damage?"

"We got here soon enough. There's light damage. It looks cosmetic to me," Rix said. "We can look at it closer after we land."

"Rix, get down!" Beverly demanded as he was walking back to the cab. Knowing better than to argue, Rix dropped and flattened out on the cargo pod just as a skiff whizzed over the top of him at three meters, which wasn't enough to do more than frighten him.

"That was close, Rix," Kel called. "I couldn't get him cut off. Do you want me to chase him down?"

"Negative," Rix said. "Matter of fact, I'm coming back aboard. I'll man the needler as we approach. Did we track that guy I hit?"

"His buddy picked him up," Kel said. "Come on aboard. I'll wait."

As Kel brought *Calypso* closer, Rix transferred to *the ship*. Once inside, he unlocked and climbed straight into the needler turret. With the short barrels of the needler lifting from their brackets, Rix spun around, targeting the closest ships harassing *Gravitational Pull*. Some of the mob tossed angry words at *Calypso*, but the message sent by the active needler turret was sufficient to turn them back home.

"Talk about chaos," Amari said after a time. "Also, Greevo wanted me to pass along his approval of you defending his wares. He also thinks you should have shot the second thief."

"When he's sailing his own ship, he gets to decide how aggressively to defend it," Rix said.

"Okay, kids, we're ten minutes out," Kel interrupted. "Amari, I'm going to have you get settled in the mooring before we commit. I want to keep our needler in play until the last moments."

"Good copy, Kel," Amari answered.

"My gosh, Driftmarket is huge. There are tents upon tents upon tents," Rix observed over comms.

"According to sources I've compiled," Beverly said, "While the predominant activity of Driftmarket is trade, there are also residences, gaming parlors, restaurants and outdoor living venues."

"What's the last?" Rix asked.

"Sports, gaming and general fitness," Beverly said. "The colorful canvas roofing comes from an early tradition created by a large freighter hauling textiles that was abandoned due to insurmountable mechanical issues. The material was sold to residents as a building material, and soon Drift Market was literally covered by it."

"What are all those blue lines between the planetoids?"

"Fluxspan rails. We'll need to avoid them," Beverly said. "They're alloy cables charged with energy so that private cars and larger public ferries can move between the planetoids. It's quite dangerous, although cost effective. I recommend avoiding anything associated with a fluxspan rail, including public ferries, which have an annual rate of collision or other injurious failure exceeding every documented safety standard within the entire Galactic Empire."

"So, you're not a fan," Rix said.

"I am not."

16

ANTICIPATION

"Did you see that!?" Kasit asked, aiming a long-range optical sensor at the approaching Galactic vessels. Mounted to a tripod and gyro stabilizers, he'd set the tracking to lock onto a cargo ship carrying two cargo pods accompanied by a small freighter with a mounted turret.

"No! I'm trying to get my HUD to link with Kha'rem's stupid scope. What did I miss?" Wagg cried.

"Nokel from the Grays just got taken out. Do you know who that is?"

"They killed a Gray?" Wagg asked. "And I've knowins Nokel. A jerk, that one is."

"Certain it was Nokel. Has that red blaze on his jacket," Kasit said. "And we be wonderin' why no Galactics come this far. We swarm them like mice to warm hovels."

"Oh, I got tele linked," Wagg said.

"What are you boys doing out here?" Kha'rem asked.

"Sorry, boss," Kasit said, straightening. "The Galactics, they got swarmed, but they defended. It's a shame. We make it hard. People not want trade wit us."

"No slang, Kasit," Kha'rem corrected. "If a Galactic wants to come to Garanod, they need to be tough. That is the way it has always been."

"It'll be a good payday for someone if the Galactics don't land at the wrong dock, or get taken before they land," Wagg said. "It's not hard to see why everyone swarms new ships."

"I need the two of you to work late today. I've arranged with *Calypso* and *Gravitational Pull* to overnight on this very pier," Kha'rem said folding his arms over his chest proudly. "Don't think I didn't hear how you told them about the long-range pirates coming their way. Turning off their electronics and taking the long road was smart thinking. As was mentioning Kha'rem as an honorable trading partner."

"They mentioned that?" Kasit asked.

"Loyalty and honor are traits I value," Kha'rem said. "It will be ninety minutes before they arrive. I will pay you double for the day if you finish the last tanks of gillet and are cleaned before the Galactics arrive."

"Double!?" Wagg asked, exchanging an excited look with Kasit.

"Standing won't stack gillet," Kha'rem said, smiling with enjoyment at the youths' excitement. He'd barely finished his statement before the two ran back into the warehouse. Walking at a more dignified pace, Kha'rem turned his wrist up to access his communicator. He tapped a request and waited.

"Kha'rem, how is it I might be interesting to you this day?" an aquamarine hologram Vesh appeared floating in the air in front of him.

"Bleca, do you have two strong backs available for today and perhaps more?" he asked.

"Loading or security?"

"Security, need twenty-six hours of coverage at a minimum. There may be opportunity for loading bonus. I do not know. Standard rate if two."

"I'll bring Spetla. Did you get the Galactic contract, then?" Bleca asked.

"Not much happens on Driftmarket that all do not soon know," Kha'rem said.

"*Calypso* and *Gravitational Pull* are unknown vessels. This causes much interest. Of course there is much talk," Bleca said. "There is a rumor. *Quibbler* returned to port without barrels for their blaster turret. When asked, angry words were given. The Galactics did not kill the *Quibbler* crew but removed their teeth. What a curiosity."

"A curiosity," Kha'rem agreed.

"There is more."

"Oh?"

"It is said that *Quibbler* did much damage. That the freighter, *Gravitational Pull*, is damaged. Black smoke billows from its engines."

"And we wonder how information moves so quickly."

Bleca laughed. "I have heard back from Spetla," he said. "We will provide a security detail. How quickly do you need us to arrive?"

"Sixty minutes. I have my store workers who will accept the moorings and if necessary, help to set up the displays. It is a good time for fresh visits from Galactics. Garanod needs the infusion of ideas and goods."

"You are a dreamer, brother," Bleca said. "I love Garanod more when I see it through your eyes."

"Garanod is a jewel that has been kept in a deep crevasse," Kha'rem said. "I do not fault those who act as savages. It is the only thing they have known. With more trade, civilization will follow."

"Be careful what you wish for, brother," Bleca said. "With civilization comes rules and taxes."

"With wise men, we can find compromise. Did you know on Galactic worlds, there are men and women hired for the security of all? These people work not for a corporation, but instead for the benefit of freedom loving peoples, regardless of affiliation."

"So you've told the story," Bleca said. "I live for my people, the Vesh. Why would I need someone else to protect my brothers and sisters? We do this for each other."

"As do the Grays and Jeshifa."

"It is as it has always been. I see no fault in it."

"Do you wish that more vessels like *Calypso* and *Gravitational Pull* would risk venturing to our humble home?"

"Well, I suppose, perhaps. I do not rightly know what it is they carry."

"Do you seek to make a point for argument?"

"I do, perhaps," Bleca said. "I understand what you say. I do not wish Garanod to change. I just wish for an easier life."

"You cannot have one without the other, brother. Think on this as we both discover what the Galactics bring."

"Let us hope."

17

LINES SECURED

From his turret, Rix watched as Amari gracefully sidled *Gravitational Pull* up next to the long pier that jutted out from a vendor's wide storefront. At least, it was his assumption that each time the color of canvas over a particular building or table changed that it represented a different vendor.

Two younger men stood at the dock's edge, ready to receive mooring lines. If the pier had been equipped with Galactic Empire standard automated piers, it would have only required that Amari initiate the sequence. As it was, she had to fire long lines, which were caught and fastened in place.

"We're secure," Amari said.

Rix scanned outward from Driftmarket in anticipation of potential danger. Aside from the spiderwebs of fluxspan rails that made it difficult, if not dangerous, to approach, nothing obviously menaced either *Gravitational Pull* or *Calypso*. Scanning the dock, he found two more men of a species he didn't recognize. They both had completely hairless aquamarine skin and webs growing between their fingers.

"Those men look like they could be semiaquatic," Rix observed.

Beverly appeared in front of him, wearing a lab coat and holding a pointer stick, which she thwacked on the nearest surface. "Why is it you are surprised at variation of species? Those men are, in fact, Vesh, which is an amphibious species."

"Habitat?" Rix wondered. "I'm not seeing any bodies of water. Living on the side of a broken planet in the middle of a nebula doesn't feel like the most hospitable place for amphibious life."

"A mystery only solved by the curious."

Rix chuckled. "You give me a hard time for being curious and then tell me that I need to be more curious. Pick one."

Beverly smacked her pointer stick again and glared at him. "Don't you like the whole mistress teacher look I have going?"

"If I'm honest, it's a little confusing," Rix said.

"Are all humans so innocent?" Beverly asked. "Also, I believe those men are the security your contact, Kha'rem, hired."

"I was hoping it wasn't the young men," Rix said. Beverly lifted the stick, but Rix cut her off. "Not that they couldn't be good at it. They just seem young to have a lot of security experience."

"Are we clear, Rix?" Kel asked.

"We're clear," Rix answered, instructing the turret to stow the needler barrels and pull the protective cowl over the gunner's nest. Free from responsibilities of the needler, Rix extracted himself and met an enthusiastic Kel in the hallway.

"This is so exciting," Kel said. "I wish we'd brought more to trade. I have no idea if your crates of old parts are going to be worth anything here. Did you at least bring some rum along?"

Rix smiled. "How about we go introduce ourselves and then see what Greevo needs?"

"That's smart," Kel said.

"Philo go?" Philo asked, joining them in the hallway.

"Maybe, but not too far," Kel said. "We don't know this area very well. Don't get lost."

"Philo no get lost. Philo need monies."

Having anticipated his friend's need, Rix had been collecting Philo's pay in small bits of precious metals, specifically platinum. He held out his hand and doled out a quarter of the backpay. "Don't spend it all right away. You need to make it last for an entire day."

"Rixy, you good people," Philo said with a giant grin on his face.

"Don't you want him to stick around to help move Greevo's load?"

"We aren't contracted for stevedore work," Rix said. "Greevo made it very clear that we were not to touch his crates."

"What's the nightly here?" Kel asked.

"Is that your question or are you asking if we're going to clear a profit?"

"Both, I suppose."

"Kha'rem is giving us both berths for thirteen hundred credits. He'll adjust if there are trades in his favor. I'm not holding my breath on that. Greevo isn't about to give up a penny to save us a dollar," Rix said.

With the gangplank extended, Rix and Kel walked off *Calypso* and onto the dock. Second in line, they were sixty meters from what looked like a store front.

"Welcome to Driftmarket," a dignified Vesh stated, bowing slightly from the waist.

"Thank you," Rix said. "Are you Kha'rem? I'm Rix Banner, and this is my partner, Kel Warp."

"I am Kha'rem of Deep Tribe. These boys are Kasit of Havenfall and Wagg of Chainreach. We will be quite accessible to you throughout your stay. If you need assistance, please contact any of us so that we might be helpful."

"I did not realize your tradition was to mention where we're from," Rix said. "Our ships sail from Patience Station in Narlux-4, which is where we reside."

"I propose a meal, that we would sit and learn of each other. Perhaps there is business to be exchanged," he said.

"We'd like that," Kel said. "Most of the load is owned by someone else, though. It's important to introduce him."

"Most interesting," Kha'rem said.

"A trading partner for the future might be an interesting discussion, though," Kel said.

"One deal does not a career make," Kha'rem said.

"Amari, what's Greevo's status?" Rix asked.

"They're getting ready," Amari answered. "You have no idea how much mess two of them can make in a very short time."

"I have some idea," Rix countered.

"Greevo is just about ready to come out," Rix said. "Tell me, do you have many Grintok out this way?"

"There is a vibrant Grintok community on Driftmarket," Kha'rem said. "Am I to understand that your Greevo is Grintok?"

"He is."

"Is he related to the Grintok of Driftmarket?"

"Not as far as I know," Rix said. "He'd have reached out, otherwise."

By the time they made it down to where *Gravitational Pull* had been tied up, Amari had exited and was staring impatiently back at the hatch. “Greevo, do not touch that,” she chided, then walked halfway back along the gangplank, only to have Greevo appear at the door.

“No need impatience,” Greevo said, tightening a cloak around his shoulders.

Amari turned and stood at the end of the plank. When Greevo approached, she held out her hand. At first, it appeared that Greevo would challenge her, but he then coughed up a piece of equipment, which he’d taken from *Gravitational Pull* as he’d passed by.

Thranga, the Grintok who’d joined Greevo when Rix had transitioned to *Calypso*, trailed behind. Wordlessly, she also set a small piece of equipment in Amari’s hand as she passed. Rix decided not to press the issue, given the gravity of the moment.

“Greevo, this is Kha’rem of Deep Tribe, the man who agreed to provide a berth for today and is providing security,” Rix said. “Kha’rem, I present Greevo of Patience Station.”

“I am honored, fellow trader,” Kha’rem said bowing. “How is it we might be of most benefit to you this day?”

“Where can Greevo set up shop?” Greevo said roughly. “Time is wasting.”

“Most trade is done in the mornings and afternoon,” Kha’rem said evenly, not the least bit perturbed by Greevo. “There are open air stalls for rent on this level, one kilometer along the inner passage. If you need help moving material, I have two for hire.”

“Where inner passage?” Greevo asked.

Kha’rem pointed back toward his shop and to the right.

“Greevo return,” he said brusquely, then walked off.

18

ARBITRAGE

"IS WHAT THEY SAY TRUE?" Kha'rem asked, watching as Greevo trundled off in search of stalls to rent. "That Mr. Greevo removed the barrels from Gray vessel *Quibbler 12A*'s particle blaster turret, instead of scuttling the ship?"

"No," Kel said. "Greevo had nothing to do with that. The ships and security are my partner's and my responsibility."

"It is true, then, that you have taken these barrels?"

"Yes. It seemed the quickest way to end the conflict without further violence," Kel shrugged.

"Admirable."

"We're traders, not mercenaries. Fighting is a game where everyone loses something," Rix said. "I don't suppose releasing the crew and ship gave us any credibility, did it?"

"Let us agree that it was an unusual approach to a difficult situation," Kha'rem said. "I take tea in the afternoon. Would you join me? We may have common business interests."

"We've attracted a lot of attention," Kel said. "I don't think it's a good idea to leave the ship."

"I can assure you, the vessels, once tied to my pier, are quite safe. I've hired additional security on your behalf." Kha'rem could see that his words weren't convincing Kel, so he modified his offer. "We'll sit on the veranda so that you may keep an eye on your vessel. Would that alleviate your concerns?"

"That works," Kel said after a moment of thought. "Rix, after we meet with Mr. Kha'rem, we'll need to do an external visual inspection on *Calypso*. We took some good hits."

"Absolutely," Rix agreed.

"Kasit, Wagg, fetch my table and three chairs."

"Four, if you don't mind," Rix added.

"Yes, that's no problem," Kha'rem said.

The two young men flashed smiles at each other and hustled back to Kha'rem's otherwise closed market.

"You have quite a lot of store front here," Rix said. "What is it you sell?"

"On Driftmarket, one barters for everything and hopes at the end of the day to have made good trades," Kha'rem said. "I am fortunate to be in the Vesh clan. We live within the Kor'vesh sea, where we tend and harvest the great kelp beds along with primarily gillet fish and shellfish of many varieties."

"That explains the smell," Kel said.

"Kel, that's not polite," Rix chastised.

Kha'rem smiled with understanding and nodded. "The musk of the sea takes some getting used to. It is a small price to pay."

The two young men had loaded a wide grav pallet with a table and chairs and were racing back across the open space. Just then, Philo appeared at *Calypso's* hatch.

"I am so sorry, Kha'rem, I did not think that our other companion would be joining us," Rix apologized. "Is it possible to get one more chair?"

"Of course. It is no inconvenience at all."

"Amari," Rix called as he sat in the chair Kha'rem offered. "Come out and join us. We have security set up."

"I'm on my way, Rix," she answered.

"How many passengers remain aboard?" Kha'rem asked.

"You're seeing my entire team, aside from Amari, who's on her way out," Rix said as Philo and Kel sat down in the other chairs. "Greevo has a total of five Grintok. Most of the trade goods in our hold and the storage units belong to him. As Kel pointed out earlier, we own the ships."

"A difficult journey?" Kha'rem asked, waving over a pair of small Grintok, who were approaching with a cart with a stoneware pitcher and cups on it.

Rix was about to answer when he noticed that Philo had frozen in place, his eyes locked on the approaching tea service. "Philo? Are you okay?"

"Rixy, Philo eyes filled," Philo said.

"How about you sit for a moment," Rix chuckled, helping Philo to a chair.

As the two Grintok approached, Rix could tell that Philo's attention was solely focused on the young woman. Despite being green-skinned and having a larger head and hands than compared to human proportions, Rix had to admit the Grintok was attractive by most standards.

"Philo want meet," Philo said. His comment earned him a glance from the pretty Grintok woman.

"Ah, Sta'ci, Dansk, thank you for the tea," Kha'rem said, as the pair added a white tablecloth to the otherwise plain table and set the service in front of them.

"Philo, you're staring," Kel whispered. "Please stop. It's impolite."

Kha'rem seemed amused. "Dansk and Sta'ci are brother and sister. They have worked for me ever since Sta'ci was pushed outside her home. They are a delight. I have raised them as my own."

"Pushed outside?" Rix asked.

"The same features that your Philo finds so attractive are the very same that caused Grintok society to reject her," Kha'rem said.

"I'm sorry to hear that."

Kha'rem lay a fatherly hand on Dansk's back. "Is it selfish that I am not sorry? I gained family that day. It was a joy."

"The cute one should come to Jump tonight," Sta'ci said quietly.

"We have barely been introduced, Sta'ci," Kha'rem chuckled dismissively. "Please, leave us to our business. Perhaps another evening, once we have come to know each other."

Sta'ci nodded and began pouring tea. "As you wish, father."

"You'll forgive the curiosity," Kha'rem said. "It is unusual that a stranger appears at our table."

"I understand the feeling completely," Rix said, studying the blue-skinned man's face. "Is your business here good?"

"It is enough to make a living for many," Kha'rem said. "Kelp and gillet are always available and provide a steady income. It is difficult, however, to get ahead."

"We know something about that," Kel said.

"It sounds there is a story, Kel Warp. Please, share."

"Independent freight hauling can be dangerous," Kel said. "We darn near spend every credit earned in repairs. And without Rix, we'd never be able to afford it."

"Rix Banner repairs your vessel?"

"Oh yeah, check this out. This is what *Calypso* looked like after our last dust-up," Kel said, holding a small tablet out to Kha'rem. "It took darn near the entirety of our savings just to afford the parts. He even had to have some of them custom manufactured. But he got us up and going again."

"That is a valuable skill indeed," Kha'rem said, eyeing Rix appraisingly. "I wondered how *Quibbler 12A's* barrels were so easily removed. I cannot think of anyone who would have taken that approach, or who would have been capable of performing that work in the great void."

"Most systems are not overly complex in their implementation," Rix said. "Those barrels were held in by half a dozen bolts each, plus some fancy wire harnesses. I slightly damaged a harness when the barrel twisted away from me, but otherwise, they're in perfect shape."

"As you might imagine, in a protected garden such as Garanod Enclave, equipment is difficult to replace and even used, potentially damaged items can often have considerable value," Kha'rem said.

"I'm not sure we want to sell them," Kel cut in. "If we were to sell them, those barrels would be back on *Quibbler* the next day, and we'd have to deal with a crew that's got an attitude."

"*Quibbler 12A* is owned by the Gray Consortium," Kha'rem said. "If you desire, I could inquire as to their interest in reacquiring their equipment."

"It's not their equipment," Kel corrected, her face stone cold. "They shot at us. We took their guns instead of killing them and slagging their ship. A good trade, if you ask me."

Kha'rem sipped his tea thoughtfully, then set down his cup. "You make a fine point, but I see value in a trade of weaponry and expertise that could settle a conflict before it grows, unmanaged. And who is this beauty that would join us?" Kha'rem stood as Amari approached.

"Amari of Patience Station," Amari said, holding out a hand for Kha'rem to grasp as she dipped respectfully. Having changed from a jumpsuit to jet black, hip-hugging pants and a strappy black shirt, she looked like she was ready to go dancing at a bar more than have afternoon tea on Kha'rem's porch.

"You not only want us to sell those barrels to Gray, the organization who attacked us, but you want Rix to reinstall them?" Kel asked. "You've got some nerve asking that."

Kha'rem looked confused as he turned to Kel. "You'd of course be paid handsomely, and an agreement of non-aggression could be drafted."

"How long would that last?" Kel asked skeptically. "They could just attack with a different ship."

"Which is their option today," Kha'rem said, unwavering despite Kel's irritation. "A pact of non-aggression is a basic tool of trade within the Garanod Enclave."

"How is it enforced?" Rix asked.

"There is no enforcement, aside from the loss of reputation by an oath-breaker," Kha'rem said. "Here, a person's word is more valuable than any legal enforcement. Once an organization is known to violate their pacts, their business withers and they are increasingly forced to make violence their primary tool of commerce. For some, this is maintainable. For most, however, it is simpler to honor your commitments."

"Does this Gray Consortium honor contracts?"

"I would not expect you to have difficulty with them," Kha'rem said. "Once your holds are unloaded, there is little residual value in attacking ships such as yours. I intend no offense."

"Such as ours?"

"Kel, let it go," Rix warned.

"No. What do you mean—such as ours?" She shifted forward in her seat, defiance written all over her face.

Kha'rem studied Kel's face for a moment and then answered. "Limited repair," Kha'rem said. "*Gravitational Pull*, your primary cargo hauler, emits a cloud of black smoke when under load. *Calypso's* hull is a patchwork of repairs. Further, you defend yourselves with skill and have defeated one of their vessels. Aside from ego, there is no reason for hostilities to continue between Gray and you. Therefore, they will accept the non-aggression pact."

"It's still a bit much to swallow," Kel said. "I can almost see selling them the barrels but actually reinstalling them feels like a step too far."

"Maybe we don't need to get through this tonight," Rix said, redirecting. "Let's talk about what we owe you for the docking services."

"That requires a discussion about currency," Kha'rem said. "Do you have any precious metals? I'm afraid Galactic Empire credits are not nearly so valuable here."

"We brought gold," Rix said.

"Ten grams per twenty-six-hour period. Are you using solid fuels or Fantastium?"

"Solids."

"Ten-kilogram blocks go for a gram of gold."

"Water?"

"Free to those who would take time to drink tea with an old trader."

"You said something interesting," Rix said.

"Oh? I do love it when that happens. I have no idea what it might have been, though."

"Galactic Empire credits aren't valuable."

"For obvious reasons.

"But people have them."

"They are known to exist."

Rix pulled out his wallet, pulled out twenty-five grams of gold coins and set them on the table. "Two full days and fifty kilograms of fuel?" he asked.

"You are officially our guests for the next fifty-two hours," Kha'rem said. "I will have Kasit and Wagg deliver the fuel first thing in the morning, if this is acceptable."

"Sure," Rix said.

"Tell me more about your interest in Galactic Empire credits."

"I'd like to be paid for the gun barrels and installation in Galactic Empire credits, but only if I get the same lopsided exchange you were just suggesting. Surely, people want to unload their Galactic Empire credits in exchange for whatever goes for currency around here," Rix said.

"Barter is our primary currency, but there is a credit system recognized by most. What is it you would ask for these barrels?"

"Just talking out loud," Kel said. "The barrels are valuable. Even in

Narlux-4 where they would be available, I imagine they're worth sixty thousand Galactic Empire credits."

"I do not think you could get that here," Kha'rem said. "Those barrels, and even the ship they were seized from, likely were not purchased."

"If I asked to exchange gold for Galactic Credits, what would your rate be?" Kel asked.

"Three hundred Galactic Credits for a gram of gold."

"How much gold could you ask for these barrels. Separately, what would you pay to have them installed?"

"I see what you are driving at, Kel Warp," Kha'rem said. "I do not have these numbers for you, but I do see the shape of an interesting transaction. Allow me to work with Gray on your behalf. I will present a deal to you that I do not believe you will be disappointed in, assuming Gray does not wish to work out the grievance less civilly."

"Aside from food stuffs, what else do you trade in?" Rix asked, redirecting.

"I have a network of friends who deal in various commodities," the trader said. "I am quite happy to make referrals depending on what it is you wish to trade. Do you have something specific in mind?"

"Old ship parts that have been repaired to working condition," Rix said.

"That is likely more interesting than you would expect. With little manufacturing in Garanod Enclave, working parts for the right machines are easily sold. Evening approaches, and the markets are closed. Tomorrow morning, after fuel delivery, I will have Kasit escort you to my friend Bha'resh. He has the means to identify your parts in a way that can be marketed in Garanod."

"Where can we get a good meal tonight?" Rix asked. "Nothing too exotic."

"There are many fine establishments. If you wish to try gillet, fresh from the sea, Fel'tesh has a grill and awning that is within the entertainment district. I would join you, but I have already made plans for this evening. Are we agreed that I will broker the gun barrels?"

"We're just getting a price, no commitments yet?" Rix asked.

"I would have more leverage if I were able to accept a deal," Kha'rem pushed.

"What's your cut?" Rix asked, ignoring the glance Kel shot him.

"Twenty percent is standard."

"If our part is less than 125 grams of gold, then we are uninterested in selling," Rix said.

"You will warrant the weapon's operational status?"

"It'll work when I'm done. No warranty, though. People are hard on equipment. I can't be responsible for that."

"Provable operational status is sufficient. I'll have something for you by tomorrow, close of business."

"Thank you."

Kha'rem stood and smiled. "Enjoy the tea for as long as you wish. Sta'ci and Dansk will clear the service later this evening, just leave everything here."

"Thank you, Kha'rem."

After Kha'rem had disappeared back into his building, Kel turned to Rix. "Do you trust this guy?"

"Like with my life? No," Rix said. "To talk to people I don't even know about selling guns I took from their ship? Sure. Seems like something a local can do better than I can."

"Arming the guys who were shooting at us doesn't seem like a great idea," Kel said, She turned her head and pointed. "And there's Greevo. Where do you suppose he got off to?"

"I'm guessing he's going to start barking orders," Rix said. "Won't this be fun?"

"I might bop him in the ear if he keeps it up. I'm about as tired of these Grintok as I can be. They go out of their way to be rude," Kel said.

"You get up move," Greevo said, still twenty feet from where they sat.

"I have this," Rix said before Kel jumped on it.

"Philo must go now," Philo announced before Rix could reply to Greevo. "Back one day, maybe two," Philo said.

"Hold on," Rix said, pulling four quarter-gram gold coins from his wallet and handing them to Philo. "Go easy on those coins, they're worth fifty credits each."

"Philo know. Philo smart," Philo answered.

"No argument here, Philo," Kel said. "Go have fun."

"Where he going?" Greevo asked, staring daggers as Philo left the table. "Time to work."

"What do you need, Greevo?" Rix asked.

"Move storage pods to new location. *Gravitational Pull* hover and drop. It work good," Greevo said.

"We do not have a mechanism to lower those cargo pods, Greevo," Rix said. "They'll break if we drop them on the ground. You need to get a delivery service to move your product. Is there a closer pier where we could tie up for unloading?"

"No. You drop. It be okay."

"Not on your word, Greevo," Rix said. You can show me this drop, and I'll let you know if I'll do it."

"Cost money, hire stevedores. Lost money. No good. Rix Banner bad business partner."

"I'm not your business partner, Greevo. I'm a freight hauler and I've done exactly that. It's your job to load the cargo pods and unload the cargo pods. And let's not forget what you have stuffed into *Calypso*, which for sure puts you well over the mass we agreed upon."

"No truth. Greevo good partner."

"Now we're playing that you I'm a liar?" Rix asked. "That's not going to work for me. Hire your workers, and if you need us to move to a temporary pier, we'll do it."

"Always hard with Rix Banner. Open *Calypso*. We start moving," Greevo said, then started barking orders to the all-female Grintok team he'd brought along. Without dissent, they started pulling grav pallets to the hold's deck and loaded them tall with crates. As soon as four pallets were loaded, Greevo's workers started pushing them down the cement path.

"This is going to take forever," Kel said.

"You know, we're not terribly busy," Rix said. "I'm going to help."

"I hate it when he gets his way," Kel grumbled.

"We can take turns watching the ships," Amari said. "When you get back, I'll switch with you."

"Okay," Kel said, slamming crates onto a pallet.

It was midnight when they finally closed the doors on the second cargo pod, which was only partially emptied. The location Greevo had chosen to show his wares was on the outside edge of a large trading square, and Rix didn't think he'd struggle to get attention. Even as late as it was, a few vendors stopped by, interested in seeing if they could get a price better than the public would see the next day. Greevo, however, was having none of it.

"Do you think Fel'tesh is still open for food tonight?" Kel asked.

"I doubt it," Rix said. All of the shops in the area had closed well before they'd finished dragging pallet loads down from *Calypso*. "Let's grab something from the ships and we can start new with food tomorrow."

By the time they returned to *Calypso*, Kitka had a large meal already in progress. The quality of the food was fully unexpected. Instead of ration bars or protein drinks, Kitka had cooked hamburgers, complete with cold bottled beers.

"This is a surprise," Rix said, accepting a plate from Kitka.

"Kitka grateful for help. Greevo not lift. Rix Banner work hard. Much faster," she said.

"Hey, what about me? I helped too," Kel whined.

Kitka's face hinted at a smile. "Yes. Kel Warp big help. Amari, too. Much food for hard workers."

"What time are you getting started tomorrow?" Rix asked.

"Greevo and Kitka leave 0400," Kitka said. "Kitka make breakfast before. Greevo not hard worker but Greevo smart. Make good credits."

"Credits are worth less here. You need more credits for each sale," Rix said, but the look on Kitka's face told him she had no idea what he was saying. "Where is Greevo?"

"Asleep in *Gravitational Pull*," she said.

Rix nodded. Greevo would be sprawled out in *Gravitational Pull's* bunk room, naked. Rix wasn't sure if he slept naked to deter visitors, or if it was just his thing. For sure, the deterrence worked well.

19

ALL ETERNITY

KASIT SLID the final two clicks back to Havenfall, smiling to himself. Playing a part in getting a Galactic Empire vessel to land at Kha'rem's dock had elevated his value with the old merchant and would likely open doors for him beyond crating gillet. With a casual flip, he released the sling's grasp on the fluxspan rail and landed softly on the spongey hillside, his arrival activating the bioluminescent fungi, as spores launched skyward.

With light feet, Kasit ran home to their hovel, but at the last moment, he felt something was off. Whether it was a smell or the wrong pattern of lights, he wasn't sure. Unfortunately, his good mood overrode the warnings, allowing him to ignore the feeling in his gut. Stepping onto the main path to the only door, he was startled to realize that a figure stood in the shadows next to the building. A small ember glowed, almost seeming to float as the figure drew a breath through a smoke stick.

"Big day?" The man's voice was raspy and low, a plume of white smoke escaping his lips as he spoke.

"You shouldn't be here," Kasit growled, gripping the sling tightly in his hand, fully intending to use it as a weapon.

The end of the smoke stick glowed again, this time twice as bright and for a longer duration. Kasit was transfixed by the deliberateness of the man's actions. Pulling the smoke stick from his lips, the man placed a finger in just the right spot and flicked it at Kasit, who had to duck to avoid the flying ember.

"Inside," Busk commanded.

Kasit's mind immediately jumped to his mother, Zenith. She should have already been home. He brushed past Busk, his stomach knotting. Inside, he found Lirren Vos and his mother sitting at the kitchen table. Fear blanketed Zenith's face as she looked at her son. "What have you done, Kasit?" she whispered.

Guilt flooded Kasit's chest. He'd known better than to take the delivery run from Grays. Doing so had made him a target, somehow, for the Jeshifa crime boss. He'd let Zenith down, and he'd invited criminals into their home in the process.

"Aww, don't be hanging all this on him, Zen," Lirren said. "It's time for the boy to grow into Gadry's shoes. It's not like you didn't know I'd be coming for him at some point." He turned to Kasit. "I told your old man that I'd look after things when he was gone."

"You don't get to use his name, Lirren," Zenith spat.

Busk stepped forward, flicking a telescoping baton out so that it extended.

"Now, now, everyone take it down a notch. I'm just here for a friendly conversation. Have you had a chance to think about my offer, son?" Lirren asked.

"No ..." Kasit stammered, looking from Zenith to Lirren and back. "I mean. I don't want to be a spy."

"That's disappointing," Lirren said. "Zen, did you know your boy is top talent among the fluxspan sliding community?"

"I know he slides," she answered.

"He more than slides. He's a damn magician on those rails," Lirren said. "I have vid of him executing a backflip between Line 146 and 182. Miss that connection and he'd still be falling. Where'd he get all that talent? I know it didn't come from Gadry. That man could trip on a clean floor. Now, put a gun in his hand and he was more than adequate as a shooter. Just not exactly graceful. Not everyone needs to be graceful, though, right Busk?"

Busk grunted but didn't speak.

Kasit stared at his mother. He'd never known what had happened to his father, but the familiarity with which Lirren spoke of him was confusing. Even more confounding was his mother not denying any of it.

"What are we going to do?" Lirren asked, taking a sip of tea. "What do you think, Zen? I say we get Kasit here set up good and proper. No reason for his talents to go to waste. Gadry wouldn't want you starving."

"I have a job," Kasit said.

"Working for that old fishmonger? What kind of life is that? Always coming home smelling like moldy kelp?"

"It's good work, Lirren. If you cared for Gadry, you'd let Kasit go," Zenith said.

"I'm not forcing Kasit to do anything," Lirren said. "In my organization, people do what they want to do. There's no forcing. There is the small matter of the expenses incurred due to Kasit's last delivery. I'm a businessman. Five thousand credits, and we're even."

"Five thousand? Because I delivered an old ledger for the Grays?"

"That ledger was mine. They stole it. You handed it over. It's costing me a whole lot more than five thousand, but because of Gadry and Zen, I'm giving you a break."

"We don't have five thousand," Zenith said, looking to Kasit for confirmation.

"Well, see, that's going to be a problem," Lirren said. "You won't slide for me, but you owe. Let's talk about how we're going to solve this problem."

"Lirren, no," Zenith begged.

Lirren patted Zenith's hand patronizingly. "Now, now, Zen. It's time for boys to become men and for men to speak. If you can't be quiet, I'll ask you to remove yourself. Do we understand each other?"

Zenith swallowed hard. "Yes, Lirren."

Kasit raised his eyebrows at his mother's capitulation. She was the fiercest person he knew, but she was scared ... for him.

"Good. Kasit, you're going to steal from the off-worlders," Lirren said. "Those Galactic Empire folks, who were curiously smart enough to avoid the boarding parties that were sent. At first, I was thinking, *what a loss. We had our shot at those cargo pods and we missed it. Now we'll have to...create another chance.* But imagine my luck! Even more curiously, the travelers decided to make a deal with, of all people, your boss, Kha'rem, for safe harbor. Do you have any idea the value of cargo those ships are carrying?"

"Looked mostly like old ship parts," Kasit said. "Fusion rods, navi-sensors, basic stuff, but lots of it. I imagine it's worth quite a bit."

"You need to recognize the part of the conversation where I'm asking rhetorical questions," Lirren said with mild irritation. "No. Boxes of old ship parts, no matter how valuable, aren't even the least bit interesting. The good news is, I know for certain you didn't look in those journals."

"I don't understand," Kasit said.

"I know. There was a communication, about an artifact from before the war, a piece of Tok electronics. You know who the Tok are, right?"

"Sort of. They're a super advanced species. Part of Galactic Empire."

"Right, Tok *are* the Galactic Empire," Lirren said, his black veins pulsing beneath the pale skin on his forehead. "I got word that a trader was coming, and they'd have a Ghostmist Navigation Cipher. Do you know what that is, kid?"

"A way to get through the nebula?" Kasit guessed.

"You're close," Lirren said. "It's more than that. It shows nav points that can put us back in Galactic Empire space. Without the cipher, ships just get lost in the clouds, their sensors all whack from the radiation and magnetics of the nebula. It's worth more than all Havenfall, to the right person. And you're going to steal it for me."

"No, Lirren," Zenith said. "You ask too much."

"If he pulls this off, he'll be set. I'll make him a lieutenant. He'll be a made man," Lirren laughed. "His debt, your debt, they'll all be paid in full. Don't you see? He already has an in. Those Galactic scum know him. He can get close and nobody will think anything is off. Like I said, I thought it was a loss, and I was going to have to do something terrible. Now this can all get fixed."

"Please, no," Zenith beseeched the men. "Kasit, don't do this. You will never escape this life. There is no way out if you do this."

"He's already been on the ship, Zen. He's scheduled to deliver fuel in the morning," Lirren said, pulling a small device from his pocket and setting it on the table. "Take this, link it to your HUD. If you get even close to that cipher, it'll light up like a bent bandiwillow."

Zenith turned to Kasit. "Don't," she pleaded. "Lirren won't kill me."

"I won't?" Lirren asked, with obvious surprise. "You overestimate my relationship with your husband, Gadry. There is only one way you both come out of this unharmed, Kasit."

"I'll do it," Kasit said, picking up the small device. "But you must promise you'll leave us alone forever once I do this. You have nothing over me or Zenith. Agreed?"

"Look who has a spine," Lirren said. "Okay. You've got me. You deliver the Ghostmist Navigation Cipher, and all debts will be cancelled between us. I'll leave you and yours alone for all eternity. Busk, write that down."

"Got it, boss," Busk answered. "All eternity."

"Oh, Kas, he'll never let go," Zenith said, tears running down her cheeks.

20

PRECIOUS CARGO

"GREEVO, GET UP," Rix said, tapping on the wall to make noise. It was 0200, and they'd just returned from delivering loads to Greevo's temporary store. That Greevo had not helped, nor even stayed to the end, grated on Rix's sense of fair play. The bottle next to Greevo's inert, naked form, however, suggested rousing the passed-out alien would be difficult.

"Let him sleep," Amari said. "We can take one more night in the pilot chairs. They're comfy enough."

"Please shoot me if I ever suggest traveling with a Grintok again," Rix said.

"You have to experience it to understand just how bad it can be," Amari agreed quietly, pulling his hand so he turned away from the sprawled, drunken alien. Gently, she leaned forward, and they lightly kissed. "Right now, I just want to sleep for a few hours."

"Same," Rix said, turning out the bunkroom lights and following her back down to the main deck. "I just don't understand how he can make a mess so quickly," Rix complained once again, kicking trash out of his way.

"An unforgettable trip that we'll laugh about in the future," Amari said, clearly trying to unseat Rix's irritation.

"I'm being childish. I apologize," Rix said, leaning over, picking up handfuls of debris and depositing them in the trash receptacle.

"It's true, but it's also warranted," Amari said with an impish grin. "You're forgiven."

Sleep came easily, but just three hours later did Kitka's noisy entry disturb them. Rix stirred as she started clanging things around in the galley.

"What are you doing?" Rix croaked out, turning in his chair. The cockpit was only a few feet from the galley.

"Big meal for big man," Kitka said. "Greevo will much trading. Family big wealthy."

"Beverly, can you help me? I'm dying here," Rix said.

"Your sleep patterns are not ideal," Beverly said, appearing in brightly colored pajamas that encased her feet.

"You're wearing Nitey Nights? You saw that ad?" Rix asked, recalling seeing the pajamas somewhere.

"This was in a magazine on your end table," Beverly said. "If you will allow, I can create a cancelling sound wave that will keep you from hearing most of the noise Kitka creates. It will not be perfect, as you are not my host, but I believe it will be enough to allow you sleep."

"Please."

Suddenly, the sounds of kitchen pots and pans clattering and food stuffs being retrieved, chopped and mixed ceased. Although those sounds were effectively muted, the humming of the ship's systems continued, providing a relaxing background noise and enabling Rix to nod off once again.

"Rix, it's time to get up." Opening his eyes, Rix found that Amari was sitting on his lap, looking into his face. Before he could say anything, she kissed him on the forehead. "Greevo and Kitka are gone. Don't get mad, but they left quite a mess. Kha'rem's helpers will be here in thirty minutes with that fuel and to help us move our crates to market."

"How bad is it?" Rix asked, rubbing his eyes.

"More than we can clean in thirty minutes," she said. "We should shower and get dressed. We can deal with Kitka later today."

"Beverly, change the access to *Gravitational Pull*. I don't want any of Greevo's people in here anymore. I'd rather sleep with Kel and Philo aboard than deal with this," Rix said. "Send a comm to Greevo to let him know of his revoked access. Try to word it nicer than I would."

"Aye, aye, Captain," Beverly said, appearing in a Naval uniform Rix recalled from his time in the service.

"Sorry, I didn't mean to order you around. Is there any way you can consider that me asking for help?"

"Message is sent," Beverly said. "Also, my feelings aren't easily hurt. If I don't want to do something, I'll likely tell you to shove it up your nose."

Pushing debris out of the way, Rix extended the shower, which took space away from the galley when in use.

"Get clean together?" Amari asked, peeling her jumpsuit from her shoulder, but not so far as to reveal anything important. "Or is that too forward for a man of Earth's 1950s?"

"Are you asking me to fornicate with you?"

"Oh, fully ruined moment." Amari rolled her eyes, ducking through the curtain into the head. "Think about word choices before we try that again, huh?" The curtain closed, and Rix heard the suit cleaner start up and the shower waters running.

"Well, hell," Rix said, leaning over to scoop up fresh debris from Kitka's cooking. "What happened there?"

"Are you asking?" Beverly asked.

"Yes."

"Amari was offering open-ended intimacy. Ordinarily, most species will experiment with this sort of intimacy before escalating to full, physical intimacy. Your word choice was clumsy and did not reflect the moment. 'Fornicate' is not a pretty word in any language," Beverly said.

"I see it now," Rix said, dumping another load of crap into the trash reclaimer. "Think I can recover the moment?"

"That remains to be seen. Can you imagine how Amari would like to be communicated with? She was offering intimacy. Were you?"

"Nope. I get it. Also, please stop. I already feel dumb enough."

"American society in the 1950s is highly repressed, sexually speaking," Beverly said. "Your responses are understandable with that lens. Try to push some of those images from your head and be a bit more 'in the moment.'"

"In the moment," Rix said, purposefully pulling off his jumpsuit. "Intimacy," he repeated.

Fingers finding their way into the seam where the curtains met, Rix slipped through the opening. Amari, soap in hair, saw his entrance and turned her back to him as she placed her head into the stream of water.

It went against everything he thought he knew about relations with the opposite sex, but instead of talking, Rix reached out and placed two fingers on Amari's back, just above the outline of her wings, which were formed into her body. Slowly, he traced the outline of one.

"Is that uncomfortable for you?" she asked.

"Uncomfortable?" Rix repeated.

"My wings. They show how different you and I are."

"I was curious about how sensitive they are. Can you feel my fingers? Does it bother you?" Rix asked.

"Your gentle touch is not bothersome. And yes, they are sensitive under the right circumstances."

"They fit you."

"That is a feature which allows me to wear normal clothing."

"No, I didn't mean it that way. They're beautiful, elegant, no—well, yes, but intricate is the word I'm looking for. So much detail," Rix said.

"You can touch them," Amari said.

Rix's fingers traced the black border of a wing. Brushing along, he realized there was directionality. Moving in one direction, he found resistance, in the other, small ridges smoothed down, making passage easy. More importantly, Amari's breathing elevated as he explored her.

"It's hard to imagine them producing enough lift for you to fly."

"That's your thought right now?"

"Yeah," Rix admitted. "I'm kind of built that way. Show me something beautifully complex and I'm going to have questions."

Amari turned slowly so that they faced each other. "You are beautifully complex, too," she said, tapping on Rix's temple. "Hold me?"

Rix wrapped his arms around her, and they stood in the stream of hot water together for a few minutes. "I'll get out first," she finally said. "You can finish up cleaning. I'll have a towel for you."

"Okay," Rix said, his hand trailing down her back as she stepped from the shower. With Amari out, Rix hurried to soap and rinse, knowing that they needed to get going. When he stepped out, Amari handed him a cleaned jumpsuit.

"Are you hungry?" she asked.

"Starving," Rix said. "I'm not having a meal bar, again, though, unless you want one."

"Let's see what the morning brings," Amari said.

Exiting *Gravitational Pull*, Rix wasn't surprised to find that the two younger men he'd met the night before were already waiting on the dock, stacks of solid fuel sitting atop grav pallets.

"Good morning, gentlemen," Rix said. "Once again with the names? I'm Rix Banner, this beautiful woman next to me is Amari."

"I'm Wagg, this ugly mutt here is Kasit," Wagg said with a big grin on his face. "Where would you like the fuel?"

"Most of it will go on *Gravitational Pull,*" Rix said. "She burns way harder than she should."

"We've seen the smoke. We thought she was on fire when she came in," Wagg said.

Rix noticed the other, Kasit, standing back, was obviously distracted, although also curious about their ships. "Let's split seventy-thirty. I'll open *Gravitational Pull's* basement and let you boys load her up if you don't mind."

"Mind? We've been wanting to get a gander inside," Wagg said. "Kasit, what in rock dust blazes has got you so quiet today? Rix Banner says we can look inside. Are you deaf?"

"Oh, yeah, cool," Kasit said, smiling politely and dipping his head in acknowledgement. "Split the load?"

"He already covered that," Wagg said, moving a stack from the pallet one brick at a time.

"I'm sorry. I'm a bit distracted."

"Late night?" Rix asked, smiling.

Kasit's heart hammered in his chest. Did this Galactic Empire alien know more than he was letting on? Did he know that Kasit's job was to steal from him, and he was prodding him?

"Not really," Kasit answered, his voice cracking. "Uh, you know. Got home, talked to mom, played some vids."

"He didn't ask for your life history, Kas," Wagg said. "Help me load this, you big oaf."

"Sorry. Okay," Kasit said.

Loading the fuel took a few minutes, but soon enough, it was done. "We got word to help you pull a load down to the market. Sounds like you have business with Bha'resh. I'm sorry Kasit is such a dud today, but he's going to help move your gear down to the market. I have gillet fish to pack this morning for Kha'rem."

"I was up late, is all," Kasit said, waving off his friend. "How many pallets of equipment are we moving?"

"Depends on how high we load them," Rix said. "Might need to make a couple of trips."

"Oh, that's okay," Kasit said, brightening. "I'll get you set up with Bha'resh, and then I can come back and grab the other pallets; make a couple of trips if needed. Just point out what you need me to bring."

"Sure, we could do that," Rix said. "Let's get her opened up."

Scanning his palm on the side of a cargo pod, Rix pulled open the hatch so they could enter the pod. Having emptied half of the pod already, it wasn't difficult to move around. Stepping in, Kasit froze for a moment as the sensor attached to his HUD squealed loudly. It took everything in him to not react.

21

SECONDARY MARKET

Rix turned to Kasit, the alarm on the younger man's wrist drawing considerable attention. "Trouble?" Rix asked.

Kasit's expression was of both confusion and panic. Tapping on his wrist, he struggled to silence his device. "No, no," Kasit said. "I ... it's just the pod blocking my communications. I should have put it on quiet." The noise abated, but Rix couldn't help but notice that Kasit held his arm at an odd angle, as if trying to hide the offending device on his wrist.

"Bring that pallet over, would you?" Rix asked, working to release the strap from a stack of crates segregated from the rest of Greevo's remaining load.

"Yes, of course," Kasit said.

"He's nervous," Beverly said, appearing on the crate in front of Rix. She wore a man's pinstriped wool suit and a fedora. "We should keep an eye on this one."

Rix nodded, unable to answer, given his proximity to Kasit, who'd unstacked one of the grav pallets and heaved it over next to Rix.

Working together, they loaded both grav pallets four crates high, which made them slightly tippy, but manageable.

"Let's go see your friend Bha'resh," Rix said, pushing the pallet in front of him to the aft end of the cargo pod.

"The remaining four in that stack are all that is left?" Kasit asked.

Whatever had been bothering the young man seemed to have passed, as he was no longer acting sketchy. "That's right," Rix said. "Those two stacks were all that I brought."

"You guys are about all anyone is talking about this morning," Kasit said. "It was a boss move to swipe Gray's particle blaster barrels. Upgrade that to legendary that you have the dangles to sell them back."

"Was that deal with Gray a bad idea?" Rix asked.

"Kha'rem will smooth that out if he can," Kasit said. "People like him. He's been around forever, so he knows how to negotiate."

"Have you ever been in the sea?"

"Kor'vesh?" Kasit asked, watching as Rix closed and secured the pod doors.

"The one where Kha'rem gets his gillet fish."

"That's Kor'vesh. No. It's not a thing people do, other than native Vesh. They don't like others in their waters." Rix nodded as the two pushed pallets down the wide passage. "We're going three levels up and then it's another kilometer," Kasit said. "Are you okay?"

"Easy peasy," Rix said. "Amari and I are glad to get out and stretch our legs. Right, Amari?" Rix asked.

"More than you can imagine. I'm tired of being cooped up in that small ship," Amari said, walking along with the two men. "Tell us, Kasit, are there other settlements in the Ghostmist Nebula aside from Garanod Enclave?"

"Yes," Kasit said. "But you can't get to them from here, if that's your question."

"I don't understand. Are they too far away?" Amari asked.

"Ghostmist messes with everything," Kasit said. "The only reason Garanod exists at all is because it's clear sailing between the jump point and here. The nebula is filled with electrical storms, magnetic field disturbances, et cetera. Point is, even if your ship doesn't get shutdown due to all of that, your sensors have nothing to hold onto, so you get lost. Ships that go out don't come back, even though we know there are at least four settlements out there somewhere."

"How does that work? Are they self-sustaining?"

"There's something called a nav cipher. It's worth as much as your ship, maybe more," he said. "That nav cipher shows the navigation lanes that lead to other colonies. The whole reason Garanod is so big is that people got this before they realized they needed a cipher. Also, this is our elevator," Kasit said, stepping over and hitting a button.

"Is this cipher a real thing, or just a rumor?" Rix asked.

Kasit laughed, seemingly caught off guard. "Yeah, for sure it's real. Every once in a while, we'll have a ship come in from one of the lost colonies looking to trade. The only way they can do that is with a cipher. They talk funny, but not funnier than you Galactics."

"And the colonists, they have these ciphers?" Amari asked.

"They did when they were taken out there. It's the only way to find anything in the nebula, even Garanod, if you don't come through the jump point like you did."

"The abundance of usable gases and warm ambient temperatures could be a significant draw. I'm not sure I'd want to get stuck here, though," Amari said.

"There's a rumor about a guy who knew how to make those ciphers but best I know he's gone," Kasit said. "Or maybe he's hiding. Who knows?"

As they'd pushed the pallets and talked, they'd run across more and more people, many of whom were carrying packages or bags already full of supplies needed for the day.

"People get up and going early around here," Rix observed.

"Not much to do in Garanod other than work," Kasit said. "The deals are better in the morning. Vendors are looking to make their marks so they can shut down early."

"Since you don't have trade partners, because of Ghostmist, is everything made here or harvested in one of the districts?" Rix asked.

"Pretty much. That's why folks are so interested in your freighter showing up," Kasit said. "Who knows what crazy stuff you guys might be hauling? Oh, and that's Bha'resh up there."

Rix followed the direction Kasit pointed to. A large, faded orange awning with dingy white stripes topped a semi-permanent structure with benches both inside and out. Like in most of the shops on that level, numerous customers milled about.

"Ah, Kasit," a gregarious Vesh man said, walking up to greet them. "I've been waiting for you. Introduce me to our new friend."

"Rix Banner," Rix said, extending his hand to the aquamarine-colored alien. Like Kha'rem, the Vesh man had no hair on his body, and his skin was so shiny, it looked like it might squeak if one ran a finger along it.

"A custom from Galactic Empire?" Bha'resh asked, extending his hand and accepting the shake.

"My home world, Earth," Rix said. "We're not part of the Galactic Empire, but that's a whole other story."

"Perhaps you will stay long enough to share this story with Bha'resh," Bha'resh said, smiling kindly as Rix released his hand. "Tell me. What brings the excitement of Galactic travelers to my humble market this day?"

"Kha'rem said you are the best," Rix said.

"Did he, now? Does this conversation have to do with the crates you have labored so hard to bring this way? Let us go inside. We will sit and drink tea as we discover if we have common interests," Bha'resh said, turning to Amari and exchanging bows with her. "Surely, a beautiful woman enjoys tea."

"Yes. Tea, and perhaps directions to where an early meal could be had," Amari said.

"Let it not be said that Bha'resh does not know how to extend hospitality to travelers," Bha'resh said. "I will send out this moment for a delightful meal. If we are unable to find commerce between us, at least we will have shared sustenance."

"You're quite the charmer, aren't you?" Amari asked, hooking her arm into Bha'resh's as they walked to his establishment.

Amari's casual acceptance of the man immediately gained her favor with him, so much so that Kasit and Rix shared an amused look, both smiling. "Did you know it was me and Wagg who sent you that comm? I didn't know if you got it, but something you said last night made me think you did," Kasit said.

"I wondered who'd sent that," Rix said. "Thank you. We'd have struggled with the flotilla headed our way."

"That's a funny word. We don't exactly float in space. It's a funny image."

"Where I come from, we don't have spaceships. The closest idea are our ships that float on top of the massive oceans of my world," Rix said, unbinding the strap that held his crates in place.

"Like the Kor'vesh Sea, but not inside the planetoid?" Kasit asked, clearly trying to make sense of the idea.

"My planet, Earth, is twenty times the size of all of Garanod Enclave, if those planetoids were pushed back together into a big globe," Rix said. "Three quarters of that globe is covered by oceans."

"And it does not evaporate into the cloud?"

"We're not in a nebula," Rix said. "Instead, the gravity of the planet is strong enough to hold atmosphere in place. The oceans do have evaporation, but those just make clouds that float over land and drop the water back down in what we call rain."

'What a strange world," Kasit pondered. "No spaceships, but people move in these boats across the seas. Does it take a long time?"

"Weeks, most of the time. We also have airplanes, which look like spaceships, but are designed to fly through our atmosphere, kept aloft by their engines and wings," Rix said. "It's more complex than that, but you get the idea. I lived in a place that, if you walked from one side to the other, it would take over a hundred days of doing nothing but walking."

"Crazy," Kasit said, setting the final crate onto the bench identified by Bha'resh. Kasit picked up one of the pallets and stacked in on the other. "I'll go back for the last crates, then?"

"You don't have access to the cargo pod," Rix said. "I'll go with you."

"Bha'resh is waiting for you," Kasit said.

"It's only twenty minutes. Hey, Amari, I'm going back for the last load, okay?"

"I'll be here."

Rix didn't miss the disappointment that flashed across Kasit's face as he spoke, though it dissipated as quickly as it appeared. The pair walked back together, continuing their chat about differences between their home worlds. Rix was keenly interested in the political and criminal factions of Garanod, and Kasit was fascinated by the expanse of the Galactic Empire. Once they were back at the cargo pod, Rix opened up and they loaded the final crates onto the grav pallet.

"Thank you for your help, Kasit," Rix said, handing him a small gold coin worth roughly forty Galactic credits.

"Wow, thank you!" Kasit answered, impressed by the size of the tip.

Rix pushed his cart back, enjoying the unusual views of the totally alien marketplace bustling to life, as it likely did every morning.

"Bha'resh has cakes and a flavored protein. You'll like both," Amari said, pushing a plate to Rix as he sat at the table upon his return. "We were just talking about how it's possible to have a successful civilization without a primary government or law enforcement."

"No law enforcement, or no *centralized* law enforcement?" Rix asked.

"Ah, a nuanced and insightful question," Bha'resh said. "We do, in fact, enforce a sort of code that, as far as I know, has never been recorded. It is up to family groups and other organizations as to how that enforcement is implemented."

"Are Vesh a family group? Or are there Vesh in other organizations?" Rix asked.

"It is both. Half of us recognize the old ways."

"When you say half, how many people are we talking about?"

"Six thousand," Bha' resh said. Rix nodded.

"Thank you for the tea and breakfast," he said after a moment, enjoying the flat cake, which had dark, sweet fruits embedded within it.

"You are certainly welcome. How long will you be at Garanod?" Bha'resh asked.

"Four more nights," Rix said. "But on this kind of trip, just about anything is possible."

"It is wise to be open to the whims of the universe," Bha'resh said. "I have to admit considerable curiosity to the contents of your crates."

"Would it be rude to start looking now?" Rix asked.

"Not at all," Bha'resh said, standing.

Rix joined him, Amari remaining behind to let them work, and with a bar provided by the alien, Rix popped the tops open on four conveniently oriented crates. "Ship parts, some new, most of them used. This crate has parts that need a little repair. I have what's needed to do the repair, but I haven't had time to get around to the work."

"You're able to repair the broken assemblies?" Bha'resh asked.

"It depends on the problem," Rix said. "But yes, for those in this crate, I just need my tools and some bench time."

"Would you accept that we lay your items out onto these benches? I assure you, no one will steal from a bench beneath my roof," Bha'resh said.

They spent the next thirty minutes unloading the twelve crates. Speaking only the efficient words of two people of similar mind, they organized the parts by function and current condition.

"What do you think?" Rix finally asked. "Can you help me find buyers for any of this?"

"We will certainly sell all of it within the next few days," Bha'resh said. "I will reach out to those I know have specific needs. We will get the best prices for those pieces. After that, I will bring in those who have the equipment that matches parts, even though that equipment is still in good working order."

"Because, you never know when you'll get a chance to find that part?" Rix asked.

"Exactly," Bha'resh said. "My part of this is twenty-five in one hundred. What currency will you accept?"

"Galactic Empire credits and precious metal would be first place for me. I talked to Kha'rem, though and discovered there's no reasonable exchange rate for Galactic credits. I'm not sure how to work with that."

"If you provide the current exchange between gold and a Galactic credit, I can translate our asking price," Bha'resh said.

"According to Kha'rem, Galactic credits don't have much value here. Couldn't we get a little more than a strict conversion, given the lack of value of Galactic credits here?"

"It is possible," Bha'resh said. "The low value is accompanied by low availability and equally low demand."

"Let's ask for precious metal, in that case, or thirty percent markup on Galactic Empire credits," Rix said.

"That approach is reasonable. Let's discuss pricing of individual items. Do you have a mechanism to easily translate grams of platinum to value you can approve for sale?" Bha'resh asked. "Otherwise, I have a computational device that will show such a translation."

"I have this," Beverly said. "Once he prices a few items, I should be able to give you expected prices for the remainder of the lot."

"My HUD is capable of making those sorts of calculations," Rix said.

The work was laborious, at first, as Bha'resh set a device next to the highest priority items and started tapping away at a keyboard that somewhat resembled a typewriter, but had unrecognizable shapes and figures.

"Thermal transfer unit for an FE-402 exhaust port," Bha'resh started. "I know someone who needs this now. I'd offer a trade of six point two grams of platinum."

"Gross is four hundred sixty-five Galactic credits, minus Bha'resh's commission nets, three hundred forty-eight credits," Beverly said. "Newly manufactured, this part costs five hundred two credits on Patience Station."

"That's a reasonable price," Rix said, considering the wear on the part.

"It should be, I know a buyer. We'll have to work harder on some of the others. Continue?"

"Go for it. I have that price recorded."

"We might be forced to negotiate, so be careful about taking that price too literally," Bha'resh said.

"I understand," Rix said. "I could take a twenty percent haircut on that trade and still feel good about it."

"Haircut?" Bha'resh asked and then chuckled as he understood. "A funny idiom for one without hair."

"Sorry."

"Oh, these linkage couplers will be a hot item. Many Galactic Empire manufactures use identical parts," Bha'resh said. "Two grams platinum each, and we'll sell out by lunch time. Perhaps we could start at two point five and see who is in greater need."

Just then, a man with burnt-orange-colored skin walked up to the benches and started picking up parts, turning them over in his hands. "Where did this come from, Bha'resh?" the man asked.

"Fresh from the empire," Bha'resh said, nodding toward Rix. "We're working through the inventory. Do you see something you're specifically interested in?"

"I'd like this power concentrator," the man said. "I'll give one hundred ninety credits."

Rix was about to accept the offer, but something in Bha'resh's posture caused him to pause and wait for his word. Bha'resh nodded. "We are accepting precious and Galactic Empire credits. I'll have to add a cost if I am to convert local credits to precious."

"Galactic? There isn't that much around," the man said. "Would you take one hundred forty Galactic Empire credits?"

"I'm afraid that is in the wrong direction," Bha'resh said. "Could you come up with two hundred five Galactic Empire credits?"

"For a power concentrator?" the man asked, taken aback.

"Yes. A refurbished and provable concentrator in immaculate shape," Bha'resh said. "Come back tomorrow, if I haven't sold it for two hundred fifty Galactic credits, I'll let you have it for two hundred."

"What about these?" the man asked, picking up three smaller parts. "Throw them in and we're getting somewhere."

"Half a gram of platinum, or fifty Galactic credits, each," Bha'resh said.

"Do you sleep well at night, charging these prices?"

"I do," Bha'resh said. "My children are fed when I make a living wage. My wife has clothing and our home has heat. Knowing the value of these parts is what makes all that possible."

"You have to give me something, here," the man said, setting the four parts together.

"Three hundred Galactic credits, or four point five grams platinum," Bha'resh said.

Rix quirked an eyebrow as Bha'resh presented the platinum exchange, which was more valuable than the credits. If the man wasn't tracking, he'd pay full price in platinum.

"Put it aside for me? I need to go back to my hovel and fetch the Galactic credit chits to see what I have," the man said.

"I will keep these for you until after the lunch rest," Bha'resh said.

This earned the trader a dirty look, but no more words were exchanged.

"You know your business," Rix said. "I expected him to walk."

"He could not. He has posted a request for that concentrator on the community board each of the last five months," Bha'resh said. "I had intended to reach out to him this afternoon."

And so the morning went, with customers filtering in as Bha'resh and Rix worked through the inventory until they were finally down to the box of assemblies awaiting repair. With tools fetched from *Gravitational Pull,* Rix sat at the end of one of the benches and continued the work he'd started on the journey over.

"What a prosperous day we've had," Bha'resh said. "Over a quarter of the parts have been sold. I've lined up many to come over tomorrow. I will be surprised if, by the end of tomorrow, we have not moved five-eighths of what you brought."

"How are we looking, Rix?" Amari asked, stretching as she stood.

"Bha'resh is quite a salesman. Our cut is six thousand two hundred thirty, if you consider a stable price for platinum exchange," Rix said.

"Rix, you are receiving a communication request. At its center, Kha'rem has extended an invitation to dinner and warns that a representative from Gray will be present," Beverly announced, having switched back to her normal jumpsuit.

"This is Rix."

"What is your status, Rix Banner?" Kha'rem asked.

"We're about to close down for the day here at Bha'resh's," Rix said. "I wouldn't mind a quick shower, but I suppose that depends on how soon we're meeting for dinner."

"Ah, very well, I did not know if you were amenable to a meal this evening," Kha'rem said. "Could you be ready in sixty minutes? I will pick you up at your pier, if it is convenient."

"We'll be ready," Rix said and closed comms. "Bha'resh, how can I help get things settled for the evening?"

"Ah, it is a simple matter of pulling closed the security screens. Your inventory will be quite safe within," Bha'resh said. "Do you need directions on how to return to your vessel?"

"No, I have them," Rix said.

"Very well. I look forward to our visit tomorrow, in that case," Bha'resh said.

Rix nodded and he and Amari excused themselves. "Was that a good day?" Amari asked. "It seems like the prices held up."

"With Bha'resh's commission, we're still up forty percent on what I could hope to get for these parts on Patience," Rix said.

"Kel, are you available?" Rix called.

"I was just about to call you," she answered. "We've got a problem."

"What kind of problem?"

"A Greevo kind," she said. "He's lost something valuable and is tearing the ship apart. He thinks we took whatever it is."

"This will be fun," Rix said. "I'm on my way."

22

BREAKING AND ENTERING

KASIT SHOOK his head as he left Bha'resh's store, tension filling every part of him. If he got caught stealing from the Galactics while under Kha'rem's guard, he would lose his job and all the goodwill he'd built with the enigmatic entrepreneur who, to date, had treated him more like a son than an employee. Lirren Vos and Busk's threats against his mother overrode any potential he had for resisting. Then, to have come so close to the item, and finding no capacity to filch it, had left him on edge.

"Where is it?" a low voice asked as a thick hand fell on Kasit's neck, just above his shoulder.

The voice belonged to Busk, and Kasit's blood ran cold. Busk had the eyes of a killer--not the sort of person one would want knowing their name, much less having an unmet expectation from. "I didn't get it," Kasit said. "It's locked up in the cargo pod."

Busk pulled Kasit to the side and slammed him into the wall. "You were within two meters. Why didn't you grab it?"

"Rix Banner and the alien woman were right there. It was in a crate. I couldn't have gotten to it without them stopping me," Kasit defended.

"Did you not bring a weapon?" Busk asked, pulling him forward just to smash him back into the wall. Kasit glanced at the passersby, each of whom looked away and hurried about their business, not wanting to get dragged into the altercation.

"I don't have a weapon. That wasn't the deal. I wasn't supposed to have to hurt anyone," Kasit sputtered.

Busk punched Kasit in the stomach, folding him over as he coughed with pain. When Kasit came up for a breath, Busk once again forced him against the wall. "You're going to put this on," Busk said, pushing a mask into Kasit's hand. "Then you're going to come up beneath that pod, cut out an access panel and get me that cipher. Do you hear me? Am I making sense to you, Kasit? Or do I need to go back and make sure Zenith understands just how badly you screwed this up?"

"No, no, I understand. Don't hurt Zenith," Kasit said.

"That's all up to you."

"I don't have cutting tools."

"Good. You're thinking it through, now. Tools are in an exchange locker on the H level, H192," Busk said. "Here's a key. Now get moving, and don't screw this up. I'd hate to have to show Zenith just how disappointed I am in you."

"I understand. Please don't hurt her," Kasit begged.

"Like I told you. that's up to you. Do what you've been told, and not only will we release your mother, but you'll make a tidy little profit. You've had your stick, maybe now you'll work for your carrot, eh?"

Busk released Kasit's neck and brushed at his shirt, as if tidying up a mess he'd neglected. He locked eyes with Kasit until Kasit broke and looked away, then he turned and walked off. Kasit slumped, his legs almost giving out from the adrenaline and anxiety coursing through his body. He rested his hands on his knees and took several deep breaths.

Setting off at a quick walk after recovering, Kasit hurried to where the exchange lockers were located. Level H was only half a kilometer away, and he easily located locker H192. With the electronic key in hand, he opened and extracted a small tool bag. Looking inside, he found a cutting rig, something he hadn't previously used, and a few other tools.

Scanning the surrounding area, Kasit immediately felt guilty for what he was about to do. He felt like all eyes were on him, but when he looked around, no one was paying any attention. He dropped the bag to his side and walked away from the locker.

As he moved, Kasit focused on his plan for gaining access to the cargo pod. In the past, he and Wagg had spent plenty of time crawling through the crisscross of support bars that held the large pier structures fronting the more industrial sections of Driftmarket. Coming from below, he looped the bag's strap over his sore shoulder and slowly climbed until he was within a few meters of the docked vessels.

Kasit sat in the cross bracing, staring out past the clutter of the markets and out into the nebula for some time. What he wouldn't give to be able to leave Garanod Enclave. Without a strong family, he, Zenith and Wagg would always be at the mercy of every criminal organization. Tears glistened on his cheeks, smearing as he gathered himself and wiped his face. He was about to cross a line he was sure he'd never come back from. Kha'rem would eventually figure out his part in the events, and then he would be banned from the only job he'd ever had.

Foot traffic above wasn't substantial. Kasit waited for a few Vesh who were passing through before he swung out to the edge of the bottom side of the dock. He then passed hand over hand on the rungs beneath the wide walk that extended to the now closed and locked cargo pod hatch.

Reaching out and clamping a magnetic hook in place, Kasit swung out and anchored his harness, allowing him to dangle beneath the cargo pod. His memory of the arrangement of remaining crates was solid, and he picked a location that he believed would not be directly beneath the cargo.

It took a few minutes for Kasit to figure out how to operate the cutting rig. He discovered it wasn't as complicated as he had expected. Moreover, the rig was designed to cut thick steel and he made quick progress, swiftly opening a section just big enough for his body to slip through. Before the cutout fell from the pod, he latched it in place using a magnetic clamp, which was connected via cable to another clamp.

He rested once the cutout was free, fighting to keep his pulse in check. Watching a temperature display, Kasit waited almost twenty minutes for the decking to cool enough that it wouldn't burn his skin through his jumpsuit if he inadvertently touched it. Slithering up inside the cargo pod was equal parts terrifying and exhilarating. He was in a place he had no right to be. If he was caught, there would be considerable trouble, but there was certainly a thrill to it.

"I shouldn't be here," Kasit whispered to himself, unable to help but voice his emotions as he pulled out the sensor he'd muted in his pocket. Flashlight in one hand and sensor in the other, he hovered over the top of the remaining crates. It was just then when he heard a commotion outside of the cargo pod. The sounds of Grintok arguing filtered in. There was no doubt in his mind that they were going to enter the pod, and his heart hammered like he'd been sprinting at top speed.

With a flat bar, Kasit opened the crate containing the cipher, cringing which each creak or clatter of the container. The device was a simple box, not much bigger than his hand. Meticulously crafted, though not much to look at, truthfully, Kasit could only wonder how it worked, but a clunk outside warned that he had no time to lose. Stashing the device in his jumpsuit, Kasit dropped his legs through the hole and clung on just long enough to attach to the magnetic clamp before releasing his hold on the cargo pod.

Voices filtered through the pod as the large aft hatch creaked open. Kasit was about to be caught red-handed, and he searched for any way to cover his tracks. It was then that he recalled the heavy cargo pads that were piled on top of some of the crates. Risking everything, he pulled himself back into the cargo pod, snatching the corner of a pad. Lights flicked on, but he had sank back through the floor, leaving the cargo pad to block the opening he'd made.

The voices grew louder as Grintok discussed which crates they were to bring back. Kasit knew that if one of them stepped through the hole, he'd be caught, so he made another bold move. Lifting the square piece he'd removed from the pod back into place, he shifted the magnetic clamps so that they held it steady, if not strong enough to hold the weight of someone standing on it. He then went a step further and cycled through settings on the cutting device, having earlier realized that it was a simple switch over to put into weld mode.

Kasit drew two short weld beads, the device making more noise than he had anticipated, and considerably more noise than he appreciated. His efforts were, to his frustration, rewarded with alerted Grintok.

"Hear that?" one asked.

"Shhh, quiet," another said. "Smell something burn?"

"No hear anything. Bad smell in cargo all time," yet another added. "Must hurry. Greevo in big hurry. Big sale. Much money."

Kasit hung frozen in place, waiting for the activity above to settle down.

"I no find case," the first said. "This crate right. No case like Greevo say."

"Oh, no. Greevo will blame. Big mad. We run."

"No. Greevo big mad, yes. Greevo make fists, yes. Greevo know not us."

Based on the conversation, Kasit imagined things were about to get quite a bit louder. With the Grintok above arguing about who would tell Greevo, he knew he had to use their noise as cover for his movements. Repacking the tool bag, he reversed his trail and ducking back beneath the dock, rushing to retreat to the dark corners. Once safe under the cover of the dock, he slowed, slinking away undetected.

23

SCENE OF THE CRIME

"Rix Banner! Thief!" Greevo spluttered as Rix and Amari entered the cargo pod, where all remaining crates lay strewn about, emptied, turned over or both. Pulling items from the crates were the four female Grintok who'd accompanied him.

The small green alien ran at Rix while wielding a metal pipe. Instead of responding in kind, Rix held his ground, wondering if Greevo would actually hit him. He did not.

"What's the problem here, Greevo?" Rix asked, already tired of the conversation.

"You took. Rix Banner criminal!" Greevo seethed.

"Took what?"

"Rix Banner take crates?" Greevo asked.

"I did," Rix said. "I had twelve crates piled against the starboard bulkhead. I've verified they contained the contents I packed. I don't have anything of yours. Of this I'm certain."

"Who else let in? Who has key?" Greevo demanded.

"Kasit was with me this morning, but he was just helping me load crates," Rix said. "He was never in the cargo pod by himself. What is it you're missing?"

"Do not act no knowing," Greevo hissed, tearing through the nearest crate and tossing the packing and contents to the deck. "Rix Banner made good plan. Steal Greevo best stuff."

"I have no idea what you're talking about. Did you maybe leave it on *Calypso*, or possibly in *Gravitational Pull*?"

"Oh, he's already looked there. Both ships are totally ransacked," Kel sighed, rounding the corner. Greevo turned toward her and glared. "Are you off your meds, Greevo?" she scoffed at him. "You need to calm down. We didn't take whatever it is you think we took. And, if you had something that valuable, you should have told us so we could safeguard it, too."

"All my crates valuable," Greevo insisted, suddenly dropping his trusty pipe and grasping a fistful of her jumpsuit as he yanked her down so they were eye to eye. "Kel Warp took! Tell Greevo where!"

It was Greevo's worst mistake so far, and Rix wondered how Kel would deal with him. Consequence caught up to the fuming green alien almost immediately, as Kel tipped her head back and then, with a quick snap, smashed Greevo's large nose with her forehead. Bone popping preceded a high-pitched keening as Greevo reeled away from Kel, releasing her jumpsuit. His heel caught on the debris left behind by his search, and he fell into a pile of packing and unforgiving spaceship parts.

"Kel Warp, no attack!" Kitka screeched. "No hurt Big Boss!"

"Big Boss better keep his grubby mitts off of me if he wants to keep using that nose to move O2," Kel said. "Nobody lays hands on me without my permission. Nobody."

Rix got between the two and knelt next to Greevo, helping him to a seated position as Amari moved to calm Kel. "Kitka, get the med kit from *Calypso*. We have a bone set kit, but we need to get it applied before his nose starts healing itself. Go, now, quick!" Rix ordered.

"He had it coming," Kel defended, clearly beginning to regret her earlier choice.

"Kel Warp strong," Greevo said reverently between gasps of air in which he, of course, couldn't help but exhale through his broken nose, spraying blood droplets everywhere.

Kel handed a cloth to Rix, which he held against Greevo's face. "Not exactly the response I'd expect from a headbutt," Rix said.

"He's had that coming for the last three light years," Kel continued, still irritated. "Wait until you see what he did to *Gravitational Pull*."

"I thought I had him locked out."

"Kitka let him in."

With a sigh, Rix waited for Kitka to return with the bone set med kit. It didn't take long. "This is going to pinch a little," Rix warned Greevo. "Kel, hold his head stable. He's not going to like this."

"With joy," Kel said, kneeling behind the still-seated Grintok and grabbing his head by the ears.

"No help!" Greevo complained as Rix moved in. Kitka and the others who'd come with Greevo crept closer, and Rix felt a hand on his arm as he reached for Greevo's nose with a rig designed to slide into the nostrils.

"Hard," Kitka advised, forcing Rix's arm forward. "Grintok, long passage."

The device slid further into Greevo's nose than Rix was comfortable with, but, as with most devices from Galactic Empire, the adjustable splint seated itself and performed diagnostics with little more assistance than the initial push into place. The sound of cracking lasted only a split second before it was covered by Greevo's howl of pain.

"Do you want to tell me what you lost? Maybe we can help find it," Rix offered after the pain killers in the bone set kit had kicked in.

"No. Rix Banner already know. Thief," Greevo said, spitting. "You owe Greevo much credits."

"Clean up this mess, Greevo. You're not leaving my cargo pod looking like this," Rix said. "And I won't tell you again that we didn't take your precious whatever-it-is." Knowing that Greevo wasn't the sort to back down, Rix motioned Kel and Amari to the aft exit, and the three exited. "Talk to me, Kel," Rix said, once outside the cargo pod. "Do you have any idea what his issue is?"

"No idea," Kel said. "But he trashed *Calypso* and *Gravitational Pull*."

"Okay, let's see what we're working with," Rix said with resignation. *Gravitational Pull* was closest, so the trio walked out onto the extended visitor's ramp and into what Rix and Amari referred to as the basement. Rix's eyes fell on open cabinets, the contents of which had been dumped on the deck. Worse, just beneath the ladder going up to the main deck, a pile of torn-open, yet uneaten, foodstuffs carpeted the deck.

"He's lost his mind," Amari observed under her breath, incredulous.

"I'm glad you broke his nose, Kel," Rix said. "Because I'm thinking about rebreaking it, now. Replacing this food will be expensive. Who knows what else he ruined?"

"This is the least offensive part," Kel warned.

Rix gingerly stepped through the piles of detritus and started up the ladder. When he reached the galley, he discovered that Kel wasn't wrong. Shredded bedrolls hung from the entrance to the bunk room, and more foodstuffs had been opened and tossed around. Even the old pilot's chairs had been slashed open, the stuffing within torn out and discarded.

"Is *Calypso* like this?" Rix asked, wishing he could avoid the answer.

"Worse," Kel said.

"Lock them out," Rix said, upset but unsurprised. "This is unacceptable."

"Good, I was going to ask."

"They can earn their way back on the ship by cleaning the mess and repairing the damage," Rix said. "We're leaving in three days. They'll need to make some choices."

"I say we leave them here."

"We need to figure out what has him turned upside down," Rix said. "Anyone have any ideas?"

"I might," Beverly said, appearing atop a mound of bedroll stuffing. She wore wooden skis, a thick coat and a knit hat.

"You're a skier?" Rix asked.

"1952 Winter Olympics are coming up in a year," she said, gliding down the white stuffing while making perfect turns.

"Cute," Rix approved. "What is it you think you know?"

"We need to ask for video from Kha'rem," Beverly said. "It is likely that someone broke into the cargo pod while we were away. But, given Greevo's search, we may infer the size of the object, or objects, missing to be of a smaller size, something that might be carried."

"I hate to point fingers," Amari said, "But I'd look at Kasit."

"Why? We were with him the entire time he was in the cargo pod," Rix said, raising an eyebrow. He'd taken a liking to the young man and didn't want to accuse him of stealing.

"We were, and he was carrying some sort of tracker," she said.

"The beeping that went off when we were loading the grav pallets?"

"That's right," Amari nodded. "He turned it off, but if you paid attention, after that, he was nervous, and he even volunteered to come back and pick up the last load by himself."

"Beverly, did you notice anything unusual from Kasit?"

"In reviewing Kasit's actions in the cargo pod, I would say that there could be a correlation between Greevo's loss and the sensor alarm that he carried," Beverly said. "Unfortunately, Greevo did such a wonderful job of deconstructing the scene, I am unable to draw conclusions as to what is missing from this morning."

"Can you look for things that might be out of the ordinary?" Rix said. "What did Kasit's sensor trip on?"

"I believe the sensor detected something inside of a crate," Beverly said. "I reviewed the data I gathered this morning, and there were no objects outside of the crates when we were with Kasit in the cargo pod."

"That's what I thought, too," Amari said.

"Well, hold on, can't we check the door log to see who entered and exited?" Rix asked. "If it wasn't us, who was it?"

"There were no other accesses until Kitka and the other Grintok showed up and discovered the theft," Beverly said.

"No accesses through the door, you mean," Rix corrected.

"A cargo pod has no other entry points," Beverly argued.

"Not usually, no," Rix said. "It's just a couple sheets of steel, though. It wouldn't be that hard to breach."

"Is that what you think happened?"

"I have no idea," Rix said. "I know how to find out, though."

"Go and look inside the pod?" Amari guessed.

"You could, but I'd look from the outside," Rix said. "It'll be obvious if someone cut in if you look around the outside. Inside, there are crates in the way. It'd be quite a lot of work to move them all. Come on."

Grabbing a line and a pair of magnetic boots, Rix exited *Gravitational Pull* and fastened the safety line he'd become accustomed to. With a broad-beamed flashlight, it took him only a few minutes to find the point of entry.

"What'd you see?" Amari asked, helping Rix up to the dock.

"Someone broke in," he confirmed, walking around to where Greevo and the other Grintok threw crates around in a desperate search. "Beverly, can you locate the breach?"

A translucent blue oval landed atop a cargo pad that had been partially kicked aside. Greevo crossed into Rix's way, but Rix pushed him aside, uninterested in dealing with the little alien any further. Rix peeled up the end of the pad, exposing an imperfectly cut opening in the floor of the pod.

"That's where your cargo went, Greevo," Rix said, pointing at the hole.

24

LIABILITY

A PISTOL APPEARED in Greevo's hand, levelled at Rix. "You responsible," Greevo growled. "Steal Greevo's nav cipher. Rix Banner give back or die today."

Faster than Rix could comprehend, Amari lunged forward, lashing out with her hand, which struck Greevo's wrist. Rix dodged, fully expecting to be fired on, but the gun remained silent. The impact of Amari's strike knocked the weapon from Greevo's grasp. Amari plucked the weapon from the space between them, smoothing out her clothing nonchalantly as she handed it to Rix.

Rix and Greevo shared a few confused blinks as they processed the shift in power dynamics. Fast as Amari's strike had been, it was equally as precise , which had allowed her to use minimal force. Both men struggled to adapt to the turn of events.

"Greevo, I'll do what I can to help you find your cargo," Rix began, gaining his footing. "But, if you were carrying something of particularly high value, it was your responsibility to let us know so we could take extra precautions. A cargo pod is hardly a high-security container, and you know it," Rix said.

"Rix Banner stole cipher," Greevo said.

"Knock it off, Greevo."

"No pay services," Greevo said petulantly. "Losses more than Greevo owe."

Rix ignored him. "Maybe we should stop arguing and see if we can get some help recovering your nav cipher."

"Shh! No name!" Greevo said. "People no know Greevo have."

"That's the problem, Greevo. We *don't* have it. And I don't even know what it is you're talking about," Rix said. "I do know that Kha'rem has guards and video monitoring. If we go to him and ask, he might be able to help."

"Him! Kha'rem stole! Too happy give protection. Too nice,"," Greevo declared.

"Buddy, you gotta knock it off with the accusation thing. You're not going to get any help if you keep that up," Rix said. "I'll call him and let him know we had some cargo go missing and how it was taken. I don't have to mention your nav cipher."

"Stop! No name!" Greevo shrieked. "And give Greevo gun. Mine."

"You lost this gun when you pointed it at me," Rix said. "I'm keeping it."

"Rix Banner thief."

"No, Rix Banner isn't giving a weapon to someone who is unstable and has threatened to shoot Rix Banner. I bet you can work that one out, if you think about it."

"Greevo no threaten shoot."

"You're still not getting the gun," Rix said, turning his attention. "Bev, raise Kha'rem on comms."

"You handled that very well, Rix," Beverly said, appearing before him in a striped prison uniform. "Before you speak with Kha'rem, I would like to ask if you know what a nav cipher is."

Rix stepped away from the encounter with Greevo and walked to the end of the cargo pod. "Really, with the jailbird uniform?" Rix asked. "And no. Kasit mentioned something about it, but I wasn't really paying attention, I guess."

"A navigation cipher is commonly used in densely packed or other difficult navigational areas," Beverly said. "If such a thing exists for Ghostmist, its value would be inestimable."

"I don't understand."

"Travel through most regions of the Ghostmist Nebula is nearly impossible. Our jump crystals placed us in a location with a line of sight on Garanod Enclave. Without that, the interference of the nebula is such that normal sensors and their positioning systems are defunct. It would be like dropping someone in the middle of one of Earth's oceans in a boat that had no windows, with compasses that didn't work."

"The cipher fixes that?"

"I haven't had a chance to inspect Greevo's cipher," Beverly admitted. "But yes. Likely, it also has the locations of other settlements and ways to escape the nebula. It's possible there's access to parts of the Galactic Empire recorded within this cipher. The possibilities are endless."

"How did anyone even know we had it?"

"That's a question for Greevo."

"I don't think he's ready to talk," Rix said. "How big of a device are we talking about? Size of a suitcase, or size of a refrigerator?"

"It could be anything, but I cannot imagine larger than a suitcase, given where it was located within the cargo pod, not to mention the size of the crate it was in," Beverly reminded him, easing some his concern. "Are you ready to speak with Kha'rem?"

"Yes." Beverly had comms pulled up the instant the word left Rix's mouth.

"Greetings, my friend Rix Banner. We were just speaking of you, admiring the courage required to cross the vastness the Galactic Empire into the unknown wilderness of the Ghostmist," Kha'rem said. "How might I be of best assistance to you this fine evening?"

"I apologize for interrupting, Kha'rem," Rix said. "We've had a break in on one of our cargo pods. A piece of equipment, valuable, by Greevo's account, was stolen. I was hoping we could gain access to your video surveillance."

"Oh, my, that is certainly distressing. Are my men not watching over your pods? How is it possible something was taken?" Kha'rem asked.

"Your men are in place. Someone came from below and cut a hole in the pod," Rix said. "They knew what they were looking for and extracted just that item."

"I see," Kha'rem said. "I will break from my friends and meet you on the pier. There is, as you have inferred, video surveillance. The coverage from below, however, is not fully encompassing. We will speak when I arrive."

"Thank you, Kha'rem. Please give my apologies to your guests for the disruption," Rix said.

"Yes. I will be with you shortly."

"What Rix Banner doing?" Greevo stormed in, gripping Rix's arm and dragging him around. "Conspire? Sell Greevo property?"

"I've called Kha'rem, and he's coming down to give us access to his video surveillance," Rix said, grasping Greevo's giant hand and prying it from his arm. "Greevo, I know you've taken a loss tonight, and I'm willing to be forgiving about your behavior to a point, but you need to get something straight. If you keep acting like an ass, you will not get any help from anyone here. Kha'rem has no responsibility for what's in our cargo pods. There are no laws here to be broken. You hid your treasure, and someone learned of its presence. Both are fully your responsibility. We had a saying in The War—loose lips sink ships."

Rix wanted to continue, but Greevo had heard enough. "Rix Banner responsible!" he stomped. "Not good cargo hauler! Greevo tell everyone!"

"Are you done with your tantrum? Because I am," Rix clenched his jaw. "You are officially locked out of both of our vessels. You have access to this cargo pod because you continue to store your goods aboard. You will remove those goods within twenty-four hours. The nonpayment threat has removed you from the return voyage," Rix said. "I'm done with you acting like a child. I will talk to Kha'rem for you, only because I would like to help recover your item. Beyond that, our business is done."

"Banner ...," Greevo spluttered. Rix had no interest in further conversation and stepped out of the cargo pod onto the pier. He could feel Greevo's eyes trying to drill holes in his back as he walked, but he did not turn around.

One of the two guards Kha'rem had assigned approached Rix. It was clear he'd received news from Kha'rem, as he bore a look of concern. "I am Bleca. I lead security for Kha'rem. What has happened?"

"There was a theft from the aft cargo pod," Rix said. "Something specific and valuable was stolen."

"The cargo pod has not been opened except by your crew," Bleca responded

"I believe that's true," Rix agreed. "A hole was cut in the floor from below with a plasma cutter. That's how the thief gained entry," Rix said.

"What is it that was stolen?"

"Greevo, the owner of the load, is not willing to share that information," Rix said. "It wasn't a large item. I don't know sizes beyond that. We're hoping security video shows something."

"Spetla is reviewing the video now," Bleca said. "Do you know the time when it was taken? That would speed our inquiry."

"No," Rix said, shaking his head. "Is there video recording beneath the dock that would have a view below?"

"No. It is not designed for that type of surveillance. Perhaps the wide angle will capture someone dipping below the pier. The thief's maneuver was quite dangerous. There is little to keep one from falling free to the levels below, and that would mean death, as it is hundreds of meters."

"Is there any chance whoever is below us would have a camera pointed up?" Rix asked.

"I will make inquiry, but it's unlikely. We are not directly above any industry; there is a yard toward center two kilometers, nothing closer."

"It is worth following up, but I understand."

"Can you be any more specific on the size of what has gone missing?" Bleca asked with little hope.

"Greevo has that information, but he is not in a civil mood," Rix said. "We'll ask him when he's more composed."

"Kha'rem has arrived," Bleca said, dipping his head toward the approaching Vesh.

"Greetings, Rix Banner," Kha'rem said. "I am grateful that you spoke with Bleca. Have you resolved anything in the short time I was en route?"

"No. Spetla is reviewing video to find a culprit," Rix said. "We're not optimistic, given the camera angles."

"Would you tell me what you know in this moment?" Kha'rem asked.

"Yes, but I cannot divulge the item without Greevo's permission," Rix replied.

"Did you guarantee security on your vessels during and after shipment?"

"No guarantee, but we feel some responsibility to make best efforts for securing items," Rix said.

"That is sensible," Kha'rem nodded.

"How about I walk you through what we know?"

Being that the details were few, the summarization took only a few minutes. Rix left out the actual name of the item stolen as he filled Kha'rem in, referring to it only as an item of high value.

"This was the only item stolen?" Kha'rem asked.

"I don't know. By the time I got to the scene, Greevo's team had unpacked so many of the remaining crates that I couldn't tell what was gone and what was just hidden in the mess. Further, we have no manifest to compare to, as Greevo didn't provide one, and I accepted that because we weren't sailing into a secured facility."

"A private load," Kha'rem noted. "I will speak further with Greevo on this matter. Given his hostility to your crew, I suggest I do this in private."

"That works for us," Rix said. "I'm done talking with him for a while. He's driving me nuts with his attitude."

"Perhaps you could prepare for our evening with the Gray representative," Kha'rem said. "I will be ready to escort you and your esteemed pilots in one hour. I understand these events are upsetting, but it would be beneficial to find a means to restore your balance. We do not want to bring angst to a negotiation with those such as the Gray."

"Message received. We'll be ready in an hour," Rix said. "Oh, also, Greevo might need some help finding lodging. He's no longer welcome on my vessels."

Kha'rem stilled for a moment. "Are you certain this is how you wish to proceed?"

"Is lodging difficult?" Rix asked. "We're packed in tightly in our ships, and we are not compatible in our hygiene. Add to that Greevo's stress, and we're better apart, I believe. Greevo knows he's off the ship. You're not delivering that news. Just a recommendation, if you have one."

"Very well," Kha'rem said. Rix sensed disappointment from the alien, but he was more than willing to live with that if it meant spending less time picking up Grintok trash and wiping grimy surfaces clean.

"Thank you, Kha'rem. I am grateful to have met you," Rix said.

Rix's statement coaxed Kha'rem's smile back to his face. "You have been a blessing to my tribe."

Walking back to *Calypso*, Rix carefully stole glances at Kha'rem as he approached a still-fiery Greevo. For a few tense moments, Rix wondered if he'd have to intervene, as Greevo gave it to Kha'rem with both barrels, furiously pointing at Rix and Kha'rem with accusation. Unable to make out the conversation, Rix was shocked when Greevo's livid babbling slowed, giving way to more rational speech.

"Will wonders never cease?" Rix said.

"What did Kha'rem have to say?" Amari asked, joining him as they entered *Calypso*.

"He and his team will get into it," Rix said. "There's no video from below, but they're going to look for any clues that might exist. Kha'rem feels some responsibility, just like we do."

"But not liability," Amari reminded him.

"I guess."

"It's important, Rix," Amari said. "You gave your best effort to secure his property in a locked and sealed container. Someone broke in, even though the cargo pod was under video surveillance. You don't owe Greevo anything."

"It still feels crappy. Greevo thought his stuff was safe. At some level, that was our responsibility."

"Right, and that responsibility was expressed in locks and finding a secure port," Kel said, joining the conversation. "We have a clause in our agreement that specifically states items are stored in our cargo pods at all facilities *at your own risk*. Cargo insurance is the mechanism required by all shippers to warrant safe arrival and delivery."

"Okay. Change of subject," Rix waved them off. "We have a dinner with a representative of the Gray organization tonight. We're all invited, including Philo. Have we seen him?"

"He's fallen hard for this Sta'ci," Kel said. "They came back by the ship for a minute to get Philo a shower and fresh clothing. I couldn't believe it. I got to talk to her for a couple of minutes. She's a sweet little thing."

"Isn't she Grintok?"

"Yes, but she doesn't act like a Grintok," Kel said. "She's all manners and sweetness. He might have met his match."

"Seriously? What will all the girls in every other port do now?" Rix asked.

"Right?" Kel asked. "There could be trouble."

Rix chuckled and then looked at Amari. "Want company showering?" he asked.

A smile played about Amari's lips. "What a lovely invitation. Yes, that sounds quite nice."

"Ugh, enough with couples already," Kel complained.

Setting his clothing into the cleaning device, Rix covered up with a towel and slipped into the small shower, which was only slightly larger than *Gravitational Pull's*. Turning the water on to a comfortable temperature, he started cleaning himself, knowing that another person in the shower would limit his movement. With water pounding on his head, he was unable to make out the conversation outside, but he could hear giggling between Kel and Amari.

"Room for two?" Amari asked, gliding into the shower with him.

"Always room for you," Rix said, trying to not to stare at the beautiful nude woman mere inches from his body.

"The awkwardness will lessen," Amari assured, placing a hand on Rix's chest and pressing up on her tiptoes to give him a quick kiss. "Thank you for being okay with this."

A million responses flashed through Rix's head. "I like being with you," he finally managed. Amari beamed.

"I like being with you, too," she said, dispensing soap into her hands and turning away from him.

"Can I wash your back?" he asked tentatively. "I'll be gentle."

"I'd like that," she breathed.

"And I'm sorry," he said.

"For what?"

"Showing ... interest, I guess."

"I imagine that's natural," she said laughing gently.

"Yeah," Rix managed.

"What do you suppose dinner will be like?" Amari asked, but before Rix could answer, she continued, "Oh, that's nice, Rix. Do that more."

Rix had been gently rubbing slightly raised lines on her back that he imagined were the support for her wings. Beneath the skin seemed to be some combination of muscle and bone, and the engineer in him was trying to identify how it might work with probing fingers.

"I was hoping this was okay," Rix said.

"Better than okay," Amari said quietly. "And I love your curiosity. Are you sure you're not a little freaked out by the differences between us?"

"You showed me before. You're just so intricate ... the detail is beautiful."

"I'll admit, that's a new response for me," she said.

"Trouble with previous boyfriends at this stage?"

"Enough that I make sure we take this part slowly. I've a healthy ego, but it can only take so much rejection," she said, turning to him.

"Do you want a minute to finish up? I'm good," he asked, wrapping his arms around her.

She leaned in and returned his hug, allowing hot water to cascade over their joined bodies. "Just a little more of this, okay?"

"Okay," he said quietly.

After a time, they separated, and Rix stepped from the shower, toweling off. While they'd been in the shower, Kel had folded their clothing and left it on the closed lid of the head.

"Getting pretty chummy, aren't you?" Kel asked when Rix joined her in *Calypso's* passenger space. He'd caught her in the middle of sweeping litter into a pile on the deck and he hastily positioned a dustpan for her.

Rix shrugged, changing the subject. “I wonder how Kha’rem is doing with Greevo.”

“Did you kick Greevo off the ships?”

“I did. He can pay for a room if he’s going to keep acting like he has been,” Rix said. “I also told him without final payment, he’s not getting a ride home.”

“I like it,” Kel said. “I wondered if we were going to have trouble with him trying to skip out on payments. Grintok are notorious for negotiating at the last minute.”

“You don’t love this deal with the Grays, do you?” Rix asked.

“No. But for the right price, I can get behind it,” she said. “How do we keep them from shooting us down with the weapons we install, though?”

“Make it part of a public agreement?” Rix asked. “Kha’rem said reputation for upholding deals is a big deal.”

“Does that extend to outsiders, though?”

“We’ll need to work that out tonight,” Rix said. “I have no idea what to expect.”

“Do you have the tools you need to install those barrels? I know you took them off, but I imagine you weren’t overly concerned with keeping them in perfect shape when you did.”

“I definitely burned through wiring harnesses and some steel knuckles,” Rix laughed. “I’ll need a shop where I can work on some parts. I imagine someone has that around here, given all of the old machines I see still functioning.”

“Make sure that’s the Gray’s responsibility to provide,” Kel said. “And we need something to guarantee our safety while working on it. This is why I hate this idea. We’re counting on them to honor a contract, but they’re shooting at us and are, by definition, our enemies.”

"But do they want to be enemies with Kha'rem?" Rix asked. "Bringing him to the table automatically puts his credibility on the line, too."

"I hope that's enough," Kel said.

"Do you think he regrets offering us a place to dock, yet?" Rix half-joked.

"Nah. Well, maybe with Greevo's attitude, but Kha'rem is set to make bank on our arrival. No doubt, he'll get a cut on this barrels deal. Plus, you have to bet he's in for a cut on the equipment you're selling through Bha'resh, too. Everything else is just the price of entry into the game."

Amari took that moment to join them. Somewhere along the line, she'd managed a change of clothing and wore a thin, gauzy dress that hung to mid-calf. The dress was cut to hint at her form without being overt.

"Gorgeous," Rix said, crossing the room to her.

"And this is why she always gets the guy," Kel said, only partially joking.

"We should do some shopping here once we get past all this business. I bet we could find you something you'd like. I have an eye for these things, and you certainly have the body for it," Amari said.

"Make it stop, please," Kel pleaded.

25

DANGEROUS GAME

As adrenaline left his system, a deep emptiness filled Kasit's chest. From the time he was old enough to talk, Zenith had talked to him about right and wrong and the personal consequences that followed. The cipher he'd stolen weighed heavily on his back as her words played in his head. Eventually, everyone would know that it was he who'd filched the artifact. There was no coming back from that. Keeping his mother unharmed, however, felt like the lesser evil. That Kha'rem would surely kick him out was simply the price that had to be paid.

Rising from the shadowed corner where he'd hidden, Kasit pushed a knot of anxiety as far from his mind as he could and steeled himself for the call. "Busk, I want to talk to Lirren."

"That's not the deal, boy," Busk said, answering his comm. "Did you get the package?"

"I have it, put Lirren on.," he said.

"You're playing a dangerous game, kid," Busk said.

"When did it stop being dangerous?" Kasit answered.

"Don't get lippy," Busk growled. "Here's Lirren."

"Trouble?" Lirren's voice questioned. "Did they see you?"

"Why would that matter, as long as you get your cipher?"

"Let's be clear, boy, I have Zenith, your mother. Don't screw this up or I swear I'll hang her dead body from the marketplace," Lirren said. "And stop referring to it by name. People could overhear."

"Let her go," Kasit said. "Let her go, and I'll hand the package over."

"That's not how this works. You hand it over. I verify it and then you get Zenith back."

"No," Kasit said.

"No? Do you need to hear her cry?" Lirren asked.

"Do that, and I'll hand it to the Grays and ask for their help," Kasit said.

"And your mother will be dead. Do you sense a pattern here?"

"You won't do that," Kasit said. "You want this *package* more than you want to hurt her. I have it. I'll give it to you, but my mother goes free now. Look, we both know I can't get away from you if you want to find me. I need to know she's okay."

"You have some guts to you, kid," Lirren said. "Part of me wants to teach you a lesson. But I'm feeling generous tonight. Busk, let her go."

"Boss?" Kasit could hear Busk's confusion.

"Let her go. Our mutual friend says he's good to his word that he'll deliver."

"But what if he doesn't have it? It could be a ruse."

"No. The package is in play. We know that much. And if he doesn't bring it to me, I'll send you to clean things up. He knows the game."

"Kid's messing with his life. Does he know that?"

"I suspect he does."

"Go home, Zen," Lirren said. "Say a word to anyone about this, and I'll make sure you all pay a price. Do you understand?"

"You promised Gadry you wouldn't come for Kas," Zenith said.

"That was years ago," Lirren said. "Gadry would have recruited Kas himself, if he were still alive."

"You're a monster."

"I hear that's your type, Zen," Lirren said. "Stop by after all this business is done. We'll grab some dinner."

Kasit could hear sounds of a struggle and his mother's objections.

"Stop! Stop it! Lirren!" Kasit yelled into the comms.

"Bring the package. I'm sending coordinates," Lirren answered, his voice dark with threat.

"Once I've heard from Mom."

"Don't mess with me, kid. I'll kill you all."

"Not if you want your cipher, Lirren," Kasit said.

"Don't mistake temporary power for real power, Kas," Lirren said. "If you run, you can't run far enough to hide from me. Bring my package, and bring it now."

"I'm coming. I'll hand it over once I know Mom is safe."

"You're as stubborn as your father. I'd hate to see that tendency get you killed, just like it did him," Lirren said and closed comms.

Kasit settled to his haunches and struggled to calm himself. He knew in that moment that he'd never be free from Lirren. Zenith's life was worth everything to him and he wondered if he and his father shared that trait too. He didn't know much about his father's death, just that there had been a betrayal and that his mother had made him swear not to live a life in the gangs.

Taking off at a jog, Kasit set out for the coordinates transmitted to him by Lirren. It would take at least fifteen minutes to traverse the path he had in mind. The act of moving and the physicality of jumping onto and sliding fluxspan rails momentarily gave his mind a moment to rest. It was on his second slide where he realized what had to be done. He both hated the idea and immediately knew it was his only way to salvation.

"Kas?" a weak but familiar voice called over comms.

"Mom? Are you okay? Are you safe?"

"Busk is following me, but I can lose him," she said. "What are you doing?"

"Delivering the package," Kasit said, never surer of anything in his life.

"I'm so sorry I got you into this," she said. "I should have run and gotten us further away from him."

"It's not your fault, Mom. Can you get somewhere safe?"

"Why? What are you doing? Give him the package. He'll be mad, but you'll be okay," she said. "Don't mess with him."

"I need to know you can get somewhere safe," Kasit said. "I'm not going to do anything stupid."

"I have a place I can go," she answered. "Kas..."

"Mom, I know. It's messed up, but I have this. Trust me."

"You sound just like your father."

"Is that bad? You never talk about him."

"No, it's not bad. You and he are so much alike; kind, trustworthy, caring," she said. "Don't let Lirren drag you in, Kas."

"I won't Mom. I have this."

26

DEESCALATION

"When we get back tonight, we're going to clean before we sleep, right?" Amari asked, looping an arm through Rix's as they stepped out onto the gangplank that ran between Driftmarket pier and *Calypso*.

"Are you sleeping on *Calypso* or *Gravitational Pull*?" Kel asked.

Amari and Rix exchanged a look and then Amari answered. "*Gravitational Pull*, we have a reasonable setup in the bunk room, as long as Greevo isn't sleeping there, too."

"I can't imagine sharing space with a Grintok," Kel said. "Speaking of, here he comes."

"What doing? Where going?" Greevo fired off as he approached the trio.

"We have dinner with a prospective customer," Rix said.

"No. Rix Banner find Greevo cargo. No have dinner!" Greevo said.

"I don't know what you think I can do, Greevo," Rix said. "I will ask about your navigation cipher and see what the people I'm meeting with think, but there's no recognized law on Garanod Enclave. We can't report theft to someone. We don't know the area, and I'm not about to run around accusing people of taking it."

"Rix Banner bad partner."

"Had I known we were carrying something of such value, we could have made other arrangements for security, but you didn't trust anyone with that information," Rix said. "Worse, you let strangers know it was aboard. What did you think was going to happen with an item of that value just sitting there, only a couple of guards at best twenty yards away?"

"Give access to *Calypso*. Greevo tired. Kitka go look for cipher," Greevo said, losing much of his bluster.

"There are hotels. Go pay for a night at one of them," Rix said. "You've worn out your welcome with us. You're not a paying customer, remember?"

"You leave Greevo on Garanod?" Greevo asked.

"No pay, no ride," Kel said, stepping in. "No pay, no sleep. I imagine you see the pattern, right?"

"Very hostile," Greevo said calmly.

"Are you serious?" Rix asked. "You've been hostile for the entire trip. You demand your way. You make a gigantic mess which you never clean up. And, you hide valuable cargo and then blame us for someone taking it after you tell others that you have it. And then you refuse to pay for the trip. You could be a whole lot more introspective, Greevo."

"Greevo not hostile. Greevo tired."

Rix could see the exhaustion in the small alien's face, and he was about to take pity on him. Kel must have seen the break in Rix's armor because she cut in. "You will make payment in full, immediately. You and your crew will clean both ships' interiors top to bottom and repair furniture and bedding. The ships will be kept this way. We will do everything in our power to find your cipher, but know this, if it is that valuable, it is likely already too far gone to be retrieved. This is your fault. These are the terms of you stepping onto *Calypso* or *Gravitational Pull* ever again. Make a decision."

Greevo hung his head, shaking it slowly in his hands. "The loss is muchly." And if the situation couldn't have gotten worse, the angry little alien started bawling, with tears and snot flowing through his fingers. "Greevo pay," he managed between sobs.

"Kitka, are you nearby?" Rix called over comms while he placed a hand over Greevo's back and tried to sooth the distraught Grintok.

"Rix Banner?" Kitka asked.

"Yeah. Could you come back to *Calypso*? Greevo is having feelings and he needs to be put to bed."

"Yes, Rix Banner," Kitka said. "No banned *Calypso*?"

"There's been an agreement," Rix said.

"I come."

"Make him sign the agreement," Kel said. "Otherwise, he'll back out."

"Really?" Rix asked. While Greevo had been yelling at him, he'd had no trouble defending himself and cutting the angry little alien off. But now that Greevo was sobbing, it felt overly punitive to force his hand to sign a contract.

"Kel Warp right. Greevo sign."

Rix shook his head in wonder as he presented the contract that Beverly wrote, spur of the moment. Greevo quickly signed the contract.

Seeing Kitka approaching from a distance, Rix couldn't have been more elated. "Kitka is here, Buddy," Rix said. "We're going to do what we can to find your cipher. I'll let you know when we get back, what we've found out, okay?"

"Rix Banner will no succeed. Cipher gone," Greevo said as he resumed sobbing again. "Rix Banner good mans." The last was apparently too much for the little green man as racking sobs threatened to pull him to the ground. Fortunately, Kitka had arrived and with strength Rix hadn't anticipated, she straightened her boss and started back across the gangplank to *Calypso.*

"Send Kitka the agreement," Kel said. "I'm not sleeping in their filth again, tonight."

"Brutal," Rix said.

"I've never seen a Grintok break like that," Amari said.

"Yeah, that was a lot to watch," Kel said. "I get the pain. That cipher would have set him good, financially. I wish we'd known. We could have come up with a better plan than leaving it in a cargo pod."

"Agreed," Rix said. "Shall we go to dinner?"

"Please," Amari said. "There's been more than enough drama for the evening."

"Funny," Rix said. "What do you suppose the Gray are going to have to say about us taking their guns?"

"They'll cry and Rix will just give them back," Kel said.

"Seriously?" Rix asked, scandalized.

"Too soon?" Kel asked.

"Tough crowd. I hope I never have emotions around you," Rix said.

"I've seen your version of emotions."

"Oh?" Amari asked.

"Yeah, he raises an eyebrow. That's how you know he's pissed."

"Oh, stop it," Rix said.

"I heard him say—oh, darn it, once," Kel continued. "And he said the 'f' word."

"The 'f' word?" Amari asked.

"*Fart*. He said *fart* and he didn't even mean stinky butt cloud. He skinned his knuckles," Kel said.

"I curse plenty," Rix said. "You just don't hear me because that's all you do."

"Ooh, nice come back," Kel said.

"You two are like children together," Amari said.

"Just him. Most of the time, I have to be the adult."

Rix rolled his eyes and pulled Amari closer as they walked. The restaurant they were headed to was two kilometers away, but the air on Driftmarket was a steady seventy-two degrees. For a time, they walked quietly in companionable silence as they enjoyed the peace around them, passing many small groups of aliens all moving about with little to no sense of urgency.

"I can see why people settled here," Amari said. "The nebula is beautiful, and if not for the thin air, it would be perfect. I suppose you get used to these little oxygen condensers after a time."

"I've been thinking. If we can line up a return load, we could make this a profitable trip for *Calypso*. How have your parts been selling?"

"Really well," Rix said. "I've sold a quarter of them through Bha'resh and already made about three quarters of what I was hoping for the entire trip. Once we're ready to leave, I'll make a deal with Bha'resh for the remainder. What are you thinking about bringing back to Patience Station?"

"For sure Kha'rem's gillet fish. His price is good per case. We could bring enough back that we could ship beyond Patience or maybe open up that boutique and sell directly to the public," she said.

"Have you heard from Philo?"

"Oh, I meant to talk to you about that," Kel said. "Yes. He wants us to meet with Sta'ci tomorrow."

"Wow, he's moving fast."

Kel smiled. "He might be, but this was more about some deal he's working on."

"I didn't know Philo worked on deals."

"He doesn't usually, but he's interested in this. Sta'ci might be more than meets the eye," Kel said.

"Grintok are good at deals," Rix said. "I don't have trouble imagining she'd have something to do with that."

"Kel was referring to her being better looking than any Grintok either of us have ever met," Amari said. "Sometimes, people, especially men, discount nice looking women as being good at business."

"Oh," Rix said.

"I have to say I'm impressed you didn't jump on that," Amari said. "Especially, given where Earth is in societal development with respect to genders."

Rix new better than to say anything on the subject. "I'm in for meeting the parents," Rix said.

"Our boy is growing up," Kel said in a funny voice.

"This is our restaurant," Rix said, pointing across a stone veranda to where Kha'rem stood inside a short stone wall, next to a table already set with plates, silverware and candles.

"Good eve, my friends," Kha'rem said. "I hope the day's events haven't spoiled your appetites. I have received word that our guest of honor, Neral Thiss of The Grays, will join us shortly."

Graciously, as expected, Kha'rem introduced Kel, Amari and Rix to the others at the table, which included Kha'rem's wife, her brother, Bha'resh, who Rix had already met and another brother.

"What a day," Rix said as he sat at the table and grabbed a glass of what he thought was water. All eyes were on him as he took a long drink. "Oh, hold on, that's not water," he managed with a short cough.

"My apologies, Rix Banner. I should have explained. Our customs are no doubt different. That drink is meant to be sipped as it has a strong mixture of alcohol. I hope that is not upsetting to the human system," he said.

"I apologize if I was rude. I was expecting water," Rix said. "Which is customary for humans. I hope I didn't break a rule or something."

"We are not standing on formalities this evening," Kha'rem said. "I was concerned for your well-being."

"Not to worry," Kel said. "This one can drink just about anyone under the table. Humans must have a second stomach for alcohol, because Korrali are the only ones I've seen keep up with him, and most of the time, he's not even trying."

"Curiosities abound," Kha'rem said. "Would you like brine to be served? It is also common on Vesh table. Filtered water is also available."

"We'd do better with filtered," Kel said. "The sodium in brine can be too much."

"Ah, we have reached understanding," Kha'rem said. "And just in time, as I see that our guest of honor Neral Thiss has arrived."

All eyes turned to the approach of a man and a woman who both looked roughly human, if not for the almost wooden texture of their skin. Both were thin and angular and slightly shorter than human, although close.

"Kha'rem, my old friend, thank you for the invitation," Neral said. Rix watched all three as Kha'rem greeted Neral and his wife. He could see both they were more acquaintances than friends and Neral's wife made no attempt to join in the greeting, although her gaze swept the table, landing on Kel first and then settling on Rix for a time before moving on.

"Welcome to our table, Neral and Shes," Kha'rem said. "Please join us. We were just bringing a container of filtered fresh. Would you like anything?"

"That is appropriate for us as well," Neral said. "And you are Kel Warp, Rix Banner and Amari ... I do not know if you have two names, Amari."

Rix stood and offered his hand for a shake. "A customary Earth greeting," Rix explained. "To show that we are unarmed and of peaceful intent."

"Ah, I was afraid you were looking to disassemble my arm and keep it to sell it back to me," Neral said.

Rix smiled but didn't have an answer. Kel, however, popped up and offered her hand as well. "I told him to behave," Kel said. "So, we're keeping that party trick to ourselves tonight."

"You are of good humor," Neral said, pulling a chair out for Shes to sit in before seating himself. "You do not hold a grudge?"

"That depends on if you intend to keep shooting at us or not," Kel said, not sitting just yet. "We don't love that."

"Funny and direct," Neral said. "Kel Warp, I believe our first meeting was not a true representation of our future meetings. Perhaps we would be better as comrades than opponents."

Kel smiled and sat. "That's what we're here to discuss."

"But first, we should start our meal with a sweet biscuit," Kha'rem said. "There will be much time ahead to discuss business."

"I agree, old friend," Neral said. "But I must know. Why did you not simply destroy my vessel, instead of neutering it? The embarrassment to my pilots was considerable."

"Surely, as a woman, Shes can answer that," Amari said.

All eyes turned to a surprised Shes whose face now bore thin smile. "An expression of power without escalation. Only a woman can be so elegant."

27

SUBTEXT OF NEGOTIATION

"Let us get to business," Neral said, setting down a trio of wooden utensils he'd used to good effect in picking up the long strands of thin green pasta that had been sauteed in a savory fish sauce. "Am I to understand you have interest in *selling* the weapons you took from *my* vessel?"

"One moment before you respond, Rix Banner, perhaps we could excuse our families who have no interest in business dealings such as these." Kha'rem stood and offered a hand to his wife, who accepted it and stood. Dearest, I thank you for gracing our table this evening."

Kha'rem's wife, who'd been quiet for most of the evening, smiled demurely and excused herself, walking off with Kha'rem's other family, except for Bha'resh, who seemed quite interested in what was to follow.

"Thank you, Rix Banner," Kha'rem said. "Please continue as you might."

"In Galactic Empire space, a vessel attacking without provocation is fair game," Kel said. "There is no limit to the damage such an attacking vessel might receive, no expectation of quarter given. When

Quibbler 12a attacked *Calypso*, your vessel was forfeit. It is only by the whim of Rix Banner that your crew was allowed to return home with a ship mostly intact. So when you ask if we would sell to you *your* weapons, you are mistaken. In the moments after your crew surrendered, having attacked an otherwise peaceful vessel, we owned *Quibbler 12a*."

"This is *not* Galactic Empire and as such your laws do not apply," Neral said with an obvious edge to his voice.

"I imagine Galactic Empire law is more restrictive, wouldn't you say?" Rix asked, his tone neutral.

"How is that?"

"Look, there's no reason for intelligent people to argue facts we all know to be true. Business is like gambling, you must risk something to make gains," Rix said. "Gray Consortium sent *Quibbler 12a* out to see if it could capture a pair of unknown ships. Your risk was that you'd lose *Quibbler 12a*, your potential gain was two new ships and their contents. Is there disagreement in this?"

Neral sat back, his eyes never leaving Rix's, as he considered the conversation. "Go on," he finally said.

"We can all agree that in deep space, especially in Ghostmist Nebula, the only law that exists is natural law—something we call on Earth, law of the jungle. That is, survival of the fittest. To Kel's point, we brought our own understanding of law to the fight, which was, we refused to attack until we were first attacked. We'll be sure not to make that mistake next time. Would you mind if I cut to the chase?"

"I am unable to translate that idiom, but I believe you are going to make an offer," Neral said. "Let's hear it."

"We took those barrels because we could," Rix said. "We didn't ruin your ship because we didn't want to stir up a hornet's nest. I'll sell those barrels and reinstall them for a price and with a few conditions."

"You are not much for negotiating, are you?" Neral asked.

"Honestly, I find it tiring," Rix said. "I know people love to barter. I don't."

"What do you love, Rix Banner?"

Rix smiled. Neral was looking for a weakness to exploit, but he wasn't afraid of the answer. "You might find this odd, but I get a huge kick out of fixing things," Rix said. "I hate it when things are broken, and when I make them work, it feels good."

"It is either brilliant to place you at the negotiating table, or madness, and I cannot decide which," Neral said. "What is your price?"

"Three hundred grams of gold," Rix said.

Shes stifled a gasp at the number.

"And your conditions?" Neral said, acting as if he hadn't heard her.

"A temporary truce between our company and Gray Consortium," Rix said. "And access to tools and a secure mechanics shop large enough to work on *Quibbler 12a*."

"There is quite a spread between zero, which I believe should be the price, and three hundred grams. Tell me why I should pay this," Neral said. "I can just wait for you to leave Kha'rem's pier and place a bounty on the return of my weapons. I would not need to go anywhere near as high as three hundred grams to focus every independent pilot on Garanod after you."

"I thought about that," Rix said. "And you're right. If they all knew when we were leaving and started at good proximity, we'd have a difficult time leaving and you might receive your weapons back, still in good shape. Although, I have to say, if it's going that way, I can guarantee those barrels won't be installable, just out of the principle."

"It's a conundrum," Neral said, shrugging.

"There's information you don't have," Kel said.

"Oh?"

"Rix Banner is a wizard with mechanical issues. Even if we give those barrels back for nothing, there's no guarantee your people will be able to get them reinstalled."

"You think we don't have talented mechanics on Garanod?"

"I have no idea, but I know that Rix is the best. Do you know of anyone on Garanod who can remove two barrels from a ship in forty minutes with limited tools and in a combat space? Maybe you've got someone like that, but I doubt it. We're offering a package deal, and it comes with the best mechanic you've ever seen.

Shes leaned over and whispered into Neral's ear. He nodded.

"One hundred grams of gold. A treaty between our organizations that includes protection for your arrival and departures. And Gray Consortium has first right to purchase all cargo aboard upon arrival."

"No way!" Kel said, pushing back from the table. "We're done here."

"Hold on, Kel," Rix said.

"No. We're not paying for protection. We can protect ourselves just fine."

"I agree. We're negotiating," Rix said and turned back to Neral. "I agree with Kel, no protection. An agreement that you won't attack our ships for the next month is all we're looking for. As for first rights, there's no universe that exists in which you attacking us somehow puts you in position to sift through our goods before others. Currently, Bha'resh is my Garanod Enclave contact. If you want to work something out with him, be my guest. Finally, one hundred grams isn't even close to the value of those barrels."

"It's a buyer's market."

"Is it?" Rix asked. "I imagine we could test that. As you know, most of the function of a particle blaster is provided by the assembly in my control. I bet there are others who'd pay just to keep those barrels off your ship."

"You don't want to do that," Neral growled. "I'm not the enemy you want. Don't underestimate Gray Consortium."

"Perhaps a break is in order," Kha'rem said. "Negotiating can be wearing."

"I don't want you as my enemy, Neral," Rix said. "But we won't be taken advantage of. We can bring value to your organization in the form of restoring weapons to *Quibbler 12a*. Further, if we part as friends, we'll find interest in letting you know what we're carrying prior to arrival, just like we'll do with Kha'rem and Bha'resh, not because they've threatened us, but because they've built trust. We're looking for partners, not threats. Don't take our decision not to destroy *Quibbler 12a* as weakness."

"There's talk of a Ghostmist Navigational Cipher," Neral said, the edge dissolving from his voice.

"Is there?" Rix asked.

"Don't play coy. There are more than a few reports that such a device was brought aboard your vessel *Gravitational Pull*. Further, there is talk of theft. Do you know anything about this?"

"I don't make habit of discussing privately owned cargo with uninvolved parties," Rix said neutrally. "I can say that there was a theft."

"And cargo is missing?"

"Honestly, Neral, I don't know. The majority of the cargo we shipped was private and without manifest," Rix said.

"A cipher would be worth a fortune. It would change the nature of our relationship if you were to bring one to me," Neral said.

"I can say with certainty that I've never knowingly had possession of a navigational cipher, Ghostmist or otherwise," Rix said.

Neral didn't speak for a moment as he considered Rix. Finally, he said, "That's unfortunate. One hundred ten grams of gold, I'll supply the mechanic's bay and my mechanic to oversee the work. I'll agree to leave you alone for the duration of this trip. It's my best offer. I suggest you take it."

Rix stood and offered his hand. "I don't love it, but you've got yourself a deal."

"This hand touching extends to contracts as well?" Neral asked, looking at Rix's hand with some disgust.

"It does. It signifies that our words are all that are required to complete this deal," Rix said.

"Very well," Neral said, completing the handshake. "I will make my mechanic and bay available at 0600 tomorrow morning. Await contact."

And with that, Neral stood, pulling out Shes's chair and then the two of them left.

"Was that weird?" Kel asked, looking at Kha'rem for confirmation.

"I would perhaps consider the successful navigation of a delicate negotiation as quite a hurdle," Kha'rem said.

"Sure, that, but he was all talkee and then he just punched through at the end and left."

"He wasn't interested in the negotiation as much as he was the cipher," Rix said. "Or that's my take. When he realized we didn't have anything to do with it, he lost interest."

"A navigation cipher has one hundred times the value of the deal you struck, to the right entity," Kha'rem said. "I would strongly bid on such an item if it were to come available."

"Are you saying he came to dinner because he thought we had a line on the cipher?" Kel asked.

"Yes," Bha'resh said. "There's no reason he shouldn't have accepted the initial offer of one hundred fifty grams and a ceasefire when Kha'rem made it earlier today. This negotiation was a pretext to discussing the rumored cipher."

"Then what was all that about protection?" Kel asked.

"Dominance move," Rix said.

"Quite right. Once he was in a superior position, he would have demanded information about the cipher," Kha'rem said.

"And now you see why we never pay for protection," Kel said, looking triumphant.

"Didn't miss that we don't get to sleep in, though," Amari said.

"Kha'rem, we need to negotiate an extension to our stay at your pier," Rix said.

"How long do you expect to stay, Rix Banner?"

"That depends on what's going on with Greevo," Rix said. "But my best guess is three days on the outside. We're not earning much while sitting here."

"I would offer six grams of gold per twenty-six hour period," Kha'rem said.

"That's a nice discount," Rix said. "Do you mind if I ask why?"

"As you so have said. We have established a bond of trust."

"We're thinking about taking a load of frozen gillet back to Patience Station," Kel said. "Is that something that is possible?"

"Very much so," Kha'rem said. "How much would you like?"

"It's more a question of what we can afford," Kel said. "Do you have a discount for bulk?"

“I do,” Kha’rem said. “If you could afford sixty-grams of gold, I would give the best possible value for two thousand kilograms of my freshest gillet packaged in forty-kilogram crates.”

“That’s a very good deal, Rix,” Beverly said, appearing on the table between them with her green accountant visor. “That’s roughly equivalent to five credits per kilogram.”

Rix nodded acknowledgement. “What kind of shelf life does frozen gillet have?”

“A considerable length of time. Four hundred days is generally the number we discuss, although if the temperature remains below zero degrees, twice that should be reasonable.”

“Let’s see how this deal with Gray Consortium shakes out, but that sounds like quite a good deal,” Rix said.

“Is this where we shake hands, Rix Banner?” Kha’rem asked.

28

TRAPPED BY CIRCUMSTANCE

"KASIT?" Kha'rem asked quietly, answering his comms while smiling across the table at his guests.

"I'm in trouble. I didn't know who to call," Kasit said, peering out from the shadows beneath the ferry platform from Driftmarket to Quiet Coil. Running every hour, the ferry was one of the least used, especially in the evening hours.

"Are you safe for five minutes?"

"Yes."

"I will ping you back," Kha'rem said, turning to his dinner guests. With their business concluded, Kha'rem understood that they likely wanted nothing more than to retreat to their ships for the evening, as he also looked forward to the evening's quiet, though he suspected it would not come for quite some time.

"Important call?" Rix asked amiably.

"I'm afraid the business of a trader on Driftmarket never ceases. I have so enjoyed our evening together," Kha'rem said, standing. "You are welcome to stay and enjoy the table for as long as you wish."

“Could we participate in the cost of the evening?” Rix asked.

“Perhaps the next time,” Kha’rem said.

Rix looked between Amari and Kel, both of whom seemed relieved for an end to the evening.

“Thank you for your hospitality, Kha’rem,” Kel said. “There’s nothing more satisfying than making friends in distant ports. We’ll get back to you on the frozen gillet. How much lead time do you need?”

“Six hours, if during working hours,” Kha’rem said.

“We should be able to make that work,” Kel said.

Kha’rem bowed, exchanged a final handshake with Rix and then watched them off.

“Trouble, brother?” Bha’resh asked, looking concerned.

“Perhaps. Will you take care of the table? I will come even with you tomorrow,” Kha’rem said.

“Of course, brother. Please call on me if you need. I am a light sleeper,” Bha’resh said.

“You breathe like the sound of a broken ventilation fan when you sleep. I can only imagine what it must take to wake you,” Kha’rem said with a quick smile.

“Be that as it may.”

Kha’rem turned and walked quickly from the restaurant. When he was forty meters from the restaurant and onto a quiet walking path, he returned Kasit’s comm.

“Kha’rem?” Kasit asked. In his voice, Kha’rem heard fear and disappointment.

“What is it, Kasit? What have you gotten into?” Kha’rem asked.

"They took Mom," Kasit said. "They said they'd kill her if I didn't take it."

Kha'rem's mind whirred as he immediately understood the situation. "Have you turned over the device?"

"I'm about to get onto the fluxspan to Quiet Coil," Kasit said. "I'm to make the drop at the stone factory."

"It is Jeshifa, then. You do not want to make that drop, Kasit. Lirren will have you killed once you do," Kha'rem said.

"He will kill my mother if I don't. There is no choice."

"As long as the cipher is in play, he will not kill Zenith," Kha'rem said. "It is too valuable to him. Do you know where they keep her?"

"He said she would be released once I turned over the cipher," Kasit said.

"Jeshifa is already the most powerful gang in Garanod," Kha'rem said. "With the cipher, they will become even more powerful. Lirren has always talked of taking over all Garanod Enclave. This will be what it takes."

"I don't understand. How is that?"

"To move through Ghostmist unhindered will bring considerable wealth in trade. With the cipher, no merchant ship will be safe, as Jeshifa's vessels will hide within the clouds and attack from cover," Kha'rem said.

"I don't know what to do," Kasit said. "I cannot let Mom down. I don't want to let you down."

"Maybe there is a way," Kha'rem said. "Have you told Lirren you have the device?"

"He knows."

"We will have to operate quickly," Kha'rem said. "Stay where you are. Give me one hour."

29

RITE OF PASSAGE

"Is that your comm beeping?" Amari asked, just as she and Rix were stepping into the shower aboard *Gravitational Pull.*

"Shoot, hang on," Rix said, tapping the earwig he used for both translations and comms. "This is Rix."

"Rix Banner, we need to meet. There is urgency," Kha'rem said. "Come alone."

"Where?"

"My office. Please, I would not ask if was not of the utmost importance."

"I'm bringing Amari and Kel. We'll be there in five," Rix said, closing comms before Kha'rem could object.

"What's going on, Rix?" Amari asked, grabbing her clothing, as she had heard at least part of the comm.

"I have no idea," Rix said. "Beverly, could you grab Kel and let her know we have something brewing? We need her to join us."

Beverly appeared in front of Rix in an all-black Mata Hari set, complete with a sequined top and a long skirt. "We're up to trouble, are we?" she asked.

"Sounds like it," Rix said.

"Are we taking bets on if it's related to the cipher?" Beverly asked.

"That's the likely case."

Amari nodded as she donned her jumpsuit, rather than the less-practical casual dress she'd worn to dinner. "Thank you for including me," she said.

Rix chuffed a laugh. "If Kha'rem knew us better, he'd never have called me," Rix said. "You and Kel are the scary ones. Not me."

"You're such a wise man for knowing that," Amari said, running a finger up Rix's throat and holding the bottom of his chin as she lightly kissed him.

"Kel has questions but is meeting us on the pier in two minutes."

After Rix yanked on his jumpsuit, he and Amari scooted from *Gravitational Pull* and were met by Kel, as expected. "What's shakin' chief?" she asked.

"I'm not sure. Kha'rem said it's urgent," Rix said.

"Something came up at the end of dinner. He was talking to Kasit," Kel said. "Want me to do some guessing?"

"I'm right there with you, Kel," Amari said.

"Thing I can't figure is why he'd call Rix if that's what's going on. No offense, Rix, but you don't exactly exude elite soldier," Kel said.

"No offense taken," Rix said, leading the trio toward Kha'rem's business. As they approached, lights flicked on in the office where they'd met with Kha'rem previously. By the time the arrived, the front door had been opened.

"Ah, thank you for coming, Rix Banner, Kel Warp and Amari. First, I apologize for calling you here at such an hour ..."

"Let's cut to the chase, Kha'rem," Rix said. "You think we can help. Let's save mea culpas and social graces for later."

"Quite so," Kha'rem said with an grateful nod. "I have learned it was my employee, Kasit, who stole the cargo from your vessel. And while I am terribly ashamed of this, to your point, Rix Banner, the situation continues to develop. Kasit's mother, Zenith, is being held with threat of death if Kasit does not deliver this cipher."

Rix nodded grimly. "Has it been delivered?"

"No. Surprisingly, Kasit thought to call me and ask for help. He has great remorse but cannot find a way to save his mother. I thought you could look at this cipher and perhaps cause it to fail, though hopefully not right away. I have heard from Bha'resh that you are indeed quite skilled with repairs," Kha'rem said.

"That's a solid plan," Rix said. "Are we certain whoever kidnapped Zenith won't harm both her and Kasit once they have the cipher?"

"Jeshifa is the organization and Lirren, who heads it, can be unpredictable," Kha'rem said. "Also, you should know that, had I known you were bringing a cipher, I would not have extended hospitality. A cipher such as this will upset the delicate balance of power within Garanod Enclave."

"I thought you said you were interested in it," Kel said. "Did that change?"

Kha'rem smiled gently. "Yes. There is a part of me that wishes for such power. When I reflect, I realize I would be inviting the ruin of my family."

"I'll grab my tools," Rix said. "Where can we meet Kasit?"

"You'll do it?"

"I'll try," Rix said. "If I can't figure it out, I can certainly disable it, which should buy some time, until they can find a way to fix it."

"I'm receiving a comm from Kasit," Kha'rem said, holding a hand over his ear.

"The moment warrants eavesdropping," Beverly chimed in, to the trio's great relief.

"They found me," Kasit's voice said in a whisper. *"I have to turn it over. They have Zenith. I am sorry Kha'rem."*

Kha'rem listened for a while longer, but Beverly was unable to make out anything intelligible. After a few moments, Kha'rem closed the comms. "I am sorry, I believe this situation has passed out of our control."

"Kha'rem, if what you say is true, we can't ignore this," Rix said.

"My friend, I appreciate your willingness to get involved in the politics of Garanod, but this is well beyond anything you can help with," Kha'rem said.

Rix looked to Amari and then Kel, who both nodded their heads just enough to communicate that they were willing to get involved. "Kha'rem, I cannot share with you how, but we can help," Rix said. "The question I have is what the actual mission is."

"Please don't underestimate Lirren or Jeshifa," Kha'rem said. "This organization is ruthless and well organized. You cannot simply approach them with your ray gun and ask for Zenith to be released, or for them to hand over the cipher."

"Wouldn't that be nice," Rix agreed. "We aren't in the business of sharing our secrets, but we ask that you would keep them should they become known. We have the means to recover the cipher. The actual question is what we do after that."

"We will get back to your capabilities, but first, let's examine the likely backlash over the cipher slipping from Jeshifa control. I believe

Zenith and Kasit would be in jeopardy once again. It is likely that Jeshifa would also seize your vessels, and there is not much I could do to prevent that."

"Why our vessels?"

"Assuming you are able to retrieve the cipher, Lirren would know that few of his enemies in Garanod have the capacity to steal from him, and those who do are unlikely to upend their already uneasy peace."

"Even for a navigational cipher?" Kel asked.

Kha'rem shrugged. "You make a reasonable point, but I am relatively certain that Lirren would start with outsiders first. His anger would be wide-reaching."

"What kind of vessels does he have available?" Rix asked. "If we got a head start, could he successfully run us down?"

"Perhaps in the short run, yes. None of his vessels are designed for long range travel, however," Kha'rem said.

"Where are his headquarters or, at least where is he most often seen?" Amari asked.

"It is too dangerous for you to go to where Lirren and Jeshifa are," Kha'rem said.

"Kel and I are veterans of a long and dangerous war, as is Rix," Amari said. "We know quite a lot about penetrating enemy positions and operating without being seen."

"I don't see how that is possible," Kha'rem said.

Amari's smile did not reach her eyes. "And that is why we are so successful."

Kha'rem looked to Rix for support. "Surely you see the insanity of this approach. How can we dissuade them from risking even more lives?"

"My friend, I have spent more than a few sleepless nights worrying. What are you thinking, Amari?" Rix asked.

"We need information," Amari said. "We need to infiltrate and locate Zenith and the boy. If they've been released, then we can focus on this cipher. I see that as a secondary objective. Bottom line is, we need eyes on before we can make any kind of decisions. But before we can do that, we need someone to point us in the right direction."

"This is what you want?" Kha'rem asked.

"You called us. If it wasn't for a solution, then why?" Kel asked.

"It is with great reluctance that I tell you these things," Kha'rem said. "There is a region on The Quiet Coil where manufacturing is common, and there are many warehouses. It is from within these warehouses that Jeshifa operates. I can help identify those that I know have been previously used, but it is possible they have moved."

"How does one travel to The Quiet Coil?" Amari asked.

"There are ferries that travel by fluxspan rail. One of the advantages of operating from Quiet Coil is that there are limited ferries. Recently, Lirren has shown interest in Kasit, as he is adept at utilizing a sling to travel the fluxspan rails without the use of any sort of ferry car. It is quite dangerous."

"Stealing the cipher could be seen as initiation into the organization," Kel said. "The pirate gangs where we come from require similar, illegal acts for entry into the organization."

"A rite of passage," Kha'rem said. "We see a similar trend here as well."

"What's your plan, Amari?" Rix asked.

"Initially, we'll gather information. That will give Lirren time to return Zenith, if he's going to do that," she said. "Is there a schedule for the ferries?"

“I can provide that,” Kha’rem said. “I am begging you to change your mind about this. I should never have involved you.” His eyes glazed over for a moment as he gestured to his HUD. A schedule of fluxspan ferries for all of Garanod Enclave appeared.

“We’ll take the 0600 ferry,” Kel said. “Rix, you can’t miss your meeting with The Grays to fix their ship, or you’ll signal that we’re up to something.”

“I hate it when you guys do this,” Rix said, giving Kha’rem an understanding nod.

“It’s amusing how often this sort of thing shows up with you around,” Kel said. “I can’t figure if that’s a good thing or bad.”

“We should get some sleep,” Amari said. “Kha’rem, you were right to call us. Please provide updates if you hear things. You should cease inquiries, however. You might provoke Jeshifa by drawing attention to yourself.”

“I will be careful.”

Walking back to their ship, Amari grabbed Rix’s hand. “You’re worried. I see it in your face.”

“Shouldn’t I be?” he asked. “Kel isn’t wrong. Putting the two of you in danger seems to be something I’m repeating.”

“I’m not sure how you can take the blame for any of this,” Kel said. “There’s a lot of injustice in the universe. Speaking for myself, I look forward to events like this where I can maybe tip the scales a bit more in my favor, morally speaking. I’ve done things I regret. This feels good.”

“But at what cost?” Rix asked.

“Have a little faith,” Amari said. “I’m more worried about you being in Gray territory without any backup. If they decide to make trouble, you’ll be on your own. Have you thought about that?”

"Why would they do that? I'm fixing their ship," Rix said, standing at the intersection of where Kel would continue to *Calypso* and he and Amari would enter *Gravitational Pull.*

"The bigger question is if Greevo's crew has done any real cleaning," Kel said. "I'm going to be pissed if I have to wade through ankle deep garbage to get to my sleeping bunk."

"We haven't been gone that long," Rix said.

"You're such a pushover."

"Goodnight, Kel," Amari said.

30

GOOD EGG

ENTERING *GRAVITATIONAL PULL*, neither Amari nor Rix were surprised to find that little had changed. “Clean the bedding and sweep?” Rix offered.

“Toss it down and I’ll run the bedding through the machine,” Amari agreed.

Rix clambered into the bunkroom and slid bedding over, dropping it through to the main level. With the bedding out of the way, he grabbed the ion-broom and started sweeping. That Greevo could make such a mess in such a short time was beyond his imagination, but the day had been long, and he could only focus on finishing the task.

“Are you ready?” Amari called from below as she started up the ladder, hoisting the bedding above her.

Rix quickly finished his sweeping and grabbed the bedding, pulling it out flat. Repeating for the linens, Amari helped finish the task and the pair flopped onto the bed, exhausted. As his last move, Rix set an alarm for 0500, which would give them just enough time for coffee and a meal bar before they had to set off for their day.

"Did we actually sleep?" Amari complained, sitting up as Rix's alarm woke them both.

"My HUD says I'm rested and ready for the day," Rix said, smiling.

"Really?" Amari asked.

"No. Not really. It's suggesting I find time for a nap today."

"Wouldn't that be nice," Amari said. "Shower?"

"As long as you're there too," Rix said. Amari managed a smile but that was about it.

After a quick shower and even quicker breakfast, Amari was out the door, wearing a non-descript jumpsuit that she said was good cover for the task ahead of her.

"Be safe, Amari," Rix said. "I hate watching you leave."

"I know. I appreciate that you trust me enough that you're not insisting to come along."

"I'm not sure how that'd work. I don't have the skills you and Kel have."

"Right." They kissed for a moment and then released as Amari made a quiet exit.

Up and full of anxiety for the day, Rix checked messages to make sure he hadn't received updates from Kha'rem. While there were some small informational updates, neither Zenith nor Kasit had shown up and if anything, Kha'rem was even more worried.

"Beverly, I'm distracted, can you help me think through what tools I need to bring along?" Rix asked. "I was thinking my normal tool bag, and the weld/cut box. Also, we have a lot of wires to fix, so that bag, too."

"That's a good start," Beverly said, showing up in her favorite Rosie the Riveter outfit, complete with red polka dot bandana. "You'll need some sort of transportation to bring the barrels over to their workshop and a lift once you get there."

"I'm hoping they have a gantry. We could work with zero-g, but that's tough for getting any kind of leverage," Rix said. "I'll start by setting the barrels on the deck of the cargo pod. Hopefully, by the time I have those down, Neral's mechanic will have shown up."

With a task ahead of him, Rix was able to put worry to the side, and he got right to work, using the straps he'd secured the barrels to the side of the cargo pod to slowly lower them to the deck. "Man, these things are heavier than I remember," Rix said. "What kind of weight are we looking at?"

"Mass is easier," Beverly said. "Two hundred thirty kilograms, each. The gravity here is sixty percent of Earth's, so weight is roughly two hundred seventy imperial pounds."

"That's not horrible," Rix said, pulling the extra parts he'd taken from *Quibbler 12a* and placing them in empty crates for transport.

"Rix Banner?" a voice called from the end of the cargo pod.

Rix stood and turned, finding a thin, disheveled young man in greasy coveralls standing at the end of the cargo pod. "That's right," Rix said. "Are you Neral's guy?"

"Petal. I'm the lead mechanic for Gray Consortium," he said. "You sure hacked up that mount on *Quibbler*. Not a good idea, you telling Neral you could get this installed. You might as well have used a cutting torch."

"I like our chances," Rix said. "Where's *Quibbler 12a* now?"

"It's over in Chainreach."

"Do you have any way to move these barrels?" Rix asked.

"No." Petal rolled his eyes. "I'm just here to oversee the work."

"Not sure you bringing a bunch of attitude is going to help," Rix said. "I can't move these barrels by myself, and I'm certain Neral gave you the assignment to help, not oversee. Now, if you'd like me to get that clarified, I can, because if we're not doing this, I'd prefer to know now. I sure won't have any trouble selling this equipment back home."

"Don't think you have that choice. You have a contract, and Grays don't put up with contract breakers."

"I'm glad you see it that way," Rix said. "Because the contract between me and Neral says he was providing someone to help, so kick in or take off. It's your call."

"You're making a mistake," Petal said, pulling his shirt up to expose a pistol in the waistband of his pants.

Rix's eyebrows raised, unimpressed as he tapped at the ray gun strapped to his side. "Make your move, Petal," Rix said. "We might as well get this out your system now."

"Are you crazy?" Petal asked, pulling his pistol out and aiming it at Rix. "I could shoot you and no one would care."

"So, I've been shot at, and shot, a number of times," Rix said. "It's not pleasant. There's a common thread that I've found between success and failure in those exchanges. Would you like to know what that is?"

"You keep running your trap and you're going to know what it feels like to be shot by me," Petal threatened.

"Right," Rix said. "You're missing the bigger ideas. The thing that gets missed is situational awareness. It's something you seem to lack."

"What in the seven lanes of hell are you ... never mind. I'll just take the barrels," he said, focusing in.

It was then that Philo swung in from behind and whacked Petal on the back of the shoulders and neck with a long pipe. "Rixy! Rixy! What's shakin'?" Philo asked excitedly. "Kel said needed help, early. How she know about bad mans?"

Rix released the strap he'd been holding and walked over to where Petal was kneeling on the floor of the cargo pod. He scooped up the lean man's pistol and pushed it into his own waist band. "I appreciate you coming, Philo. We're going to head over to Chainreach and install these barrels back on *Quibbler*."

"Man's here to take big guns?" Philo asked.

"Nah, he's just got an attitude problem," Rix said. "Would you mind grabbing some flex cuffs from *Calypso?* I don't think our new friend, Petal, is feeling extra helpful today."

"You can't do this," Petal said. "I'll kill you."

"You're going to need to work on that situational awareness idea," Rix said. "Now, how about you let me know where we're headed so we can get on with our morning?"

"Are all Galactics this crazy?" Petal asked.

"Probably not," Rix said. "But I'm not even from Galactic Empire. I'm just a visitor. And, for what it's worth, I'm willing to give this whole thing another try, because I doubt you want your friends to see you walking in with handcuffs when we get back to your shop."

"You wouldn't dare."

"I would. And like I said at the beginning, if you lose the attitude, we'll get along just great. What do you say, are you interested in giving this another try?"

"Sure. What do I have to lose?" Petal said glibly.

"I have conditions," Rix said. "I don't mind people making a mistake, once. It's repeated mistakes that I try to avoid. You don't get to threaten me or Philo, and you'll help me in any way I ask, as long as what I'm asking isn't unreasonable."

"Okay, give me my gun back, then."

"Maybe in a bit," Rix said. "Show me you're a good egg and I'm sure we'll soon be fast friends."

Rubbing his wrists where Rix removed the handcuffs, Petal stared at Rix as if daring him to make his next move. "Now what?"

"Do you want to give me a destination on Chainreach?" Rix asked. "Philo, we'll just take the stack of storage pods with us."

"Where we're going, there won't be enough room for your entire ship," Petal said.

"Oh? How much room are we talking about?"

"Not enough for those container pods."

"How about just the ship?"

"Should be okay."

"Okay, Philo, let's tie these cargo pods off and detach," Rix said.

"Yup, yup," Philo said with enthusiasm.

As expected, Petal didn't provide much help in separating the hauler from its cargo pods, but it wasn't an unfamiliar process and Rix and Philo managed it easily enough. "I'll move *Gravitational Pull* around to the back of that pod and we can lash the barrels to that short platform where the cargo rails connect. Does that sound about right to you, Philo?"

"Yup. Rixy move ships. Philo make sure not get too close."

It was with some trepidation that Rix hopped into *Gravitational Pull's* pilot chair. Sailing through the vast expanse of space was one thing. Tight maneuvering next to a pier was another thing entirely.

"Beverly, can you show me closeup controls? I don't want to bash anything."

Beverly appeared with a leather cap, wearing goggles and an aviator's jacket. "Yes, Rix. We'll move down to one tenth scale. Everything will take ten times as much as you're used to. Let me know if you'd like to scale up."

"First, nice Amelia Earhart," Rix said. "Starting main engines."

The motor struggled, not unlike an old carberated engine that wasn't getting enough fuel. Rix manipulated controls that shifted the mix of fuels and the motor chugged to life, spewing a dark, smoky cloud across the pier.

"Grumpy man is waving arms. Want talk," Philo said.

"Beverly, can you get him on comms?"

"Working on it," Beverly said.

Rix pushed forward on the stick and inched *Gravitational Pull* away from the cargo pods, still connected to their frame rails. "Petal, what is the issue?" Rix asked, slowly turning *Gravitational Pull* away from the pier. Unlike Kel, Rix had no interest in rotating over top of the cargo pods like Kel would do, instead, he turned the utility vehicle around, as if he were driving the cab of a semi-truck.

"Your engines are smoked. This thing isn't going to make it to Chainreach, much less back to Galactic space," Petal said.

"Ordinarily, I'd agree with you," Rix said, gliding along next to the cargo pods, checking the standoff distance he struggled to maintain. "She's just got an attitude. We'll be fine."

"Some mechanic," Petal grumbled.

Rix grinned as he slid *Gravitational Pull* around the end of the last cargo pod and backed into place, all the while watching Philo in addition to his monitors. "Stop, Rixy. Touches in one meter. Drifting still."

Rix checked the distance between his vessel and the stationary cargo pods. Indeed, he was closing the gap. Tapping twice, he threw a fresh charcoal cloud onto the pier and with Beverly's help, brought *Gravitational Pull* to a stop, relative to the pier.

"Mooring lines extended," Rix said, watching through cameras as Philo expertly tied off the ship.

"Secure," Philo announced.

Rix left *Gravitational Pull's* powerplant running, even though he had plenty of charge in the vessel's large batteries. The effect was that wafts of smoke continued to waft across the pier. Walking back out, Rix found that he was two meters away from the back of the cargo pod.

"Hey, Philo, buddy, I need to get closer to touching. Would you loosen those mooring lines and let me tap her back?"

"Can do, Rixy," Philo said, unwinding one of the two lines, which he slacked and then retied, moving to the second line he'd tied. "Go, go. Room now."

Spatially, Philo nailed the lengths and as *Gravitational Pull* tugged against the mooring lines, the small, aft platform Rix planned to tie the barrels to just barely contacted the pod, although that contact gouged the edge of the pod.

"With the two of us, this should be manageable if we drop a grav pallet in the middle," Rix said, sliding a pallet to Philo. "I'll lift this end, push that under, please?"

"Yup, yup," Philo answered.

It took only minutes to get the first barrel settled on the pallet and slid over to where they lashed it in place. Repeating for the second barrel took another twenty minutes, but then they were done. Closing the pod, Rix stepped onto the pier. "Your turn, Petal. Where are we going?"

"I'll fly it in."

Rix shook his head. "You can ride and point, but you're not sailing my ship."

"It's tricky, and you don't look too steady with it," Petal said. Rix motioned for the surly mechanic to follow him and Philo back into the ship. "What a dump. Is this how you people live?" Petal wrinkled his nose.

Rix grunted a laugh. "It has been on this trip," he said. The trip over to Chainreach turned out to be more a lesson in visually locating and avoiding the fluxspan rails than any sort of tricky sailing. And though Petal's instructions were minimal, they managed to arrive without any major incidents.

"You're in my shop, now," Petal said as Rix settled *Gravitational Pull* in next to the mechanic's bay adjacent to a thin pier made for smaller vessels.

"Good, why don't you walk me through it so I can get an idea about how we're lifting those barrels into place? Do you have gravity control?" Rix asked.

"We can reduce to near zero. There'll still be some pull, so be careful. Massive objects moving at slow speeds cause a lot of damage," Petal said.

"Okay, what about your tools?"

"You don't have your own?"

"Is this how you want this to work?" Rix asked. "The reason we're in this hangar is because I'm a visitor and don't have my shop available. I *do* have some of my own tools, but no doubt I won't have everything. If you actually help out instead of grumping at me every time I ask a question, we'll get this done and you can have your life back. Or we can argue about every darn thing and take all day. Make a choice, Petal."

"You don't get to boss me around."

"Turn down the gravity," Rix ordered, making up his mind. "If I need tools, I'll just start opening drawers. Don't get in our way."

"You ..." Petal started but then stopped for no reason Rix could imagine.

"Philo, grab the chains from deck three. They're in the starboard storage compartment at the bottom. We'll get you on top of *Quibbler*. You can reach that support to secure your chains. We'll lock the barrel in place."

"Yup, yup, Rixy," Philo said blissfully. Rix followed the exuberant little alien back into the ship, where he grabbed the tool bag that he'd repacked for the operation. By the time they were back in the mechanic's bay, Petal had reduced the gravity so much that Rix had to switch over to the magnetic clamps in his boots, which made climbing *Quibbler* a much easier process.

"How are you getting the barrels up there?" Petal asked, curiously.

"We have some work to do up here first," Rix said, pulling out the electrical tools at the top of his bag. Taking the barrels off, he'd severed about a hundred electrical connections.

"That's a rat's nest," Petal observed, climbing up next to Rix and looking into the control box.

"But that's the majority of the work," Rix said. "Do you have a size-two boltgun? I kept the bolts, and then we only need to replace the control box lid with a custom top."

"You're going to manufacture the top for the control box after you reconnect all those wires? That'll take you hours to make those connections. And how will you even know if you got it right?"

"Colors and positions," Rix said. "The control box has diagnostics that will tell us how we're doing, too. The interface is standard for my diagnostics reader. I figured that'd be the biggest problem, but we're okay."

"You're crazy. This needs a full replacement. You can't fix a mess like this."

Rix nodded but didn't answer. After seeing what he'd left behind, he was even more confident that the repairs, while laborious, were well within his reach. "Help me get that barrel up so Philo can lock it in place?"

Petal managed a long sigh but didn't otherwise object. Unlashing the starboard barrel from *Gravitational Pull,* the two men slowly guided the barrel into the shop, careful not to gain too much momentum as they moved. As massive as the barrel was, with the miniscule gravity, it became a game of nudges and tugs that finally saw it slide in close to where it belonged.

"What now?" Petal asked, still not believing Rix could accomplish the job.

"We need to build a bridge so we can lock this barrel in place, but up about six inches," Rix said. "Do you have some metal scrap I can work with?"

"I don't know what you're trying to do," Petal said.

"We can't bolt the barrel in place, it'll get in the way, and I won't be able to fix the connections. Also, I can't afford to have the barrel moving around. With some scrap quarter inch, I can use the existing bolt holes, but raise them out of the way, and keep them from floating away and snapping all our good work."

"This will never work," Petal said. But even though he was pessimistic, he clambered down the side of the vessel and walked Rix over several bays where there was a pile of junk. "Can you find what you need here?"

"This should do," Rix said, pulling a long piece of scrap three-eighths steel. "I'll have to cut it down."

"Do you have a pattern? We have a jet over here," Petal said.

Beverly appeared in her Rosie the Riveter outfit. "Ask him what standard for the drawing," she said. Rix did as she asked, and a moment later, he had specifications, which he flicked to Petal.

"You just had those?"

"We've known we were repairing this for a while," Rix said. The statement wasn't exactly an answer, but he wasn't interested in giving any more details than necessary to the surly mechanic.

"Give me a minute," he said, grabbing the scrap from Rix. It took closer to thirty minutes, as Petal discovered he didn't have the credentials to use the machine, and then realized he wasn't placing the material in the machine correctly.

"That's perfect," Rix said, inspecting the metal risers. "Thank you, Petal."

"Sure."

Twenty minutes later, with the first barrel fixed in place, Rix started the long process of locating and attaching wires, a task that, without Beverly's ability to highlight matching pairs, would have taken forever, as Petal had assumed.

"You're going too fast," Petal said. "You can't possibly be getting that right."

"Errors are possible," Rix said. "Let's get my scope connected and put it into electronics debugging mode. This model has a trace function that'll tell us what's disconnected. We can also set it to find crossed connections. Maybe you could experiment with that, some."

"I don't know what you're talking about. Diagnostic scope for wiring? That's nuts," he said.

"Try it," Rix said. "You might appreciate knowing how to do this at some point."

"I'll hook it up, but it's a dumb idea."

31

HERDING CATS

It was 2100 when Rix settled *Gravitational Pull* next to the pier adjacent to Kha'rem's dock. Earlier, Amari had told him that they'd returned to *Calypso* and had news. The plan was to meet with Kha'rem to strategize on what, if anything, was their next move.

"Did you get paid?" Kel asked first thing when Rix arrived.

"One hundred ten grams, twenty-four karat gold," he said, holding up a pouch. "We'll have to talk about how much we want to put into return cargo. With Greevo paying his bill, we're going to do alright this month."

"Yeah. How much are we going to spend on repairs when we get home?" Kel asked.

"Both ships need work."

"I have deal I want talk about," Philo blurted out.

"Philo?" Kel asked. "What kind of deal?"

Philo sighed. "Big deal. Need monies. Have maybe partner."

"Do we have time to talk this out before we meet Kha'rem?" Rix asked, accepting a warm hug from Amari as they welcomed each other back.

"Is fifteen minutes enough?" Kel asked. "I imagined you wanted a shower when you got back."

"Philo isn't often excited about deals. I guess I'd like to hear about what he's got going," Rix said. "Is the galley clean enough for us to use?"

"Barely," Kel said. "They cleaned it like a bar. Amari and I have been wiping surfaces, but it's just okay."

The four filed back into *Calypso*. To Rix's eyes, the interior was good or even better than he'd remembered seeing it. There was no trash piled anywhere, and the floors even appeared to have been vacumed and dusted. However, when the light was just right, he saw several spots where the finish looked tacky, and upon inspection, it was discovered to be messy.

"Not a bad start, at least," Rix said, settling onto a stainless-steel stool next to the galley table. "Tell us about your deal, Philo."

"Four broken close ships," Philo said. "Buy. Repair. Sell. Make good money. Cheap here."

"Close ships?" Rix asked.

"Runabouts," Amari filled in. "Messenger craft, local space deliveries, passenger shuttles, that sort of thing. Every station ends up with a graveyard of these kinds of ships because fixing them can be a pain and buying new isn't that expensive."

"And you want to buy four old, broken ships, Philo? Would you fix them yourself, or is that a group project?"

"Us," Philo said, a little frustration showing on his face at his inability to communicate well. "Rixy. Kel. Philo. We fix. We sell. Split money. Good money."

"Have you looked at them?" Rix asked.

"Philo looked at many many. Philo pick four, maybe five," Philo said.

"Do you have a number?" Rix asked, which added to Philo's frustration as he didn't understand the question.

"Money. What do they want you to pay?" Kel asked.

"Not figured," Philo said. "Sta'ci want buy some. Be partner."

"Would we be fixing them here?" Rix asked. "I'm not sure we want to stick around that long."

"Maybe Sta'ci come to station. Maybe talk to Kels."

"Philo, is Sta'ci your girlfriend?" Kel asked, the pitch of her voice climbing as she spoke. "Is Sta'ci going to be the end of the crazy bachelor life for you?"

Philo's face flushed, and he looked at the floor. "Need good deal on brokens, so fix and make business. Kels help get good deal?"

"We need to talk to Sta'ci and see how much she wants to be involved," Kel said. "If you two buy the broken ships and do most of the work, that seems like a good business for you. Is that something we could help with, Rix?"

"I'm always up for helping a friend figure things out. Maybe we could go look at the runabouts you've picked, and we can get an idea of what it'll take to fix 'em," Rix said. "I'd be happy to help with that."

"Rixy and Kels good people!" Philo exclaimed, hugging them each before bounding from the room.

"Hey, while you were gone, Greevo took the remainder of their crates down to the bazaar," Kel said. "Or that's what I think, anyway. Everything has been taken out, and the last user code entered was Greevo's."

"Sounds good, let me get a quick shower and we'll go talk with Kha'rem about what you guys found," Rix said. "I assume you have something interesting to look at."

"We do," Amari said. "It's going to take some work to find where they're keeping the cipher, but we know where Kasit and his mother are."

"They're being held?" Rix asked, pulling off his jumpsuit. He'd brought a change of clothing with him, and he slipped into the head while Amari took his dirty clothing with a promise to clean it while he was in the shower.

Instead of eating at the restaurant where they'd previously met, Kha'rem asked the trio to meet with him in an office within his warehouse. Joining them was Bha'resh, but no others.

"I'm intensely curious of the news you have brought," Kha'rem said. "I have listened today. There are rumors of a break in at Jeshifa but somehow there is no evidence. Was this you, Kel Warp?"

"I don't know of these reports," Kel said. "But here's what we do know. Kasit and his mother Zenith are being held in a low security setting. We imagine they're being held more on the fear of being caught than actual, physical security. It would not be difficult to extract them."

"From observing, however," Amari stepped in. "We believe that once they are extracted there will be a strong response from the organization to find them."

"What of the cipher?" Kha'rem asked.

"We didn't directly find it," Amari said. "To do so would have tipped our hand as to our presence. Kasit and Zenith should be extracted before we attempt to locate the cipher."

"That's difficult," Kha'rem said. "If you make a play for those two, certainly Lirren will know that the cipher is at risk. The device will disappear."

"So that's the rub," Rix said. "It we go for one objective, the other might become unreachable."

"There will be no safe place for Kasit nor Zenith if they are broken out from Jeshifa control," Bha'resh said. "And, if your crew is associated with having helped with their escape, Jeshifa will come for you, regardless of Kha'rem's original offer of safety for your vessel."

"I cannot stand directly against Jeshifa," Kha'rem said. "Lirren's forces are too many. Did you get any sense of the danger Kasit and Zenith are in?"

"They're being treated reasonably well, but locked up," Kel said. "The guards made it seem like they would be locked down for an extended time, perhaps as long as a couple of weeks. There was talk that the pair won't ever be released, and that at some point they'll have to 'make tough decisions.'"

"As in, be killed?" Rix asked.

"Yes," Amari said.

"Getting them away from Jeshifa will be a trick, even if we take the cipher," Kel said. "Let's set that aside for a moment. Let's say we help them escape. What then? Where do they go? Can you hide them, Kha'rem?"

"For a time," Khar'em said. "Garanod Enclave is not such a large place that they would not eventually be found."

Kel looked at Rix and shook her head. "I know what you're thinking," she said.

"What?"

"That we could smuggle them out," Kel said.

Rix sighed, defeated. "I was."

"That's taking on a whole lot of trouble we didn't sign up for," Kel said. "We don't have responsibility in this."

"We brought the cipher," Rix said.

"Greevo brought the cipher," Kel corrected. "I'm all for doing a good thing, but if we smuggle them out, that cipher is as good as gone. We also burn Garanod as a shipping destination. Jeshifa will eventually figure out it was us."

"What are your thoughts about this, Kha'rem?" Rix asked.

"The only reason that Kasit and Zenith's lives would be endangered is that Lirren does not wish others to know he possesses the cipher," Kha'rem said. "Also, Kasit must have refused to join Jeshifa. As for plans to rescue Kasit or Zenith, my approach would be to negotiate with Lirren. I do not have high expectations for such a negotiation."

"That was a brave stance on Kasit's part," Amari said. "I am not quite as worried about returning to Garanod after a rescue, mostly because with the cipher, there will be a strong shift in power on Garanod to the Jeshifa organization. With an ability to hide in the nebula's clouds, a Jeshifa attack vessel would have significant advantage on an attack. My point is that without control of the cipher, Garanod will not be a friendly destination."

"That's a good point," Kel agreed. "We're back to looking for the cipher, then."

"I believe that's right," Amari said. "We'll set off early tomorrow morning."

"It is too dangerous," Kha'rem said. "You were fortunate to have traveled to Jeshifa territory and returned. It is unlikely you could do this more than one time."

"Bha'resh, how did sales of our goods go, today?" Rix asked.

"You have raised an additional twenty-five grams of gold. Most of your better items have moved already. There is a buyer who would purchase the remaining for twenty grams," Bha'resh said.

"That sounds a little slim," Rix said. "I was expecting we had at least sixty grams left, before the twenty-five was collected. That leaves more like thirty-five grams worth on the table."

"If sold individually, I agree," Bha'resh said. "I might be able to move him to twenty-seven grams, but he won't go much higher."

"Twenty-seven is a good number," Rix said. "I'd go as low as twenty-five if that gives you some negotiating position."

"Thank you. Our dealings have been fair and profitable for all involved. It has been a pleasure," Bha'resh said, dropping a small pouch of gold on the table. Rix picked up the sack and counted out fifty-two small, gram sized bars.

Rix smiled, understanding that Bha'resh had already completed the deal and was simply allowing him to catch up. "It's been a pleasure working with you," Rix said.

"I hope it has made this journey a worthwhile endeavor."

"We're doing okay," Rix said. "There is quite a lot of risk, but if we're able to make it home safely, it will have been quite a good trip for us."

"You have moved beyond the conversation of Kasit and Zenith," Kha'rem said. "Please explain."

"We're going back to Chainreach tomorrow," Kel said plainly. "We're going to find the cipher, and once we do, we'll make some decisions about next steps."

"But the danger," Kha'rem argued.

"The danger is real, Kha'rem," Amari said quietly. "The issue is that when you add the impact of the cipher to the equation, we're talking about a whole lot more than two innocents being kidnapped. Jeshifa will use that cipher to bring pain and death to many more than Kasit and Zenith. We are responsible for bringing this cipher to Garanod Enclave, therefore, we will fulfill our responsibility by retrieving or ruining it. If Kasit and Zenith can be saved, that will be a secondary mission."

Kel raised an eyebrow at Amari's decisiveness. "And that, my friends, is what we call the final word."

"I offer to you whatever support you may need," Kha'rem said.

Amari picked up a sandwich and held it in Kha'rem's direction. "This is a great start. I'm starving."

"Then, let us eat," Kha'rem agreed, following her lead and loading a sandwich onto his own plate.

"What are you up to tomorrow, Rix?" Kel asked, as if they hadn't been talking about stealth missions and threat of death to hostages seconds ago.

For a moment, all Rix could do was stare at his friend and then he finally shook off the discordant thoughts. "Well, I thought I would go with Philo and Sta'ci to look at a pile of old runabouts he's looking to buy and fix up."

"Geldat Visor?" Bha'resh asked.

Rix glanced at Bha'resh. "I guess I don't know. Philo said he found a whole lot of junked runabouts and thought four or five of them looked repairable."

"Geldat is the same who purchased the last of your supply of parts," Bha'resh said. "When he was in, he mentioned interest from outsiders in some of his vessels that no longer ran. I thought it to be Greevo as there was a Grintok woman involved. You're saying that your man, Philo is involved with Kha'rem's Sta'ci?"

"Oh, this should be good," Kel said, rubbing her hands together. "Yes, Philo was smitten by her when they met not twenty meters from where we're sitting just now."

"What do you feel about this, Kha'rem?" Bah'resh asked.

"Sta'ci has my blessing to venture out."

"Is Geldat a tough negotiator?" Rix inquired.

"He enjoys negotiating. He'd given me an upper price he was willing to pay for the remainder of the parts, which is why I was able to close the deal this evening," Bha'resh said. "I stretched him by a single gold gram. He has already responded that he will cover that difference. You might consider that tomorrow as you negotiate." Rix nodded, making a mental note.

"Have you thought more of your departure date?" Kha'rem asked.

"I bet we're not quite as desirable a tenant as we once were," Rix snorted. "We've brought trouble to your pier."

"We have enjoyed your visit. And we will welcome you upon your next visit," Kha'rem said, smiling. "But I would be lying to say I was not eager to see you on your way home, and all of this business completed with none injured."

"I'll speak to Greevo," Rix said. "I believe he intends to sail back with us. Are you okay if I give you an answer on departure tomorrow? I'd like to get sailing the day after tomorrow, if everything works out, but it could be another day after that."

"Certainly, that is fine," Kha'rem said.

Rix covered a yawn, and when he realized Kha'rem was looking at him, he gave a sheepish smile. "Sorry about that. It's been a long day. Perhaps we could talk more tomorrow, after the girls have had another shot at looking around."

"I have questions about how they were able to travel to Chainreach and penetrate the defenses of Jeshifa," Kha'rem said. "But I don't believe you would discuss these matters with me or Bha'resh."

"Don't take it personally," Kel said. "You already know more than we'd like. The fewer people who are aware of our activities, the easier it will be for us."

"I understand," Kha'rem said. "Take the sandwiches back to your ship and eat at your leisure. I believe we have covered the important topics for this evening."

"What time are you going over to Geldat's yard?" Bha'resh asked. "I'll come along and we can deliver the parts he purchased from you. It might ease the conversation of negotiation."

"You're welcome to come along," Rix said.

"Do you have transportation?" Bha'resh asked.

"I don't even know where we're going," Rix said. "I imagine we could take *Gravitational Pull*."

"Contact me when you know when you'd like to leave," Bha'resh said. "I have a people mover that will be easier to travel in."

"I'll let you know shortly," Rix said. "Thank you."

And with that, the trio walked out onto the veranda in front of Kha'rem's warehouse. "Do you get the feeling Kha'rem knows more than he's sharing?" Kel asked.

"He seems like an upright sort of fella to me," Rix said.

"Those don't need to be conflicting ideas," Amari said. "Kha'rem knows many things he hasn't shared with us. I too, believe he has more information of Jeshifa's plans for the cipher. I cannot determine if that is a competitive issue between Kha'rem and Jeshifa or if it is concern."

"Kha'rem was straight with us regarding his interest in the cipher," Rix said.

"No need to get defensive," Kel said. "We've got our butts hanging out in the wind a bit. I'd like to make sure all the people on our side are working out of the same playbook."

Rix nodded. "I wish I could come along with you. I do not love the danger you place yourselves in."

"It's more than danger," Kel said. "It's fun, too! Imagine the thrill of being able to look like someone else but having no idea how they interact with other people. It's a big mind game trying to read their faces and how they talk to figure out how not to blow your cover."

"That's not making me feel better," Rix sighed.

"She knows," Amari said, looping an arm around Rix's. "She's trying to get you stirred up. We are both experts at avoiding conversations that expose us. Traveling together, we're able to protect each other even more by creating minor diversions. Trust me, Rix, we are very good at this, and we do not need protecting."

"But that's always been my job. I make sure people are safe," Rix said. "Even in the war, I had to pick up a gun more times than I'd like to admit. I always ended up in the action."

"Sounds like that's what you're missing," Kel said. "Sorry, pal, we were born with our skills. You're just going to have to live with us going out on our little missions every once in a while."

"I just saw Kitka go into *Calypso*. I wonder if that means Greevo is back?" Amari wondered, changing subjects.

"Oh, good, I'd like to see what he's looking at for travel plans," Rix said. "I'd like to shove off in thirty-six hours, give or take."

"That lines up with what we told him, originally," Kel said.

A wave of sour smells greeted them as they entered *Calypso*. Entering just aft of the combination crew quarters, galley and open space, they immediately found that Greevo and his four companions were taking up every available space. At the galley, Kitka worked over a large bubbling pot that periodically spewed out a clump of gooey green material, most of which landed back in the pot, while some, simply landed on the bulkhead adjacent and behind.

"Ugh," Kel complained. "I hate it when they make this crap."

"Greevo, could I have a word?" Rix asked, finding the curmudgeon lounging on the dilapidated couch.

"Have you found my cipher?" he asked with obvious irritation.

"No. I'm afraid you'll need to make an insurance claim on that," Rix said.

"No insurance. Rix Banner bad partner," Greevo grumbled.

"Be that as it may," Rix said. "We have plans to leave in 36 hours. Can you have your business concluded within that timeframe?"

"I cannot leave without my cipher!" Greevo spluttered, sitting up as flecks of whatever he'd been eating flew across the space between them.

"Do you have cargo you'd like to return to Patience Station with?" Rix asked. "If not, your final bill for transport is sixteen thousand credits. We'll need that deposit approved pending Galactic Empire exchange prior to you disembarking with us."

"I haven't sold all of my goods," Greevo further complained.

"Greevo, was it your impression that we would stay here indefinitely? I'm burning precious metals for every day we're tied up," Rix said. "Do you need a recommendation for a partner who can help move your products?"

"Forty-six hours," Greevo shot back. "We cleaned. You promised."

"In forty-six hours, you will pay sixteen thousand credits or hand over equivalent precious metal exchange," Rix said. "If you want to negotiate space in my cargo pods, you need to start talking as I'm lining up loads for the return trip."

"How much space you have?" Greevo asked.

"Right now, I'm using about a third of a pod," Rix said. "By this time tomorrow, I might fill them completely. Get me your space requirements by mid-day tomorrow and I'll get you a price."

"Covered by original contract," Greevo said. "There is no mention of price for return cargo."

"Right, because you wouldn't commit, so there is no available space unless you pay for it," Rix said and when Greevo started to object, Rix held his hand up. "We're not arguing about this, Greevo. Get me your requirements, I'll give you a number."

32

BUYING JUNK

"Good morning to you, Sta'ci," Rix said, eyeing the small Grintok woman. Although she was shorter and green, she was good looking by most human standards. More importantly, she seemed to look at Philo with great fondness.

"Good morning, Rix Banner," Sta'ci answered in her high, reedy voice.

"I hope you don't mind, but I had dinner with Bha'resh last night and invited him along. We have a delivery to make out at Geldat's," Rix said.

Sta'ci exchanged a look with Philo, then took a half-step toward Rix. "We need to be careful in showing our interest to Bha'resh," she said. "He might bid against us, making our price higher."

"I'll ask him to stay out of the bidding this morning," Rix said. "Would that help?"

"Yes."

"Philo, talk me through this. You want to buy a bunch of old runabouts, fix them up and then sell them for a profit?" Rix asked.

"Yes, Rixy!" Philo shouted as a small hover craft approached the pier from the opposite direction as the marketplace.

Rix looked from Philo to Sta'ci and back. "Where are you setting up shop?"

"Philo talk to Rixy about this. Philo use small part of Rixy shop?" Philo asked.

"On Patience?" Rix asked.

"Yes, yes, Rixy."

"What about Sta'ci?" Rix asked, turning to the young woman. "Are you coming back to Patience Station with us?"

"I apologize. We are speaking out of order," Sta'ci said. "We were going to ask what the cost of a crew berth would be to Patience Station. I am considering moving there."

"To start a business? Hang out with Philo? Both?" Rix asked.

Sta'ci's green skin darkened on her cheeks. "To start a business with Philo. You should know, there is little opportunity on Garanod Enclave for a Grintok of low caste. Even so, I am hesitant toward an arrangement that makes me beholden to someone else."

"Such as through rental payments for shop space and a place to live?" Rix asked.

"There is more. I have only capital for one vessel, but I've identified four or five that I believe are repairable and would be desirable," she said. "Philo believes you might have interest in investing in our little company."

"I see," Rix said. "What kind of capital are you hoping to raise for investment, and what are you expecting to return?"

Sta'ci smiled, realizing Rix was taking them seriously, and her face relaxed. "Geldat has not individually priced the derelict and junked vessels in his yard. I do not believe he has even created an inventory.

Philo and I scoured his yard and found five vessels, all mounted atop Marfos frames and with Norwed power plants, which was our search criteria. As scrap, those vessels could fetch between three and ten grams of gold. I would offer thirty-eight grams for five vessels."

"Then all we need to do is haul them back to Patience Station, fix them and sell them for more than we've put in," Rix said. "You'd need Kel and me to invest twenty-eight grams of gold, cover transportation and provide storage and a workspace."

Philo's normally happy-go-lucky face fell as he listened to Rix enumerate the costs associated with the venture. "Bad idea," he said, voice thick with disappointment.

"No, Philo. Not a bad idea. Before you say more, Rix Banner, let us go look at these vessels. You are an unparalleled mechanic. Your opinion is valuable," Sta'ci said.

"I didn't want to interrupt," Bha'resh said, stepping out of the hovercraft. "Greetings Sta'ci, Philo. I have heard that you are considering a business deal with Geldat."

Philo nodded. "Sta'ci is big thinker on deal."

"A formidable negotiator, no doubt," Bha'resh said. "Would we all like to load up and take a trip?"

"Let's go," Rix said.

The four of them climbed into Bha'resh's spacious hovercraft, with Rix in the front and Sta'ci and Philo in the back.

"We're about thirty minutes out," Bha'resh said.

"Is there any chance Geldat will see you as a competitor for Sta'ci and Philo's negotiating?" Rix asked. "I'd hate for him to play the two of you off each other."

"Honest and open conversation. How refreshing," Bha'resh said. "While I have found treasures in Geldat's yard in prior years, I am in no market for a new vehicle. I will make this well known. Do you mind if I ask what you're looking for?"

Rix turned around in his seat. "That's all you, Sta'ci," he said.

"Our criteria are commonality of components," Sta'ci said. "I have spent much time searching and comparing units in Geldat's yard. Marfos frames with Norwed power plants are common starting points for the cosmic runabouts common to Garanod Enclave."

"I agree that is a common configuration," Bha'resh said. "I do not understand the interest caused by the commonality."

"Swapping components. If we are able to move components between frames, perhaps we could end up with three working vessels of the five we purchase. At eight grams gold per junked vehicle, we only need fourteen grams gold on three of the derelicts to make a profit. Fourteen grams for an operable runabout is a very low price. We should expect to collect twice that, if not more."

"Ah, there is the risk you are assuming," Bha'resh said. "Repair is not certain for Geldat's grounded fleet of peculiarities. Repairing three might cost you even more in parts than you could ever make."

"Yes," Sta'ci answered.

"That is quite an endeavor," Bha'resh said. "Consider coming by the shop. It is likely I have parts you will need."

"Thank you." Sta'ci gently dipped her head in a slight bow.

Rix decided it was a good moment to change subjects. "How populated is Garanod Enclave? It's not looking like there are many homes located this far out."

"It is difficult to live too far from the populated regions," Bha'resh said. "The atmosphere is breathable, but little grows other than fungi, and while many are edible, one cannot survive long on fungi alone. Even so, there are many settlers scattered across the surfaces of all five district masses, but less than a percent of any of it has been civilized."

"Geldat is in an unsettled area?"

"Yes, his yard is at the beginning of the vast wastelands of Driftmarket."

"Does he have to worry about bandits, much?"

"Any who have looked to steal from Geldat in the past have found he is not soft," Bha'resh said.

33

PHONE A FRIEND

Dozing in and out, Kasit's was pulled from sleep as his attention was drawn to the soft turn of the door latch where he and Zenith were being held. Tapping his mother's leg, he woke her from a similarly light sleep. She raised her head from where it rested against him. Without comment, she glanced at him and followed his locked stare to the opening door.

"When are you going to let us out? We've done everything you've asked," Zenith asked, recognizing the guard who stepped in.

"You need to be quiet," the guard said, lifting a finger to his mouth. "We're friends."

Behind the first guard, a second stepping in wearing unusual clothing, oddly similar to Kasit's.

"You're not going to cross Lirren," Zenith challenged, though she lowered her voice.

"We don't have time for twenty questions. If you want to gain your freedom, you must listen to me," the guard said. "Can you at least do that?"

Zenith and Kasit exchanged confused looks, then Kasit turned back to the guard. "What's in it for you?"

The guard's smile was inine. "That's a better question than you realize. Kasit, you need to accompany me to hatch 12A, where I've stored your fluxspan sling. You'll make a run over to Driftmarket and then to Geldat's junkyard, where you'll find Rix Banner. You need to convince him to come back with you. We have a job for him. You need to do this and not get caught. Do you follow what I'm saying?"

"Rix Banner? If he can escape, just let him go. Lirren can do what he wants with me," Zenith objected.

The second guard turned to Zenith. "This isn't the moment where we debate tactical plans and feel all warm and fuzzy. Do you want to live? If you do, Kasit does what's been outlined. We'll take care of the rest. In the end, you'll have some hard choices to make, but this isn't the moment."

"Like what?"

"Look, I know this is a lot to take in," Kel said, changing from the shape of the second to Kasit's. "And if you tell anyone about what's happening, there'll be big trouble for you." She waited for Zenith and Kasit to look at her long enough to watch the transformation. From history, she knew people needed as long as a few minutes to accept what they were seeing. She hoped the mother/son pair were quick learners because she continued. "I'm going to stay here so Kasit can fetch Rix. My partner..." she motioned to Amari as the first guard, "will take care of things here. The plan for saving you guys looks a lot like people not figuring out anything has happened. And trust me, we're good at this."

"I ... I don't understand," Zenith said.

"That's the great part of this plan. You don't need to," Kel said, sitting next to her, looking very much like Kasit as she patted her leg. "Also, it's kind of important that Kasit and I aren't in the same room at the same time, so we kind of need to get this show on the road. Kasit, do you know what you're doing?"

"Uh, well ...," he stammered, looking to his mother for confirmation. Zenith shrugged her shoulders, just as unable to process the moment as her son. "12A, you've stashed my sling. You want me to find Rix Banner at Geldat's yard and bring him back. But what if he doesn't want to come?"

"We'll have to take that chance," Amari said as the first guard. "But I like your chances. I left a cloak with a hood at the hatch. Take it with you. We can't have anyone from Jeshifa recognizing you. That'd cause trouble."

"You have ninety minutes," Kel said, smiling as Kasit looked at her, clearly confused by the fact that he was looking into his own face.

"Go!" Amari urged, pulling Kasit to the door and walking him out.

"Wait," Zenith hissed, hurrying over to the door where Kasit had just about been pushed through. "They'll see him out there."

"Not our first rodeo," Kel said. "And if you're wondering, if you act all nervous and draw attention, you put us all at risk. Your job is to sit, defeated on that bench, just like you were when we came in."

"Kasit ... I love you," Zenith managed before she allowed Kel to lead her back to the bench and sit her down.

"I ... I know," he answered and then turned as Amari closed and locked the temporary cell.

"You need to get tough now," Amari said, leading him quickly through the hallway. "This is no time for second thoughts. You have one mission. Get to Rix Banner and bring him back. Screw that up and this gets messy for everyone."

"What does that mean?"

"People start dying, Kasit," Amari said with a hard look. "That's what we're trying to stop, here. More people dying."

"Okay, I got it," he said, turning to stairs that would take him to the twelfth level. "Go back. I have this."

"You've got this when you're outside and moving," Amari said. "And stop running. It attracts attention."

Together, they moved downstairs to the twelfth level and turned, running directly into a pair of Jeshifa gang members.

"What are you doing down here?" the bigger of the two asked.

"If it was your business, you'd be doing it," Amari said as the first guard.

"Don't be talking like that to me," the man said menacingly. "I'll knock that ugly teragut seed off your shoulders like its ... soft."

"I'm fully insulted," Amari said, shaking her head ironically. "Decide; get in my way or move on. I have business."

"You're doing something you're not supposed to be," the man said, reaching for his pistol.

Amari flicked her hand first in his direction and then in the direction of his partner. Neither reacted other than to step back, expecting something violent to happen and perhaps surprised that nothing, aside from an itch on the side of their face presented itself. The man who'd challenged them finished drawing his weapon.

"Don't do that," Amari said.

"Why?"

Stepping toward him she grasped the hand holding his weapon and twisted, somehow managing to keep the pistol from firing. Angrily, and slowly, the man started to react, but just then the chemical she'd flicked into his face acted and he crumpled into her.

"You're in no shape to be firing weapons," she said, helping him to the ground. "Catch him, Kasit. We'll store them in the bathroom, up here."

"Did you kill them?" he asked, horrified.

"No. But the less you know about all that the better. They'll wake up in an hour, with headaches and a loss of memory," she said, pulling the big man into the bathroom and into a stall where she set him face down, with his chest resting on a toilet that needed servicing. "Bad luck on that one," she said. "Kas, do the same with yours."

"Okay. What's with putting them over a toilet?"

"They'll likely have upset stomachs. Different species react differently. It's handy for the story if they toss breakfast, though."

"You could have broken out Mom," he said.

"Right. Not your day to make plans," she said, leading him from the bathroom and out to the hatch. "Get Rix. Come back. Don't screw up."

Kasit crouched and picked up his sling. "How did you get this?"

"So many questions, so little time," Amari said. "Go."

Kasit shook his head and took off at a light jog, pulling the hood of his cloak up. Fully unnerved by the events, he struggled to get his bearings and had to crouch by an abandoned shack. Ten minutes prior, he'd been in Jeshifa's custody and now he was free, but running a mission for someone who could change their appearance? Was it some sort of fancy technology? His clone had looked all too real.

"Wag, are you there?" Kasit called over comms. "Don't let anyone know you're talking to me, but I need the fastest jump route to Driftmarket, near Geldat's junkyard."

"What in the seven moons?" Wag came back in a whisper a few minutes later. "Word is you got caught up by Lirren himself."

"I'm in trouble. I need that route, and you need to be quiet about it."

"I have you, brother," Wagg said. "I'm just glad to know you're alive. Kha'rem is worried. Everybody is worried. What happened?"

"Long story," Kasit said. "You wouldn't believe it, even if I told you. But I'm in a spot. Talk to me."

"Send a location."

"Here."

"What in the seven moons are you doing on Chainreach? You're escaping Jeshifa? You have some big crazy ones, brother."

"Stop talking, Wagg. Someone will hear you. I only stay alive if you stay quiet."

Wagg's chuckle came through the comm line. "That's a heck of a thing to bet on, but I got you. Okay, you have six minutes to take the 547 fluxspan to Quiet Coil, but you're going to jump to Driftmarket 941 at the junction twenty kilometers. Are you up for that? Otherwise, I can get you a link in Havenfall. It'll cost you thirty-five minutes, though."

"I'm good," Kasit said, scurrying from cover toward the fluxspan ferry terminal and the 547 line. Because the ferry from Quiet Coil to Havenfall was outgoing, there would be passengers lining up within just six minutes. It was likely those travelers were Jeshifa, which could be trouble for him. Pulling his hood even closer in, Kasit raced forward. If ever there was a time to be bold, this was it, and he ran like demons chased him, which wasn't far from true.

Kasit didn't hesitate as he ran beneath the ferry terminal. With sling in hand, he leapt into space, flinging his lifeline out over his head and over the fluxspan rail, grasping the ever-familiar cable as it swung predictably around. Expecting relief, he found no comfort as he slid along the fluxspan rail, which was once the pinnacle of his personal freedom. He realized that joy had been ruined by Lirren, and he wondered if it would ever return.

Sliding along, he focused on his connection with the Havenfall 941 line. In truth, there was no connection beyond the close traversal of the two fluxspan rails and the periodic joints that allowed long tethers to hold the rails in place. At these joints, there were three-meter, square connectors that were flat on top. A talented fluxspan rider could leap from one rail to a connector below, if his timing was good. Of course, missing that jump would likely become the jumpers last feat.

Kasit watched carefully as his HUD showed a countdown to the release of his sling. Under normal circumstances, releasing a sling wasn't difficult. Making sure to do so with milliseconds of wiggle room made it a whole lot more exciting. Releasing just a little late, Kasit, twisted in midair and flattened out his body. He landed on the back side of the rail connector and slid, jamming the edge of his sling's body into the metal surface and slowing just enough to stay atop.

"That was exciting," he said to himself. Taking a minute, he checked his gear and made sure his sling hadn't been fouled in the fall. With a few quick steps, he jumped off the side of the connector and swung his sling around the rail, proceeding toward Driftmarket.

34

DEAL INTERRUPTED

"HOW BIG IS THIS PLACE?" Rix asked as Bha'resh turned onto a bouncy road that cut through what looked much more like a dump than a junkyard to him as mountains of trash were piled on both sides.

"This isn't Geldat's yet. But he's got a big place just another couple of kilometers up here," Bha'resh said. "Are you sure you want to sell all these parts, now? Several of the items you're selling could be useful in repairing cars like what you've described."

"Two different transactions," Rix said. "Anything I'm selling here, we can pick up back on Patience without too much effort."

"It's hard to imagine a lack of scarcity like that," Bha'resh said.

"Funny," Rix said.

"How's that?"

"Patience Station has a level of scarcity I've never encountered and yet you look at it as being wide open."

"Is there anything you can't get if you're willing to pay enough?" Bha'resh asked.

"On Patience? No," Rix said. "At a minimum, we have the industrial manufactories. The cost can be prohibitive, though. Now, on Earth, where I came from, this kind of technology isn't possible at all. We've just started launching satellites into orbit. Apparently, that's one of the first steps toward space flight. But the technology we have is available to most people, provided they have money. Food, housing, all that isn't hard for most, at least in my country."

"Country is like a district?" Bha'resh asked.

"Except with individual governments and militaries. Earth has a lot of people compared to Garanod or Patience."

"What's a lot?"

"Two and a half billion and growing fast," Rix said.

"That's huge," Sta'ci marveled. "How did you feed them all?"

"Big farms. And we don't always do that great of a job of feeding everyone. That has more to do with governments failing people than not having the capacity," Rix said. "Earth has its own share of problems, but space to grow and people to work are not on that list."

"Here we are," Bha'resh said as the mounds of trash on the side of the narrow road diminished, giving way to piles of junked vehicles that were lined up in neat rows. "Sta'ci, do you have a map of where your specific treasures are located?"

"Do you promise that you will not undercut my bidding today?" she asked. "I was worried to travel out here with such a renowned trader."

"That's a generous statement," Bha'resh said. "No, Rix already broached this topic with me, and honestly, diving through the junkyard has little interest to me. I'm much more likely to ask Geldat to locate a part for one of my customers than to come looking for it of my own volition. I will not interfere with your trading."

"Thank you, Bha'resh. I will remember your kindness today."

"You are an unusual Grintok," Bha'resh said. "I had heard that you do things differently. You are quite pleasant to work with. Maybe we can find business together in the future."

Sta'ci exchanged a look with Philo and leaned over to give him a quick kiss on the cheek. "Perhaps. For now, I am interested in this partner," she said. "Here is the map of the vehicles Geldat has listed."

"I'll let Geldat know we're going to cruise his yard before we stop in and talk to him," Bha'resh said, turning off the road and stopping about halfway down one of the half-kilometer long aisles.

"Some of these have seen much better days," Rix said, jumping out to look at the vehicle identified. "Not much on this but frame and powerplant. The body is completely roached out."

"Roached is a funny translation," Sta'ci said. "Philo is very good with body work. Did you not know?"

Rix thought about it for a moment. Philo had been a tremendous help in fetching and playing second fiddle that he hadn't considered he might have a specialty with a task that wasn't often what *Calypso* needed. "I guess I've seen him do some hull repairs, but nobody likes doing those."

"Did you look at the clean lines?" she asked. "He showed me videos of recent repairs."

"Oh, that's right. I'm sorry, Buddy. I was just running around so much that I didn't think to step back and admire your work," Rix said.

"All good, Rixy," Philo said, pulling a panel off so they could look in at the gravity repulsors. "These no good."

"How would you price this, Sta'ci?" Rix asked.

"Seven grams of gold," Sta'ci answered. "As you have noted, there is not much beyond frame and powerplant. Between us, though, I believe some of these components could be repaired if given attention."

Rix nodded, scratching some notes. "Next?"

The group moved through Bha'resh's yard, stopping periodically, finding some of the vessels in a variety of levels of repair, sometimes agreeing with Geldat's listing, sometimes not.

"You were in the yard for quite some time," Geldat, an older Vesh said. "It is good to see you, Bha'resh. Introduce me to all but Sta'ci. We have been introduced. Greetings to you, Sta'ci."

Sta'ci bowed slightly and smiled. "Greetings to you, Geldat. Thank you for allowing my visit."

"It appears that we have friends in common. Although, with the manners you have shown, you would have always been welcome."

Sta'ci blushed a little and shifted closer to Philo. "Thank you."

"Bha'resh, are we to conclude our business before we start anew?"

"The crates are in the vehicle. Tell us where you would like them placed," Bha'resh said. "We can settle funds at six-day morning drinks."

"Very well. Just inside the shop would be most helpful," Geldat said. "While you do so, do I have business with you, Sta'ci?"

"My partners, Philo and Rix Banner should be part of this business," she said.

"Let us start and once they have completed moving the crates, they can join us."

"Yes. As you wish," Sta'ci agreed.

There were only three, repacked crates of parts left for Geldat and Rix and Philo got right to moving them, moving one between them at a time. When Bha'resh offered to help, they turned him down as they were comfortable working together.

Having not travelled far, they found Geldat and Sta'ci nearby, seated at a Garanod equivalent to a picnic table beneath a wide, open-air awning. Looking over Sta'ci's shoulder, Rix found the list of vessels was well more than the four or five she'd originally suggested, although they'd visited each of them in the yard.

"Do you have funds to purchase all of this, Sta'ci?" Geldat asked.

"I imagine that has to do with the prices you would ask."

Geldat sighed. "I suppose that is a fair assessment. If I were to sell them all to you in this moment, you could have all nine for one hundred seventy-five grams of gold."

"That is certainly a generous offer, honored Geldat," Sta'ci said.

"Thank you."

"I have limited room and budget. Which of these vessels are the gems that have brought your offer to this number?" she asked. "I certainly see considerable value."

"Well, 19-F needs only a few parts to run once again. Why your partner might have even sold such a part to me, this day," Geldat said.

Sta'ci scrolled the list to show a well-weathered runabout that Rix had wondered about. He didn't think he'd brought everything required to get it back on the road, but Geldat was right, he had brought parts compatible with it. "What do you feel this is worth in current condition, with the knowledge that you have the capacity to restore it."

"Restored, it is worth at least 75 grams. The parts and labor are perhaps 20 grams of that, however."

"If we removed from the list, would you say you are willing to part with the remaining for 120 grams?"

"Well, I guess I'm not sure if it can be repaired so easily," he said.

"There is risk. I understand. Our venture is about taking risks," she said. "What is your second most cherished?"

"Is there a number you're working on?" Geldat asked. "I feel like you have a plan to negotiate with me until I am too tired to continue my day."

"I had thought all Vesh liked to negotiate and bargain," Sta'ci said.

"And I thought all Grintok were abrasive and ugly. Perhaps there is variance within our species."

Sta'ci grinned at his pushback. "You enjoy negotiating, well enough. Your tactics are more subtle, and I feel I am learning from a master."

"Your words are sweet. I am also old and have experienced much. I will not be swayed … much, by talk such as this."

"I have an idea that might sweeten the pot some also," Rix said.

"Oh?" Geldat said.

"I know the part you would put in the vehicle from 19-F. It'd take me twenty minutes to install it, but you give Sta'ci credit for the work when I'm done, how about?"

"That is indeed interesting," Geldat said. "Let us add that to the offer on Sta'ci's side. But let's now speak as common folk. What is the capital you have available? I will give you a reasonable price if it is enough for three or more."

"Rix Banner, you know the capital I have available. I believe you and Philo have discussed a potential loan. What is the number we can give to Geldat?" Sta'ci asked.

"Sixty grams for five vessels and I'll put that part into 19-F," Rix said. "You should know that Bha'resh is my primary trader for parts when I visit again, if that sways your interest."

It was at this moment that the sight of a cloaked figure running along the dusty road toward them caught their attention.

"Who in the purple mountains could that possibly be?" Geldat asked.

35

HANGING OUT

"RIX, THAT IS KASIT," Beverly said, appearing in a WWII Army Corps uniform. "I have used a private communications channel. He is here to fetch you. It is critical you do not expose his identity."

Rix pulled sixty grams of gold from a pouch and handed them to Philo. "Buddy, there's my share. You and Sta'ci make your best deal."

"Who is that?" Geldat asked.

"Someone I wasn't expecting to meet up with," Rix said. "I must go and that person needs privacy. It's important. Please."

"You are acting strangely, my friend," Bha'resh said.

"Bha'resh, I need you to trust me. You, of all people, know that these are tense times. Help me in this moment. Also, I'll be available tomorrow morning to repair that vehicle if that ends up as part of the deal. Sta'ci, that install is worth a minimum of 3 grams and I'll need transportation."

"I understand."

"Geldat, will you excuse me? I'm afraid there are issues of critical importance that have my attention."

"I must say that you have piqued my curiosity," Geldat said.

"If you could resist that, I'd be grateful," Rix said to which Geldat nodded with a small grin of understanding on his face.

"Let me drive you," Bha'resh said. "I will not ask questions. Time may not be your friend this morning. Geldat, old friend, I will return as soon as is possible."

"Yes, yes. I was due for a tea just now, anyway. You will miss the sweet biscuits I baked just this morning."

Rix looked between Kasit and Bha'resh's vehicle and then nodded. "I can't imagine this isn't critical," Rix said, climbing into Bha'resh's vehicle.

Lumbering across the uneven road, Bha'resh's vehicle, equipped with gravity repulsors caused the speeding vehicle to bob along as if on a pitched sea. As they approached, Kasit pulled his hood tight around his face and looked away.

Hopping out, Rix grabbed the young man's arm and stood away from the vehicle so he wouldn't expose him. "What are you doing here?"

"You have to come with me. These ... they did things I don't understand. It was like looking into a mirror," he said.

"And they said to come get *me*?" Rix asked incredulously.

"Yes. They kept Mom there and sent me."

"Two of them?" Rix pressed for intel. "How far?"

Kasit shrugged. "Quiet Coil. You're not going to like it."

"I never do," Rix said. "Bha'resh will drive us. Tell me where to go. You'll lay in the back of the car, behind the front seats."

"There is a fluxspan terminal five kilometers from here. It is the only one that's even remotely close," Kasit said.

"We're taking a ferry?" Rix asked, opening the back door to Bha'resh's vehicle.

Kasit climbed in, keeping his head low, although Bha'resh didn't once look back.

"Like that," Kasit agreed.

"Where to?" Bha'resh asked as Rix slid in beside him.

"There's a fluxspan ferry terminal about five kilometers from here. Do you know of it?"

"I do," he said. "The ferry isn't for another hour, though."

Rix nodded as understanding dawned on him. "That's just great."

"Is there a charge?"

"No," Rix said.

The drive was short and Bha'resh stopped a hundred meters from the terminal, preferring to let Rix and his mysterious passenger out, well away from where they would run into people who might be interested in a chat.

"Go in peace," Bha'resh said.

"Sta'ci might need help in the negotiation," Rix said, pulling a sleeve of tools from his tool bag. "Can you watch over her and Philo for me?"

"I will," Bha'resh said. "Perhaps we could have dinner this evening."

"I'd like that," Rix said over his shoulder, following Kasit, who was already moving toward the terminal. He hustled to catch the narrow young man. "What's going on?"

"You know everything. They sent me to bring you back. They wouldn't let Zenith go until I brought you," he said.

Rix nodded. "Then you did the right thing."

"What are you doing with that?" Kasit asked, pointing at the sleeve of tools Rix carried on one hand.

"If they need me, it's not because of my good looks or persuasive nature," Rix said. "If they asked for me it's because something's broken or needs breaking. So ... tools."

"We're already going to be overweight for my rig," Kasit said, turning suddenly and stopping them both. He roughly grabbed the belt around Rix's waist and tugged violently. "Do you think this can hold your weight?"

"No," Rix said. "Why?"

"My sling is only good for one. I need a sling to hold you," he said.

"Do you have any line?"

"Some, why?"

"Hand it to me."

Kasit pulled a length of rope from the pack connected to his sling and gave it to Rix. "Give me your tools. I'll carry them."

"Do you need a recommendation on strong harness from your rope?" Beverly asked.

Rix nodded, not wanting to let Kasit know he was talking with Beverly. A short video played on his HUD, and he could see the value of the harness construction.

"It won't be pretty, but this should do," Rix said, looping the rope around his legs and waist until he had a secure harness.

"How do you know how to do that?"

"Let's go," Rix said.

"Right. When we get to the rail. You're not going to do anything until I'm sliding. Once I start sliding, you *must* jump off the edge, or we could get fouled when my weight finally pulls you off. Trust me. You will not fall."

"But what if I do?" Rix asked.

"Fall? Why would you do that?"

"Rope breaks."

"Oh. You're dead, then. You'll eventually crash into a cliff wall. There are big outcroppings, but you'll for sure die on impact."

"You're not very good at this whole soothing thing, are you?" Rix asked.

Kasit led Rix beneath the ferry platform and pointed at the fluxspan rail. "Okay, so, this one is a little higher than I thought. We're going to have to run, together. When I say jump, you jump. Got it?"

"You've got to be kidding me," Rix said, looking over the edge of the chasm separating Driftmarket from other planetoid hunks of Garanod. A stiff breeze howled up the rock face, although with the light atmosphere, it wasn't nearly as impactful as Earth winds could be.

"No and you need to jump. We have exactly one shot at this," Kasit said.

"Oh, my good Lord," Rix said. "This is our best plan?"

"Or you could take the ferry and meet me there. It'd take about three hours for you to traverse."

"How long for you?"

"Twenty minutes. Your people sure thought this was urgent, though."

"Dang it!"

"Let me know when you're ready."

Rix scoffed. "That's not likely. Okay, on three we start when you need me to jump say—*one, two, jump*. I'll jump right as you say it. Got it?"

"Easy enough," Kasit agreed. "We go, now!"

With only a short run of line between them, they raced forward. Rix struggled not to entangle with Kasit and his heart was pounding when he heard; "One. Two. Jump!!"

Rix gave it his all and watched as Kasit leapt into the air, flinging a line from his sling. It was going well until Rix's less athletic jump caught up with them and Kasit was yanked downward. Surprisingly, the young man did not panic but rather allowed himself to fall a moment as the line swung around and at the last minute, he caught and secured it.

"That's sliding, baby!!" Kasit howled as the harness around Rix's midsection snapped to his full weight, causing his hand to lose contact with the rope and he swung, upside down. "What are you doing?" Kasit called. "My rig can't take this swinging. Stop! Now!"

Rix caught the rope with his legs and stabilized, even though he hung upside down. "Beverly, help me get straightened up."

"You are stable and I do not believe you are flexible enough to reach the rope while hanging upside down. This is not a long trip. You should simply enjoy the view," Beverly said, floating along next to him in her Amelia Earhart flight suit.

"I can't enjoy the view. I'm upside down," he lamented. "How long?"

"Seven minutes," Kasit called. "The landing isn't going to be great with you hanging upside down. At the last minute, you might want to lift your head."

"Fine. Give me a three count," Rix said.

"We have a couple of minutes," Kasit said. "Isn't this great?"

"No."

Time passed and finally Kasit gave a warning. "Ten seconds to landing. Lift that head if you can. I'll try to make this as light as possible, but with the extra weight, we're coming in fast."

All Rix could see was the fast-approaching terminal with hard edges everywhere. Struggling, he released his legs and kicked at the rope, which earned him an irritated howl from Kasit. The move, however, allowed him to pendulum around. Wildly, he grabbed at the line between him and Kasit. He missed and was starting to rotate back to his upside-down position when his boot heels knocked against a very hard surface.

"Frak!" Kasit exclaimed as the pull against them gained force. Expertly, he flung open the traveler, which connected sling to fluxspan rail. No longer holding onto the rail but still connected to each other. The two tumbled in a mass of legs and arms until they came to a rest.

"For Pete's sake," Rix groaned, having taken multiple body shots from Kasit's arms and legs, not to mention the uneven ground they'd tumbled across.

"Not blassin," Kasit said with a mix of anger and pain.

It took the pair a few minutes to separate. Once they had, they sat for a moment. "Are you okay?" Rix asked.

"You're not very good at sliding rails."

"No. Seriously?" Rix asked sarcastically.

"One more to go. We need to be better. Quiet Coil isn't a place we can be screwing around," Kasit said.

"Good pep talk."

"I don't know what that means."

"No surprise. Where are we going?" Rix asked.

"Follow me. Can you run two kilometers?"

"At some pace, sure," Rix said.

"Let's go." With the combination of a cheap oxygen condenser, the limited atmosphere of Garanod and the exertion, Rix was struggling to breathe when Kasit finally slowed. "You are not in very good shape. Catch your breath. We cannot approach the terminal breathing like a crazy person."

"Fine," Rix said between ragged breaths. "Also, you're an asshole, kid."

"I wondered how long it would take for you to show who you are," Kasit said.

"Just ... shut ... up ... and lead," Rix struggled to say.

"Fine. This way," Kasit said. "Also, you need to get upright this time. We can't arrive at Quiet Coil looking like it's our first day. They'll pick up on that in a minute."

"Like I'm doing anything but my best," Rix grumbled, following Kasit around the ferry terminal which already had a handful of people gathered.

"Ferry is here in five. We'll follow it out," Kasit said, slipping into the shadows beneath the platform.

Their next jump was only marginally better than their first. This time when Rix found himself upside down, he kicked his legs and managed to grasp the rope connecting him to Kasit and sit into the cradle made of rope.

"Frak, could you swing around anymore?" Kasit asked angrily.

"I'm done," Rix said, looking out to the horizon. The distances between the large planetoid districts were surprisingly small, on a planetary scale. With less volume than Earth's moon, the scant kilometers between was almost imperceptible from space. Sliding between, however, gave a much different view of things and Rix could imagine why it was interesting to a young man like Kasit.

“Terminal in two minutes. When we get there, pull your legs up and meet the ground with knees bent,” Kasit said.

“As opposed to getting dragged along the ground?”

This apparently caught Kasit’s good humor and he laughed. “It’s a whole lot nicer this way,” Kasit agreed.

“I’m going to have bruises for days.”

“Yeah, let’s try to avoid that. Ten seconds. Legs up.”

As landings go. It was anything but elegant and at the last, the rope between them ended up being their downfall, causing them to trip over each other and land in the sandy dirt of Quiet Coil.

“I thought we had it,” Rix said.

Kasit set to unclipping the rigging and freeing himself from Rix. “I don’t think that’s a skill we want to get much better at,” Kasit said. “The chance of the rig breaking is a whole lot higher than you might think. And nobody comes back from a fall.”

“How are we meeting people?” Rix asked.

“No idea. My job is to get you to Jeshifa’s warehouse. After that, I have no idea.”

“They have to be watching for us,” Rix said. “Lead the way.”

“You certainly have a lot of faith in your people. Coming with me was a dumb idea. Jeshifa are bad people.”

Rix nodded. “We don’t always make the best decisions for our own wellbeing, but if war taught me anything it was that doing the right thing has a cost. Let’s hope it’s just bruising this time.”

“Mom and I are screwed,” Kasit said. “It’s not like we can hide from Jeshifa. That’s why the security is so lax around our cell. Where could we go? What I don’t understand is why you’re helping. I stole from you. Now you’re helping me.”

"I don't like being stolen from," Rix said. "But I also understand that good people will do bad things if they're pushed hard enough. Taking your Mom was apparently the right button for you."

"I'd do anything for her."

"I get it," Rix said. As they'd been talking, they'd freed Rix from the harness and rewrapped and stowed the lines. "How far."

"Two more kilometers. Not far. We need to keep to shadows, though. There's no valid reason for us to be where we're going," Kasit said.

"As long as I'm not running," Rix said, earning him a grin from Kasit.

It took thirty minutes to stealthily cover the two kilometers, and they arrived at the large door, leading into the lower levels of the warehouse.

"Do you think we should go in?" Kasit asked.

"That depends. Do you know where we're going?"

"Kind of."

"Beverly, can you find them?" Rix asked quietly.

"Not if we're outside the building," Beverly answered, still in her Amelia jumpsuit.

"Let's go inside. They'll have a plan better than just sit outside the door."

"I hope," Kasit said.

Rix shrugged and unlatched the door. Movement on the other side surprised him. "Hey, who is that?" a gruff voice asked. Suddenly, the door was yanked open and Rix found himself staring at two men, one of whom was holding a pistol on him. "What are you doing out there?"

Rix took in the scene, the men were smoking the equivalent of cigarettes, and he go a strong whiff of alcohol. In response, he plucked the Starfire ray gun from his belt and held it to his side. "Catching you two," Rix said, narrowing his eyes. "Kedge said I'd find you messing around down here. I guess I'll have to let him know he was right."

"Not if I shoot you."

"Oh, sure, that'll go over well. It's not like Kedge won't remember he sent me looking."

"He's right, Guave," the other man said.

"Who's this Kedge? I don't know any Kedge."

"He's related to Mexu," the other man said.

"Just go back to work," Rix said. "You keep this to yourself, and I'll give you a pass, for a price."

"For what?"

"What you got?" Rix asked.

"Twenty grams silver," the second man said.

"Make it thirty."

"Guave, do you have ten? I only have twenty."

Guave holstered his pistol and pulled coins from his pocket. "Here's eight," he said angrily.

"Sorry man. Here's twenty-five," the second said.

"Get gone, already.

The two men gathered their smokes and alcohol and walked away. "I'm telling you there's no Kedge. That guy is full of waste."

"No, I know the name," the second answered. "We don't need more trouble. They're already looking at us."

From the hallway, another man suddenly appeared. "Nicely done, Rix," the guard said. That the guard was wearing the same jumpsuit Amari had put on that morning was all Rix needed to recognize her. "I thought for sure they weren't going to buy that."

"A lot of soldiers like to find places to screw off," Rix said. "Cigs and alcohol are classic tells."

"I didn't think you had any game," Amari said. "I stand corrected. Now, let's move. We need to get Kasit back to the cell."

"You said you'd let us go if I helped."

"We will," Amari as the guard said. "But not yet. If you go now, Jeshifa will just come find you. Let us do what we need to get done and then we'll get you out of here quietly. Have you thought about where you want to go once you're free?"

"No. But we can lay low in a few places," Kasit said.

"That's hardly a strategy," Amari said, turning to Rix. "We should take him and his mom back to Patience. They've no chance of survival here."

"How about we talk about that after we get out of here. I assume you have a job for me," Rix said.

"I love that you're perceptive like that," Amari said, leaning in as if she was looking for a kiss. Of course, all Rix saw was a scruffy guard looking to get fresh.

"Knock that off, already!" he said. The guard smiled and Rix shook his head. "That's not okay."

"First things first. Kasit, you need to deal with the fact that we're taking you back to your cell," Amari said. "You decide to do something different; you won't get our help. Do you understand?"

"I understand."

"Good."

The path back to the cell was without other Jeshifa and Amari unlocked the door, and let Kasit and Rix back in.

"Gang's all here," Kel said, already shifting her face from Kasit's to the first guard she'd mimicked.

"What now?" Rix asked.

"Stay put and act like a guard," Amari said. "Kel and I are going to grab that cipher and bring it back."

"And then what?" Rix asked.

"Have you not been talking to Beverly?"

"No?"

"The two of you are going to reprogram it so that it seems to work."

"I have no idea how to do that."

"It's possible," Beverly interjected.

"We'll be back," Amari said as she and Kel slipped from the room.

"What are your plans for us?" Zenith asked warily.

"I guess we're talking about taking you back to Patience Station with us," Rix said. "That sounds kind of crazy, though. Once they figure you're missing, it'll be hard to leave."

"Do we get a say in this?"

"Are you asking if we're kidnapping you?" Rix asked. Zenith nodded. "No. We're not kidnapping you. If you want to hide out around here, that's entirely your choice and will be safer for me and mine. What do *you* want to do?"

"I never thought we'd have to leave," Zenith said. "Especially not to Galactic Empire."

"What's wrong with that?"

"Poverty and corruption."

"For sure it's safer than here," Rix said and then realized his experience didn't exactly line up with that statement. "At least for you guys. We have a lot of things going on back there. We can hopefully get you guys started on something where you can make some money and have a life."

"Who are those two?" Kasit asked. "They change shapes."

"We don't talk about it," Rix said. "It's dangerous for them that people know about their abilities. It can get them killed. So, you need to learn how to keep a secret."

"I can keep a secret."

"Don't bring it up, again, then," Rix said. "And hand me my tools."

"I'm not sure I want to live near you," Kasit said. "You have a lot of anger to work through."

"It's not anger," Rix said. "I don't like being here. Kasit, the things you did put my people in danger. I agreed to help, and I'm on board, but you need to stop acting like ... I don't know how you should act, but you're damn irritating."

Kasit nodded and sat on a bench opposite Rix. For several minutes, they sat in quiet until finally, Kasit spoke. "Do you feel better getting that off your chest?"

"Sure do."

36

GOLDEN RULE

RIX RESTED his back against the wall opposite the cell and tried to adopt the look of a bored thug who had been pressed into guard duty. After several minutes of shifting uneasily from foot to foot, he realized he had no idea how a thug guard might look and decided his best bet was to get comfortable.

Steps in the hallway drew his attention and his heart rate sped up. Nervously, he double checked the ray gun at his side. He had no desire to start a fight, but he also knew he had no place within Jeshifa.

Men's voices filtered down the hallway as the footsteps grew closer and Rix struggled to hide his nervousness. Through the clear window into the cell, he saw Kasit trying to get his attention. Looking at the young man, he found Kasit was giving him a signal to calm down, patting the air between them. Rix rolled his eyes and shrugged.

"Hey, where's Quince?" one of the two men who'd just turned the corner asked.

Rix looked from Kasit over to the approaching men, both of whom were armed. Rix's mind spun with possibilities, but no words formed and soon the situation turned awkward.

"Are you stupid? I asked you a question," the speaker asked, grabbing Rix by the shoulder. "What are you doing here? Where's Quince?"

Rix blinked and entertained a few responses. Nothing made sense.

"You broke him," the second man offered.

"Something's not right," the first said jostling Rix even harder.

The physical contact seemed to do the trick and Rix shook his head. "Man, get your hand off me," Rix said lazily but firmly pushing the man's arm. "I don't know no Quince and I sure as fargen don't know you."

"How do you not know Quince?" the first asked, his eyes narrowing suspiciously.

"I just came in. They said I had to pull guard duty. All I've done so far is sleep and watch these two sleep," Rix said. "Worst job of my life."

This seemed to get the man's attention. "Plenty of good people out there would like this job. You should be grateful."

"You here to relieve me?" Rix asked.

"Don't you know your schedule?"

"No."

This earned him a derisive chuckle. "Well then, I guess you're still on. If you see Quince, tell him we're looking for him."

"I don't know who you are," Rix said.

"No. But Quince will," the first said, turning and walking away.

"Fino," the second man said. "Tell that to Quince."

Rix waited until they were out of earshot and sighed. There was something about subterfuge that spun him up like nothing else, and he wondered how Amari and Kel dealt with it so easily. There was an art to deception that mystified him.

With the adrenaline leaving his system, he looked for and found a chair he could drag into the hallway, allowing him to sit. Kicking back the chair, he leaned against the wall and struggled to bide his time, something he was about as good at doing as pretending to be someone else.

Thirty minutes later, more footsteps echoed down the hallway. Rix stood and worked on his story. He was a new guy and had been assigned guard duty. He couldn't remember the name of the person who'd brought him in, but his buddy Fino had put in a good word for him. He hoped using the name of one of the men who'd just visited wouldn't come back to bite him.

As before a pair of men rounded the corner. This time, one of them was carrying a worn leather small case. "Any trouble?" one of them asked.

"No," Rix answered.

The men approached and one of them smiled. "You don't know who we are, do you?" Kel's voice asked from the stranger's mouth.

"Aw, crap," Rix said. "You changed clothing."

Amari handed the small case to Rix. "We need to either disable this or take out something important, but have it look like it's still working," Kel said.

Rix nodded and entered the cell where Zenith an Kasit had come to the door to check out the recent commotion.

"What's going on?" Kasit asked.

"Relax," Kel said, her face transforming back to normal. "It's us."

Kneeling on the floor, Rix opened the case. "Beverly, do you have any ideas?"

Appearing next to the case as a wild-haired professor wearing a lab coat, Beverly peered into the case. "I can confirm that's a navigational cipher of some sort," she said. "Can't tell for sure if it's tuned to Ghostmist Nebula."

"There's no manual," Rix said. With tools from his tool sleeve, he started releasing fasteners that held the covering bezels in place. Seconds turned into minutes as he methodically deconstructed the device, creating a trail of removed parts on the floor next to him.

"Are you sure you know what you're doing?" Kasit asked, crouching next to him and looking into the device.

"Funny. I have no idea what I'm doing," Rix said.

"Then… what are you doing?"

"I'm going to let the cipher tell me what to do," Rix said, placing a final molded cover onto the floor. After a short time, Rix shook his head. "I recognize a power circuit, but that's about it. What do you have, Beverly?"

"The components look to be purpose built," Beverly said. "Without a sophisticated probe and more time than we have, I cannot tell."

"Nothing elegant, then," Rix surmised.

"What are you saying," Kel asked.

"We can disable. That's not hard. Making it look like it's working is," Rix said. "How much power do you think this draws?"

Kel answered his question, even though she knew the question was targeted at Beverly. For his part, Rix didn't even process her answer.

"Not more than forty watts," she said. "See how thin those lines are?" Highlighting through Rix's HUD she illuminated the power leads exiting a battery compartment.

"That's the weak point," Rix said, pulling out his pocketknife and extending the blade. Reaching in but not touching he asked, "what would happen if I nicked just a bit out of that line?"

"It would be obvious to anyone who was looking," Beverly said.

Rix nodded and rummaged through his tool sleeve. Not finding what he was looking for, he turned the sleeve upside down and dumped the contents. "There you are."

"What is that?" Kel asked.

"Would you believe a fishing weight?"

"A what?"

"A crappy electrical conductor," Rix said, extracting his soldering gun and sucker bottle. Heating up the power line, he extracted what he imagined to be an analog to solder, fully ruining the electrical circuit after clipping out the existing conductor. Then, he lay a single strand of extremely thin copper wire in the gap. Finishing the task, he melted the lead of his fishing weight back into place so that it covered the line. "It's not perfect. If someone looks hard, they'll see it."

"What did you do?" Kel asked.

"That piece of copper and to some degree the lead too, will let the unit power up," Rix said. "But over time, it's going to have too much load and overheat. That will melt the lead or it'll just break. The overheating should ruin the components on the other side of this board. As it is all of this tech is so thin and fragile, it won't take much to break it."

"You're confident?"

"That it'll fail? Yes. Confident on when, I'm not. Confident they won't figure out what I've done. I don't know how to know. There aren't too many who are willing to work on equipment like this," Rix said, setting the last piece he'd removed back into place and re-seating the fasteners. "It seems to be a lost art."

"Lost art?" Kasit asked. "You removed forty things from that box and put them back in. How do you know what to take out and what to leave? That's crazy to open a box like that."

Rix shook his head. "The thing is, I don't know what needs to be removed or what doesn't. I just keep taking things apart until they make sense. As long as I remember how to put it back together, it doesn't matter what I take apart. And before you ask. I have a method on how I place things I've taken off so I know what order to put them back."

"I saw you being careful on how you were ordering the parts," Kasit said. "I wondered if that was on purpose."

"You've a good eye for detail," Rix said. "Don't be afraid to experiment."

A few minutes later, Rix stowed his tools and closed the case.

"You're done?" Amari asked.

"I am."

"Give us twenty minutes," she said.

"And then what?" Zenith asked.

"We're going to break you out of here," Kel said. "Kasit, I assume you can figure out how to get your mother home in a way that doesn't attract much attention?"

"After it's dark, sure," he said. "Are you going to make trouble?"

"No," Kel said. "The best extracts happen without anyone knowing."

"What about me?" Rix asked.

"When we get back, you should be able to just walk out of here and take a ferry," Kel said. "It's not like they're monitoring people leaving. Kas and Zen would attract attention, but you're just one more guy out walking around."

"I don't love the plan, but I understand," Rix said.

"You're so brave at so many other things," Kel said. "Why is this the thing that bugs you?"

"I'm terrible at lying."

"No lie," Kel said. "You're done with your business and headed back to Driftmarket if anyone asks. The best stories are true ones."

"But what if they ask what I was doing?"

"You were looking at some equipment, but you decided you didn't have any further interest," Amari filled in. "If we don't raise alarm bells, no one will ask."

"Where are we to go once we leave?" Zenith asked.

"Reach out to Kha'rem," Rix said. "He's going to hide you for a while. You'll have some decisions to make after that."

"Like running away to the Galactic Empire with you three?"

"Exactly like that," Rix said.

And with that, Kel and Amari left with the case and Rix returned to the hallway. Aside from feeling nervous and pacing, the time was uneventful and the girls returned, as promised, twenty minutes later.

"How'd it go?" Rix asked.

"As far as we know, no one is the wiser," Kel said, her face started to shift and her resemblance to Zenith increased.

"I'm going to walk the two of you out," Amari said, staying in her guard uniform. "There's a utility room you can hide out in until dark. Reach out to Kha'rem once you're somewhere safe. Got it?"

"It can't be this easy," Zenith said. "What happens when they come back here, looking for us?"

"You'll be in this room," Kel said, her face about a third of the way to Zenith's appearance.

"And how will you escape?"

"Leave that to us," Amari said.

"I'm not sure if that's comforting or not," Rix said, still getting used to the idea that his business and romantic partners were both more competent in these matters than him and even worse, they seemed to enjoy it.

"Let me walk you out," Amari said, still in the guise of a guard.

"Oh, I forgot to ask. Do you know a Quince? There were a couple of guys looking for him."

"Did they say why?"

"No, but they didn't seem too upset about things. I said I didn't know him," Rix said.

"Well, that could be a wrinkle. Quince is one of the guys we're mimicking," she said. "I'm Quince."

"Where's the real Quince?"

"Nearby," she said. "He's ... let's say, under the weather."

"Did you hurt him?"

"Do you want to know?"

"Not *now*, no," Rix answered. "But I'm part of this."

"Still alive," Amari said. "He'll make a *mostly* full recovery." Rix bit his tongue, afraid to ask more in that moment. He did, however, wonder what *mostly* meant.

"See you back at the ship," Kel said. "Are you going to get that gillet?"

"Yes. Philo is bringing Sta'ci back to Patience," Rix said. "They're also looking to buy a bunch of small runabouts that need work done. That Sta'ci has a mind for business and Philo couldn't be more smitten."

"I love that for him."

Rix followed Amari out of the cell and instead of leaving through the lower levels, she lead him straight up and through the main warehouse. "Are you nuts?" he asked nervously.

"Stay calm," she said. "We're not doing anything wrong."

"If that guy sees me …," Rix said and then clamped his jaw as the man who'd challenged him about Quince earlier saw them and beelined his way over.

"I thought you didn't know Quince," Fino said.

Amari gave Rix a skeptical look. "What's your issue, Hugene?" she asked. "Why would you tell him that?"

Rix paused for a moment as his adrenaline spiked again. With both of them staring at him, he felt considerable pressure to answer. Finally, he decided to punt and go with the truth. "I didn't know your name was Quince," he said struggling for sheepish in his expression. "Sorry, Fino. Sure. I've seen this guy plenty."

"Seriously, you forgot my name on your third day here?" Amari as Quince asked. "That's completely uncool. I know yours, or do I have it wrong? Your name is dumbass, right?"

Rix sighed. "No. Look. I'm sorry."

"Let me deal with this, Fino. Meet me back at the cantina in like ten minutes?" she asked. "I need to take care of this guy first."

"Grab me at Hogial's tonight. I'll be there most of the night. I just wondered where you got to."

"That's sweet, you checkin' up on me," Amari as Quince said. She then pulled Rix along and moved toward the main entrance to the warehouse. "Do you know where you're going from here?"

"How do you know what to say?" Rix asked in a harsh whisper. "Wasn't that risky?"

"People are basically the same everywhere. You can't talk all formal like you do. Play with people a little. It puts them at ease and it makes it easier for them to believe you."

Rix shook his head. "No way would that work for me."

"You'd be surprised."

"Rix, there are three ferries accessible from this location," Beverly said, appearing in her jumpsuit and bomber jacket.

"Amelia Earhart," Rix said. "Let's go to the second closest. I want to get a bit more walking in before we must be close to other people."

"What, no kiss before you leave?" Amari asked.

Rix turned and almost considered it but the fact that she looked like a scruffy thug finally resonated with him and then he saw her smile. "You're such a turkey," he said and then stalked out of the main entrance, momentarily unconcerned for the people around him.

It took over half a mile of walking before Rix's heart rate settled back to a normal tempo. On an alien planet in the middle of an exotic enclave, Rix couldn't have felt more anonymous. Even so, his hand brushed the ray gun more than a few times for reassurance.

Not knowing how the ferry worked, he wondered what it would cost for traversal. He'd received a few coins while exploring and had brought them along, unsure if they'd be necessary. The ferry, which was to Havenfall, used about a third of his coins and took forty minutes to traverse, giving him time to choose which ferry he'd take back to Driftmarket. This time, he found that an extra kilometer of walking would put him on a ferry to Driftmarket, close to where Greevo was selling his wares.

Exiting the second ferry, the familiarity of Driftmarket was oddly settling for him. It had taken the better part of three hours and evening was rapidly approaching. When he arrived at Greevo's booth, he found that only Kitka remained.

"Rix Banner, are you here to purchase items?" Kitka asked with a hint of a smile.

"No, I happened to be in the area and thought I'd drop by. Are you having success with sales?" Rix asked.

"Garanod Enclave ripe," she answered. "Greevo need more parts. Selling good."

"That sounds hopeful," Rix said. "Speaking of, I was looking to talk to Greevo. I still don't know if you guys are coming back to Patience Station with us."

"I no understand the alternative," Kitka said.

"Your boss does," Rix said.

"Would explain? Perhaps Kitka negotiator."

"Oh, nothing to negotiate. He can pay what's due, and I'll be happy to bring you back," Rix said. "And, if he wants to bring back a load, I'm going to need to know what it is and negotiate for mass. I have my own cargo that we'll be loading tomorrow."

"When *Calypso* leave?"

"Tomorrow at end of day. Greevo knows all about this. He talked to me about it."

"But no pay."

"That's right."

Kitka nodded her head. "I find money. Give to Rix Banner."

With that, Rix turned and walked on to Bha'resh's shop, which was only another kilometer. He was greeted with a big smile when he entered.

"Rix Banner. I will admit to having concern for your well-being," Bha'resh said. "Is all indeed well?

"A work in progress," Rix said. "My part is done, though. Now I just get to worry."

Bha'resh nodded. "Will you need help with any activities later this eve?"

"Not me, specifically, but others are likely to reach out," Rix said.

"That is anticipated."

"How did things go with Philo and Sta'ci's negotiations?" Rix asked.

"You are in for a treat," Bha'resh said. "We had quite a busy day, and I very much enjoyed the enthusiasm of this unexpected couple."

"Philo's a good egg," Rix said. "I don't know Sta'ci that well."

"She negotiates as a Grintok, but without the frustration that is often felt when dealing with the pugnacious species," Bha'resh said. "She is a credit to Grintok."

"I assume we have transportation to work on?" Rix asked.

"Loading is the task, Rix Banner. We were able to secure transport from Geldat, and by morning, Philo and Sta'ci's load will be sitting atop the pier next to your vessel," Bha'resh said.

"This should be interesting," Rix said, scratching his head.

"Is everything okay, Rix Banner?" Bha'resh asked.

"I think so," Rix said. "Do you ever have one of those days that gets off the rail right from the start?"

"It has been quite some time since I have had the sort of excitement your visit has brought," he said. "I have enjoyed the change. Perhaps it is best experienced in small doses."

"Yes. Not like today, which was a firehose," Rix said.

"Will we see you this evening for a meal?"

"I don't think so," Rix said. "It's our last night in port, and I'd like to make sure we keep things locked down."

"Perhaps Kha'rem and I will bring dinner to you, in that case. We have so enjoyed our time together," Bha'resh said.

"I'll be there. Thank you for your help, today, Bha'resh. This would have been much more difficult, likely unachievable, without your wisdom and generosity," Rix said.

"There is a Vesh parable that speaks about extending to others that which you would also benefit from."

"Back home, we call that the golden rule. Do unto others as you would have them do unto you."

"This is well stated."

37

MORAL CRISIS

"May I speak with you, Rix Banner?"

Rix startled at the tall alien standing in shadows. "Kha'rem, I didn't see you there."

"My apologies for the subterfuge. We have matters of import. Might I beg your attention?"

Only twenty meters from *Gravitational Pull*, Rix tapped a button on his HUD, checking the ship's occupancy. "Step inside my office?" he asked, gesturing for Kha'rem to follow.

"I will admit curiosity with your Galactic vessel."

"Prepare to be disappointed," Rix said, opening the lower hatch and then looking back to size up Kha'rem. "This is the mechanical room. It might be a tight fit."

"Ah, I see," Kha'rem said, awkwardly twisting but following Rix onto the stairs leading to the main deck. "Please do not be offended, but I would find this vessel stressful on a multi-day journey."

"The word you're looking for is claustrophobic," Rix said, pulling a folding chair from the bulkhead and opening it. "Are you someone who drinks coffee in the evening?"

"Your hospitality is welcome," Kha'rem said, gratefully sitting.

Rix started the coffee and then pulled out another chair so they sat on opposite sides of the narrow galley table. "Would you like a meal bar? I particularly enjoy the berry ones."

"I have had sustenance for the evening," Kha'rem said. "Please eat, you have had a busy day."

Rix set a meal bar on the table and then turned back to finish the coffee. He slid the coffee into place and sat. "What's on your mind?"

"Are we entirely alone?"

"We are."

"I thank you for the rescue of Kasit and Zenith. I had thought them both lost. It says much of your character that you would become involved in their plight," Kha'rem said.

Rix, uncomfortable with the praise, shifted uneasily in his seat. "Thank you, Kha'rem. I suspect that's not why we're having coffee so late in the evening."

"You are correct, and you must be exhausted, so I will get directly to the point," Kha'rem said. "I will sell to you the load of gillet at half price, thirty grams of gold. This is an incentive to secret away Zenith and Kasit."

"Won't Jeshifa search for them?" Rix said flatly. He'd thought a lot about bringing the pair back to Patience Station. While docked at Driftmarket, Jeshifa would not have trouble gaining access to their ships and if the fugitives were found, his crew would suffer unimaginably.

"That Jeshifa rests is most unusual," Kha'rem said. "All I ask is that you consider it."

"Their release came at great risk, Kha'rem," Rix said, pulling a handful of gold slivers from a locked drawer. He counted sixty grams and pushed them to Kha'rem. "We are interested in two thousand kilograms of your frozen gillet. Let's decide tomorrow by midafternoon about bringing them aboard."

"You are, of course, right. I respect the responsibility you have to your crew," Kha'rem said splitting the gold into even piles and pushing one back. When Rix looked at him questioningly, his answer was straightforward, "let's resolve the situation with Kasit and Zenith before full payment. When would you be open to receiving your gillet?"

The pair were disturbed by loud sounds from outside of the craft. "What in the heck," Rix said. "Excuse me."

Without waiting for Kha'rem's response, he rushed over to the nearby pilot's seats and slid into place. Tapping on the controls, he brought up a view of the pier, fully expecting to see a Jeshifa invasion force.

"What is it, Rix Banner?"

Rix chuckled, his jangled nerves releasing slightly. "I need to deal with this. Geldat is dropping off Philo and Sta'ci's broken runabouts."

"Of course. Our business is complete," Kha'rem said. "Do you plan to load them still this evening?"

"Is it okay if I leave them on the pier for the night?"

"Yes, my friend," Kha'rem said gently. "I have a mobile lift that I would lend if you would find value in this?"

"That'd be a big help. I don't think any of these runabouts are moving," Rix said, pushing up from his seat.

Outside, he found Geldat had arrived with a long trailer that was haphazardly loaded with seven vessels that all looked like they'd seen better days. "Hello, Rix Banner," Geldat said. "And evening's greetings, Kha'rem."

"Evening's greetings, Geldat," Kha'rem said.

"Where would you like these?" Geldat asked.

Movement caught Rix's eye and he found that Sta'ci and Philo were hurrying from *Calypso*.

"Rixy! Our little ships come!" Philo said with obvious excitement.

Sta'ci, more reserved, nervously looked at Rix. "We used all our bargaining. I hope you do not mind," she said. "I have obligated you for a repair."

"Oh?" Rix asked, remembering that he'd offered to install a part onto one of Geldat's vehicles.

"The blue Nogg at the front," Geldat confirmed.

"Do you have data sheets on it?" Rix asked.

"Yes. It is a lot of detail. I am not certain how helpful it will be, though."

"Very," Rix said, accepting a small data chit.

"In cargo pods, Rixy?" Philo asked.

"Not yet," Rix said. "We have gillet to load tomorrow and we'll need to see if Greevo is bringing anything back."

"They not all fits," Philo said. "Need big strappys."

"We'll get it figured out," Rix said. "Let's just unload them here, Geldat."

"What of the Nogg? Should I bring back to my yard for your repair?" Geldat asked.

"You did right to bring it," Rix said. "Unload it closest to the gangway. I'll get started on it as soon as we're unloaded."

"This evening?" Geldat asked

"That's the thing about space freighters," Rix said. "By tomorrow evening, we'll be sailing through the deep dark, and all we'll have time for is sleeping."

"Ah, I suppose that is right," Geldat said.

With a gesture, Geldat urged two younger Vesh to exit the larger vehicle that had pulled the trailer to join them. Speaking too quickly for Rix's translator to pick up, he set his crew to work. Excited for the start of his new venture with Sta'ci, Philo joined right in.

Sta'ci placed a small hand on the back of Rix's arm, gently gaining his attention. "He's sure excited, isn't he?" Rix asked.

"Yes. We both are," Sta'ci said. "I want to thank you for your faith in our endeavor. It is a rare friend who offers finances with so little information. Tell me, Rix Banner. Are you our new partner, or are you a financier?"

"How would you like to see this go?" Rix asked, accepting eight grams of gold back from the sixty he'd invested.

"Would a twenty five percent return on your investment within eighteen months be suitable? I expect there to be shipping costs to consider, as well," she said. "We should also factor in the expenses of an additional passenger."

"Additional fuel for sure," Rix said. "Could we make a deal to have you plan and procure food for our return trip? That'd certainly cover room and board."

"I had hoped you would find productive work for me on our trip to Patience Station," she said.

Rix handed her the six grams of gold back. "I'll send you a passenger manifest along with a travel plan and required food items."

"I accept this proposal," she said, extending her hand to shake. When Rix looked at her with question, she answered, "Philo taught me this is how humans conclude successful negotiations."

"Glad to have you aboard, Sta'ci," Rix said and then he turned to Kha'rem who looked like he was ready to leave.

"You are quite busy as one would expect from space faring traders," Kha'rem said. "We will speak of our matters tomorrow at midday when I bring your crates of gillet for the return trip."

"Thank you, Kha'rem," Rix said, glad to reduce the load of people to deal with by one.

And with Kha'rem gone and Philo busy unloading the smaller vehicles, Rix made his way back into *Gravitational Pull* where he combined the sleeve of tools he still carried back into his tool bag. Knowing it would take some time to unload the vehicles from the rickety transit, Rix grabbed the meal bar sitting unforgotten on the galley table and hungrily ate, washing it down with coffee. By the time he made it back out to the pier, Philo and Geldat were down to two vehicles, one of which was Geldat's Nogg.

"Harder to load than unload," Geldat observed as he spooled out the winch cable holding the last of Philo's vehicles in place. "Do you wish me to unload the Nogg here or is there another location?"

"I suppose here is as good as any," Rix said.

Geldat agreed and waved one of his helpers to pull the transport forward so the Nogg could have a clean piece of the pier to sit on. "I will contact you tomorrow to see about your progress. The parts are in the aft section. Please contact me if you find issues."

"Can do," Rix said, pulling a handful of magnetic lighting dots from his bag. After reviewing the vehicles diagram in conjunction with the parts Geldat had provided, he started strategically placing the lights for illumination of the workspace.

"You do not waste time. Are you working this evening?" Geldat asked.

"No time like the present."

"Would you welcome a second pair of hands? I am quite interested in seeing how you will install the hydrogen compensator with only a bag full of tools."

Rix reviewed his HUD, suddenly worried that there was a trick to the installation. There would be quite a bit of disassembly, and he'd have to field cut fresh gaskets on reinstallation, but it wasn't anything beyond his comfort. "An extra pair of hands will be valuable. I have a way I like to do this. Are you willing to let me take lead?"

"Oh yes," Geldat said. "I am just here to offer help if requested."

Rix had heard the statement before and wondered if he'd have trouble with Geldat not taking direction. That he was the customer still held value to Rix. "Beverly, do you have a good feel on steps?" Rix asked.

"Pardon?" Geldat asked.

"Just talking to myself," Rix said.

"Oh, am I part of you, now?" Beverly asked with a pretend pout. She'd switched to her Rosie the Riveter outfit, as was common when they worked on projects. "I don't even have my own identity?"

"A most valuable part," Rix said, trying to placate.

"You're not very good reading women," Beverly said with exasperation. "I am showing a parts blowout of the first stage of disassembly. I propose you line them up in the aft compartment ... the boot as it were."

"Are you English already?" Rix asked, recognizing her term.

Beverly smiled.

"I ... are you still speaking to yourself?" Geldat asked.

Rix ignored the question as it was late and he had no interest in trying to make up excuses for his talking with Beverly. "I have a plan for how we lay parts out as we remove them from your subcomponents. It's critical we follow it. Here, I'm sending you the layout."

"You are very precise," Geldat said. "You would not like working in the yard."

"Why is that? I love old vehicles," Rix said.

"There is no precision. You would be working forever to achieve such."

"I thought your yard was quite sensibly laid out," Rix said. "The problem of new items coming in once you've filled a homogeneous area is a tough one."

As he spoke, he started pulling parts off and handing them to Geldat, who, for his part started taking them back and lining them up on the boot's metal flooring. Several times, Rix had to take a minute and reorganize the parts.

"I am sorry, Rix Banner. I just do not think the way you do," Geldat said.

"You're doing just fine and I appreciate you," Rix said, moving to the next subcomponent.

Minutes turned into a couple of hours and finally, Rix had removed the actual part, a fouled hydrogen compensator. "If you put this in a bath of solvent, you could get this cleaned up and usable again," Rix said, holding up the part.

"If you would like to keep that part once my Nogg runs, it is yours for free," Geldat said. "I have never seen someone work so steadily on a single problem. I understand how it is you are successful in this work."

"It's all about breaking down big problems into little ones," Rix said.

"Yes, I suppose it is."

"And now, we reverse the process," Rix said, laying out his blank gasket material and laying the part atop it. With a special scribing tool, he outlined the gasket and then finished the job of cutting. With a special sealant, he replaced the compensator and started bolting and screwing parts back together.

"One down one more to go," Rix said.

"It is 0100 in the morning, do you intend to keep working?" Geldat asked.

"I do. That compensator was the hard one. This next part will take maybe ninety minutes," Rix said. "I can grab some coffee if you need?"

"It is I who should be grabbing stimulant drinks for you."

"Sleep is overrated," Rix said.

It was 0300 when Rix stepped back, wiping his hands on a dirty cloth and stuffing it into his back pocket. At some point, Geldat had taken a seat in the Nogg's front and fallen asleep. Rix gently grasped the Vesh's shoulder and gave him a light shake.

"Is there ... what ... how am I here?" he asked, struggling to wake. "Rix Banner, oh, with a plea for mercy I ask that we wait until morning to continue."

"No need. She's all fixed. Light her up, she'll have some pep in her," Rix said.

Tapping the power buttons, Geldat smiled as the console lights turned on and gauges came to life. "You are truly a master of vehicles," he said. "I wondered if you'd be capable of such work. You should stay behind. I have an entire yard of vehicles that would benefit from your hand. There would be great pay in such a venture."

Rix smiled. "Sorry, we're leaving in fourteen hours, give or take. I have my own cats to herd."

Geldat smiled. "Then understand you have made more than a deal today. You have made a friend. Please visit Geldat when you next return."

"I will, Geldat," Rix said. "Now, go home and get some sleep."

For the umpteenth time, Rix checked messages, hoping that Amari had reached out to him. She hadn't, and while he trusted her to take care of herself, he still worried.

"You need rest, Rix," Beverly said when Rix tripped over an uneven portion of the pier, even though he caught himself.

"Hard to argue with that," Rix said. "What do you think of Kha'rem's idea."

"To provide shelter for innocents who will be murdered because of the greed of immoral thugs?" Beverly asked, floating along next to him. She'd switched from work clothing to a long nightgown with pink bunnies on it and her hair tied up in rollers.

"You've made your point," Rix said. "I like the rollers. *I Love Lucy*?"

"Very good guess," she said. "And, have I? Because I thought that was what we did. We help people who can't help themselves."

"There will always be people in trouble," Rix said. "Do we need to help all of them?"

"No, but do you want to turn your backs on them?"

"Of course not."

"You've answered your own question."

"There is a lot of risk."

"Coming to *Garanod Enclave* was a lot of risk," Beverly said.

"Wake me up a 0700?" Rix asked, closing the hatch to *Gravitational Pull* behind him and climbing up the ladder. Climbing into the sleeping bunk, above, he sat and pulled off his boots. He'd planned to take a shower, but the cushion looked too inviting. Mentally, he promised himself he'd only rest for a moment before he showered. Four hours later, he heard Beverly's gentle alarm calling him to awaken.

"You're killing me here," Rix complained. Rolling over, he pushed up to a seated position.

"Humans need at least seven hours of sleep for proper functioning," she said, still in her jammies and rollers. In addition, a stethoscope hung around her neck, and she had a white lab coat.

"Is Greevo still over in *Calypso*?" Rix asked.

"Yes. It does look like they are preparing to leave for the morning, however."

"He can't make this easy," Rix said. "I'm tired of chasing him around."

"I understand," Beverly said as Rix pulled his boots on. "At least you did not change out of your clothing last night."

"Small blessings," Rix grumbled, sliding down the ladders one after the other. He tromped across the pier, where people were just starting to move around and jogged down the gang plank to *Calypso*.

Entering, he almost ran over Kitka, who was at the hatch, exiting. "Rix Banner, Greevo wishes words."

Pushing down his irritation, Rix worked around Kitka and then another of Greevo's helpers. Entering the passenger area, he noticed that while it was far from his standard of clean, it was more picked up than usual.

"We will pay to return to Patience Station," Greevo stated with no preamble.

"The time for that is now," Rix said. "And how much mass in cargo are we hauling for you?"

"You intend to make Greevo pay cargo?"

"Let's pretend we're like every other freighter in the known universe. So yeah, how much cargo?"

"Greevo has fifteen tons of cargo."

"What kind of volume is that?"

"*Gravitational Pull* has much room," Greevo said sending a load plan for his cargo. The load he had would fill most of both cargo pods.

"That's fine, but you can't put anything in *Calypso*," Rix said. "Have your load on board by 1500."

"Rix Banner not good businessman. Greevo need 1800."

"No," Rix said. "I have other cargo to load. I'll use the space if you're later than 1500."

"Not like Rix Banner."

"Sure," Rix said, flicking an invoice for nineteen thousand credits, or one hundred thirty-five grams of gold. "Pay before you leave this morning, or the cargo pods will be locked when you return."

Greevo made a big show of his displeasure but pulled out an electronic pad, tapping on it. Rix received a notification of credit exchange for 19000 and a warning that until they returned to Galactic Empire space, the exchange would not be finalized.

"Thank you, Greevo," Rix said. "Now make sure this place is cleaned up before you leave for the morning. I'd hate to add a surcharge for cleaning."

"Bad mans," Greevo grumbled.

The words were water off a duck's back for Rix as Greevo had complained for the entire duration of the trip. Instead of reacting, he turned and exited, knowing he had plenty of work in front of him for the day.

"Kha'rem, are you to work yet?" Rix called over comms.

"Yes. Sleep has been difficult," Kha'rem said. "Have you thought of my offer?"

"Thirty grams gold for the gillet we agreed upon is reasonable," Rix said.

"Oh! I see," Kha'rem said. "I will need three hours of preparation and then I will have my hands load it. I assume there will be power available. The gillet must remain frozen and my crates will keep the temperature within the correct range."

"There's power available," Rix said. "You care to know that our departure time is 1900, provided my people return on time today."

"Yes. We will certainly be sad to see you leave," Kha'rem said. "It is not often one finds a new friend and you all will be missed."

"I feel the same," Rix said. "Would you mind if I came over to your shop so I could use that portable lift you were talking about. I'm going to have to stretch the cargo rails out to load Geldat's vehicles."

"Yes. Of course. Please come to my office. I prepared an extra meal portion in anticipation of your last day."

"You're a lifesaver."

38

SEARCH AND SEIZURE

RIX HAD two of the five vehicles loaded onto *Gravitational Pull's* extended rails when he received an urgent communication request from an odd source labeled Chiren Glasti.

"This is Banner, go ahead," he answered, waving at Philo to start lashing the last vehicle into place.

"Heya sweet cheeks. How close are you to pushing off?"

Rix recognized the voice as being Kel. "Greevo has two hours left before he has to be fully loaded," he answered. "*Gravitational Pull* is running heavy. Is that going to be a problem?"

"One never knows," Kel said. "They found a couple of the thugs we put in cold storage. There's quite a bit of activity around here."

"Are you safe?"

"Funny," Kel said.

"It doesn't feel like a *funny* question."

"I understand. Yes, we're safe. We're working out details on when we should head that way. With the increased security, it's likely they'll figure out that we're gone sooner than we'd hoped."

As they were speaking, Rix noticed that Greevo's team was approaching on the dock, pulling heavy stacks of goods behind them. "Well, Greevo is looking to load. I'd say we're scheduled for departure at 1600."

"Does Philo know that's when we're leaving?"

"He's working with me, I'll make sure Sta'ci knows. He listens to her," Rix said.

"I imagine," Kel said. "Do us a favor and don't come outside the ship under any circumstances after 1530, unless you hear otherwise, okay?"

"Would it do me any good to ask why?"

"Not really."

"Who is Chiren Glasti?"

"Lirren's main squeeze," Kel said.

"You're in their apartment?"

"That's a leap. We could be using her comm from anywhere, but yeah, she was handy and we don't think Lirren will be back to the apartment for a few hours, what with all the trouble."

"Do you need anything else?" Rix asked, shaking his head.

"What, does getting ready to shove off makes you busy, all of a sudden?"

"Loading two ships and wrangling Greevo makes me busy," Rix said. "We're not pushing off until you two are loaded. So do what you need to but get back safely."

"Aww, you do care."

"Most of the time," Rix said, jumping from Kha'rem's portable lift and meeting Kitka, who was in the lead.

"Halo, Rix Banner," Kitka said.

"Looks like a big load," Rix said. "How'd you guys do with your market?"

Kitka's face showed a slight smile. "Good profit in long distance," she said. "Greevo still feel pain in stolen item. Grumpy, grumpy."

"That makes sense," Rix said. "It's a tough loss if it was that valuable. I wonder how they could have known that you even had it. Even I didn't know it was aboard."

"Mistakes. Greevo talks much."

Rix nodded. "Are you going to be loaded by 1500 like we talked?"

"Yes. Much work. We make Rix Banner deadline."

"Make sure everyone is on board by 1500," Rix said. "I'd hate to leave anyone behind."

"Yes, Rix Banner."

No more was Rix done speaking with Kitka than did Philo and Sta'ci climb off the aft of *Gravitational Pull,* having strapped down the first two of five vehicles.

"Need Philo run lift?" Philo asked. "Philo good."

"Yes. In a minute," Rix said. "Sta'ci, are you packed up so we can push off from the station at 1500 this afternoon?"

"I will visit my family one last time, but I should be back to *Calypso* before 1500," she said. "Is there a problem?"

"There are a lot of moving parts, but we don't want to miss our departure window," Rix said.

"I sense tension. Is Kel Warp and the other woman in some sort of danger?"

"They're just finishing up some business," Rix said.

"We will not be late," Sta'ci said, standing straight.

"Good. Philo, go ahead and bring that next one over," Rix said.

"Yup, yup."

The extended rails were good for three vehicles which made Philo's shift to the lifter well timed. Strapping in the third vehicle easily, Rix then had to guide Philo to stacking the fourth on angle, so it rested on the aft-most cargo pod, which hindered loading Greevo's cargo, but only to a small degree. The fifth vehicle was loaded directly atop the cargo pod and Rix ended up welding braces at various strategic points to fully secure the unwieldy load.

"Could you take that lift back and let Kha'rem know we're ready to start loading his gillet into *Caylpso's* hold? I want to check on Greevo's crew," Rix said. "Sta'ci, are we still on schedule for that chandlery delivery at 1400?"

"I will check, Rix Banner," Sta'ci said. "Do not worry. I will make sure they deliver on time."

"Thank you, Sta'ci."

A pair of grav pallets were en route from Kha'rem's warehouse and in that moment, Rix realized he hadn't verified the condition of *Calypso's* hold. Jogging away from his conversation with Sta'ci, he bounced down the gangway to *Calypso* and entered. He pushed from his mind the condition of the passenger compartment and turned aft, getting stopped at the hold's locked door. It took a moment to enter, and when he did, it was just as he'd feared. Greevo had started stacking crates inside.

"Philo, could I get your help?" Rix asked. "I'm in *Calypso's* hold. I have a bit of a problem."

"Rixy! Yup, yup. Philo coming!"

Rix couldn't help but smile at the irrepressible alien's good humor. Struggling to keep a good mood, he pulled a grav pallet from the starboard bulkhead and dialed down the artificial gravity to twenty percent normal.

"How can we help?" Sta'ci asked, as she and Philo entered through the forward hatch.

"I have two thousand kilograms of gillet that needs a home in here," Rix said. "Greevo wasn't supposed to be stacking in *Calypso*."

"He was irritated that there was not easy access to *Gravitational Pull's* aft cargo pod," Sta'ci said. "I overheard him speaking to Kitka about this."

"Where take?" Philo asked as he helped Rix stack three crates atop a grav pallet.

"Pier next to *Gravitational Pull*," Rix said. "Drop them off, and we'll make a big stack. Damn, this is a lot of work. I don't think we have time."

"There is a professional organization that works with loads," Sta'ci said. "I would imagine for a fee, they would manage your cargo holds."

"It's such short notice," Rix said.

"Yes. And that might add to the cost. Would you like me to see if they have any opportunity to help?"

"I'd need them in the next thirty minutes," Rix said. "Make the call."

"What are you willing to spend?" Sta'ci asked.

"Five grams of gold?" Rix said, quickly calculating.

Sta'ci nodded as she connected comms and walked forward to not be further interrupted. As she did, Rix caught Philo's eye as he watched her leave. Philo's grin spread across his entire face. "Philo did good. Sta'ci best girl."

"She's all that," Rix said. "What are you going to do about all of your other friends at all the other ports of call?"

Philo shrugged. "Sta'ci say one girl. Philo say okay. Other girls be sad, but not too sad."

"Fair enough," Rix said. "Let's keep moving, okay?"

The pair pushed the grav cart out and across the loading ramp which was adjacent to the pier. It was a forty meter walk to *Gravitational Pull*, where they unloaded. Turning back, they returned to the hold and loaded another stack of crates when Sta'ci returned.

"Stevedores required seven grams gold and will have a crew here in twenty minutes," she said. "The need a load plan."

Just then the first of the gillet crates arrived. Unlike the tool crates, which were roughly a meter in each dimension, the gillet crates were fifty percent bigger and had blinking lights around the top.

"Rix Banner?" a skinny, young man asked, looking skeptically into *Calypso's* cargo hold.

"That's me," Rix said.

"People call me Wagg. I'm supposed to help you load these, but we have eight more back in the warehouse. There's no way these are going in and they need power."

Rix extended his hand and smiled reassuringly. Wagg accepted the handshake limply, clearly not familiar with the tradition. "What we have here is a SNAFU," Rix said. "That's Army speak for things not working out the way they should, but it's normal."

"Kha'rem says you need a meter of clearance on the horizontal and that they can't be stacked," Wagg said, clearly not following.

"Sta'ci, get those stevedores and tell them we'll go ten grams if they can get here ASAP," Rix said.

"I have it," Sta'ci said, turning away from the conversation.

"Wagg, just set the gillet crates there on the pier, and grab the rest of them," Rix said. "I have a load crew coming."

"Kha'rem wants me to stick around until they're all loaded," Wagg said. "Stevedores won't want me getting in their way, though."

"How ever it needs to work," Rix said.

"Philo and Sta'ci go foods?" Philo interrupted.

"Do they need us to pick up?" Rix asked.

"Yup."

"Yeah, sure, go," Rix said, checking the time. He was down to seventy minutes to meet his own deadline, and he still hadn't heard more from Kel or Amari. Further, he hadn't heard from Kha'rem about Kasit and his mother.

"Where did my nicely ordered life go?" he wondered out loud. "Beverly, can you scan this space and help me work on that load plan?"

Beverly appeared in front of him in a clean jumpsuit that had *Calypso* emblazoned over her right breast. Wearing safety glasses and a hard hat, she held a clipboard. "Do we know if we have all Greevo's load?"

"We should be able to tell once we get a look inside the cargo pods," Rix said.

"I will send a query to Kitka," Beverly said. "Show me what's already loaded in *Gravitational Pull's* cargo pods. Also, is there a reason you have not extended the side loading ramps for the cargo pods? It would make loading easier."

"Has Greevo not been using those?" Rix asked. "I've never been around when he's been loading."

"No, he did not know of them."

Rix shook his head and set into a jog and once again bounced along the gangplank to *Gravitational Pull's* cargo pods. Opening, he found each of the pods about two thirds full of haphazardly stacked crates.

"What a mess," he lamented.

"I calculate that there is at least seventy cubic meters yet to arrive. There is room to load the remaining, even given the chaos we see," Beverly said.

"But we can do better, right?"

"For ten grams of gold and an hour of work by professionals, you can do quite a lot better," Beverly said. "Also, Kitka has responded. They are bringing the second to last load up from the market just now."

"Does she know she's talking to you?"

"No, I am impersonating you."

"That works," Rix said. "Tell her to stack on the pier. There's no sense in having them make the mess worse."

"Are you learning anything about freighting on this trip, Rix Banner?" Beverly asked.

"More than I'd like," Rix said.

"Rix Banner?" a bulky alien with longer than and thicker than average, hairy arms asked in a deep voice.

"That's me," Rix said, stepping out from the forward cargo pod onto the pier.

"You've quite a mess in there," the alien observed.

"My mistake," Rix said. "I allowed a customer free access."

"We'll appreciate the work," the alien said. "Payment up front."

Rix pulled ten grams of gold from his belt and handed it to the alien. “I have crates in the freighter, *Calypso*, that need brought back to the cargo pods. These cargo pods need to be restacked first, though. There’s also seventy cubic meters on the way up from the market.”

“As long as they get here before we’re done, we’ll get them loaded,” the alien said, gesturing to the trio who’d accompanied him. “Kha’rem’s gillet is loaded on the other freighter?”

“I have a plan,” Rix said, flicking Beverly’s load plan.

“Well, that makes things easy,” he said. “Just keep your people out of our way and we’ll have this done in fifty minutes, give or take.”

Rix checked the time. He had exactly twenty minutes of breathing room if the stevedores kept to their word.

“The holds are yours,” Rix said, backing out.

“We’ll get to it.”

A shout from a distance caught Rix’s attention. Greevo, sitting atop the load being pushed by his crew, gesticulated wildly. “And one more time with Greevo,” Rix said, frustration clear in his voice.

“Just explain that you have professional loaders,” Beverly counseled.

“Sure,” Rix said. “Because he’s all about listening.”

It turned out that Greevo, while initially irritated, was accepting of the stevedores when he learned that Rix was footing the bill for their labor. And after the Grintok contingent dropped off their load, they were off again to the market for the final bits and pieces. With nothing more to do, he headed back to *Calypso’s* bridge to start running system’s checks and to validate fuel and coolant levels.

Entering the bridge, he startled when he found a figure sitting in the pilot’s seat. The figure turned, having heard Rix’s entrance. It was none other than Zenith.

"What are you doing here?" Rix hissed. "You can't be here. You're visible to anyone with decent optics!"

Zenith smiled and even as she did, her face melted until it was Kel's. "Man, are you tightly wound or what?" she asked chuckling.

Rix started sputtering a response but then he felt hands on his waist as a soft form hugged him from behind. "Don't be mad. Kel's just playing with you," Amari said quietly as her lips came close to his ear, her voice but a whisper.

"You almost gave me a heart attack," Rix said.

"Did we?" Kel asked, still laughing.

"Yes."

"You're not making your 1500 schedule," Kel said. "Those holds are a mess, and you have crap everywhere."

The feel of Amari's arms around his waist sent a calming wave through his body and he relaxed for just a moment before responding. "We're closer than you think," Rix said. "How much time do we have before we have to worry about Jeshifa organization coming for us?"

"They're already out looking," Amari said. "Kel and I made sure to show our faces a couple of times over on Chainreach and then again on Havenfall."

"Something is going on out on the pier," Kel said. "Grab a weapon."

"Crap," Rix said, his hand immediately testing the presence of his ray gun on his belt.

Pulling longer guns from the armory cabinet behind the pilot's chairs, Amari and Kel both armed themselves. The three of them raced to the pier to find a four, armed men standing next to the load of crates still on the pier.

"What's going on here?" Rix demanded, realizing that he'd met one of the men while in the basement of the Jeshifa warehouse.

"Stay where you are," the leader of the group said, raising a weapon as the others tore tops off crates and made hasty searches of the open crates.

Rix exchanged a look with the stevedore lead who'd stepped away from the contested crates. The look told Rix what he needed, which was the stevedore wasn't getting involved.

"Do you intend to search every damn crate? That'll take hours," Rix said. "What are you even looking for?"

The Jeshifa thug Rix had briefly met in the warehouse gave him the stink eye but clearly couldn't put together where he'd seen Rix before.

"Not your problem," the Jeshifa leader answered.

"Cod, search the ship," the leader said and Rix was concerned that it was in fact the man who would sooner or later remember where he'd seen Rix. "Take the captain and keep an eye on him."

Rix was about to correct the misunderstanding about Kel vs him as captain but thought better of it.

"You can see all of everything from out here," Rix said. "You're not going in my ship."

"I can get more men here if this is going to be trouble. I'm sure they'd love to look through your crates," the man said. "Or get a good feel for your ladies. If you have nothing to hide, smart money is let us do our job."

Rix sighed. "Come on, Cod. Let's get this over with."

"Do I know you from somewhere?" Cod asked as he waved a gun at Rix and motioned for him to go in the ship.

"That's unlikely," Rix said.

A text showed on Rix's HUD as he walked.

Amari: Can he make you?

Rix was surprised that Amari had any idea what was going down and then when Beverly answered for him, he was equally surprised.

Beverly: Yes. Rix ran into him in Jeshifa compound.

Amari: Disable him quietly. I'll take it from there.

Just like that, Rix thought. He was supposed to dispatch a man who had a gun leveled at him. How was that supposed to work?

"Didn't I see you out at the warehouse a couple days ago?" Cod asked.

"We picked up supplies from a number of vendors," Rix covered as he led Cod forward to the bridge. "You probably want to look at the smuggler's trunk on the back of these pilot's chairs. You gotta get down there to see in, though. Right through the armory locker."

"You need to stand back," Cod said.

Rix backed away and held his hands up. "Look. We don't need more trouble. We're just trying to get out of here," Rix said. "I'm no threat to you."

"Best keep it that way," Cod said, kneeling and opening the locker Rix had pointed to. As he did, Rix nudged the bridge door closed. "I don't see no panel." Cod pulled out of the locker, obviously irritated.

"That's because there isn't one," Rix said.

Cod, understanding the deception, lunged for Rix.

Firing on someone who wasn't directly threatening him was a line Rix had not previously crossed. In the moment, though, with his heart hammering in his chest, it only took Cod's actions for Rix to fire.

39

AYE CHI MAMA!

RIX: AMARI, I HAVE A PROBLEM.

Amari: Dead or what? I saw the flash.

Rix knelt by Cod, first securing his weapon. After that, he checked his pulse and didn't find anything, but he discovered Cod was breathing, so he marked it up to being poor at checking for a pulse.

Rix: Not dead. Probably needs medical attention.

Amari: I'm coming in.

Rix: How? They're not going to like it.

"Searching crates takes time," Amari said, already appearing next to him. "Take his clothing off."

Rix shook his head. He wanted to question Amari about her next actions, but he already knew what she was up to, so he got to business.

"Where can we stash him? What if the other guy comes in?"

"Pirates are lazy," Amari said, already halfway transitioned to Cod's image. "Put him in one of the chairs and tie him up."

"I can see why governments would be looking for you. This whole thing is crazy."

"Yes," Amari agreed. "Also, don't watch as I change. It will cause you trouble in how you perceive me."

"Fair warning," Rix said, handing her Cod's clothing without looking directly at her. "What will you do?"

"I will help finish up the task of searching our vessels and once we leave, I will find a way to separate myself from the others," she said. "Also, hand me ten grams of gold. Do you have that much?"

"I have more," Rix said, fishing in his pocket for gold.

"Make it twenty, then," she said.

"What are you thinking?"

"Cod is unlikely to leave this ship without taking something. A payday will help them all to move along," Amari said, completing her transformation to Cod.

"What should I do?"

"Cod would most likely require you to accompany him. We will continue to search the ship and make a mess as we go," Amari said. "How do you feel about a bit of a shiner? Perhaps you struggled when I found your gold stash."

"Really? You're going to hit me?" Before he could finish his sentence, Amari lashed out and caught Rix's cheek with Cod's weapon. Bright lights flashed in Rix's vision, and he grunted at the pain. "What the hell!?"

"Ooh, I must have got you good," Amari as Cod said approvingly. "You never swear. And get your hands out of that. We need blood on your cheek to sell it."

"You get scarier every day."

"Practical is the word you're looking for," she said. "Now, let's trash this place."

The pair worked together to make a real mess of things and worked their way through *Calypso's* hold. As Amari as Cod rifled through crates in the hold, Rix noticed that Greevo had returned, although he stood off, keeping well away from the ruckus.

"What'd you find?" the lead pirate asked.

"Ship is overloaded with crap. I don't know what these Galactics find so interesting about worn-out old parts and pieces. No stowaways, though and I'm going to need a shower. I have gillet fish all over me," Amari as Cod grumbled as she approached the lead pirate. From her pocket, she pulled half of the gold and palmed it to the man.

"All of it," he said with a whisper loud enough for everyone to hear. Amari reached back in and pulled the remaining gold and handed it over. "That's better. All right boys, finish up. There's nothing here."

It was with some consternation that Rix watched Amari leave with the remaining Jeshifa crew. Greevo decided that was his best moment to get involved, but Rix shut him down with a withering look.

"I hate to be this guy, but you're in no shape to be loading gear in this moment," the lead stevedore said with an apologetic look.

"You're right," Rix said.

"I'll give you a break. If you can get this cleaned up by 1700, we'll be back and I'll only need another five grams to pay the boys," he said.

"That's more than fair," Rix said.

"I don't know what has Jeshifa all worked up. I've never seen them take after a freighter like this. I imagine it had something to do with your departure time being close to some sort of trouble," he said. "You handled it right. You must go along with what they say or it gets real bad."

"Thank you," Rix said.

"How can we help," Sta'ci asked, as she and Philo approached next.

"Greevo, how do you want to handle your crates. Can we help repack, or do you want to do it?" Rix asked.

"Why did this happen, Rix Banner?" Greevo asked.

"I don't know and we can discuss later," Rix said. "Right now, I want to get packed up so we can get on the road."

"There is no road. All our equipment is spread out on the pier."

"Do you want help or not?"

"Yes. Help. Rix Banner is bad at business."

"You keep telling yourself that," Rix grumbled, although in this case, he felt Greevo wasn't entirely wrong. Jeshifa's shakedown was directly related to their involvement in rescuing Kasit and Zenith.

"Rix Banner, we will accept help," Kitka said, stepping in.

The work was neither difficult nor interesting but with everyone pitching in, the crates were soon re-packed, with only a few broken items discovered in the process. Once they were done, Rix sent a message to the stevedore, who promised to return as quickly as possible but no later than 1700.

"Rix, did you know there's a guy tied up in the bridge?" Kel asked, quietly pulling Rix aside.

"I do. Is he awake? I need to get in there and get him some medical," Rix said.

"Oh, he's awake," she said. "I gave him a sedative that will help him forget the day. We just need to figure out how to get him unloaded before we take off."

"Won't that be a little suspicious?"

"Not if you stick around a few more hours."

"I don't follow."

"No, but you will."

"What do you want to do with our extra time?" Kel asked.

"Greevo and crew owe us some cleaning. *Calypso* is still an absolute mess," Rix said.

"They're not exactly good at taking direction. Even Kitka seems unable to understand basic cleaning," Kel said.

"I have an idea," Rix said. "Sta'ci can I talk to you a minute?"

"Sure Rix, what's up?" she asked cheerily.

"This might be the kind of trouble you don't want to get involved in, but I'm going to ask and you can tell me to go pound sand," Rix said.

"That's a funny saying," she observed.

"It'll make sense," Kel added.

"Here's the deal, we're having trouble getting Greevo and his crew to understand what we mean by keeping things clean. I'm wondering if we're not successfully communicating because they're Grintok and I'm human, or if there's another problem."

"You would like me to get involved in your dispute with Greevo?" she asked.

"I suppose that's the sum of it."

"You are not asking me to pay for my transportation from Garanod Enclave to Patience Station," she said. "I believe it is quite reasonable that you ask for my help to negotiate with Greevo and his team. Yes. I will help. What is the standard you are trying to enforce?"

"Keeping the place picked up. Dishes cleaned after use. Trash in the recycler. Clothing put away, hallways cleared and bathrooms clean," Rix said.

"I understand," Sta'ci said. "And you have negotiated this with Greevo in the past?"

"It's part of our contract."

"Please send this to me," she said. Rix flicked the contract to Sta'ci, and she read it for a few moments. "There is language that is potentially subject to interpretation, but I will clear this up."

"Do what you can," Rix said.

Returning to *Gravitational Pull*, Rix set to the work of cleaning, which for the most part, he didn't mind. The short-haul freighter had often been at the bottom of his priorities and hadn't received the level of cleaning he felt it deserved. As he worked, he wished he had access to the painting rig stored back in his shop on Patience.

"A man who cleans. That's a good start," Amari said, startling him as he had wedged himself behind the pilot chairs and was picking up decades of old trash and dust.

"Just a minute," he called, not willing to stop working.

"Your stevedores have returned," she announced.

"Are they loading?" he asked. "I gave them a plan."

"It didn't look like they had questions," she said. "I can see why they get paid so much. They're ridiculously strong and handle those crates like they're boxes of shoes."

"I need to pay him," Rix said, wiggling out, having moved all the junk out so he could pick up the pile.

"That's disgusting," Amari said.

"I found this," Rix said, proudly holding up a small pistol.

"Seven Point energy weapon," she said. "Stuns most species on contact. Does it have a charge?"

"No idea," Rix said, handing it to her.

"It's dry, and this place is looking fantastic. Are you working out your angst with cleaning?" she asked.

"Why do you think I'm angsty?"

"You're not?"

"Everything is hard today," he said. "Greevo, Jeshifa, ... well, that's about it, I suppose. Oh, and Kha'rem. Somehow, we're picking up Kasit and Zenith, but he won't tell me how and doesn't want us talking about it. How's that supposed to work?"

"He's a smart guy. Play it his way. I don't think he means any harm," she said.

"It doesn't make things easier is my only point."

"Soon, we'll be bobbing along in the deep dark, and you won't have a care aside from Greevo messing up all your cleaning efforts," she said.

"Shoot me if I do a deal with him again," Rix said.

"Are you going to come out okay on this deal?" she asked. "Financially, that is?"

"I think so," Rix said. "Let's make it back to the Narlux-4 system before we make any final judgements on that."

"Fair enough," Amari said. "Jeshifa is giving up their search for Kasit and Zenith for tonight. It sounds like they think they're hiding on Havenfall somewhere, which makes sense. That's where their hovel is."

"Let's go see how the loading is progressing," Rix said. "Do you have any thoughts on how we'll get Cod out of the bridge without everyone aboard knowing what we're doing?"

"That'll cost you more money," she said. "Offer to pay for a meal to make up for the inconvenience."

Rix nodded, grimly reaching into his pocket for gold slivers. "Will three grams do it, you think? I can ask Sta'ci to escort them and pay."

"Sta'ci? Is she up for that sort of thing?"

"She's been kicking in—wants to pay for her ride back to Patience by helping out."

"Sure, why not? Oh, I have two grams for you. It was Cod's cut of your gold," she said, digging out a couple of gold slivers from Cod's clothing.

Returning to the pier, Rix discovered that the stevedores were nearly done packing and he made his way over to the lead. "I sure appreciate you coming back, tonight."

"I hope you didn't get set back too far on your schedule," he said, accepting payment plus two additional grams in tip. "That's mighty kind of you."

"You and your boys have been the bright spot in the day," Rix said. "It was well earned."

As Rix was talking with the stevedore, Amari had offered to negotiate with Sta'ci to see if she'd accompany Greevo and crew to a nice dinner. Exchanging a glance with Amari, Rix could see that Sta'ci was enthusiastic for the expanded responsibility.

Thirty minutes later, only Rix, Kel and Amari remained on *Calypso*, where they met in the bridge to discuss their issue.

"How do you suppose we get him out of here?" Rix asked.

Cod, who was awake, thrashed around, likely expecting that they were talking about killing him.

"Cod, listen to me," Amari said. "We're going to free you from the bindings and you're going to change back into your clothing. You're going to accompany us to a bar in the market, where we're going to get you nice and drunk. At some point. Once you're drunk, we'll leave you to your business. If you make trouble, you won't like how it goes. Nod if you understand."

"How do you want to do this?" Kel asked.

"Prostitutes," Amari said.

"Perfect," Kel said, turning her attention to Rix. "I'll get changed. Can you handle getting Cod into his clothing? He's going to be a little wobbly."

"Wobbly?"

"Yeah, we can talk about it later."

Rix started cutting the man's bindings and Cod, who apparently didn't get the wobbly memo, tried to muscle his way around the three of them, only to end up face first on the deck. Amari smiled sympathetically as she pulled off Cod's clothing and changed into a small bundle of clothing she'd brought along.

"Gosh, that's quite a look," Rix said as Amari shifted her visage to that of another, more buxom, younger and less restrained woman.

"Aye chi mama!" Kel announced, appearing as a shift from her normal self with revealing clothing.

Rix helped Cod into his clothing and pulled him to his feet. "Have a good time, Cod," he said. "I won't be sorry to see you go."

"Oh, Cod is going to have a marvelous time, isn't he Kel?" Amari asked.

"The best," Kel said, sashaying up next to him. "Let's go, big boy."

Rix shook his head as he watched the two of them escorting Cod from the ship. A few minutes later, he received a ping from his incoming messages.

Amari: I know this is a lot to take in. Are you doing okay with all of this?

Rix: There will be drinking involved once we're free from this place.

Amari: I'll join you, but you're not freaking out?

Rix: Sure, I am, but it's manageable.

Amari: I could use some close time with you once we're underway. This whole thing got a bit more out of hand than I thought it would.

Rix: That's the nature of conflict.

Amari: Indeed.

And for the first time in many days, Rix had the run of the ships to himself. That Sta'ci had been successful in encouraging Greevo's crew to clean up after themselves was a blessing, but there was still a smell, so Rix moved from *Calypso* back to *Gravitational Pull*, where he poured two fingers of the closest thing to whiskey he had from a quickly dwindling bottle.

"Rix Banner, this is Kha'rem, do you have a moment to speak?" Kha'rem asked over comms about thirty minutes later.

"Go ahead, Kha'rem," Rix said.

"I believed you would be underway by this time. I have seen much activity. Is there anything I can do to help?" Kha'rem asked.

"We need two more hours? Is that okay?" Rix asked.

"Yes, my friend, that was not my concern."

"I assume you saw that we had visitors," Rix said.

"It appears they did not find reason to remove property from your vessels."

"They were happy to help themselves to some of my gold," Rix said. "But, otherwise, no, they did not remove anything else."

"There is private talk of Jeshifa making a journey to a distant colony," Kha'rem said. "Lirren, himself, will be leading a trio of vessels."

"Kind of makes me wonder why they need to keep things quiet, in that case," Rix said.

"I suspect that was a short-term interest," Kha'rem said. "Once they begin their journey, it will no longer be a mystery as to where the unique device brought from the Galactic Empire ended up."

"I have questions that don't belong on the wire. Are you around to talk?"

"No. I have taken a sabbatical to the Kor'vesh sea," he said. "I did not care for interest Jeshifa was bringing to my door."

"I'm sorry for our part in that."

"You did not bring trouble to my door. Trouble was here and you were unlucky enough to find it," he said. "I do hope you will return one day. Safe journeys, my friend."

"Thank you Kha'rem."

Rix settled back into his chair and sipped his whiskey, knowing the quiet he was enjoying would soon be disrupted. And forty minutes later, he was not wrong as Sta'ci, Philo and Greevo's crew returned.

"Rix Banner!" Greevo demanded, banging on *Gravitational Pull's* hatch. "Let me in."

Rix shook his head. He'd enjoyed the quiet and knew better than to expect more. He made his way down and opened the hatch. "What do you need, Greevo?" he asked.

"Rix Banner good man to buy Greevo and Greevo people a good meal," Greevo said. "Greevo like Rix Banner."

Rix looked around to see if anyone else was around to hear the conversation. They were alone and by the sounds of things, Greevo's crew were loading into *Calypso.*

"That's ... surprising of you to say," Rix said.

"Hard trip. Greevo know this. Time to go home. Greevo tired. Greevo sleep long."

"We'll set sail shortly, Greevo. If you want to head up to sleep, go ahead," Rix said.

"Greevo bring Kitka?"

"Choice is yours," Rix said. "Just keep the place clean and we'll be fine."

"Yes. Yes. Greevo know clean."

Rix shook his head questioningly but wasn't about to ruin Greevo's good mood by pushing him any further. Tapping out a quick message, he checked on Amari.

Rix: Are you guys doing okay?

Amari: Just finishing up, here. Our boy Cod was a cheap drunk.

Rix: Greevo has returned and we're all loaded. Come home when you can.

Amari: Home is such a nice word.

Nervously, Rix waited for the girls to return, but true to Amari's word, twenty minutes later, she and Kel both found Rix in *Gravitational Pull,* still wearing their alluring clothing.

"I've missed you," Amari said, embracing Rix, her breath smelling of alcohol and clothing of dank smoke. Rix wasn't about to turn her away and enjoyed their hug if not the lingering smells.

"Yeah, me too," Kel said giving Rix a lop-sided grin and opening her arms for a hug. Rix knew she was messing with him but pulled her into a three-way hug, which she accepted and seemed to appreciate, even though she'd started it as something of a joke.

"Are you good to sail, Kel?" Rix asked.

"Your girl took the brunt of the drinks," Kel said. "I'm good. When are we leaving?"

"We'll do a role call once you're back on *Calypso* and then we'll get underway," Rix said.

"Did we ever figure out what Kha'rem did with Kasit and Zenith?" Kel asked.

"I imagine he's taken them out to the Kor'vesh sea," Rix said. "He made it sound like he'd let us know at some point, but I don't know much beyond that."

"If it's all the same, I'd like to move as soon as we can," Kel said. "This place has a strange way of trying to hold onto us."

"I couldn't agree more," Rix said.

"Give me fifteen minutes to get a shower and get settled."

"Take thirty," Rix said. "I'm going to see about getting Amari into the shower, too."

"Good plan," Kel said, leaving down the ladder and out again.

"Take a shower with me," Amari said, running a finger along Rix's chin.

"Greevo is up in the bunk and Kitka is on her way over to join us for the trip," Rix said.

"We didn't get any time to be close this trip," she complained. "Travelling with Grintok aboard a tiny ship is definitely not romantic."

"I know," Rix said. "Come on. I'll jump in with you, but we need to be quick. I don't want to be here any longer than we must."

"Okay, but you're kind of a spoilsport."

"And you're kind of drunk."

Amari shrugged. "Sacrifices were made."

40

AMBUSH

"KHA'REM, we're thirty minutes from pushing off," Rix said, honoring the Vesh's request for notification. With Kitka and Greevo in the bunkroom above fast asleep, he and Amari sat in the pilot's chairs, although Amari had been nodding off, which caused him some surprise when she asked a question.

"What do you suppose he did with Kasit and Zenith?" she asked.

"He's hiding them," Rix said. Amari leaned forward and set the comms to monitor several local bands. "What are you doing?"

"Jeshifa uses open comms to direct some of their security forces," she said. "I might have snagged their encryption codices while in Lirren's quarters."

Rix nodded as chatter on the radio spiked.

Speaker 1: We have a sighting. Megix and I are on the move.

Speaker 2: Provide updates. Base out.

Speaker 3: Looks like those Galactics are getting ready to shove off. Are we in pursuit?

Speaker 2: Intercept at four hundred, as planned. Boarding team, load up.

"Well, shoot," Rix said. "Beverly, send that over to Kel."

"I have it, Rix. Four hundred is probably four hundred thousand kilometers," she said. "With that Ghostmist Cipher, they'll be able to stay in the clouds and ambush from cover."

"Unless we modify our flight path. That cipher doesn't let them see through the cloud, does it?"

"Well, that's kind of the point, Rix," Amari said. "I thought you disabled it."

"I did, but it'll take a bit of use before it stops working," Rix said.

"Define *a bit*," Kel said.

"A couple of hours, maybe?"

"That could be a problem."

"I understand. We should expect they're tracking us. My biggest concern is that *Gravitational Pull* is fully loaded and we're not going to be even remotely maneuverable," Rix said.

"I have an idea," Kel said.

"Let me guess, I'm not going to like it."

"You, for sure, are not going to like it and it's pure genius, if I do say so myself."

Rix laughed. "I'm afraid to even ask."

"Let's get rolling," Kel said.

"Twenty minutes. Kha'rem asked for a full thirty minutes."

"I don't like sitting here. Are you even listening to that Jeshifa conversation? They're looking for Kasit and Zenith. I'd like to move while they're distracted with all that."

"Sounds like there have been sightings," Rix said. "That works in our favor."

"Twenty minutes. Not a second longer, okay?"

"Yeah, that works," Rix said.

They passed their time listening into various Jeshifa conversations, but, in the end, nothing much came of it. Finally, it was time to depart.

"Kha'rem, it's been a pleasure. We'll see you next time," Rix said as he released the permanent mooring lines and then retracted the gangplank that had been extended to the pier.

"Take care, my friend. I have a message for you that is coded to be accessible once you are back in Galactic Empire territory. I hope you find time to return. You have added richly to that which is Garanod," Kha'rem said.

"That's kind of mysterious," Amari said. "Why does he want us back in Narlux-4 before we listen to his message?"

"Kha'rem likes his secrets," Rix said, shrugging. "Kel, I'm at full power, pulling away from Driftmarket. Dang, but we've never accelerated this slowly, before."

"You're like an old family junkship. Don't worry, you'll get where you're going. It might just take another day or two," she said.

"Are you seeing any pursuit?" Rix asked, once they'd reached a thousand kilometers of separation from the broken planetoid.

"Maybe some looky-loos, but they're mostly keeping their distance," she said.

"At this acceleration rate, we're looking at three days to the Narlux-4 transition," Rix said.

"Sta'ci says she planned for a full two weeks of food, so we might as well take it easy," Kel said. "I've set a four-hundred-thousand-kilometer mark as where I'm expecting Jeshifa to break from cover and jump us. I have a plan, but I need *Gravitational Pull* to build up a head of steam, first."

"So mysterious," Amari said.

"You know me, I do like a well-timed surprise," Kel said. "We'll check in in forty-five minutes."

"Copy that," Rix said.

Finally, Rix had a chance to do something he hadn't since arriving in Garanod Enclave, and that was to relax. With *Gravitational Pull*'s engines steadily churning away fuel, which left a billowing black cloud behind, there was little to do aside from sit.

"I miss good beer," he said, casually.

"I'm sure there's good beer somewhere," Amari said. "You didn't like that ale that Petju imported from Marska? She was so proud of it."

"It wasn't bad," Rix said. "It's just not the same. You know how that goes."

"I've been thinking, I wonder if we should take a trip back to Earth and let you settle some things. You could let your family know you're alive," Amari said. "You could even get some beer."

"Maybe I could buy hops and barley seeds so we could source our own at some point," Rix said.

"If you had that, could you make your own beer?" Amari asked. "Look who I'm talking to, of course you could. But, is that what you want to do with your time?"

"I'm spit balling," Rix said. "Isn't it illegal to land on Earth due to the quarantine?"

"Yes, but also, it's not heavily patrolled," Amari said. "And you have a reasonable claim in that you're from there. I'm not sure anyone can stop you from going home. Now, if you start sharing technology secrets, you might get in trouble with Tok. But if we go in discretely, we'll get away with it."

"I'd like to raise some money and get it to my old landlord. He had insurance on the diner building, but that doesn't always cover everything. Oh, crap, I totally forgot to pay Thudd that second installment. He warned me we'd be good friends but that wouldn't stop him from charging me late fees if I was out galivanting around the galaxy," Rix said.

"Does this qualify as a galivant?" Amari asked.

"It might. I totally meant to set up a payment, but I have so much tied up in this trip, I was short on credits," Rix said. "He said the late fees were sizable, ten percent or so."

"That sounds like Thudd. The man likes to make his money. Are you going to be okay when we get back?"

"I'll make a payment once we're in Narlux-4 space," Rix said. "I just wasn't thinking about the fact that we'd be out of range of Galactic Empire communications."

"Quite a change from 1950s Earth. You are a spaceman for sure, now," Beverly said, appearing on the forward bulkhead in a brilliant red mid-calf-length dress. "You didn't have electronic banking at all back home. Now, you're relying on it."

"You have me there," Rix said. "Also, I don't recognize your outfit."

"Rose Devore Grace dress," Beverly said. "I saw it in one of your magazines."

Rix was about to respond when Kel cut in. "Rix, I'm about to execute that plan I've been hatching," she said.

"Oh?" Rix asked.

"You're going to cut your engines and shut down everything but life support. And that includes external transponders and everything," she said.

"Going dark won't help. If they're tracking us, they'll know where we're headed," Rix said.

"That's fair," Kel said. "But humor me."

"I guess," Rix said. "When can we turn them back on?"

"Wait until we come back," Kel said. "There's nothing we can do about Jeshifa tracking *Calypso,* but we have teeth and we're not so loaded we can't cause trouble. I was thinking, though, maybe you'd like to come over and man the needler, just for a couple of hours. I know that pulls you away from Amari and you don't love it, but it's our best play."

"I don't even know what the play is. Jeshifa is going to find us. They're already tracking," Rix said.

"Have a little faith. I'll send Philo and Sta'ci over to keep Amari company," she said. "Cut your engines. I'm going to raft up with you."

"Are you okay with this, Amari?" Rix asked.

"Kel only has so many good ideas in a day. You have to trust the ones that show up," Amari said.

"I heard that, Amari."

"You were supposed to. I was being supportive."

"We'll need to talk about what you think supportive sounds like," Kel said.

"Let's wait to see how this turns out, first," Amari said. "It might not be that necessary."

"Ladies. Enough, already," Rix said. "I'm cutting power. Go ahead and initiate your approach, Kel."

Calypso easily navigated around *Gravitational Pull* until the middle hatch was adjacent to *Gravitational Pull's* lower hatch in the basement. Rix pulled out a retractable safety line and clipped it to his vac suit before exposing the basement to the thin atmosphere of the Ghost-mist nebula. Pushing off gently, he glided to *Calypso* and inelegantly struggled for a moment as he caught the external grab bar and settled. Clipping the line onto *Calypso*, he entered the airlock and cycled it.

"Have you done many spacewalks, Sta'ci?" Rix asked noticing the small alien looked greener than usual.

"I have never been out in space before."

"It's easier than you think," Rix said, clipping a safety line to her waist. "If you get in trouble, less movement is better than more. Just ask for help and Philo or I will come get you. Otherwise, just hand-over-hand until you get over to *Gravitational Pull.* Watch how Philo does it and then you do it just like that only slower. We're in no hurry and speed never makes this better."

"Okay," Sta'ci stammered.

"You've got this," Rix said, placing a hand on her shoulder.

They both watched in silence as Philo expertly traversed the line and landed on the side of *Gravitational Pull.*

"He's sideways," Sta'ci said.

"No gravity. There is no up or down," Rix said. "That won't make sense today, just focus on Philo."

"Okay," she said, tentatively pushing off. Rix knew she'd been listening to him when he watched her take her time crossing over, with the entire trip taking several minutes. "I made it!" she exclaimed when Philo was finally able to reach her. "I did it!"

"Great job, Sta'ci. You're a natural," Rix said and then closed the hatch after disconnecting the safety line and stowing it.

"Are you aboard, Rix?" Kel asked.

"I am. Do you want me in the needler or on the bridge?" he asked, entering the passenger compartment, which was cleaner than he'd ever seen it. "And, what happened in here?"

"Bridge, and happened in where?"

"The galley, it's spotless," Rix said.

"Oh. Sta'ci happened," Kel said. "You never see her yell, but I'll tell you, those other Grintok snap right to it when she starts handing out assignments. I'd love to know what she's doing to make that work."

"She seems so mild," Rix agreed, settling into the pilot's chair next to Kel. "So, tell me what your big, secret plan is. And why didn't you want to tell me over comms?"

"I got to thinking. If we could listen to Jeshifa comms, what if they could listen to us?" she said.

"Hard to argue that," Rix said.

"We're going to push *Gravitational Pull* in a different direction," Kel said.

"Push?"

"Yeah, push."

"I'm not sure there's a good place to push on *Gravitation Pull*, especially with all that mass aboard," Rix said. "We'll use mooring clamps and as long as you don't go more than twenty percent thrust, we'll be okay. Beverly check my numbers, would you?"

Beverly appeared in the same red dress. "You didn't say if you liked me in this dress, Rix."

"It's a lovely dress, Beverly," Rix said. "It pulls out the highlights in your hair."

"You're just saying that. I don't have hair and I for certain do not have highlights."

"All the same," Rix said, not backing down.

"Well, that is kind of you to say," she said. "Twenty percent thrust is acceptable if we just use magnetic mooring clamps from both vessels."

"Can you organize that, Rix?" Kel asked.

"Aye, aye," Rix said. "Amari, without discussing it, could you mirror our action here?"

"That's kind of vague," Amari answered a moment later. "And I will if I can figure it out."

Rix launched the magnetic mooring lines, which thumped against *Gravitational Pull's* cab and cargo pods. With heavy winches, the slack was pulled from the lines until both ships were pointed roughly in the same direction. "Now your turn," Kel called.

Without further communications, *Gravitational Pull's* mooring clamps were deployed in much the same manner. "Are we good?" Amari asked.

"Well done." Rix closed comms and looked at Kel. "Now, what?"

"We put *Gravitational Pull* on a new course, but only *Calypso* will show a signature of moving," Kel said. "We'll make a few course adjustments and then release *Gravitational Pull*. After that, we'll make a few more course corrections and by the time Jeshifa shows up, if they show up, our ship will be a distant memory."

"And we collect *Gravitational Pull* once we know things are in the clear," Rix said. "That works great unless Jeshifa waits us out."

"Well, we'll make sure they have no interest in that," Kel said. "Remember. Without having to defend *Gravitational Pull*, we have real teeth. Especially with you in that needler turret."

"You're buttering me up," Rix said.

"Maybe a little. I still like our chances, though," Kel said.

With the two ships joined together, Kel turned twenty degrees to starboard and powered up *Calypso's* engines. With the combined mass of the two vessels and only twenty percent engine output allowed, the process was excruciatingly slow. Every ten minutes or so, Kel would make a new, seemingly random adjustment until an hour had passed.

"Release them," Kel said. "Hopefully Amari knows better than to give away her position by chatting me back in this moment."

"It seems like this would be right in her wheelhouse," Rix said.

"I have no idea what you're saying."

"She doesn't need a comm from you to figure out to release her clamps," Rix said, his point accentuated by a sudden lurch caused by *Gravitational Pull* releasing and both ships drifting away from each other. "And how will we find them once we're done with Jeshifa?"

"We know where they're going," Kel said confidently.

"How soon until we think we'll run into Jeshifa?" Rix asked.

"I'd say anywhere from an hour to two," Kel said. "I ran a simulation putting us out to four hundred thousand kilometers, given *Gravitational Pull's* load. We' reach that in sixty-five minutes."

"Crazy trip, so far, right?" Rix said.

"Did we make any money? I'd hate to think we did all that for nothing," she said.

"I'll let you know when Greevo's check clears," Rix said. "In my mind, he's figured out a way to get out of paying. I don't know if that's true, or not. I'll believe the deal is good when I have the credits."

"Let's say his money is good. How are we cutting it up?"

"I figure we split into shares. The ships both get two shares, captains get two shares, crew each get a share. So, Philo and Amari get a single share, we put two shares into *Calypso's* repair budget, same for *Gravitational Pull* and you and me each get two shares. That's a total of ten shares. Each share is worth 1,900 credits. Does that work for you?"

"An interesting way to hand out money, but I don't have any immediate objection. Where'd you get this model?"

"Old Earth sailing ships assigned shares based on position, to include owner, captain, etc.," Rix said. "I stayed away from complexities and decided to treat the ships as individuals because we know both will need work once we return."

"Let's socialize it with Philo and Amari. Are we not paying Sta'ci anything? She's doing a good job keeping the Grintok in line."

"And she's getting a free ride back to Galactic Empire," Rix said. "I don't mind if we want to give charitably, but her having a seat is a gift."

"Bubba, you can be kind of cold. Has anyone ever told you that?"

"I guess it's just how I think of things. I probably am cold."

They continued to chit chat and at sixty-eight minutes, a ship appeared from a large, cauliflower lobe shaped cloud.

"Now that's impressive timing," Kel said. "I missed by three minutes."

"I'm heading back."

"That's smart. Go ahead and unlimber the turret. They might as well know we mean business," Kel said. "All hands, please take a seat and strap in. We have a hostile ship in the vicinity."

Rix scrabbled up the ladder into the needler turret and strapped in. As soon as he was settled, he raised the turret and spun it around once, checking the stock of needles and running a startup diagnostic.

"I'm good to go, Kel," he called over tactical comms.

"We have comms incoming. Stay on the channel," Kel said.

Rix tapped a paddle, and the needler turret spun so it was oriented on the nearest enemy target, in this case, the approaching Jeshifa vessel.

"Galactic Empire vessel, *Calypso*, you are ordered to heave-to," Lirren called.

"*Jeshifa-One,* that's not going to happen," Kel answered. "Also, you need to work on the creativity of your ship names."

"Your vessel *Gravitational Pull* appears to have gone missing. We offer our services to help you find it. We are the only vessel capable of traversing the Ghostmist Nebula and our services will cost you compliance with our directives."

"Gee, thanks," Kel said. "Still no on the whole heave-to, thing. We lost *Gravitational Pull,* that's kind of her problem, not ours. We're headed back home and aren't looking for any ice-cream cones or whatever it is you're selling. Now, shove off, or we'll get into this like we did with The Gray, only this time, we're not giving back your guns once we emasculate your ship."

"You have one chance remaining, or we take no pity on your crew, once you are captured," Lirren said haughtily.

"I sure hope you're good at sailing that old rust bucket, because we're not standing down and I've been spoiling for an even fight. You're no longer back home, Lirren. There's nobody out here to save you."

"You have miscalculated," Lirren said.

"Let's do this," Kel said, and pushed the accelerator to maximum.

41

UNDER THE SKIN

"*JESHIFA-ONE* HAS AN ENERGY CANNON TOP, center. No other weapons detected," Beverly said over tactical comms.

"Rix, tell me if that cannon is powered up," Kel said. "And hold on, we're going to see just how good of a pilot we're dealing with."

Calypso raced toward *Jeshifa-One* and Rix counted down the seconds to when the larger ship would come into range of his needler. "Beverly, help me find a weak spot; power, engines ... whatever we've got that can end this quickly."

"*Jeshifa-One*'s critical systems appear to be well armored as is the cockpit," Beverly said. "I suggest that you hit them amidships and dump their atmosphere by puncturing living spaces. This will slow movement within."

"That's hardly a winning shot," Kel said.

"I'll continue to assess for weakness. We need time, Kel, and more views that are close in," Beverly said.

On the tactical display, *Jeshifa-One* was shown with many splotches of green highlighting showing where armor had been skimped on. Rix stabbed a finger at one of the forward most sections, relatively near the bridge, his reasoning being that even if he had no impact on the bridge directly, the chaos might prove distracting as well as pull atmosphere from the ship.

"Shallow angle from their keel, Kel. I'm trying something," Rix instructed.

"Good copy, they'll try to roll to orient that nasty blaster cannon on us," Kel said. "Things might get a little jerky, but we have plenty of needles, so don't spare 'em."

Rix weighed her statement. He had about seven hundred kilograms of needles, which sounded like a lot, but he could easily blow through them in ninety seconds of continuous fire if he wasn't careful.

"Good copy," Rix said as Beverly projected his chosen target onto his HUD. She also updated the needler automatic targeting so that the lever slap Rix used would recenter on that one location.

As Kel had predicted, *Jeshifa-One* attempted to roll in place as the lighter, faster *Calypso* raced into battle. True to her word, Kel's adjustments were jarring and Rix struggled to stay on target. Once in range, Rix opened up with a three second burst, each pause allowing him a chance to adjust and reacquire his target.

"*Jeshifa-One* venting gasses, no structural damage detected," Beverly announced over comms.

Just then *Calypso* shuddered as an energy bolt furrowed a trail across the starboard, aft section. "They tagged one of my engine power transfers," Kel said. "I'm not sure how long it's going to last."

Rix searched the available targets as *Calypso* flipped tail for nose and accelerated back into the fray. "Kel, I can end this," Rix said. "Pass below and flip so *Calypso* is oriented to *Jeshifa-One's* aft."

"Fast would be good."

"Can you do it?"

"Yes, but how does that help. You have the same view of her underside, either way," Kel said.

"I need you to sit in the pocket for five seconds or so, so I need you to accelerate hard once you flip," Rix said.

"You're nuts.

"Right, can you do it?"

"And keep them from rolling over on us without them getting a firing solution?" Kel asked. "You're asking a lot."

"Agreed," Rix said.

"Shoot, okay, ten seconds to flip. Be ready. I don't think I can do this twice," she said.

"When they roll, let them," Rix said. "I have this."

"And if you don't, their energy cannon is going to get a free shot at us," Kel said.

"I guess we better both do our jobs then," Rix said.

"You're a mechanic!"

"Right. That's why I'm asking you to do this."

"Lords of Gavenar, fine! But just so we're clear, it is NOT a good day to die," she said. "I'm about to have two credits to rub together. I just want a couple of days with money in my pocket."

Rix didn't feel it necessary to respond and watched with anticipation as *Calypso* approached *Jeshifa-One*. Instead of firing right away, Rix awaited the maneuver they'd planned out.

"Hold onto something, we're flipping around!" Kel said as she end-for-end rolled over and twisted, orienting *Calypso* directly beneath

Jeshifa-One and in the same line of travel. With engines at maximum, Rix was pushed back into the crow's nest chair, his vision blurring. He struggled to gain control even as *Calypso's* original inertia caused them to continue sliding back, behind *Jeshifa-One* which was trying to barrel roll and bring their energy turret in line.

Rix managed a glance at his target and pulled the needler barrel up at a sharp angle, aiming at the cockpit instead of any unarmored target.

"What are you doing?" Beverly asked. "Their bridge is fully armored. You'll never penetrate that glass."

"I'm counting on that," Rix said, stitching a line of needles at an oblique angle next to the cockpit glass. As expected, the majority of his assault was easily repelled by armor and angle. But suddenly, *Jeshifa-One* stopped its barrel roll and listed to starboard. "Get cover, Kel!"

Without hesitation, Kel adjusted *Calypso's* flight and ducked beneath the pirate ship.

"*Calypso,* this is *Jeshifa-One,* stop firing!" came the call over comms. "We're breaking off our attack and propose a ceasefire."

"Oh, hell no," Kel said. "We have them on the ropes! What did you do?"

"Take the ceasefire," Rix said. "I didn't disable that ship or its weapons. I just gave them a bit of a scare. We're still badly outmatched."

"But we can take them. That wasn't even Lirren talking. You cut the head off the snake!" Kel said. "Let's put them down!"

"To what end? We'd just run survivors back to Garanod and what, scavenge their ship?" Rix said. "Get some status from them."

"*Jeshifa One* provide a sit rep. If we don't like what we hear, we're boarding and taking prisoners. Do you read? Send videos to back up your claims," Kel called.

"*Calypso,* we have multiple injured and our boss, Lirren, is dead. Even worse, his dumb, fancy box is smoking and we can't see how to get home," came a worried voice. "We're at your mercy."

Moments later video from the inside of *Jeshifa One* started streaming onto *Calypso's* tactical displays. Recognizable, but also horribly disfigured, Lirren Vos's body was one of the first images they saw. The damage on the bridge was considerable, to include the smoking remains of the Ghostmist Cipher.

"Gah, turn it off and fine. *Jeshifa One,* we are providing a direct course to Garanod Enclave. Do not vary from it or you'll be lost again. You will keep your transponder active and retreat at full power. Any diversion from this course will be considered hostile, and we will respond as such," Kel called. "Also, you will put the remains of that Cipher out your airlock with a transmitter on it. Will you comply?"

"We're complying now," the young pirate answered.

A blinking transmitter appeared next to the ship just before *Jeshifa One* powering up engines and hastily retreated from the combat zone.

"That's better," Rix said. "I hope they didn't get our engine too badly. Pull up next to that cipher. It looks like its seen better days."

"Okay, we'll snag it, but you have to tell me what you did? It looked like you missed with everything. Did you see something that made you think that'd be a good shot?" Kel asked.

"No, but also, I've worked on enough of these ships to know that the transition between that glass and the fuselage is a weak spot. Maybe not dead on, but you were so close, I thought it possible to send a few needles under the coping if any part of it was loose. Once those needles were in the bridge, they would have bounced around until they found something. It wouldn't have taken more than one or two to cause chaos. They're moving fast and are meant to ricochet."

"I'm glad you're on our side, in that case," Kel said. "How long do we want to wait to retrieve *Gravitational Pull*?"

"Act like we're following them back to Garanod but keep our distance and let them pull away. That's roughly in the right direction to grab *Gravitational Pull*," Rix said.

"Good call, setting course in now," Kel said. "Go

42

EPILOGUE

"YOU'RE BRILLIANT. Has anyone told you that before?" Amari asked.

"I don't know about that," Rix said, grabbing a wet cloth and dousing the fire he'd started on the paint while welding a quick fix within *Calypso's* engine compartment. There was more damage that needed attention once they returned on Patience Station, but the field repair was all he thought necessary to continue the journey.

"Kel told me about how you found a weakness in their armor. I looked at the scans. There was no way to see any of that," she continued.

"The word you're looking for is lucky," Rix said.

"Sure, lucky, as long as you admit you had a plan and it worked out," Amari said.

"My plan was to try to fling something down the hallway and hope it went into the engine room," Rix said. "It was a last-minute thought to try to get under that bridge glass coping. If they hadn't rolled over like they did, things might not have gone so well."

"I talked to Kitka. They'll take the next shift so we can get some rest," Amari said. "Do you feel like you'd like a nap? You've been going for about twenty hours."

"I could sleep," Rix said. "We still have two full days to get to the Narlux-4 transition. I hope it's an easier trip than what we've had so far."

"One thing at a time," Amari said.

Returning to *Gravitational Pull*, Rix was met by Greevo and Kitka, who were standing with their backs to the pilot's chairs. Inwardly, Rix groaned. No doubt Greevo would have a complaint, but it was Kitka who spoke first.

"We have cleaned the bunkroom, and your bedrolls are laid out," Kitka said. "When you awake, we will have breakfast waiting."

"Well ... wow, thank you, Kitka," Rix said.

"Rix Banner protect Greevo shipment. Rix Banner good man. Get sleep. Long sail," Greevo said.

Rix shook his head in confusion, but tiredness pushed him to action, and he climbed the ladder up to the bunkroom where he gratefully collapsed, waking up some ten hours later, with no reports of incidents or threat of being followed.

It was at this point that space travel started once again living up to its reputation. Three-hour shifts were shared by the four passengers and even though living space was crowded, a general ease settled over the cabin. And it was without event that they arrived at the location where transition back to Galactic Empire space, specifically the Narlux-4 solar system, was possible.

"Feels like there hasn't been a whole lot of fanfare about our return," Kel said.

"Were you expecting a parade?" Rix asked. "I've been in one. They're kind of cool."

"You were in a parade?"

"Our town celebrated the end of The War," Rix said. "I got to ride on a float. I'm not seeing anything like that here."

"Maybe back in Narlux," Kel said. "Snuggle in close, otherwise you might not get transitioned."

Rix let Amari, who was the better pilot, approach *Calypso* for transition. Unlike other transitions, leaving the Ghostmist Nebula for Narlux was eventful, in that the gas cloud they'd been living in for the better part of the last two weeks was suddenly replaced by a starfield.

"That doesn't get easier, does it," Rix asked, rubbing his stomach.

"For some people it never does," Amari said. "Given you started at such a late age, I doubt you'll ever enjoy transition."

"Neat," Rix said sarcastically.

"Hey Rix," Kel called over comms. "We might have a problem over here. Would you mind making a quick space jump and come visit us?"

"I'm on my way."

"Bring Amari."

Rix and Amari exchanged looks and then moved with speed to suit up and EVA over to *Calypso.*

"Lucy, we're home!" Beverly called with a Cuban accent, wearing a 1950s housedress and a scarf tied in her hair.

"What is it with you and pop culture from my home?" Rix asked.

"It's fascinating. Everything is a little moral story. Even the magazine advertising projects a story. I love it," Beverly said.

"*I Love Lucy* is way different than Amelia Earhart circumnavigating the globe," Rix said. "One is real the other is made up."

"Both have story value," Beverly said.

Upon entering the passenger compartment, Rix found Kasit and Zenith sitting hunched at the galley table with Kel and Sta'ci talking to them.

Kel acknowledged Amari and Rix, "they were stowed in a compartment beneath one of the gillet crates. The cold leached, we're working on some minor hypothermia. Auto doc says they'll need medical back at Patience, but they mostly just need to rest. Did you know about this? You don't look that surprised, Rix."

"No, but I wondered. Kha'rem under charged for the gillet. He used the price we'd discussed if we brought Kasit and Zenith aboard but then didn't say anything more. His reluctance to talk to me after that had me wondering what all the hush-hush was about."

"Are you taking us to the Galactic Empire?" Zenith asked, her body shuddering as she did.

"You're already there, sister," Amari said, patting Zenith on the back. "What do you think about that?"

"Safer for Kasit," Zenith said, coughing uncontrollably as she continued, "Lirren had his hooks in."

"Don't talk. We've got you," Kel said. "We'll make bunk room for you. Or you can sit out here, whatever you like."

"No boxes," Kasit managed, also struggling to breathe through chattering teeth.

"We understand," Sta'ci said.

"We'll be pushing our atmospheric regeneration hard between here and Patience," Kel said. "We might need you to come over and do a carbon scrub, Rix."

"How about I do that now, before we get underway, again. Kha'rem had a video message for us for once we were back in Galactic Empire space. I suppose we should play it. Maybe it'd be best in the bridge. I'm not sure if there's any private content."

Kel nodded and moved to the bridge with Rix and Amari. Rix had Beverly play the video on the forward displays.

"Rix Banner, by now, you have discovered the stow-aways. Thank you for bringing them to safety. You will find thirty grams of gold in the same compartment where they were resting. It is not as much as I wish, but it is what I can offer to help them start a new life. I hope *Calypso* will return to Garanod. My pier will always be open to you, Rix Banner and you as well Kel Warp. Blessings to you."

"Short and sweet," Kel said. "We should find that gold. I'm not saying there are sticky fingers aboard, but you never know what someone will do with that kind of gold available."

"Agreed," Rix said. "I don't think this changes our plans. Kasit and Zenith will have startup money. We can help them learn to live inexpensively on Patience. That's about what we have to offer, don't you think?"

"Thirty grams will be a good start," Kel said. "Heck, it's more than I'm going to make on this run."

"We haven't sold the gillet," Rix said. "And we might be going into a fix-it business with Sta'ci and Philo."

"Doesn't that compete with your shop?" Amari asked.

"It would if I was ever home long enough to open my shop to outsiders," Rix said.

"Good point," Kel agreed.

"Do you have enough room to keep them comfortable on *Calypso?*" Amari asked.

"We'll be tight. We were already tight, but it's doable. Especially since we're only six days from home and we have no more jumps left," Kel said.

"It's going to be a long six days," Rix said. "How about we grab some dinner with you guys before we go back to *Gravitational Pull*?"

"That's a good choice, Sta'ci is a marvelous cook," Kel said. "We've been eating well."

"Kitka has been making breakfast," Rix said. "I have to say, bringing people along who know their way around the kitchen is worthwhile."

As promised, Sta'ci's dinner was better than anything they'd come to expect from spaceship fare and Rix and Amari were in a good mood returning to *Gravitational Pull.* Unfortunately, Greevo and Kitka had chosen to swap rest schedules and had left a message asking Rix and Amari to take their shift.

Settling into his chair, Rix checked the balance of his accounts. Two urgent messages showed that he was late on commercial space rental and his mortgage. Checking his balance, he realized the error that he hadn't set anything to automatically apply his Council Seat salary to the mortgage, which explained the nearly ten thousand in credit balance in his private account.

He paid both bills, dropping his bank balance back to 6,200 credits and then checked on Greevo's invoice. He wasn't quite sure what to think of things in that Greevo's 19,000 credits had moved as agreed. He got right to paying out the crew, with 1,900 to each Philo and Amari, 3,800 to himself and Kel. With 7,600 moving to the business account for repairs to both ships.

"What are you working on?" Amari asked. "Oh, I just got paid. I wasn't expecting that. And especially not that much."

"It's fair," Rix said. "Make sure you spend as much and as widely as you can on Patience. It's not enough to make things go, but it'll help the overall economy. They say money moves up to six times when it enters a township."

"Who is they?"

"Not exactly sure," Rix said.

"Are you doing okay, financially?"

"Well, yes, better than I was."

"Mind sharing numbers with me? I'll go first. These 1,900 credits bring me to 2,850," she said.

"So, I have those manufactory patterns that are still making me money. Add that to salary for my council seat and various trades, I'm sitting at thirteen thousand, give or take. My business, which I share with Kel, is at twenty-five thousand."

"Where did twenty-five thousand come from?"

"The parts I sold through Bha'resh plus the ships' share of the contract with Greevo," Rix said.

"Sounds like you're rich to me."

"You mean spread thin," Rix said. "My monthly payments just for space are over six thousand. I can't afford to take my foot off the pedal even for a minute."

"You stress about this too much," Amari said. "Having no money isn't fun, but you still survive if you know how to hustle."

"I guess this is my hustle," Rix said.

"Wait, what about the gold you're holding, don't you have some left?"

"Thirty grams that I didn't add to totals," Rix said. "So roughly another five thousand credits."

"What are you going to do with all your newfound wealth?"

"First things first, *Calypso* needs a comprehensive overhaul. *Gravitational Pull* needs new engines and a power plant," Rix said. "Although,

I hate the idea of long haul with her. So maybe we should look at a new, bigger vessel."

"Can you afford that?"

"I don't even know who sells used freighters," Rix said. "Or, if Kel would be open to the idea."

"She is loyal to *Calypso*," Amari said. "I don't blame her, though. It treated her well when no one else would."

"There's this thing that's been bothering me," Rix said.

"Oh? What's that?"

"You and Kel have special skills that should have ensured you didn't have to put up with bad people, but you did," Rix said.

"And you want to know why."

"If you're willing to talk about it."

"Bad people don't show up with a sign on their forehead telling you that's who they are. My ex didn't start out being awful. He also could be very charming and attentive. As long as I was with him, I didn't have to worry about living. My kid was safe. I was safe and it was a small sacrifice that every once in a while, he'd turn into a psycho. I loved him."

Rix nodded empathetically. "I've heard that can be a thing," he said. "And now, do you think you still love him?"

"I love who he was," she said. "I love who we were together when it was good. Are you asking if he was around would I want to be with him?"

"That's hypothetical," Rix said. "Do you have an answer?"

"No. I don't like who I was with him. I gave up parts of me to make the peace. I lost important parts and I'll never go back to that again. Do you miss Cranberry Cove, Wisconsin, Earth?"

“Some parts of it. I didn’t have a person, so it’s different for me,” Rix said. “I was making something of my shop, and the diner was growing, too. I had a lot of my capital tied up in both of those things, but I could see that was going to turn the corner in a few years. It was exciting to be part of.”

“You do miss it. We should go back for a visit, then,” she said. “You can make a list of all the things you want to do and the people you want to visit. Wouldn’t that be fun?”

Rix paused for a while and the nodded. “You know what? I would like that.”

But of course, that’s another story, entirely.

43

FLYING SAUCERS AND CHROME PLATE

WHAT FOLLOWS IS a preview of the fourth novel in the *Spaceship Mechanic* series titled *Flying Saucers and Chrome Plate.* The full novel will be available later in 2026.

Chapter 1 - Homecoming

"Patience Station, ho!" Kel called over comms. "Are you picking her up yet, Rix?"

While *Gravitational Pull's* sensors were only useful within a few hundred kilometers, the cobbled together long-range sensors and navigation systems kept him and Amari up-to-date on their general position within a solar system. So, while he knew their relative position, none of the ship's systems had any sort of physical confirmation.

"Negative, I'm showing we're still out forty minutes, give or take," Rix answered.

"And here you thought *Gravitational Pull* wasn't going to make it."

"I feel like you're jinxing a perfectly good homecoming, Kel," Rix said. "And me without any actual wood to knock on."

"You don't really do that, do you?" Kel asked.

"Sometimes," Rix admitted. "What do you suppose Atom has been up to since we left?"

"I suspect you're not going to love how things look when we get back," Kel said. "How much money did you leave him with?"

"Twenty credits to spend daily with Petju and another five credits spending money," Rix said. "I'm hoping he couldn't get into too much trouble."

"I guess we'll see," Kel said. "Did you let him know we'll be docking soon?"

"I sent a message but haven't heard back, yet. It's late, though, he's probably asleep," Rix said.

"How do you think he's going to react to that photonic barrier firing up and the bay doors opening?" Kel asked.

"I guess we'll see," he answered, allowing comms to close as the conversation waned.

Rix felt Amari's hand in his own. The trip to Garanod Enclave had been long, and stressful. Between fending off pirates, dealing with a recalcitrant customer, cramped conditions and stowaways with prices on their heads, there had been no part of their voyage that had been relaxing.

"Have you heard from Thudd about your apartment?" Amari asked. "I know you've been working through some Station Council issues with him."

"The apartment is complete. He was asking about furniture, and I told him we'd probably want to pick that out on our own," Rix said. "There's something else, though."

"What's that?"

"You and Hutari have six weeks before Patience Council is going to start charging rent on Sable territory apartments," Rix said. "You should have received a letter by now."

"We did," she said. "Hutari is looking for something smaller. We're not in a position to pay eight hundred credits a month for Shixen's old space."

"You could move in with me," Rix said and then immediately regretted it as he saw Amari's face fall. "Or not ...," he hastily added.

"Rix, I love what we're doing here," she said, pointing first at herself and then at Rix to indicate their new couple's status.

"I sense a but."

"Do you really not know what I'm thinking?"

"We'll I guess I don't think it's a moral thing," Rix said. "Maybe you think Hutari wouldn't feel welcome. I assure you, she would be. I think she's great."

"That's not it," Amari said with a sigh, and she waited a moment to give Rix another chance.

"Your relationship with Shixen has you worried about sharing space," he finally said.

"Yes. The Council does know that most people don't have money for rent, right?" she asked.

"That's not just in the old Sable territory," Rix said. "Sixty percent of station inhabitants are on some sort of modified payment schedule. The letter should have included an application for that."

"It feels bad to ask for charity. Not everyone makes money as easily as you do," she said.

"Patience Station needs money for upkeep."

"And Council salaries."

"Are you looking to fight about this?" Rix asked. "How are my finances part of the problem. I'm working hard to survive. You know that as well as anyone."

Various emotions flickered across Amari's face as she considered her next response. She finally sighed again. "You're right, I shouldn't take out my irritation on you. It's just ... I don't know, everything is hard. I thought with Shixen gone, things would get easier."

"Have you checked in with Skef?" Rix asked, more than interested in changing subjects. "The farms might be generating revenue by now."

"We're meeting first thing in the morning," Kel said. "Hopefully it's good news."

"I'm thinking about offering Sta'ci a job," Rix said.

"Oh? What kind of job?"

"Business manager," Rix said. "I'm getting tied up managing all these smaller concerns, like figuring out what Atom's up to and other stuff."

"Mostly managing Atom?" Amari asked.

"Geez, I suppose that's right, at least to start with," Rix admitted. "But, we'll have that new business with her and Philo to deal with."

"Can she be a business manager and a partner? Wouldn't that be a conflict of interest? How much would you pay her?"

"It'd be part time," Rix said. "I'm thinking two to three hours a day, probably forty-five credits."

"That's quite a commitment if you intend it to be ongoing employment," Amari said.

"It would free me up to make trips and she could help arrange smaller jobs for the shop," Rix said. "I need my investment in Atom to start making sense financially."

"I thought that was charity."

Rix searched Amari's face for double meaning and not finding any he continued. "Charity is a strong word. I'm willing to deal with Atom's personality and learning style, but at the end of the day, I hired him as a mechanic or mechanic's helper. Sta'ci, with my and Philo's help, will start to figure out what jobs Atom can do and what is too big. His body work, for example, is first class. He welds, fills and paints exceptionally. In the same vain, he might also weld next to sensitive equipment because he's in a hurry. That will require ongoing management, but I know he can more than pay for himself, especially if I have someone like Sta'ci watching him."

"You have a lot of faith in her. What if she's not up for or interested in the job?"

"There are more people who can do what I need," Rix said. "We just need to find them."

"What about Kasit and Zenith? Bringing them to Patience Station isn't really saving them from anything but Jeshifa," Amari said. "Without jobs, they're going to be just one more family who needs help."

"Kel and I talked about Zenith helping her out with a boutique," Rix said. "She has experience in trading."

"Do you have enough trade goods that you could pay her enough to stay alive?" Amari asked.

"The initial answer is no," Rix said. "But she and Kasit have some startup money. Kel's boutique would help extend that. If we sell the frozen gillet at retail, there's more money than what you might think available. She could also help sell our produce if Skef doesn't have it all spoken for."

"You're putting yourself in a position where a lot of people are coming to depend on you," Amari said. "Are you sure that's the life you want to lead?"

"At home, we have a saying that goes something like – a good man doesn't stand by when people need help. That's a paraphrase, but that's kind of how I'm looking at this. There is so much opportunity that I just don't think people are seeing correctly. We just need to get things started by opening doors. Maybe some of my micro-businesses fail, but I think the people involved are better for the experience."

"Like my farm project," she said. "I guess I'd never have thought to work on it at the scale you've brought, and then to make it some sort of kit is so interesting."

"That was a collaboration between you, me and Skef," Rix said. "Everyone brings a new idea to it. If I disappeared tomorrow, you and Skef could just keep running with it. So no, I'm not terribly worried about people depending on me, because I'm trying to not make success dependent on my constant contribution."

"It's hard for me to complain, given the fat stack of credits sitting in my pocket, just now," she said. "I also don't want to be tied down. I want to get out and adventure!"

"Like sailing a passel of Grintok out to Garanod Enclave kind of adventuring?"

Amari's good humor returned and she smiled. "That's more of a *lesson learned* sort of thing, but yes, similar to that, but without the smelly Grintok living on top of us."

"I don't know, even with all the drama, it's going to pay off better than any mission we've had, before," Rix said. "Maybe Greevo is exactly who we should be targeting."

"It might be time to find yourself a new girlfriend, if that's what you're thinking," Amari said.

"Want to look at beds and linens with me? I doubt we can get them manufactured yet tonight, but I'd really like to sleep in a real bed at some point," Rix said.

"You can sleep in my apartment tonight, even though you and your council cronies are kicking me out in a few weeks," Amari said.

"Maybe that is just a ploy to get you."

"What, make me destitute and homeless so I'll come running to my big, fearless man?" Amari asked with a mocking tone.

"If it works, who's to argue."

"You're incorrigible."

"I try. Oh, look there," Rix said. "We've got comms from Patience. How about you grab that."

"We're not done with that conversation," Amari said, tapping the console to bring up comms. "This is *Gravitational Pull*, go ahead, Patience."

"Mom! You're alive!" Hutari's voice filtered over comms.

"Was there a rumor otherwise?"

"Most of the time, you send a message so I don't worry," Hutari said.

"No comms where we were," Amari said. "Do we need a nav plan to Level 8 private pier?"

"I'm clearing both *Calypso* and *Gravitational Pull* to Level 8. What in the world are you hauling, by the way. Your mass readings are way up."

"Grab a visual," Amari said. "You'll understand. We did a bunch of trading and are way over loaded. Dravari would bust us if we tried to dock anywhere but patience. No part of either ship is qualified for the loads we're hauling."

"Sounds like a lot of people around here will be excited. Did you bring me anything special home?"

"Aside from me and Rix?"

"Yes. Aside from you two."

"What do you feel about frozen fish?" Amari asked.

"You're no fun," Hutari said. "Next time you go on a big, exotic adventure, I'm expecting something cool when you come back. Don't disappoint me again. Got it?"

"I read you," Amari said. "What's your schedule. Rix and I are going to crash at the apartment after we do a bit of unloading."

"I'm on for the next six hours. I was sleeping in your bed. I hope that's not a problem for Rix."

"He'll be fine. Trust me, you'll be the cleanest person we've shared a bed with lately."

Rix chuckled ruefully and it was just then that Patience Station popped into view in the distance. "There she is," he whispered.

Thirty minutes later, *Gravitational Pull* shuddered to a stop next to the pier outside his mechanic's bay. With Philo having already offboarded from *Calypso*, Rix deployed mooring lines, which were expertly lashed into place bringing a sense of finality to the long trip.

"What workin', Rixy?" Philo asked in his broken speech.

"I'd like to give Greevo access to his goods. We'll need to unload the runabouts you and Sta'ci bought back on Driftmarket," Rix said, referring to the five junked small vessels they'd purchased with the intent to repair and resell them once back on Patience. While Rix had funded a good portion of the venture, he'd made it clear that it was to Sta'ci and Philo to make a business of it.

They'd no more than started working on the first set of straps when Greevo emerged from *Gravitational Pull* carrying an open bag with clothing and food supplies overflowing. That the foodstuffs had been purchased for the trip, he decided he didn't need to make an issue of what otherwise felt like steeling to him.

"What are your plans for unloading, Greevo?" Rix called after the Grintok. For Greevo's part, he simply ignored Rix and trundled into Rix's shop, through the brightly lit photonic generator. "For the record, that's the kind of conversation I need Sta'ci for. I hate chasing people to get answers."

"I understand," Amari answered and helped as Rix tossed a long strap to her.

"Big Boss?" Atom's shaky voice called out a few minutes later. "Big Boss, home?"

"We're unloading, Atom. Come on out and help us," Rix said.

"Atom very tired."

"Work comes before sleep, Atom," Rix said, hooking a line Philo had extended from the gantry crane that had been pulled over to the shop's space-side entrance. With little gravity, the crane provided a semi-fixed point to steady the small vessel's movement. It was a slow process, but one that was not prone to vehicles getting out of control.

"Are we keeping these all in your shop, Rix?" Sta'ci asked.

"How about we do that until we get a good inspection and come up with repair plans," Rix said. "Then we can move them out onto the pier, or even into the cargo pods, depending on how quickly we'll get to them."

"I understand. That's generous of you," Sta'ci said as Atom walked up to her. "And who is this?"

"Atom," Philo said. "Him good friend."

"Nice to meet you, Atom," Sta'ci said. "Do you work here, too? I've heard a lot about Rix Banner's shop."

"Atom live in shop. Atom mechanic," Atom said beaming with pride.

"Atom, I wonder if you would go up to the top of that cargo pod and help Rix Banner unload," Sta'ci said.

"Atom strong. Atom go."

Rix looked on in amusement at Atom scrabbled up next to him requiring no more encouragement.

"What have you been up to, Atom?" Rix asked. "Were you able to retrieve any of those subsystems I had on your list?"

"Atom work whole time Big Boss gone. Piles big big now."

"That sounds amazing," Rix said. "I can't wait to see what you've accomplished."

"Some trouble. Old stuffs break easy. Hope Big Boss not be mads."

"I'm sure we'll get through it," Rix said. "Grab that strap, and pull it around, would you?"

Atom got to work as Rix asked and with a third pair of hands, the broken vehicles started slowly but steadily getting unloaded and organized within the shop. As Rix worked on this, Kel started loading grav pallets with the small crates of goods she'd purchased.

"Do you have thoughts on where we should stay tonight?" Zenith asked on a comm channel which included Kel, Amari and Rix. "I have a prompt asking us to register with Galactic Empire. It looks like that's a requirement for use of any station services."

"You'll need to register, but it's just a formality," Kel said.

"You're welcome to stay aboard *Gravitational Pull* for a couple of days while you get settled. We have some leftover food, even and I have plenty of rations in the shop," Rix said. "It's not much, but it's something."

"Are you certain?" Zenith asked.

"Those are the most logical choices," Kel said. "You don't want to spend money on a hotel stay. You'll want to get an idea of where you want to live and all that before you start blowing your startup money."

"Did you talk to Zenith about your boutique, Kel?"

"I did, but we should get her and Kas hooked up to the employment boards. They might want to do something else."

"It's just an idea," Rix agreed as they pulled the last of the five vehicles into the shop and closed the outside bay doors. Glancing at the piles of reclaimed parts, he quickly came to an understanding that Atom hadn't been overly productive in his absence. "Kasit, I know you're not afraid of work, have you done much mechanical work?"

"Not really," Kasit said. "What are you thinking?"

"I have some derelict freighters that we're parting out and scrapping metal from," Rix said. "It's hard, irritating work, but there's money in it."

"Any job is better than nothing," Kasit said. "At least to start with."

Rix marveled at the youth's new-found humility. "So, how about we get together later this afternoon, after we get some rest, and we can talk about what we're really doing."

"Okay."

"Rix, Kel, thank you," Zenith said. "There's no reason for you to have taken up our cause. We're lucky to even be alive at this point and trust me when I say, we won't forget your kindness. How can we ever pa you back?"

"The best payback is you guys getting on your feet," Kel said. "Everyone here has run into hard times and one point or another."

"You both have access to the station through the public entrance at the end of the pier," Rix said. "Tomorrow, well, really later this afternoon, we can start getting you all settled. Including you, too, Sta'ci."

"If acceptable, I'd appreciate a bunk aboard *Calypso* for a couple of days," Sta'ci said. "I am not sure that I am ready to live with Philo just yet, even though I find him quite adorable."

"Hansum," Philo corrected.

"Oh, yes, and handsome, too."

"I'll find you this afternoon, Sta'ci," Rix said. "I have some business I'd like to discuss if you're amenable."

"I am, of course, interested enough for discussion," she said. "Would you like me to interface with Greevo for the offloading of his goods?"

"You're offering?"

"You've been more than generous. Consider it a gesture of my appreciation," Sta'ci said.

"That would be fantastic," Rix said.

"Can we stop by the farm and then check out your apartment before we head to my home?" Amari asked, her eyes gleaming with excitement.

"Of course," Rix said, shouldering the ruck that held his clothing and personal items from *Gravitational Pull*. "Lead the way."

Crossing through the public station hallway over to Bay 808, where the hydroponic farm was located, they were immediately greeted by the bright grow lights spilling from the four, rectangular farms. Amari dropped her bags and ran to check out what Skef and Rook Hadden had growing.

"They have three generations of micro wheat berries growing in this farm, alone. I can't even calculation how many meters of wheat have been planted," Amari exclaimed with excitement.

Beverly took this moment to appear, wearing overalls and a straw hat. She took a position as if she were sitting on top of a tall rack that held large trays of ten-centimeter-tall micro wheat plants. "Two hundred square meters per farm with the nine racks planted like they are," Beverly said, picking at her teeth with a piece of straw. "I believe you are looking at harvest in three days on the oldest generation. Tell me, Rix, have you considered how you will dry the berries?"

"It hadn't even crossed my mind," Rix said. "I'm guessing you have an idea for this?"

"I suppose you could lay them out on the platters and dry one of these farms out," she said.

"Or?" Rix asked, hearing a *but* in the conversation.

"A drying machine," Amari said. "It's a bit more capital but if we want to mass produce micro wheat, it's going to be a thing."

"Sounds like a conversation with Skef. Good news is, I just checked, we still have eight hundred credits in the capital account."

"I'll leave a message for Skef," Amari said, grabbing Rix's arm and jumping with excitement. "This is really going to work. We're going to have fresh wheat on Patience!"

"And we still have that sorting and grinding machine from before. We could sell it as flour and make an even bigger profit," Rix said.

ACKNOWLEDGMENTS

To Jordan Olsen for excellence in editing and word-smithery.

To my beta readers: Carol Greenwood, Kelli Whyte, and Lyle Clingman for wonderful and thoughtful suggestions. It is a joy to work with this intelligent and considerate group of people.

Finally, to Elias Stern, cover artist extraordinaire.

ABOUT THE AUTHOR

Jamie McFarlane is the father of three and lives in Lincoln, Nebraska. An avid runner, scuba diver and hiker, Jamie enjoys the active life writing fulltime affords him.

Word-of-mouth is crucial for any author to succeed. If you enjoyed this book, please consider leaving a review, even if it's only a line or two; it would make all the difference and would be very much appreciated.

FREE DOWNLOAD

If you'd like to receive automatic email when Jamie's next book is available, please visit http://fickledragon.com. Your email address will never be shared and you can unsubscribe at any time.

For more information
www.fickledragon.com
jamie@fickledragon.com

ALSO BY JAMIE MCFARLANE

Spaceship Mechanic

1. Boltguns and Duct Tape
2. Jump Drives and Coffee Stains
3. Ray Guns and Late Fees
4. Flying Saucers and Chrome Plate (Late 2026)

Junkyard Pirate Series

1. Junkyard Pirate
2. Old Dogs, Older Tricks
3. Junkyard Spaceship
4. Junkyard Veterans
5. Junkyard Raiders
6. Junkyard Ghost Ship
7. Junkyard Commandos
8. Junkyard Mercenary
9. Junkyard Saboteur

Oldest Starfighter Series

1. The Oldest Starfighter
2. Rogue Commander

Privateer Tales Series

1. Rookie Privateer
2. Fool Me Once
3. Parley
4. Big Pete
5. Smuggler's Dilemma
6. Cutpurse

7. Out of the Tank
8. Buccaneers
9. A Matter of Honor
10. Give No Quarter
11. Blockade Runner
12. Corsair Menace
13. Pursuit of the Bold
14. Fury of the Bold
15. Judgment of the Bold
16. Privateers in Exile
17. Incursion at Elea Station
18. Freebooter's Hold
19. Black Cutlass
20. Privateer's Supremacy

Space Troopers Series

1. Rebel's Call
2. Rebel's Run
3. Rebel's Strike

Privateer Tales Universe

1. Pete, Popeye and Olive
2. Life of a Miner
3. Uncommon Bravery
4. On a Pale Ship

Henry Biggston Thrillers

1. When Justice Calls
2. Deputy in the Crosshairs
3. Manhunt at Sage Creek

Witchy World

1. Wizard in a Witchy World

2. Wicked Folk: An Urban Wizard's Tale
3. Wizard Unleashed

Guardians of Gaeland

1. Lesser Prince

www.ingramcontent.com/pod-product-compliance
Lightning Source LLC
LaVergne TN
LVHW020040110826
845155LV00029B/564